CRANE
The Left Handed Gun
THE BEGINNING

By Dave Lodge

Published in 2018 by Dave Lodge

This book comes from conversations and discussions on my
planned story in 1960 with my late father Ted Lodge.

ISBN: 978-1-9998936-8-2

Book Design by Russell Holden
www.pixeltweakspublications.com

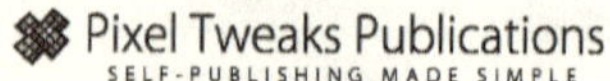

Printed by Ingram

This book is dedicated to my lovely wife Margaret as always, because she is my reason, for attempting to do anything in my life. Thank you Margaret for all you do, have done and continue to do for me.

CONTENTS

CHAPTER 1

If Tony Crane had known the kind of hell his life would bring to those who cared for him, he would have thrown his guns in the horse trough, saddled his horse and ridden out on the road to nowhere. He would have done this long before the following events took place.

As it was, the day that young Tony's world changed forever started like any other for Tony on his Pa's scrub farm on the edge of a desert in West Texas. The whole family were up before first light, Pa and Tony stumbling, with tiredness would go out to the barn together. There was plenty of work to done, stock had to be fed and watered, earth needed to be ploughed, fences had to built and mended.

By the time their first jobs were done they were starting to feel awake and alive. Neither of them ever complained it was just the way things were. The family enjoyed a good life, if a hard one. In the years they had been there the crops had never failed and they all enjoyed good health. Tony's Ma kept good food on the table and their cabin was spotless. His and his pa's clothes were clean and well looked after. Compared to many who farmed the land, they enjoyed a good life. After all Tony's Pa said, the pleasure that came after a days work in the fields was the most satisfying that he had ever known. To sit on the porch and reflect on life, was joy that all men should aspire to achieve.

Like most boys Tony had a dog, his Pa brought the dog home one day when Tony was about two years old, it was only a pup and they had great fun together while they were growing up. As the dog grew it used to chase jack rabbits and sticks that Tony threw for him, and it was always ready to play. Good times, but now the dog was getting old so he just ambled around behind Tony, or more and frequently he just slept on the porch. This was just as well really because now Tony was getting older, his chores didn't leave him much time for play.

As a fourteen year old boy who thought he was a man, Tony seemed to have been doing his chores for so many years, he felt as though he was doing them in his sleep. So it was on this fateful day, it started just like any other. Having walked from the cabin with his Pa, Tony stopped at the barn, his first job was to milk the only cow that they had and take the milk in to Ma so that she could make the breakfast that they would enjoy about four hours later. Then his Pa moved on out to the corral to get their plough horse ready for a hard day in the field, Tony would feed the few stock animals they had, pigs and such and then clean out the barn. This had been the normal daily routine for a long time now, Tony thought it had started with the milking when he was six or seven and the jobs had just increased as the years had gone by.

Tony looked at his father's back as he walked away from him, Len Crane was the biggest man Tony had ever seen, In his boots he looked to be 6ft 11in tall. Tony knew him to be 6ft 8 or even 9ins in his socks, Ma made all their clothes and she had measured them both so he was sure of his Pa's height. His Pa's shoulders were so wide he had to turn sideways to walk through any door, and of course he had to lower his head. Tony's Pa was lean and hard, made that way by the years he had worked and at times fought to make his way in life.

There were marks on the barn door that his Pa had made to record Tony's height through the years. It was clear that Tony would not make his Pa's height. He thought he would make maybe 5ft 11 or 6ft when he was full grown. But what Tony would have was his Pa's width of shoulder. That was clear, because the frame was there but there was not much weight on him yet, Tony was lean and spare, but he was very strong. He took after his Pa who had a massive strength, Tony had seen him lift things with ease, on his own that two normal sized men would struggle to pick up.

Tony's Pa said that Tony was like his own Pa who was long dead, having been killed in a cattle stampede. This had happened not long after Tony had been was born so he didn't remember much about his Grandpa. Pa told Tony that his own Pa was much stronger than him, with a strength that came from something inside, a force of will that had to be seen to be believed. He went on to say that Tony had it. Tony's Pa warned Tony that he would have to be careful not to abuse that strength as he could make trouble for himself and others.

Tony didn't really understand what his Pa was telling him, he just took his strength for granted, so unusually for him being a boy who would argue at the drop of a hat, Tony kept his own counsel and carried on regardless.

Father and son were alike in some ways, going about their daily work quietly and efficiently, steady you might say. Surprisingly for Tony, they shared something else speed of movement, not all big men have that. They didn't use all the time, but when they needed it, Tony's Ma said they were both like a blur sometimes when they moved. Also and this seemed a silly thing, Tony's Pa showed him that they could catch flies out of the air, because they both had very quick hands. Although Tony didn't realise that there was anything special in this, he thought everyone could do it.

The other thing Tony used his hand eye co-ordination for was throwing a knife, he had a strange technique he would hold the knife by the handle, with the point down, then he would let it go forward in one fluid motion. When he did this he could pin fat blowflies to fence posts, he never missed. His pa said he had never seen anything like it. Pa was sure no pistol fighter could draw faster than Tony could throw that knife. Pa should know because he had known a few pistol fighters in his day.

Tony and his Pa shared the same colouring, olive skin and shoulder length dark hair their eyes where different though Pa's eyes were a shade of grey, Tony's were like his Ma's, his were blue. They were very different though, because where hers were soft and sparkled, smiling all the time, Tony's were flat sometimes devoid of expression and they looked like steel when he was annoyed.

Now Tony's pa told him that Grandpa had lived with the Comanche' for a time and married one of the women in the village. She had been a great beauty by all accounts but she had died giving birth to Pa. So that was where Tony and his Pa got their colouring from it would seem. Tony supposed that this relationship made him about a quarter Comanche, for all the difference he thought that it made.

There was one very big difference between Tony's Pa and him. Tony had never seen his Pa lose his temper and he never seen him lift his hand to anyone, least of all Tony. On the other hand Tony had a quick temper, and if there had been anyone around to fight with he would have got himself into trouble. So while he had no one to fight when he lost his temper, Tony was always breaking things, doing damage. Because of this Tony was a handy carpenter, because his Pa made sure that he repaired or remade the all the items he broke.

Tony thought that he must have got his temper from his Ma because she would shout and throw things if she was annoyed. Ma was small maybe 5ft tall and very pretty and she was always laughing and she loved to dance. She had blonde hair to go with her blue eyes and a great personality. Most unlike Tony who spent a lot of time sulking.

His Ma and Pa never argued, it was clear that Ma would sometimes have liked to but, Pa would just say, we ain't having this conversation, Mae, then he would just go and do something else. Ma would try to carry on arguing with herself but after a while they would both just be carrying on as though there had never been a problem.

All in all life was pretty good, times were hard, but they were not poor. Ma had taught Tony to read and write and do some work with numbers, apparently not all boys his age were so lucky. Although Tony didn't appreciate his luck when he was stuck inside during what would have been his free time. There was precious little of that when he had finished his chores. Tony's Ma said it was important, that he was literate and his Pa didn't complain about the time spent learning, as long as the work was done. To be fair his Ma made things interesting, she knew how to teach because she had taught school in her home town before she had married his Pa.

Pa and Tony would sometimes go out with rifles to shoot something for the pot. Tony was good at this because his hand to eye co-ordination was excellent. His Pa said he was instinctive, Pa was pretty good himself, so he must have known what about he was talking about when it came Tony.

When Tony finished the other chores which included feeding a few calves that the family were rearing for a local rancher. He would feed the hens, clean out the barn and chop some wood just the normal things that kept the place running, his time was his own. Then Tony was really happy, because he got to work with his colt. So far the colt had been to young to ride but Tony had been working him out on a lead rope and it was going well, Best news of all Pa had said Tony could start trying to ride the colt over the next couple of days.

This colt was special, Tony knew it was. Now every boy thinks that his first horse is special but this colt really was special, perhaps different would be a better description. The reason being was that his breeding was strange. The Colt's sire was a wild stallion that had broken into their corral one night. The Colt's mother was their plough horse, she was to different, part French Percheron and part Shire. The result was a very big colt indeed and very strong one. He would not be winning races, but as Tony's Pa had said, "What would what would a farm boy want with a race horse?"

The Colt was a dark bay in colour, in fact Tony would

say black, and took his colour from his mother. He had huge muscles that bunched and rippled under his skin when he made the slightest movement. He had the most unbelievably long mane and tail they flared out behind and around him when he ran. Pa said he would be bigger than the stallion who sired him by maybe another two hands which would make him about nineteen hands. It seemed to them both that you would only ride this horse if he let you. Pa had made a conversion to a saddle so the stirrups hung lower so that Tony would be able to get up there. Because Tony didn't really bend his knees when he rode it would work, if he didn't fall off. Pa rode long stirrups as well, but then as Tony says he was really tall.

The colt liked to nuzzle and push Tony whenever he came near him. His temperament was good but he had been known to lose it. One occasion, a wild dog got into the corral late at night and attacked their plough horse and the colt, the colt had trampled the dog and picked it up in his jaws and thrown it across the corral. This showed he had a really wild streak but for some reason Tony felt he didn't want to break him of it.

The thing was that after he had been in the corral with the plough horse Pa caught the stallion and then he had gentled him. After that he used him as his saddle horse. Pa didn't believe in breaking the spirit of any creature. Having said that for some reason the wild stallion didn't have the wildness about him that the colt did. Pa said he had a feeling that the stallion had belonged to someone before as he took to the saddle quite easily. This was often the case in those days, wild horses might be caught and broken in, then get free and roam again, before being recaptured. Or a horses rider might be killed by outlaws or Indians and the horse would then run free. Sometimes horses were stolen, but of course that was likely to be a hanging offence and that would not be sensible way to get a horse.

Pa's Stallion was a fine looking animal, nigh on 17 hands high, light chestnut in colour almost to the point of gold, Tony would have said that he was a Palomino if the mane and tail had been white. He was a strong quick animal with muscles rippling under his skin. The colt couldn't be kept in the same corral as the stallion, Tony and his Pa found that out when the colt was only about six months old, he was always trying to kick and bite the stallion. Pa said that this was because he, was feelin' his oats, wanting to show he was top man, which he clearly wasn't at that time.

Tony was a sensible lad and he could be trusted, so on this particular day his Pa said," I need you to go to the town, Jacksboro', and pick up the seed I ordered. When you get back we will be able get a crop in tomorrow." Tony saddled up Pa's horse and rode in town moaning to himself all the way. He could have been working with his colt instead he was being treated like a kid, sent on errands, this wasn't right because Tony knew he was a man. He had worked himself into a real state by the time he reached town.

CHAPTER 2

Tony rode along the street into town ignoring his neighbours shouted greetings, he was not in a pleasant mood. He dismounted in the street outside the store, then tied the horse to the hitching rail and stepped up onto the side walk. Tony strode forward towards the entrance to the store, head down. He walked straight into someone, he was knocked back, almost falling. He looked up and a big overweight guy glowered at him and swore. Tony then tried to walk round him, the guy wasn't having any of it. He put his hand on Tony's chest and swore at him, calling him stupid. Tony tried to step away but the big guy swung at him with his other hand, if the blow had landed the fight might have ended then.

Tony didn't know how it happened, but instead of ducking away he stepped in and grabbed the big guys arm, with both hands, one at the wrist one at the elbow, he yanked down hard against the guys elbow joint, Tony must have moved fast but he felt that time seemed to be standing still. He heard a scream, it must have come from the big guy, because the joint in his elbow had snapped. Tony let go and the big guy dropped to his knees. Tony spoke for the first time, saying "Just leave me alone next time!" Very slowly because he was in great pain, with his good hand the big guy reached for the pistol on his hip. Seeing this

Tony kicked him under the chin, and the guy sprawled out on the side walk, unconscious. Tony was completely bewildered, how could this happened? He had just wanted to get his Pa's seed.

There was suddenly a lot of noise and shouting, a blow then Tony was lying on the ground in the street. He got back up on his feet ready to fight back and then punches were flying left and right. The whole thing was bewildering Tony got a few good licks in but finally the weight of numbers drove him down to his knees, then on the periphery of his vision he saw a length of four by two and then he didn't see anything else.

Tony came out of the darkness in a rush, hands pushed him down, as he swung his arms in defence, the voice he heard was calm, "Easy boy" he heard that voice say. "Don't call me boy" Tony replied, his voice sounded thick and everything seemed far away. As he gradually returned to full consciousness Tony took in his surrounding, he was lying in a bed with a plain white counterpane, as his eyes cleared and he looked around the room. The room was sparsely furnished, it contained just the bed he was lying on, a chair by the bed and a small table. The sun was streaming in through the window which had some drapes on either side, he had never been much good with what they call fripperies, so Tony didn't pay much attention to the curtains.

Tony heard the voice again, "Good to see you open your eyes, that four by two hit you so hard I thought you might not." Tony turned to one side to look at the person who spoke. Waves of pain shot through his body, he gasped, fighting to keep from crying out. He succeeded then he saw, the man who had spoken to him he searched his memory, It was a man who he had seen around town but never spoken to. The man spoke "I'm Doc Evans, I know your family, you are Len and Mae Crane's boy, aren't you?" "Yes" he said, "My name's Tony." Then he asked, "Why am I here?" The doctor replied,"You took quite a beating, it was so bad it would have killed some men, never mind a boy." "You managed to upset seven of them, starting with the guy whose arm you broke." "Seven, huh," Tony replied." "My lucky number."

The Doc said, "You won't think so when I tell you your injuries." "You have a broken right hand, broken ribs, various cuts and bruises, but the worst thing was your head, I didn't think you would come round." "It has taken you two days to regain consciousness." Tony tried to get up, the doc put his hand up, saying, "Whoa, you won't be going anywhere for a while yet."

"I have to get up because Pa's waiting for his seed, we've got planting to do." "He's waited two days already" the doc replied, another couple won't harm. Tony shook my head, "Two days and he didn't come for me?" "That's not right." "It's OK" Doc replied, "The Sheriff sent a deputy out to your place to let them know."

Tony sat up fighting back the pain and swung his legs round so as his feet touched the floor, he stood up, he felt dizzy and sick, then he swayed and almost fell. The doc put his arm out and Tony leaned on him till the room stopped spinning. He stood there in his long underwear, "Clothes, I want my clothes." He said. "OK, if you insist, but I warn you, you are far from right." The doc replied. Tony struggled into his clothes, he couldn't bend to put his boots on so the doc put them on for him.

"Thanks, for taking care of me." Tony said. "I have to get my horse and the seed." He left the room and found his way across the hall through the outer door into the street. Tony heard the doc call, "Your horse is at the livery stable." He kept walking along the side walk. Every step was shaking his head to pieces. Tony got to the livery, he stepped down into the dusty street, he walked through, the double doors. When he got inside he saw the livery man, old Amos, with the gimpy leg, forking hay into a stall. Tony leaned on the wall, he felt real bad. "I've come for my horse Amos." He heard the words, come from his lips but they sounded very far away. "Looks like I had better saddle the horse for you," Amos said. Tony nodded slowly as he staggered away.

Tony saw a trough of water and staggered over to it plunging his head into it, up to his shoulders, the cold water took his breath away. He lifted his head out of the water and just stood there dripping, the water running down his shirt. He started to feel better, Tony looked up and saw Amos with the horse, "Thanks" he said. "Tell your Pa, he owes me a dollar, next time he is in town" said Amos. Tony nodded and led the horse out in to the street, down towards the store. He walked the 50 yards or so, as he didn't think that he could manage to get up into the saddle. Then he tied the horse to the hitching rail. He used the rail to pull himself up on to the side walk, and walked on into the store.

The store keeper, whose name was Al saw Tony come in to the store and spoke to him, "I suppose you want your Pa's seed Tony?" "Yeh,"Tony replied. "Nothing to pay," The storekeeper said "Your Pa covered it." Going on to say, "How are you?" "You sure took a beating." Tony just shook his head took the bag and walked back into the street. He stayed on the side walk, untied the horse turned him sideways on to the street and tying the reins round the saddle horn somehow pulled himself into the saddle, he moved the horse up the street and started heading out of town.

Tony leaned the bag of seed on the saddle in front of him unwound the reins and held them in one hand. The horse plodded up the street, as he passed the sheriffs office the sheriff, Ben Shaw stepped out in the street and got hold of the horses bridle, stopping Tony's progress. "I'm only going to tell you this once Crane, leave town and don't come back." "I don't like your Pa, never have, you are worse you are a bad seed and trouble will come wherever you are." Tony looked right through him, then jerked the horses head out of his grasp, and carried on out of town.

As Tony slowly rode home he prepared himself for his Ma and Pa's disappointment in him, he knew he was in the wrong, he had let his temper get him in to trouble. Pa had warned him, but he hadn't listened, he was lucky to be alive. As he got near their farm Tony saw a rider coming away from it and he was coming lickety split. As the rider got up to Tony he pulled his horse to a stop. It was the sheriff's deputy, Don Liston, "Don't go no further Tony, it's too awful, come back town with me, we will get the sheriff." Tony put his horses shoulder into the deputy's horse, pushing him out of the way. As painful as it was Tony galloped towards the farm, not prepared for the sights that would greet him.

The first thing Tony saw was his Ma lying in the yard, she must have run from the house to help Pa because she was lying beside Tony's rifle. She had fired it and Tony could see she had tried to reload, but she had been shot from distance, one side of her face was blown away. Tony flung himself from the saddle, dropping to his knees, the seed bag burst spilling as it hit the ground the bile rose in his throat as he scrabbled in the dirt towards his Ma, and he vomited. There were dry harsh croaks coming from his throat. Tony couldn't speak, his heart broke right there in the dust, it was to awful and Tony knew that life as he had known it was over.

Tony got to his feet, he had never felt so weak, he turned towards where he could see three male bodies and that of his dog lying by the corral. Three, Tony thought, How? He knew Pa would not have a gun with him,so what had happened? He got over to where they were lying, and looked down.

The first thing he saw was that one of the guys was shot in the shoulder it looked bad, Ma must have got him, but the bullet hadn't killed him, the man's neck was at an impossible angle Pa had like to tear his head off, his neck was completely snapped. The other guy looked like he'd been crushed in a stampede, His Pa had broken near every bone in his body. He still had hold of him. Pa had bullet holes in his back at least ten or twelve, so there must have at least four men, or if there were three one of the man had carried two pistols. Judging by the boot prints, Tony was inclined to think that there were four or more.

Tony sank to the ground and just sat there, He cried, until he could cry no more, the sobs that came from him were harsh and dry. Then it was just his shoulders heaving as he sobbed in silence. Tony looked over at the dog, he could see that there was bloodstained denim in his mouth, this showed him that the ever loyal dog had fought right to the end, there were three bullets in him.

Tony didn't know how long he sat there but the day was changing to dusk when he heard hoof beats come into the yard. The Sheriff's voice sounded behind him, "Hell of a thing, looks like Len killed these two with his bare hands, I knew he was a dangerous man, definitely not the kind of man you want in a civilised place." Tony felt rather than heard a low growl in his own throat, the second man's pistol was lying by his left hand, he grabbed it and turned, firing in one movement, the horn flew from the sheriff's saddle, bits of it going everywhere, his horse reared up on it's back legs, throwing him to the ground, where he lay stunned. Tony was still moving, all pain forgotten he turned to the deputy arriving just behind the sheriff.

The deputy's hand had gone to the butt of his pistol, "I wouldn't do that Don," Tony rasped,"It could be the last move you ever make." "Just take that pistol out slowly and drop it on the ground." "Easy boy," Don replied, "I know that your hurtin' but you need to calm down before things get worse." Anyway one lucky shot don't make you a pistolero." "Just drop the pistol on the ground unless you want to find out how lucky I could be, and don't call me boy." Replied Tony. The deputy eased the pistol out of it's holster and let it drop. It was awkward but Tony used his right hand which had the arm in a splint to pick up the pistol and push it into his belt.

Tony moved round to where the sheriff lay on the ground and took his pistol, dropping the one he was holding because he realised he had fired the last bullet in the chamber, when he hit the sheriff's saddle.

So Tony thought I have been lucky twice, once by hitting

the saddle and once when Don failed to realise that Tony was holding an empty pistol.

Sheriff Shaw groaned, saying "I broke my damn shoulder falling from the horse, you need to help me up." "No" Tony said, "The first thing that is going to happen is, Don is going to help me get Ma and Pa to the cabin." "We'll take Ma first," Don went over to her and gently picked her up, Tony was glad the state he was in he would have had to drag her, she didn't deserve that. Tony called to Don, "Put her on the big bed." Don nodded and kept walking towards and into the cabin. He came out, walking back towards him, saying, "I can't lift your Pa Tony, he is just to big." Tony nodded, saying "We will have to drag him, I can only use one arm"

Tony pushed the pistol in the other side of his belt. This was the time he could be jumped but Don just didn't seem inclined to try. They wrestled his Pa clear of the other corpse, Tony had his left arm under his Pa's right armpit, Don did the same on the other side. Tony gasped with pain from his chest and ribs as they started to move towards the cabin, his whole body felt as if it was on fire. Somehow they made it to the cabin and inside. With a real struggle they got him on the bed beside Ma. Tony was drenched in sweat and panting hard. They turned and went outside Tony pulled one of the pistols out of his belt.

As Tony and Don got back to the sheriff Tony spoke to the sheriff "Right Don catch up your horses, it's time for you to go." Don said, "I think you should know Tony, it was those seven guys you crossed in town did this, they may come back." Tony stumbled, he felt as If he had been kicked in the stomach, through gritted teeth Tony said, "There's only five now." "Just get your horses and get off the farm!" "I ain't finished with you Crane" snarled the Sheriff, "Oh but you have," Tony replied, "Don't give me reason to come looking for you."

Shaw looked from Don to Tony in disbelief, "They should have killed you in the street the other day" he spat. Then he said, "When I told them who you were and were you lived, they should have waited till you came home, and finished the job." Tony's face drained it's colour, he put the pistol back in the right side of his belt, handle facing left for a cross draw and pulled the other out of his belt throwing it on the ground in front of Shaw.

Tony had never felt so calm, "Pick it up," he said quietly, "You wanted the whole family dead, finish the job yourself." Tony turned his back and heard the sheriff scrabbling in the dust, Tony thought to himself as he felt the wind of the bullet that he didn't care about miss him on the right, Shaw will have thought I would turn round to the right because the bullet the sheriff had fired he didn't care about missed him to the right, that was because Tony had spun left, his pistol was already in his hand Tony fired as part of the same movement to the left The bullet hit the sheriff in the throat, Shaw's pistol slipped from his hand he was dead before he hit the ground. Tony wondered how he had managed to get away with his stupid move. He really had thought the sheriff would finish the job and kill him.

Tony heard the deputy, Don gasp,"My God." Tony turned towards him, pushing his pistol back in his belt. "Do you want the same chance I gave Shaw?" Tony asked. "No, No way, how did you do that, when your right hand is broken ?" "Well neither of you thought to ask before it was to late for Shaw," replied Tony, "The fact is that I am naturally left handed, although having said that, in normal circumstances I'm just as good with my right hand."

Don just stood there, holding the reins of both horses, there was shock etched on his face. Then he spoke "About the sheriff, I'll tell them in town how it was but I don't know what they will do, they may send some one after you." "It doesn't matter," Tony replied, "Shaw killed my Ma and Pa same as if he pulled the trigger himself, so I don't regret shooting him." Then after a moment he added,"I was just as responsible, I should have walked away when that guy in the street pushed me, I didn't and I caused all of this." Tony picked up his dog with some difficulty, it was awkward due to his right arm. Then he walked to the cabin and laid the dog in the place on the porch that he always liked to sleep. Then he went on inside the cabin, as he went inside he picked up a candle holder and candle from the shelf on the wall. He picked up a match and struck it on the wall,the match flared in the darkness, Tony lit the candle and carried it with him.

As he walked across the room Tony looked at his Ma and Pa lying on the bed, surprisingly he felt nothing, all emotion was gone from him, he didn't know it he was in shock. Tony turned and walked to the cupboard beside the fireplace, he opened it and looked on the shelves inside. Tony picked up his Pa's saddle bags, as he looked along the shelves he saw his two Sunday go to meeting shirts and the black pants he wore with them, also the real nice belt with the fancy buckle was on the shelf with them, Ma and Pa gave him that last Christmas—undershirts and underdrawers, a couple of pairs of socks a couple of clean rags, he don't know why and a cake of lye soap, he picked these things up and stuffed them all into the saddle bags.

He put the saddlebags over his shoulder then picked the candle and holder up again and recrossed the room to the fireplace. He walked as if in a dream.

Tony moved to the right of the fireplace, then he bent down, dropping onto one knee, he gasped in pain due to his broken ribs. As he recovered, from the shocking pain he put the candle and it's holder down on the floor Then Tony pulled his pocket knife out of his pants, he opened the blade and prised up the two floorboards that he knew to be loose. As the boards came free Tony folded the blade of the knife back into the handle and put it back into his pants pocket. Tony put his hand down under the floor and got hold of the small leather pouch that was down there he pulled it out and put it in his other pocket. He didn't look in the pouch he knew what was in it, five 10 dollar gold pieces, Pa's rain money.

Tony put his hand in the hole again and brought out a heavier package, it was wrapped in oily rags,he unwrapped it and he looked at it, it was his Pa's pistol belt, put away under the floor because as he had said "A farmer don't need no pistol." Tony slid the pistol out of the holster and looked at it, the gun oil glistened in the dark, he slid it back into the holster. Tony had never known why Pa had ever needed a pistol, but he was sure he knew why he did. Tony put his hand in the hole once more and came out with two boxes of shells, these things went in the saddle bags.

Tony stood up and strapped the pistol on, Pa was left handed like him, it felt heavy but it felt right. His damaged right arm made fastening it difficult but he succeeded It felt funny when he found that the pistol belt fit, because nothing else of Pa's ever had. Tony left the tie strings trailing down his left leg, because he just couldn't fumble to tie the strings with his right hand the way it was.

Tony turned and walked towards the kitchen area, there was a shelf Pa's watch was on it, he picked the watch up and put in the saddle bag. Then Tony picked up the coffee pot and emptied the contents on the floor, got a couple of bags of coffee, some beef that his Ma had jerked and then dropped them in a burlap bag along with some cans of beans. There was a tin of coal oil for the lamps on the shelf, Tony took it down and shook the contents round the floor. Then he went back and picked up the burlap bag, saddlebag, the candle holder and the candle, he lit the candle. Tony walked back to the door, stopped turned and looked round the room seeing nothing. Tony put the candle down on the floor then, kicked it over and watched as the flickering flame caught on the coal oil. Then he turned and stepped out across the porch past the dog and down the step into the yard.

Don was standing there looking at Tony, he had put Sheriff Shaw across his horse, tying him across the saddle like a dead calf. The whole of the inside of the house seemed to be burning now, he looked at Tony and said one word, "Why?" Tony knew what he was asking. "There's nothing here for me now, I'm moving on." "You going after the other five?" Don asked. Tony just looked at him and then said "Yup." "They will kill you" Don said. Tony looked at him and said nothing. Don carried on speaking "They are real mean guy's, one of them is called Mexican Joe, he is a half breed, he really is a natural born killer, I could see it in his eyes." Tony still said nothing, "Can you track Tony," Don asked. Tony shook his head. "How are you gonna find them then?" Don continued

Tony replied "They took my colt and the plough horse, they will want to sell them, they can't go back town so they will have go North, there is nothing in any other direction that's close enough to make it worth while." "Then I know one has broken arm, I broke it, You tell me one is called Mexican Joe, I have enough information to find them." "If I kill them, or if they kill me, I don't care, it really doesn't make any difference, none of us will be any loss." Don looked at Tony, shook his head then, he mounted his horse and rode out of the yard, leading the sheriff draped across his horse behind him.

Tony watched him go in the light from the fire. He walked his horse to the water trough, in spite of the gunfire the horse had never moved, because Tony had left the reins trailing. Tony put the saddle bags on the back of the horse then he turned and walked to the two dead men, Tony bent down with an intake of breathe caused by the pain his ribs, he took off their pistol belts, one was also wearing a shoulder holster, Tony looked at it saw how it worked and with a struggle put it on, he pushed one of the pistols in to it, after first checking the loads. The cabin was burning brightly now, lighting up the whole yard and in the fires glow Tony noticed one of the men was wearing new boots, they looked to be his size, so he took them. He checked their pockets, between them they had 11 dollars and a few cents, he took that.

Tony found that one had a Bowie knife and a throwing knife. There was also a mother of pearl handled straight razor Tony took them all. There was a hat, lying on the ground Tony's size, black it suited his character, he would have that. One of the men who hadn't been shot, just crushed to death in his Pa's hands had a hip length black jacket,under his slicker coat, he took of the slicker then the jacket– surprise, surprise the jacket fitted Tony. The other surprise was that the jacket had a pocket in one sleeve with a double barrelled derringer in it. Tony checked the pockets of the slicker coat and found reloads for the derringer he transferred them to his possessions. Then Tony picked up the dropped rifle checked the loads and put in the saddle boot on his Pa's saddle.

When Tony was sure the men had was nothing else he needed he left the bodies for the buzzards thinking, we all deserve to eat. Then Tony went to the water trough and filled a couple of canteens, then he hung them from the saddle horn. Leaving the dead rider's pistol belts, pistols, Bowie knife, throwing knife, straight razor, boots, the hat and the jacket on the ground beside the trough.

After that Tony went into the barn let the calves out and drove them off. He got the three legged stool and a bucket, Tony sat on the stool and milked the cow, she was bellowing and in pain she was glad of the relief. She was a good cow and she had always been fine with Tony. When she was milked he turned the cow loose and drove her off.

One of their neighbours would find her and they would have a good cow. As Tony was filling two more canteens at the pump he saw Pa's slicker coat hanging on the barn door it was to big but he took it with him, it would keep him warm on a cold night. He carried the slicker coat and some piggin' string with him as he walked back to the horse. Tony threw the slicker coat down, then he put the things that he had left on the ground in it and wrapped them all together, tied the bundle up with piggin' string and tied the bundle on the back of the horse behind the saddle. Then he walked back over towards the barn, when he got there he set fire to it, put on his new hat and rode out.

When Tony turned looked back a few minutes later, he saw that the whole sky looked red. Tomorrow there would be nothing to show that the Crane family had ever lived there. There would just be a pile of ashes, drifting in the breeze.

Tony rode North following the trail of the men who he was cursed by his own actions to find. Tony Crane the farm boy had ceased to exist. The boy had become Crane, he was a 14 year old killer and a robber of the dead. No wonder Sheriff Shaw had said that he was a bad seed, as he rode Crane had no doubt that the sheriff was right

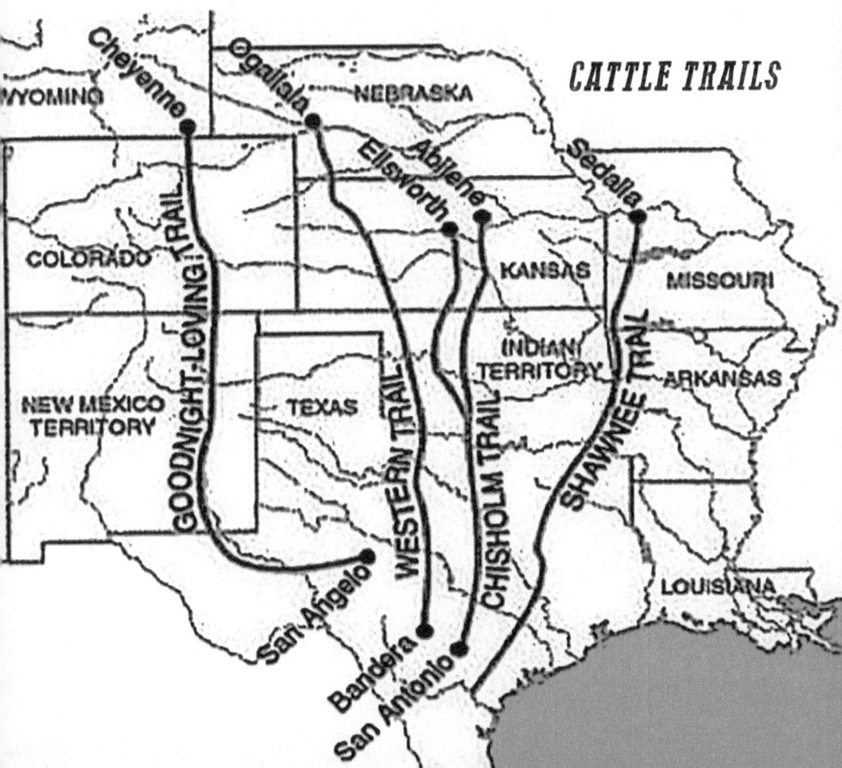

CHAPTER 3

The four men sat round their camp fire and cursed, "Damn that family." The one with the broken arm, whose name was Colin said "I can't believe it the kid broke my arm, then that damned dog bit me and tore my pants and then his Pa smashed up my face, and killed Griggs and Walsh." "We should have killed that kid before we left town."

Mexican Joe, laughed, "Don't worry about a stupid farm boy, he was probably addle pated before I laid that four by two across the back of his skull, he will sucking soup through a straw by now." "Yeh," Said the broken armed fat Colin, as his friends called him, "You're right he's nothing, the big problem is that colt, he's a killer if ever I saw one, we might be better to put a bullet in him now. "No need for that" said Lattigo, the others looked at the lean scar faced man, "I can break any horse, even one as big as him." "I'll start the job in the morning."

Utah the other man, who known by no other name except the place he came from, shook his head, "I'd be careful he doesn't break you," he drawled. Lattigo, stared at him, then he spoke, spitting to words out staccato, "Break Me!" "There ain't no man nor horse can do that job!" "Don't forget I shot Kirby for arguing with me before we got here, I don't mind killing someone else." Utah got up slowly, shrugged his shoulders and walked away from the camp fire into the dark.

Mexican Joe said, "I think we should turn in, you three seem a leetle mite jumpy." He stood up threw the dregs of his coffee from his tin cup, picked up the coffee pot and emptied that on the fire, steam rising around him as he turned away, a man who was used to others doing what he said.

Utah was already in his bed roll, Lattigo and Colin moved towards theirs, Colin mumbling "I gotta pee first," heading further into the darkness. "Damn it," he muttered, "This is difficult with one hand." The others heard the urine splashing on the ground. Then Colin made his way to his bed roll, there was a thud and a curse as he hit the ground "God dammit" He cursed. Three voices answered in unison, "Shut up, you useless bum." "I can't help it" Colin whined, "I ain't got no balance with one arm." The others ignored his reply and the camp went quiet.

There was a thunder storm that night the, lightning flashes were lighting up the sky, the rain came down heavy enough to cause a flood, dry creek beds that had not seen water for months filled and overflowed running fast, the land was soaked, and so were the men who slept on it. The four outlaws them were cursing and moaning, there would be no coffee for breakfast because there was nothing dry to start a fire. Their clothes, boots, blankets everything they owned had been soaked because they had camped at the bottom of a slope and the water had run down and pooled around them. The four argued among themselves, they were small minded men who held everyone and everything but themselves responsible for any misfortune that befell them.

They had been eight when they left Mexico but as he said, Lattigo had killed Kirby before he got to Jacksboro.

One of the big things that galled Colin particular was that they had been avoiding settlements and towns along the trail they had travelled through Arkansas. They had been keeping away from people altogether, just because Mexican Joe said they should. Colin commented on this and he and Lattigo started pushing each other, arguing back and forth. Lattigo was goading Colin, trying to force him into going for his gun But Colin who was a bully and a coward by nature and although he would happily back shoot Lattigo, but he did not want to face him in a stand up pistol fight. So he snivelled and weaselled his way out of the argument

Lattigo looked at Colin sneering at him, saying, "Lily livered scum." He took out a monogrammed leather tobacco pouch and cigarette papers. He took a paper shook tobacco on to it and rolled a cigarette. Then he struck a match on the seat of his pants, because they were wet it didn't light, just fell apart. He cursed and getting a another match, he found a rock with a dry edge struck the match against it and when it fired up he lit the cigarette.

Utah as usual stood off away from the argument, he was a quiet taciturn man who kept himself to himself, he didn't seem to belong with this group of men. Circumstances as they say had led him to this point in his life. He was not a happy man in his present company, in fact in better times Utah had been a well respected law man. He really needed to find away to ride away from the other three men, he had thought this more and more since Mexican Joe had shot the pretty woman, back at the farm when she had tried to help her husband.

Utah had really admired the farmer, he died fighting never taking a backward step, he showed no fear even though he had no weapon to defend himself. The kid to, was like his father brave, kept getting up in the face of insurmountable odds, when they had kept hitting him knocking him down and kicking him. These people Utah was riding with made him feel ashamed, that he hadn't helped the boy or his Ma and Pa later. He questioned himself, When had he become less than a man? Then he asked the silent question, *Could there ever be any way back, to humanity?*

As he ruminated on the problem, while half listening to the ongoing argument,between Lattigo and Colin, he heard Mexican Joe's rasping voice say, "If you pair of scum don't quiet down I'll kill you both!" Lattigo spun towards Mexican Joe lips twisted in a bitter snarl, "You are gonna get what you want if you keep crowdin' me, only you will be the one killed.' Lattigo walked away only stopping to pick up his saddle. Mexican Joe watched him a sardonic smile playing around his mouth, he looked at the other two, "He's right, I will have to kill him one day," he paused then added with a smile, "Soon."

Lattigo walked on in to the clearing where the horses were hobbled, the colt was shifting his feet from side to side, ears back, nostrils flared and eyes rolling. Lattigo looked at the colt and said "That finishes today, I'm going to ride you until you break or die."

The colt danced sideways it's feet were tied with hobbles. Lattigo got his rope from the saddle throwing the loop over the colts neck he pulled it tight, he got to close and the colt lunged to wards him and colt tried to bite him, Lattigo lashed the colts face with the quirt that was hanging from his wrist, the colt went wild, trying everything to get to him, but the hobbles held. Lattigo threw the other end of the rope over a nearby tree and tied it off, the colt still fought hard but he couldn't stop the saddle being thrown onto his back and then the girth was tightened The colt whipped his head right and left the saddle was his enemy and the colt danced from side to side. The Colt already wore a bridle that the outlaws had used to lead it away from the farm, the reins were tied off around it's neck.

Lattigo was working fast now, he unfastened the hobbles grabbed the saddle horn, and vaulted up into the saddle. The colt exploded screaming into the air, it reared right up, front hooves pawing wildly at the air. There was no rope made that could hold this colt and sure enough the rope snapped as came tight. Sensing that it was free the colt reared again even higher this time, it kept rising, going over backwards, The extra strain snapped the girth on the saddle, Lattigo fell from the saddle and the colt landed on top of him. He was likely dead in that moment but with unbelievable speed the colt was on it's feet, rearing in the air it repeatedly rose and fell it's hooves crushing and breaking Lattigo's body. Utah and Mexican Joe burst into the clearing, the colt spun when he heard them, laid it's ears back and ran at them, they dived away landing either side of him and the colt kept running, Colin, fat and slow got there late arriving in time to see the colt go.

The other two got up, and the three of them walked to where Lattigo's broken body lay. They looked down at him in disbelief, then Utah spoke,"Well he met the horse that broke him." Mexican Joe, spun away from them, saying over his shoulder, "Shut up, we need to break camp and get away from here." He was clearly shaken by this turn of events.

The three outlaws packed their stuff saddled up and rode away leading the horses belonging to Lattigo and Kirby and the Plough horse. Three bitter and lonely men each with their own thoughts. "Colin finally spoke, "I'm glad to see the back of that Colt. I think it would kill us all if it could." The other two silently nodded and rode on.

CHAPTER 4

Crane was cold and wet, but the sun was shining, Pa's big slicker had kept most of the water off him. As a farm boy he would have been glad to see the rain a few weeks ago, but things change. After riding for over a month without seeing anyone and making several dry camps he had camped up on a bluff, looking down on what had been a dry creek bed last night, so at least the water ran down the creek bed which was now a swollen river. That was his third bit of luck, if he had bedded down on the low ground as he had a few times along the way, he would likely have drowned. They say it is better to be lucky than just good. Crane don't know about that, he only knew that luck can run out. The other two bits of luck he had involved the first pistol that he had picked up.

When Crane had fired the pistol at the sheriff who was on his horse in Crane's home yard, it was the first time he had ever even held a pistol never mind fired one. Crane had hit the smallest target, the saddle horn, when he fired if he thought at all he thought he might hit the horse, as it was if he had fired any higher he would have missed everything. Then when he had challenged the sheriff to a pistol fight he had turned his back then spun and drew on the sheriff, he could have caught the pistol in his waist band, or he could have turned into the sheriff's bullet. Then when he fired at him his shot was rising, once again he was shooting high. A habit like that could get him killed, not that he cared.

Crane decided that he must look a real sight so, he took the splint off his right hand maybe his arm it wasn't broken at all, perhaps it was only strained it had only been the deputy who said his arm was broken. Crane hadn't waited for the doctor to tell him much. So he decided to wash in the river, using the lye soap that he had brought from the kitchen at home. Physically Crane was feeling much better and he was moving with more ease now. Being young he supposed had made sure that he was healing quickly, feeling better everyday.

Crane picked up and threaded his good leather belt through the loops on the black pants then put them on, cinching up the belt. He put on a clean shirt, before he fastened the sleeve on the right arm he strapped the throwing knife there, it slipped down into the palm of his hand when he flexed the muscle in his forearm. Crane pulled on the new black boots that he had taken off the guy who had been shot, they had spurs fastened to them, but someone had replaced the spiked rowels with silver dollars. Crane liked that because there was no way he would be raking a horse's side, to make him run. The boots fit real good and made him about an inch and a half taller with the heel. He had never had a pair like them before, he had only had his lace up work boots.

Then Crane put the shoulder holster on and covered it with the short jacket another good fit and it wasn't heavy material either. He put one of the pistols he had claimed from the fallen men in the shoulder holster after first making sure it was loaded, the jacket was a loose enough fit to hide the pistol from view.

Crane picked up his Pa's pistol belt and put it on, it was made to fit low on his left hip, this time he managed to fasten the leather thongs around his leg, the holster felt snug against his thigh. He picked up his Pa's pistol once again, thinking that he would have to stop thinking that it was his Pa's, because these things were his now. Crane checked that the pistol was loaded and slid it into the holster, he pulled it out again a couple of times,the pistol literally jumped into his hand as if it belonged there. When he was happy with it's feel, Crane holstered the pistol and pulled the loop over the hammer that would keep the pistol in place when he was riding.

Crane got the Bowie knife in it's scabbard and slid it in to the top of his left boot, it flt snug against his calf. Then Crane pulled his pants legs down over the outside of his boots, no one would know it was there. Having the knife in his boot gave him what his Pa had told him once was an edge, his Pa had said he knew a guy who lived by that ideal, in fact his name was Edge. Crane put the straight razor in his jacket pocket, then put the pouch with the gold pieces in to his left front pants pocket the other money in the right front pocket and his pocket knife in his jacket.

The jacket a small pocket on the inside low down, the derringer fitted very nicely in there, it gave him another edge, so he decided to keep it there and not in the sleeve. Crane ran his fingers through his long damp hair then put the black hat on, running his fingers round the brim. He filled his canteens from the creek, he was loaded for bear, it was time to saddle up and ride on. Crane was riding the Shawnee Trail, up through Indian Territory, he did not know it but he was reversing the journey his Pa had made to get to their farm a few years before. Crane was just drifting, but at the same time he was also searching for the men who killed his family and stole his colt. He just had to keep moving

Crane's horse plodded on through the heat of the day, he looked at the sun, it looked to be about noon he saw a few trees ahead with buzzards circling overhead and angled his horse towards them. As Crane got there he saw a the broken body of a man lying on the ground, Crane's eyes scanned the area and he saw the end of a broken rope that was still tied to a tree, there was a saddle with a broken cinch strap lying on the ground. The earth was churned up and hoof prints could be clearly seen on the damp ground. The picture told Crane a story, A big horse had trampled this man to death. It did not take much imagination for him to come to the conclusion that this was one of the men who had killed his Ma and Pa. The likely hood was, that this poor fool had tried to ride Crane's colt and paid the price.

Crane looked at the body, he hunkered down and looked closely at the bloody remains there was a lot to see. The top pocket on the man's shirt was, like much of his clothing was shredded but there was a leather pouch which had pretty much survived hanging from the shredded cloth. It was covered in blood, Crane picked it up and rubbed it on the ground, he could just make out some letters on it, LATTI, this could be the guys name Lattigo maybe, for all the difference it made to him. Crane could see that there were 3 or 4 silver dollars on the ground in the area where the guys pockets might have been, so he picked them up and put them in his pocket, he just thought, one more dead.

At that moment Crane heard the thunder of hooves, he spun around reaching for his pistol, but he was to slow, Crane was knocked from his feet/ Lying on the ground he looked up and saw that his colt was standing over him. The colt lowered his head and nuzzled his face, Crane struggled to my feet, "Well" He said, "I never thought to see you again." The colt pushed his head against him, it was pleased to see him. Crane stroked the colt's face and thought to himself we could all do with water. So he walked back to his horse lifted his canteen of the saddle horn, and took out the cork.

Crane then picked up his hat from where it had fallen and poured water into it both horses drank from it in turn, when they were finished he took a couple of swallows from the canteen himself and then after pushing the cork back in the top he hung the canteen back on the saddle. He put his hat back on, then he made ready for the midday camp. He took the saddle off his horse and used the blanket from under the saddle to dry the sweat from both the horse's backs. He didn't want these horses getting saddle sore, even though he didn't know when or even if he could ride the colt.

Crane lay on the ground, He had no concerns that his horse would wander because he had left the reins hanging loose on the ground the colt had made it clear that he wanted to be where he was so Crane left him free. Crane lay down with his back against his saddle, pulled his hat down over his eyes and dozed. About an hour had passed when he was awakened by the colt making a hell of a racket. Then a boot hit his already sore ribs, he came up with a roar and found himself looking straight into the twin bores of a double barrelled shot gun.

"Well lookee here" the guy holding the shot gun said, "It seems we got ourselves one these kids who wannabe one of those hell raising Missouri Raiders who tore things up things up along the border for so long." Crane looked around and he saw two more men stationed off to the left and right of him. One of them had his hands full because he had made the mistake of putting a rope on the colt. The colt was stamping and lunging up in the air, hooves flying. The guy had looped the rope round a tree but he couldn't tie it off, with all the prancing and dancing the colt was doing the guy had no chance of ever doing it.

The first guy spoke again, "Just take that pistol out real slow and throw it over here, you can follow it with the one hiding under your arm." Well Crane was known for his quick temper but he is nobodies fool and with two guns on him he thought it best to comply. Crane looked at the guy with the shot gun, he had it cocked and Crane knew it would cut him in half if he pulled the trigger. Moving slowly he threw his side arm to the left following it with his shoulder pistol. This decision not to throw them straight line out in front of him, might just save his life down the line.

On the periphery of Crane's vision he could see and hear the colt getting wilder and wilder. Crane could tell the two guys covering him were becoming more and more distracted, He knew if he was to have any chance at all, the next few minutes would be the time to make his move.

What the hell he thought I'm only going to die once.

Crane reached his left hand into the small pocket inside his jacket his fingers closing on the but of the derringer he kept there, at the same time he took a step forward, saying "I've got fifty dollar gold pieces here." As he did this with the derringer in now in his hand he deliberately stumbled, falling to his left turning his body the same way. Crane heard the blast of the shotgun and the crack of the pistol on his left and felt a burn on his right arm and the right side of his face.

As Crane hit the ground he fired the derringer at the guy on his left who stumbled as the bullet hit him but kept hold of his pistol. Crane's right hand closed round one of his own pistols, he was aware of the most incredible noise, it sounded like a herd of horses plunging, stamping and neighing, not just the colt.

Crane shot the guy on the left hitting him in the throat he was rolling moving all the time, wondering about the shot gun, he came to a sitting position his pistol levelled facing in that direction. What Crane saw was a shock, from his position the ground he could see the biggest horse, a roan, that he had ever seen in his life just bringing his hooves down on the body of the shot gun guy. Atop the horse with the reins in his teeth and a pistol in each hand, was a tall spare man.

Crane suddenly remembered the guy who was trying to hold his colt he rolled ready to fire knowing that he would be to late. Crane was lucky again, the colt had done the job for him, the broken body of the man lay at his feet as the colt stood back wild eyed and snorting. Crane turned back in time to see the tall guy dismount. When the man got down from his horse Crane could see he wasn't as tall as he thought, in fact he wasn't as tall as Crane maybe 5ft 8 or 9 inches, certainly no more.

Under his hat the man's long hair was brown, he had the blackest eyes that Crane had ever seen. His face showed the signs of battles fought. He had a deep knife scar in the left corner of his mouth and a scar that may have been from a bullet across his right cheek, the man sported a moustache. The man opened his mouth, "You have got what you can't buy son," he drawled.

Crane looked at him bewildered, "What?" "You've got that mean streak that only comes out when all is lost and you think your going to die." The man replied. Crane just said, "That and dumb luck," Crane then went say, "Where are their horses?" "They are still running I shouldn't wonder, they took off when I rode in" Said the man adding, "these dammed fools left them loose, they were just Crow baits anyway."

The guy looked around, "These guys have been trailing me for about a week" he said. Then he asked, "You got a name?" "Without thinking the reply came, "Crane." Then he asked, "You? Josey Wales" The man replied. Crane looked at him in disbelief, "I've heard of you, why did you help me?" Crane asked.

"I was helping myself," Wales replied, "As I said these people had been on my trail for over a week and I wanted to avoid being shot in the back, so I turned around on them. Then I saw that they had come on you so I watched, when you made your move I thought I would even things up. You are a pretty good pistol fighter but I notice you shoot high, that could get you killed one day." "That would be no loss." Crane replied. "Yeh I can see that in you" Wales affirmed.

"Why were they trailing you?" Crane asked. Wales gave him an appraising look, then said "For the $3,000 reward." He paused then drawled, "If you are interested in collecting." Crane shook his head,replying, "No interest at all, I only have one purpose in my life and that is to find the men who killed my folks." "Ah" said Wales, "You are on the vengeance trail, I know that route." "My wife and boy were murdered sometime back, before the war. I find someone involved in that now and again, so I keep riding on. I've nowhere else to go, no other reason to be" adding, "That's why I got into the Border War and rode with Bloody Bill Anderson."

Crane replied, "I think my Pa spent some time with Anderson, Ma said one time that he had been a guerilla fighter, but he never told me about it. He never carried a pistol in the time I knew him. He just worked hard and put food on the table. Him and Ma always worked hard, then I got them killed." Crane said bitterly. The two men were reloading as they talked. Wales nodded, "I like to see that in you, I've seen good pistol fighters die when they forgot to reload."

Wales looked at Crane, then he said, "Your Pa carried a pistol damned well when he rode with us and he twice killed a man with his bare hands, when he looked like he'd get killed in knife fights." He never knew when he was beat, biggest strongest man I ever saw." "You can make that four." Crane replied, "He killed two of Mexican Joe's gang with his bare hands when it looked like he should have already been dead."

"Yeah he had that in his eyes" replied Wales. "One thing I don't understand kid, you say you got them killed?" So Crane told him about the fight in town. Then about how he had found them and how he killed the sheriff. Wale's looked at him, then he slowly said, "You're wrong boy," "What do you know about it?" Crane spat, then he said "Don't call me boy." Wales looked at him with those flat black eyes, "That temper will get you killed boy," he stated. Then he said, "If you want to hold back on dyin', for a minute I'll tell you why it ain't your fault."

Crane looked at him not trusting himself to speak, he knew that he was closer to death in that moment than he had ever been. Wales carried on speaking, "If you hadn't gone town that day, those riders would have still gone to your farm, only difference being, if you had been there, you would have died with your parents." "Some things just happen, you can't change them, though you might make them worse."

Crane thought about it, Wales was right, Crane had been blaming himself for what was quite simply fate. He spoke, saying, "So I guess I'm not fated to die today." "Me neither" Wales replied. "You?" Asked Crane, "Oh Yeah," he replied, "I would surely kill you in a pistol fight but, you are first one I've met in a long time who like me would die to kill his enemy, you would take me on your way down." Crane just looked at him, because there was nothing to say.

They were silent, then Wales said, "That colt is going to be bigger than my Roan, I saw him kill that feller, he is a war horse like mine, always loyal to one person and he has the instinct to kill, you find horses like that, once in a generation." "You two are a good match." Then Wales asked, "You got coffee son?" he drawled, "I never talked so much in my life, my mouth is bone dry." "Sure," Crane said, "I'll light a fire and make some."

As they both moved away from the battle ground and Wales unsaddled and they worked in silence, Crane making the coffee. Wales came over to Crane with his canteen and a rag in his hand, "Better try and clean up the wounds on your face and arm. Your jacket will make good waistcoat, it's no good with one sleeve and your shirt can be ripped up as a bandage for your arm." Wales dabbed the wet cloth on Crane's face, Crane pulled away as it stung, but Wales kept at it. Then he said"There are a couple of pieces of shot in here, I've seen wounds like this before, it will likely heal with a blue scar, you don't look so pretty now."

Wales helped Crane to get out of his jacket his right arm and shoulder were stiffening up. Then Crane shooked the shoulder holster and took off the shirt. Wales looked at Crane's arm, then put the blade of his knife in the fire, he looked round and picked up a small piece of wood, he handed it to Crane, saying "You will need to bite on that, because I've got to dig for a couple pieces of buck shot"

Wales pulled the knife out of the fire Crane put the wood in his mouth and bit down, Wales got to work. It hurt like hell and Crane thought his jaw would break and all his teeth to, as he bit down. Just when he thought I can't take it any more, Wales was finished. He got up walked over to his saddlebag and came back with a bottle of Rye. He took the cork out and splashed it over the wound on Crane's arm as Crane yelped Wales poured some down the right side of his face. Crane cursed, "Dammit!!" Wales smiled and took a swig from the bottle, then said, "Here

40

take a swig, Crane did coughing and spluttering, It was the first time he had tasted alcohol and he had never tasted anything so bad. Wales took Crane's shirt tore it into strips and bandaged his arm.

Crane got another shirt from his saddle bag and put it on, then buckled on the shoulder holster. He then got out his knife, Wales smiled when he saw it in Crane's boot, but said nothing as Crane cut the tattered right sleeve off and then the left one and put the resultant waistcoat on. He returned the knife to it's place.

Crane went to his saddlebags taking out and throwing Wales a can of beans and they sat with their backs against their saddles opened the cans with their knives and ate the beans in silence while the coffee bubbled on the fire. Wales got his own cup from his saddle bags and they poured the coffee and let it cool.

They dozed in the afternoon sun, they knew that they still had something to do as the buzzards circled overhead. So after awhile they got up and walked to where the bodies lay. First they gathered the weapons and any reloads dead men had. The Shotgun was done, the Roan had smashed the stock and flattened the barrel. Crane picked up a couple of knives, Wales looked at him saying, "You are good, you never leave anything you might use." The two men went through the dead men's pockets and shared the money that they found. "You don't mind robbin' the dead boy?" He asked. "Way I see it if you're dead you're dead, someday it'll be me, anybodies welcome to what I've got when that day comes." Replied Crane

"Well," said Wales, "I guess I'll drift boy, You know how it is I always ride alone, characters like you and me seem to wind up getting our companions killed. Just one last thing I have an old Indian friend name of Lone Waddy, now he says that we should all endeavour to persevere, think on it."

With that Wales saddled up touched his fingers to his hat and rode out.

After he had gone Crane thought how many times he had called him boy and son. He thought to himself, "I must be growing up, I didn't take offence." With that in mind Crane set about breaking camp.

CHAPTER 5

Crane rode on through the darkness, the colt following behind him, his thoughts playing around with the things that Josey Wales had said to him. Maybe I am growing up because he repeatedly called me boy and I didn't react. Other things Josey said made Crane look at my situation, the more he thought about the more he realised Wales was right, Crane wasn't responsible for his Ma and Pa being killed. Those men were travelling North looking for easy pickings, they were just drifters, who made their way by stealing from others. Those kind of people don't need a reason to rob and kill, they do it because they can. Crane realised that he was wrong to blame himself or the sheriff for their deaths, but, having said that,Ben Shaw had bad mouthed Crane's Pa and he clearly wanted to kill Crane, so what happened to him was as Crane looked at it now, just fate.

What was done was done and Crane's way forward was set, he had nothing to go back for, like Josey Wales it was the vengeance trail for him, he would not be swayed, he would just ride on. Crane dozed in the saddle trusting his horse to find the trail. Then he woke with a start, the horse had stopped moving and was just standing. It was dark very dark and they were in a clearing surrounded by trees. Crane's horse had made the decision that they would go no further that night. Crane slid down out of the saddle and set about making a camp. He unsaddled the horse rubbed him down gave him and the colt a drink from his hat and then took a drink himself. Then using his saddle as a pillow Crane pulled his Pa's slicker over him, put the pistol from his shoulder holster on his chest and went to sleep.

Crane slept long and deep awaking mid-morning, feeling refreshed and less sore than previously. He had a swallow of water and began breaking camp. He had two horses to attend to because the colt now had to be considered a horse. He responded well to Crane's company and displayed his usual affection for him. Crane thought that maybe this afternoon he might try riding him. After all he needed to know if he would be riding him or letting him go. Also Crane knew that he could not continue with two stallions without problems coming sooner rather than later, because as they went along each one would be vying for superiority.

Crane rode on through a group of trees, almost a wood really, as he came out of the trees he found himself in a rather sparse meadow. Right, Crane thought this would be a good enough place to try and ride the colt. He dismounted and took the stallion's saddle off, as always rubbing the sweat from his back with the blanket. Crane left his reins trailing, He knew the horse wouldn't stray.

Going over to the colt, Crane put the saddle on and tightened up the double girth and lowered the stirrup leathers as far as he could, then he pushed his weight down hard with his hand on the stirrup. The colt stamped his feet and whickered. Crane felt good about making the effort to ride him, he was sure that they had built a bond starting from when the colt was foaled. There was nothing that Crane had seen in the colts actions towards him had changed his opinion that he would be able ride him.

Crane decided the best way to get up into the saddle was to grab the saddle horn and vault up when the colt stepped forward as Crane was sure he would. Well, was Crane in for a surprise? Because when he gripped the saddle horn the colt lowered his left side by bending his knees, Crane vaulted up into the saddle with amazement and prepared for the explosion of power as the colt did his level best to unseat him. But nothing happened the colt just stood there, Crane patted his neck and urged him forward with pressure from his knees. The colt went forward at the walk, Crane couldn't believe how calm he was it was if he had been ridden for years.

The next twenty minutes were spent with the colt being put through the changes of pace, from walk through the trot, canter and gallop. This horse was truly amazing, Crane really felt as though he had been riding him for years. Crane dismounted took his saddle of and rubbed him down, then gave him a drink of water from his hat. As he was doing that Crane noted that he would need to find water very soon.

This had turned into a very good day for Crane, he was happy for the first time since he had left his home behind him. It seemed the hours put in the lunge line and just making a fuss of the colt had been well spent. There was still daylight so Crane re-saddled the horse and rode on.

The days turned in to weeks, the months into more than a year as Crane drifted and meandered across the land. Very little changed and he had found no sign of the men he was following. Having said that he did find the plough horse on a scrub farm, the farmer had bought the plough horse from three mean looking men. He said, that as he hadn't any money he paid them with supplies. He had thought at first they would kill him but they were half starved and one of them who he heard was called Utah had told the other two that for once they should do the right thing. The farmer went on to say that if they hadn't let him have the plough horse, they would have to kill and eat it, the men were starving. The plough horse knew Crane and the colt, he thought that she knew the stallion as well, but she just ignored him. Crane was surprised that he hadn't had more trouble with the two stallions but so far they had remained aloof, they just ignored each other.

The farmer and his wife fed Crane and watered his horses. Crane having told the farmer his story assured the man that he wouldn't want to reclaim the plough horse. This was great relief to the farmer. Before he left the farm Crane traded the farmer a rifle and ammunition that he had picked up along the way, for some cans of food and dry goods. Crane was riding the colt all the time now, but he was not ready to part with the stallion.

As Crane rode away he thought to himself, well at least I have another name now, Utah. Crane pondered about how strange it was that this man Utah had talked the other two riders out of killing the farmer and his wife. If this man had a conscience why was he riding with the men that Crane thought of as scum? Also why hadn't he stopped Mexican Joe killing Crane's Ma and Pa. Questions which troubled Crane because he couldn't find an answer

CHAPTER 6

The three men were arguing again, the usual self absorbed attitude to life led to the vitriol that was coming from Mexican Joe and Fat Colin, Utah was becoming more and more frustrated with them, he knew he couldn't take much more. Colin whined, "It ain't fair Joe keeps saying we can't go into a town because maybe the law knows who we are, we are going nowhere just drifting round." Utah replied, "If you want to hang by your neck until you are dead, go to any town, ride back to Dallas it ain't to far you won't be missed by me." Mexican Joe snarled, "I run you guys, I tell you what to do, nobody is going any where, unless you two are ready for Boot Hill!!" His right hand hovered over the but of his pistol. "I'm getting tired of your threats, I suggest you choose your next words or actions very carefully, replied Utah." "Never mind all that" said Colin, "We have been running from that kid Crane for nearly four years now, every where we go we hear that he was hunting four men now he is hunting three men, we must be the three men he wants." "Then on top of that people say that this Crane is lightning fast with a pistol and he is riding that devil horse that killed Lattigo, I'm telling you the kid just can't be human, Josey Wales is telling people that he was glad to ride away from him. "So Joe, if you are our leader when are you going to do something about this kid?"

Mexican Joe looked at him through narrowed eyes, "If it bothers you we will circle back and you can kill him, from ambush if you like." Colin looked back at him saying, "About time, I'll do it I owe him!" Utah remained silent keeping his thoughts to himself. The rumours they had picked up on trail led him to believe that this ambush plan was a big mistake, the kid would likely kill them all.

The three men saddled up and rode out, for the first time in a long time they had a purpose and a direction. They had been riding for about half an hour when they saw rider coming towards them. They stopped and let him come to them. As he got closer, Colin spoke, "I know this guy, they call him Lucky Tom Salt, he lost an ear wrestling a bear." Mexican Joe and Utah looked at him with expressions of humorous contempt. Mexican Joe, spoke, "What's lucky about losing an ear?"Colin replied, "Someone shot the bear before it killed him." Mexican Joe just snorted "Huh."

Salt was riding a Calico Pony, it pranced stepping sideways as it approached and the three riders could see the lack of an ear on the left side of Salt's head. Worse to see was the raked scars down the side of his face that stretched under the collar of his shirt. The left side of his mouth was dropped and badly scarred. His clothes like theirs were tattered, torn and grimy.

Salt saw Colin, his mouth twisted in a sneering smile, "Hey fat boy long time no see" "Don't call me that," whined Colin, it ain't my fault that I am big boned." Salt ignored the reply saying,"Where are you fellers going?" Again it was Colin who replied, "We are riding to kill a man, he is very cunning he crept up on me, and broke my arm. "Mexican Joe burst out laughing, "haw haw" he rasped,

"Then he said, "Every time Colin opens his mouth he lies, we're going to kill the schoolboy who broke his arm when Colin tried to face him down.

If what I've heard on the trail is true, it'll be a kid called Crane who kills the three of you. "I saw Josey Wales a while back and he said the kid was chained blue lightning with a pistol and he simply don't know when he is beat, he eats pain like candy and if he don't kill you, that horse of his will. Wales said if he owned the horse he would call that black horse Death Dancer, he says the animal is bigger and deadlier than his own horse and we all know what a warrior that roan horse is."

Mexican Joe, snarled "Keep your opinions to yourself, otherwise you will wish that bear had hold of you again." Salt just looked at him, then he said, "I guess I will ride along with you, I would admire to see how you handle this job. So now four men rode on with Crane as their target. Somewhere on the trail Crane rode in ignorance of the fact that the tables had turned, because after four years of him being the hunter he had become the hunted. Once again Utah was left with his own thoughts, he was not surprised to hear Josey Wales opinion of the kid. Crane clearly was his fathers son,he had his mothers spirit as well, he would never forget the determined way that she came out their the cabin to help her man.

It was late in the afternoon when they saw a lone rider on a huge horse in the distance, there was no doubt that it would be Crane. Mexican Joe circled of to right intending to come at Crane from behind. Utah dropped back thinking to himself, this is it, this may be my last chance to do the right thing. Colin seeing this sneered, to Salt,

"Don't mind Utah he's yeller, the question is are you in?" Salt looked sideways at him, "Yeh I'm in you'll never do it alone, you are no use in a fight."

Suddenly the air was split by the sound of Utah's pistol, one two three shot's he fired and the sound of his voice shouting, could be heard. "Crane ambush in front and behind." Adding, "I am Utah so that Crane would hopefully react quickly." Colin cursed, "Damn it! Damn that Utah" He turned and fired not seeing what he hit, because all the hounds of hell seemed to have come to call, right in front of him and Salt.

Crane for it was indeed him, with his reins in his teeth and a pistol in each hand was charging towards them on this great black stallion, who was no longer a colt, but Colin knew the horse, because it was the colt that they had stolen and that it had killed Lattigo. In a flash the horse was on them rearing up in the air. Dancers hooves caught Colin's horse full in the face and the stricken mount dropped like a stone. At the same time Colin was struck by a bullet from Crane's, left hand pistol. Horse and rider went down, Colin was dead before Crane's stallion trampled over him. Salt spun away hit in the left shoulder, shot by a bullet from Crane's right hand pistol.

Utah was on the ground trapped under his horse, Colin's wild shot had killed it, he saw the stallion racing towards him, time seemed to stand still and he waited for the death he knew was coming. Crane was riding like a demon, he was showing incredible control of his stallion, just using his knees and the horse turned and spun away back towards Salt who was still mounted on his Calico pony and trying to bring the terrified animal under control, sadly for him without success, as Crane thundered back towards him on Dancer. The Calico pony was out of control and the frightened animal put his foot in a gopher hole, Salt was tipped over his horse's head falling out of the saddle. There were two loud cracks, one as the horse leg snapped, it didn't suffer because one Crane's bullets hit between the eyes, as it was falling, killing the horse stone dead. The other loud crack was Salt's neck breaking as he hit the ground, landing head first.

Crane looked round at the fallen riders, he holstered his pistols and returned the reins to his hands and turned back to Utah who was still lying on the ground, trapped under his dead horse. As Crane got back to Utah he saw that the fallen rider had managed to pull his rifle from it's saddle boot and was trying to use the rifle as a lever to get the horse off his leg. He wasn't having much success. Crane dismounted and took the lariat from his saddle horn. With an effort he lifted the dead horses head and put the loop round it then still holding the rope he turned and leapt in to the saddle wrapping the end of the rope round his saddle horn. Crane used his knees to get the black stallion to back up, as he did so he saw that Utah was levering a shell into the chamber of the rifle. As Crane's pistol sprang in to his hand, knowing that he was to late, he heard two shots and a scream of pain came from behind him, he dropped the rope and turned in time to see a rider racing away. Crane knew he could not hit the rider from that distance with his pistol so he turned back to Utah lying on the ground. "I think I owe you my life, twice," Crane said as he jumped down from the Black Stallion. Crane was reloading his pistols as he walked towards Utah, saying, "I will help you now."

Through gritted teeth Utah spoke, "You owe me nothing and now you know who I am you will kill me anyway." The pain was clearly worse now the horse was off him. Crane said, "That leg is clearly broken, I will try and set it and then we will talk." He turned and walked round looking for suitable wood for splints. As he looked he went and picked up the run away rider's pistol, he saw that the man's thumb was with it, The pistol was useless the cylinder flattened so Crane threw it down. He continued to look for straightish pieces of wood to use for a splint.

Crane came back and hunkered down beside Utah's leg, "I think it's as straight as it's gonna get," he said. "I'll just splint it" Needing something to tie the splints together, Crane got up and went over to Colin's body, he heaved him round and took off Colin's jacket and shirt. Then taking Colin's shirt with him Crane walked back to Utah, tearing the shirt in strips as he went. When he got back he hunkered down and lifted Utah's leg and started to put splints on. There were groans, from Utah as Crane laid strips of cloth under Utah's leg, Crane lowered the leg as it as gently as he could then using the two lengths of wood as splints, Crane used the cloth strips to bind the wood tightly to Utah leg.

Utah said, "You need to be aware that it was Mexican Joe riding away, he will be back." Crane smiled, "Not for a while," He said. "You managed to shoot his thumb off, it is lying on the ground over there." "His first job will be trying to avoid bleeding to death." "I don't know how I managed that, I couldn't really aim with you and that damned big horse of yours in the way." Utah replied." Crane looked at him and said, "I am a great believer in dumb luck."

Crane busied himself unsaddling his horse and making camp, he lit a fire using brushwood and put coffee on to boil using water from a near bye creek. Then he went over to Utah's dead horse and with a struggle took the saddle off. He walked back to Utah turned the saddle so the underneath was up facing up and then dragged Utah into a sitting position with his back against the saddle.

Crane put his saddle down near Utah's and said "We will have some coffee and you can talk. He looked in Utah's saddlebag finding a battered tin cup, he got his own cup from his saddle bag. When the coffee was ready he poured two cups and brought them over, then sat down. "Let's talk" he said.

Utah said, "My name is Utah and I was with Colin and the others the day you got kicked half to death on that street in the dirt town near your farm. Then I was there with them when your Ma and Pa got killed. I can tell you I never hurt you in that street fight, I can also tell you that I never fired a shot at when we were at your farm. None of that means anything because I never tried to stop the others doing what they did, so I want you to know that I'm guilty and I'm ashamed."

Crane drank from his cup and looked in the fire before speaking." A man called Wales educated me about fate, he explained some things don't change because they are fated to happen." "You couldn't have stopped them and if you had tried they would likely have killed you" "If that had happened, you couldn't have saved my life twice today, so I would say we are even friend." "The other thing is that until I called on a farmer a while back, I had never heard your name, so that was lucky, because when you shouted your name, I knew from what the farmer said that you were different from the others. Mind you when you chambered that round in your rifle, I thought I had made a fatal mistake."

Then Crane looked over to the creek and saw that both his horses were drinking. Content that all was well he pulled his hat down over his eyes and went to sleep. Sensing that the conversation was over, Utah stayed in his sitting position, thinking about what Crane had said, then as he to began to doze, Utah thought how lucky he was because when he shouted the warning to Crane, he was sure he would die. Now Crane had spoken to him using the word friend. Strange how things turn out Utah thought as he fell in to a restless sleep.

Utah awoke early next morning to the smell of fresh coffee, he looked around. He was feeling really ill and in pain. He looked up saw Crane who spoke to him saying, "You are running a fever, you really need a doctor. So I've made a litter that I will attach to your saddle, when I put it on my other horse I will take you to the outskirts of the nearest town and send you on in." "The people there will take care of you, I can't go in." "I've been in a couple of trading posts but I steer clear of towns, after I killed our local sheriff I will be wanted." He brought coffee for both of them and then sat down next to Utah.

Utah looked at Crane and said, "I heard the stories that people tell about you on the trail, but you ain't looked in a mirror recently." "I can tell you that you ain't the kid they might be looking for." "You have the scars on your face and a different look in your eyes, from the one you had back then, added to that you have really filled out." "Four years ago you were a very strong boy, today you are clearly a very powerful man, you are maybe five eleven to 6ft in height but the heel on your boots will make people think six foot 2 or 3ins. It is clear to me that you are strong like your Pa was and if you live another twenty years you will grow even stronger." "So the only way people will know you is by your name, there is no doubt, you can go town."

Crane did not speak, he just began breaking camp. Then he saddled his black stallion. He came back to Utah, Gently lowered him to a lying position and took the saddle putting it on what used be his Pa's stallion. Then he put the litter poles that he had cut in the stirrups and tied them there with the piggin' string from long ago. He had used his Pa's slicker to make the litter by tying it to two sapling poles he had cut with his knife. Then he had used a blanket tied to the sapling with Colin's jacket used to strengthen it in the middle. Crane picked up Utah in his arms like a baby and put him on the litter. Then he walked around the corpses of Colin and the guy without the ear shooing the buzzards into the air while he checked their saddlebags and clothing for useful goods.

Crane came back to the horses and put what he termed the spoils of war in to his own saddlebags. Then he mounted Dancer and rode out at the walk, the horse with the litter shied a little at the strange weight behind him then followed on at the walk. Utah groaned then settled down as the rocking motion put him to sleep. Behind them the buzzards settled to their work, anyone coming along that trail in a month or two, would just find white bones and maybe a few rags to show that horses and men had died there.

CHAPTER 7

Crane stopped the horses on a bluff and looked down on the town of Dallas, thinking to himself, this is the moment of truth, he wondered should he ride in or let Utah go down alone? Then he thought, if it is my destiny to die here, so be it there was no need to keep fate waiting. He used slight pressure from his knees and his horse moved forward, he heard the other horse move off behind him. He walked the horses steadily down the side of the bluff riding down into the main street of the town. Anybody looking would see that Crane and his wounded partner, because such circumstance had made them partners, albeit maybe only temporary, had ridden in from the south, there was nothing else for them to know.

Seeing the livery stable on the left side of the street Crane stopped his horse, the hostler came out, a slim man came out maybe sixty five years old, he sported what Crane had heard called the winter plumage, that being grey hair on his temples the rest of his hair still black. The two men sized each other up, the hostler spoke, "I'm Larry, Larry Richards, what did you say your name was?" Crane looked him up and down, replying "I didn't, I'm looking for a doctor, has this town got one? "Yes sir," Larry replied "You can call me Larry, I'll take real good care of your horses.

"Where is the doctor?" Asked Crane. "Over there, about a hundred yards up the street on the right, he has a shingle out, you can't miss it Doc Black, most folks call him Chris, he is a real friendly feller." Crane nodded, saying "I'll be back. "

Larry watched as the horses plodded up the street, he thought to himself, "This is a strange man, young but with a look in his eyes that is very reminiscent of the border raiders who had filled the town with fear a few years back." Yet as Larry turned to go back in the stable he felt there was something different, something that set this stranger apart from all the different men who came and went passing through this town on their way to who knows what. I should know Larry thought I fought with and against some really dangerous men during the war between the states. Larry had done some Indian fighting to a few years back, so people might be surprised if they knew the story behind this chatty friendly man who looked after the towns horses.

Crane stopped and dismounted outside the doctors office, he left his mounts reins trailing, he knew better than to tie him up. He went to the litter behind the other horse not tying him either, Crane knew his horses wouldn't stray. As Crane looked down at Utah who was delirious muttering and twisting around it was clear he was in a bad way. So he picked him up and carried him in to the doctors office, finally laying him on what seemed to be the examination bed.

Crane heard a voice off to one side of him say, "Can I be of help?" He turned and saw a tall broad man with long black hair, who looked more like the pistol fighter he had once been, than the doctor that he was now. "My friend has a broken leg" said Crane. "I'll take a look said Doc Black" He moved forward looking at the dishevelled man, "I see you've used a makeshift splint, that will have to come off." As he worked quickly Crane noticed the doctors hands, they were huge, he had long fingers yet you could see they were gentle like a musicians.

"I'll leave him with you and go and put up the horse's back at the stable." Said Crane. "Yeh, OK" said Doc Black, "If you got a coupla dollars for my work it would be appreciated." "No problem." Replied Crane and left two dollars on the table by the door on his way out.

Crane walked out on the street, mounted his horse turned him round and rode back to the street to the livery stable, his other horse followed. When Crane got there he stepped down and walked to the other horse removed the litter, and then took off the saddle, rubbing the sweat dry with the horse's blanket as usual. As Crane turned to his own mount, Larry came up and said, "I can do that for you.." Crane spoke, "Not if you want to keep running this place you won't, this horse don't take kindly to being touched by anyone but me." "OK, I'll put the other one in a stall." Larry replied. Crane said "No I prefer them in your corral, they ain't used to being kept inside." "OK" replied Larry. He led the first horse in to the corral opened the gate and let him in. Crane unsaddled his horse rubbed him down and led him in and closed the corral gate. Then pulled the litter apart throwing the slicker and the jacket over the rail. He stood the to poles up against the livery stable wall, then he rolled up the piggin' string and put it in his saddlebag.

Crane asked, "How much to keep the horses here?" "Sixty cents a day and I'll feed and water them." Replied

Larry. Crane fished in pockets and gave him six dollars, "That should do for a few days till I see how my friend Utah is getting on." Larry took the money and put it in his pocket. "Just make sure you feed and water them from outside the corral, "Said Crane." "Sure no problem" Replied Larry while he was filling the trough by working the pump beside it. As the water splashed in to the trough, the horses ambled over and drank. At the other end of the trough Crane plunged his hands in to the water following up with his head and shoulders. He shook his head and brushed his hair with his fingers. Larry let the water from the pump run over his own hands.

Larry spoke saying, "You wanna eat?" "I've got a pot luck stew on the stove" "Don't mind if I do" replied Crane." Following Larry into the barn and through on to his living quarters. They went into the one room cabin and Crane sat down at the makeshift table, making use of a long bench. As Crane sat down Larry put two tin bowls and spoons on the table. Then he carried a pot over from the stove and ladled stew from it into the bowls. Larry then brought a hunk of bread to the table sat down and pulled the bread apart, giving Crane half. Then the two men ate their food in silence.

CHAPTER 8

After they had eaten Larry looked at Crane and said, "Do you want to bed down in the barn?" "There will be no charge." Crane feeling very weary, said "yes" and thanked Larry as they walked back into the barn. He climbed the ladder up in the hay loft and quickly fell asleep. Larry went back got the dishes and washed them. Then he put some feed in the corral for Crane's horses then he bedded down the horses that he had in the livery barn, after that he retired to his own bed.

Crane woke in the morning to the smell of bacon cooking, this was a smell he hadn't enjoyed for more than two years. He got up climbed down the ladder and walked to the trough and plunged his head into the water came out snorting and pushed his fingers through his tangled hair. Crane thought to himself that a bath and a shave should be on his list of things to do. Larry came looking for him saying, "Morning, friend, I've got some bacon and beans back here for you, there's even a couple of eggs and hot coffee." Crane followed Larry through and sat down at the table, as he began to eat he said, "After sleeping on the ground for three years and more and living on mostly cold beans and the occasional jack rabbit stew, I'm really feeling that I am living the high life." Larry smiled and said, "I thought you must have slept well, because it almost noon now."

They ate in silence for a while then Crane said, "I need a bath and a shave." Larry replied, "You should see the barber, John, his shop has a bath house behind it." Then he went on to say, "We know who you are, Doc Black came by earlier said your friend is doing well and he talked a bit about you, all good in case you wondered." "I doubt that" replied Crane." "I have to tell you we've heard of you before Crane," Larry said, "But in this town we judge a man by how we find him while he is here." Take our sheriff Big John McCane people say that he was one of the border raiders a while back but he has been good for the town, so his past can stay in the past."

"We'll see" said Crane, "I guess I'll go and have that bath and a shave." He walked up the street seeing people who tipped their hats, smiled and said "Hello," it all felt very strange.

When he arrived at the barbers, he was the only customer, "What can I do for you?" the Barber asked. "Name's Eckert, John Eckert." Crane replied, "I need a bath and a shave." "Yes sir" said the barber, "Just sit in the chair and I'll shave you while the boy fills the bath with hot water" He shouted, "Hey Joey, fill the bath and keep the hot water comin'"

"Sure Pa" the youth answered. Crane hung his hat and side arm on the hat stand by the door. He drew his shoulder pistol and sat own with the pistol on his chest, hands over it. If the barber thought this was strange behaviour he said nothing. John put a cape over Crane's shoulders and chest it hung down onto his knees, "How about this hair cut?"

He asked. "Sure" said Crane "tidy it up, but don't cut it too short." The barber got to work, shaving Crane's face and cutting his hair. He soon found his idle chatter was ignored so he shut up.

When John had finished, cutting Crane's hair, Joey returned, "Your bath is ready." Crane looked at him, then he said, "Do you think you could go to the store get me some clothes?" "Sure" Joey replied. "So do you think you can guess my size?" Crane asked him." "Yeh no problem" said Joey. Looking Crane up and down. Crane gave him ten dollars, saying, "Shirt, pants, socks and underwear if you can. The youth left on the run. Crane then asked the barber, "How much do I owe you?" "Dollar fifty cents" came the reply. Crane handed over two dollars saying, "Keep the change." Then he picked up his hat and pistol belt up from the hat rack and walked out to the back for his bath.

There were two tubs of water out back, side by side, one tub had a cake of soap on a small table beside it. Crane put his hand in the other, tub it was ice cold clearly to rinse of the scum from the warm bath. Crane started to peel off his clothing, ready to get in the bath as he did so Joey came back with his new clothing. Crane took the clothes from him and held up the items against him, by the look of the things, it seemed the youth had done well,

The pants were dark grey and the shirt was plain navy blue, there was also a blue neckerchief in with the socks and underwear. Crane put the new clothing on a chair that already had two towels on it that seemed to have been put there for the job of drying himself, he put the towels on top of the clothes. Joey said, "I have a dollar three quarters change for you," "Keep it, you earned it." Crane replied.

Crane finished taking his clothes off, dropping them on the floor put one of his pistols on the small table beside the bath and then slipped into the warm water. As he did some of the water slopped over the edge of the bath, out onto the hard packed dirt floor. Crane noticed a scrubbing brush next to the soap and set about making good use of both the scrubbing brush and the soap. He soaped his hair and slipped under the water to rinse the soap off. By the time he was finished bathing, there was a heavy scum all around him. Crane got out of the tub and climbed into the other one, drawing in his breath as the cold water surrounded his body, he slid down and rinsed his hair thoroughly. Crane climbed out of the bath and towelled off, he put on the new clothes. He was pleased because the pants and shirt fitted him very well. When he was dressed he tied the neckerchief loosely round his neck. Crane thought he looked half human and he felt invigorated. It felt really good to be clean again.

Crane rubbed the dust off his boots with his old shirt and put them on. Then he put the knife back in the top of his boot. He put his shoulder holster on and replaced the pistol in it. That done he buckled on his side arm, then he picked up the self made waistcoat, noticing as he put it on how, short and tight it had become, it was half way up his back and it no longer allowed him to fasten the single button. With this done Cane checked the derringer, straight razor and fifty dollar gold pieces were in place in the pockets. Crane then picked up his old pants and emptied the pockets of loose change, transferring it to his new pockets then he threw his old pants on the pile with his old shirt socks and underwear. Crane felt pretty good as he picked up his hat and walked back through to the front of the barber's shop.

John Eckert, was waiting for Crane, "Sit down sir, I will just tidy the hair now for you." Crane sat down saying, "Burn the old clothes for me will you?" "Certainly sir," replied John busying himself with scissors and comb. Crane looked in the mirror seeing the blue scar down the side of his face, then for the first time he took in the hard angles on his jaw line and cheek bones. Even Crane's parents would not recognise this man as the fresh faced boy who had been their son. The barber worked quickly and when he finished Crane gave him a dollar, saying, "Thanks Mr Eckert." "Thank you" replied the barber, "You should call me John." Crane nodded at him then put on his hat and walked out the door.

When he got outside Crane crossed over to the other side of the street and walked into the doctors office. As he went through the door, he saw an very attractive dark haired women with smiling eyes coming through from the back. "Hi"she said, "You must be Crane, I've heard a lot about you." Crane looked at her Saying "And you are?" "Vanessa" she said "Ness to my friends, I'm Doc Blacks woman" "Right" said Crane "It's good to know you." Ness added "I've been nursing your friend, he is doing well, the fever has broken and he is not in so much pain," I do the nursing for Chris's patients when it's needed"

Can I see Utah?" asked Crane. "Sure you can." Said Ness, "Come on through." She turned and walked through to the room where Utah was sitting propped up in the bed. He looked at Crane, saying, "I'm being well looked after here, I ain't slept in a real bed in an age." "Me neither" said

Crane. In fact I still don't know when I'll sleep in one." He smiled, maybe the first time in more than three years, it felt strange. It looks like you will be laid up for a while yet compardre, but at least you'll be getting good care and good food.

Utah's face lit up, "I can't get used to how friendly you are towards me." He said. "Well"said Crane "You are my friend, I never had one before," feeling a bit embarrassed he went on, "Well if you are OK I'll move on out." Crane turned around saying, "Thanks Ness," He put his hand in his pocket and came out with five dollars, "Please give this to the Doc for me." Ness took the money, "You are rare one, in paying people usually don't, Chris has to manage on very little." Having said that the towns people support him where they can."

Crane decided that he would call on the Sheriff, before the Sheriff called on him. He paused as he came out onto the board walk looking up and down the street until he saw the shingle with Sheriffs Office written on it, then he turned and walked towards it. When he got there he walked in and spoke to the man behind the desk. "Would you be the Sheriff?" The man behind the desk stood up, Crane watched him as he seemed to keep rising forever. This man was huge at least as big as Crane's Pa, he was certainly heavier. Crane's Pa carried no weight, he had been made spare and lean by hard work on the farm. This man was six foot seven maybe six foot eight inches tall, he carried no fat but he had muscles that were bulky and rippled in his chest and shoulders, he stood there on powerful legs. The sheriff had a handsome strong face under a mop of black hair. His eyes twinkled and sparkled as his lips parted in a smile. "Yes I'm Big John McCane, he said and I'd say that you are the guy they call Crane." He held out a huge hand Crane shook it.

Crane said "Well this is a welcome I didn't expect." McCane said "Take the weight off."Pointing to a chair. Both men sat. "The things men have said about you are clearly true," Said McCane. "Josey Wales told me you would be a good man to ride the river with." "Well sheriff said Crane. "Call me John" said the sheriff. Crane started again, "Well John, you can call me Crane, nothing else fits anymore." "No problem," John replied. Crane then said, Look I need you to know that I shot the last sheriff that I met." "Oh I know that" came the reply from Big John. "But that sheriff was crooked and everyone knew that, your home town has been a better place since he's been gone." "If you hadn't done the job somebody else would." "The deputy Don Liston, who by the way is the sheriff there now, told the townspeople how things went down." "It seems to me that you gave him a better than even chance, so that incident won't give you any trouble especially not in this town."

Crane was amazed that this huge man was being so kind to him. "Well I never expected to hear anything like this, it has to be said that I have killed some other people." "Yeah Big John replied, "Josey told me about some of them and so has your friend Utah, it seems people make the mistake of thinking you will be an easy target." Crane shook his head saying, "I've been reckless and just plain lucky, I don't know how I got away with some of the fool plays I've made." "I just seem to go to this real strange place in my mind were time slows down, yet I move faster." Big John smiled, "You have what the Indians call the warriors way, you are born with it and you will live and die by it's code." "Some people don't want you around in peace time but if there is war those same people don't want to be without you."

"Well" said Crane "I guess I will mosey on around town, that is if you are happy for me to stay in town for a while?" Crane let the question hang. Big John replied, "No problem, you are a quiet man and trouble might follow you but I don't see you looking for it here." Then he said, "Stop by again and I will take you to meet my wife Susan and the boys, let you see the reasons why I settled to town life." "I'd like to do that" Said Crane, as he got up and walked out the door.

As he walked down Main street Crane thought to himself how different these last few days had been, what at one time he thought might be called normal. Crane wondered if he could live with normal after these years on the trail. As he walked Crane found himself at the general store, he thought I could do with another outfit of clothes. After all he had lived in the previous set for more than three years, he didn't want to do that again.

As he walked into the store Crane was greeted by the man behind the counter "It's Neil" the man said "Neil Crossland, me and my wife Maureen run the store,." Neil looked Crane up and down, "I see the clothes fit pretty well" he said. "They do" said Crane. "That is what I am here for, I need another outfit" "No problem at all" Neil came out from behind the counter, he was a stocky man who moved well around his own environment "I have to two prices for everything one for credit customers and one if you have dollars."

Crane said, "I have dollars, I haven't spent anything for three years, but if I keep on the way I have since I came town I will be broke." Then he said, "I will take underwear, socks pants, a shirt make that two, shirt and pants the same colour as these I am wearing now and I could do with a short jacket. Because I have torn and outgrown this waistcoat. He looked down at the heel of his boots adding, I had better have new boots as well. Neil moved quickly round the shelves talking to himself as he took clothes off the shelf.

Neil piled the clothes up on the counter, he looked at Crane, Saying, "That hat has seen better days" he scanned the shelves and got a dark coloured Stetson down and put it with the clothes. Now a jacket he looked towards the back and called out, "Dave," then said to Crane, "my friend Dave he does great work with leather." A heavy set man came through from the back, "Dave" said Neil "This is Crane, he wants a jacket, if you don't mind bring him the one you made last year for that feller who never came back." While Dave was gone Neil got a pair of hand tooled boots down off the shelves, "here" he said, "these will fit you, Dave made these as well."

Crane sat down on a nearby stool and took off his old boots, he put on the new ones stood up and stamped his feet, they were a good fit. He said to Neil, "You have a good eye for size." "Comes with the job" Neil replied.

Dave came back into the store carrying a dark but not black hip length leather jacket. Saying, "Try this for size." Crane removed his waistcoat and put it on the stool, he took the jacket and was amazed how light and soft the leather was. He shrugged it on,it felt as though he was just wearing his shirt, he checked the inside for pockets and found that it had some useful ones. The jacket hung well hiding his shoulder holster and the centre fastening was easy to close, Crane moved his shoulders the jacket felt good. "How much Dave" he asked "It's yours" replied Dave "The guy paid me in advance and he never came back." Crane held out ten dollars, "Take it please," he said. "You can call it luck money" Dave took it "Thanks" he said with a smile.

Crane emptied the pockets of the waistcoat, he took one of the fifty dollar gold pieces from the pouch before putting the pouch in a pocket. He turned to Neil "can you throw these boots, the waistcoat and the hat away for me?" "Sure" Neil replied, Crane took off his hat and put it on the counter picked up the new one and put it on, he took it off again played with the brim a bit and put it back on. "Right Neil, how much do you want?" Neil's hands ruffled through the clothes making calculations in his head then he spoke, "Twenty three dollars sixty cents, I'll throw in a couple of neckerchiefs and we'll say twenty dollars for cash." Crane gave him the fifty dollar gold piece, Neil opened the drawer under the counter and counted out thirty dollars and handed them to Crane, "Thanks" said Crane, putting the coins in his pocket. Neil put the clothing on a sheet of brown paper, wrapped the paper round and tied it with string, then he handed the parcel to Crane. "Thank you" said Crane and then he left the store.

CHAPTER 9

Crane ambled down the street heading back to the livery stable some time had passed and the sun was starting to go down. He arrived back at the corral and his black stallion came over to the corral rail to see him, the horse lowered it's head and Crane rubbed it;s forehead. As he did he thought to himself this day had been the longest time that he had been parted from his horses.

Crane felt really strange not being in the saddle all day, every day, but before he could think more on the subject he heard Larry's voice saying. "Wow!" Don't you look fine?" Crane felt his face go warm and he coloured up, "No more" he said, Larry laughed and held his hands up, "OK, all I meant was you sure scrubbed up well." Crane smiled ruefully, "It really seems to be my day for getting compliments." "I think I go to your outhouse before I embarrass myself." He walked away.

As Crane walked through the stable out and off to the side were he found the outhouse. Crane went inside made ready and sat down, he drew his pistol from his shoulder holster and held it pointing at the door. This was not the time to get careless he wouldn't be the first pistol fighter to be shot in an outhouse. He finished up, holstered his pistol and came out. The foetid atmosphere was claustrophobic, Crane preferred the outdoors for this purpose.

Crane wandered back until he found Larry, then he asked him about the saloon in town, he needed to know if Mexican Joe was around and he thought that the saloon would be a place that the killer would hang around. Crane asked, "Larry have you seen a guy with the thumb missing from his right hand?" Larry shook his head, saying, "No, I haven't, and I think I would have remembered something like that." They continued to chat for a while and then Crane said "I think I'll saddle the black and ride him out, he really needs the exercise."

While they where still talking Crane busied himself with saddling and bridling his black stallion. Just as he was swinging up into the saddle Crane saw Joey the barbers son running up to them. He was short of breath but he managed to say, "There is trouble, real trouble Sheriff McCane is facing down about fifteen riders at the other end of town. From what we can tell it seems that these riders are going to rob the bank. My pa, Mr Crossland Mr Selley from the store have taken their pistols and gone to try and help the sheriff stop them. Pa told me to ask if you and Larry would come."

As Joey was speaking they could all hear the sound of gunfire, with no hesitation Crane turned his horse towards the sound. He jammed his reins in his teeth and drew his pistols while he was racing up the street. Crane with Dancer fully at the gallop covered the ground in no time. When Crane got there the scene unfolding before him was crazy. The sheriff and his men were pinned down behind a horse trough, the raiders were still mounted and they were shooting holes in the trough. The water was running out of the trough out in the street. Some of the raiders saw Crane approaching at speed and they turned galloping their horses towards him. They were firing wildly, their voices raised, they were shouting, "It's only one man take him down!!"

Crane and the stallion met the onrushing riders head on, his stallion was screaming it's rage. The raiders parted allowing Crane to pass down the middle, but one of the leading riders was to slow in getting out of the way and his horse and Crane's stallion with Crane firing right and left collided with the horse and rider. The raider and his horse went down under the flying hooves of the stallion. Crane's stallion plunged and reared still screaming in it's rage as they continued towards the main bunch of the raiders, there were bullets grazing the horse's skin driving him even wilder.

Crane was ice cold in the heat of battle and he put one pistol in his holster, while loading the other. As Crane rode towards them the lead was flying all around him as he arrived fast. Crane's new hat flew from his head and he felt a burning sensation. He didn't feel it but his face was wet, in fact blood pouring down his face. The blood was pouring from a crease on his skull. Crane drew his lips back in a snarl as he ploughed into the raiders in front of him. Again and again he fired right and left he was only using one pistol. But the stallion, Dancer was creating havoc. Horses and men were falling, screaming as their bones broke. It was as if he, Crane could not fail to do damage, as long as he kept moving. Someone, one of the raiders, was trying to turn and run, as he did so he sobbed, "Oh sweet Jesus, it's the devil himself." One of Crane's bullets took him in the eye and silenced him, he was dead before he hit the ground.

Suddenly Crane was through the crowd of horses, his great black stallion with his mane and tail flying in the breeze, reared up and spun back towards the battle. Crane's pistol was empty and he let it go, and it fell to the ground, Then he released his throwing knife from his arm and threw it the nearest man, it took the man in the throat and that man went down, dying as he fell to the ground. Crane grabbed his derringer from the pocket and fired it just as a bullet hit him in the chest high up on the right side he fell backwards from the horse hitting the ground hard.

Although he was stunned, Crane's left hand fumbled for the Bowie knife in his boot. A wounded man, who fallen from his horse, had got to his feet and was standing on the ground. He threw himself at Crane, going straight on to the Bowie knife. The man fell on top of Crane, he was dying, as the blade slipped between his ribs and pierced his heart. As he landed on Crane he bounced because he was a bigger and heavier man than Crane. Then for Crane everything went black. The warrior was done, Crane, was down and out his valiant fight was over.

Dancer was enraged, now he really lived up to his name, Devil Dancer he reared and bit and kicked at anything that moved men fell back the horse gave none of them time to reload. One man who had rode forward from the back looking down at Crane, who lay motionless, "I will finish him!" He said, the rider aimed his pistol down at Crane, but before he could pull the trigger a shot rang out and the man fell backwards out of the saddle. A tall lean man dressed in black, spoke quietly, almost to himself as he fired at another rider saying, "That man on the ground deserves an edge."

The Sheriff Big John McCane, Neil Crossland, Dave Selley and John Eckert were already in the fight, Larry Richards had arrived on his buggy and he had been using a rifle to great effect. Also there in the street even though he was on a crutch was Utah, firing from the hip, with a pistol, he was making his presence felt. He had Doc Black at his side and the Doc was using his pistol to great effect showing why he had been one of the most feared pistol fighters in Texas and Missouri.

The raiders who could still ride, did just that fleeing from the brutal crossfire. The street was littered with the dead horses and men who lay where they had fallen. Chris the Doc said "My God you hear it but you can't believe it until you see it" "To ride in to the guns of fifteen or twenty men, with no thought for your own safety takes a special kind of man." "I saw Josey Wales do this once but this was even more, Josey just charged one way, to break out of an ambush. This kid was riding to save us, because we would surely all have died here today, he turned his horse and attacked again" "True" replied John McCane, did you see the way Crane was coolly reloading while the lead flew around him and that stallion was plunging and rearing under him.

The tall man in black spoke, "This kid lived and died my way, I never saw man who kept finding a way to fight, when he was out of ammo and he still had something to fight with." Big John looked at the man who had spoken "You are Edge" he said, "I know you, this town is getting crowded with pistol fighters." Edge for it was he, the former Captain Josiah Hedges, who had joined the fray to help Crane, spoke again, "Who was this kid ?" "his name was Crane "replied Big John McCane. Edge nodded and said, "I've heard of him, he really was one of the special ones."

The men kept walking towards were Crane lay, his great stallion stood head bowed beside him. All it's spirit seemed to have gone from it now, the horse's eyes were dull and listless as it allowed Larry to lead him away. Larry took the horse to the hitching rail where then he tied the reins. There was a strong smell of cordite and blood in the air and there still dust swirling around, kicked up by the feet of galloping horses.

Utah his eyes blinded by tears, looked down at Crane saying, "That kid was more of a man the day he was born than most of us will ever live to be." "Amen to that" Came the reply." A couple of men lifted the body of the man killed by Crane's Bowie knife off Crane. Then the Doc knelt down beside Crane, all the other men with the exception of Utah, whose broken leg prevented him doing so, did the same. They were all paying a silent homage to the great fallen warrior. Doc Black looked down on the mask of blood that was Crane's face and despaired, how could this have happened?. Why he thought did such a good man like Crane have to fall to the border scum?

CHAPTER 10

All the men rose to there feet and stepped forward on either side of Crane's motionless body, ready to carry him to the undertaker's office. None of them had ever felt such misery, Neil Crossland said "I only met him once but I liked him." Dave Selley replied "Yeah I liked him to, I can't believe it, Crane gave me luck money and now his luck has run out" Doc Black spoke, "Don't be to sure that he is gone, he shouldn't be but I think he is still breathing, they all looked down at Crane's bloodied face and sure enough a bloody froth was bubbling on his lips. The Doc spoke again, "A bullet must have got his lung, we had best get him to my place." "Crane may only have a slim chance of survival but it's better than no chance." John, Dave, Neil and Larry picked up Crane and carried him down the street to the Doc's place, each man had prayers in their hearts

Ness was waiting in the Doc's treatment room, when she saw the almost lifeless body of Crane being laid on the bed. "What can I do?" she asked, Bring me some boiling water,my instruments and then pray." Replied the Doc. Then he went on to say to those who had carried Crane in, "You need to get out!," "I will need space." The men filed out, Big John McCane paused and asked. "Do you think that he live?" "Only God knows the answer to that" replied the Doc. Big John left the room with sadness in his eyes.

Ness came back into the room, she had boiled the water and sterilised the instruments. She laid them out on a clean white cloth which she had put on a table beside the bed. Doc said "please help me get his jacket off." Together they lifted Crane up and somehow got his arms out the sleeves, then they cut Crane's shirt and the top half of his long underwear from his body. When they had done this they could see the entry wound. It was a blue pucker hole in Crane's chest, they lifted him and turned him, when they did it was with relief that they could see an exit wound. This wound was bigger and it had jagged edges. "Praise the Lord" said Doc, "He may just have a chance." "We will need to clean and disinfect his wounds and dress them."

Together they worked swiftly, the Doc decided to stitch the exit wound, when he had done this he poured a liquid solution of disinfectant on both wounds, applied an antiseptic cream to them and then he applied dressing. He bandaged all the way round Crane's body. "Now" he said to Ness, "We need to look at his head wound, he was wiping blood away, when he did he could see that a bullet had torn a furrow along up the side of Crane's head. Knowing that the bullet hadn't come out he probed with his fingers along Crane's skull, then felt a lump near the crown of his head. "I don't believe it" Doc said, "The bullet hasn't broken his skull it is lodged under the skin" The Doc then applied pressure with his thumb and the bullet popped out. Taking it from him Ness put it in a bowl on the table.

"You will have to shave his head before we will be able to dress this wound" said the Doc. Ness set to work first with scissors and then with a razor, she did a quick and efficient job. Then the Doc cleaned the wound, applied antiseptic and bandaged Crane's head. Ness washed Crane's face and neck cleaning away all the dried blood. Throughout all of their joint ministrations Crane remained motionless, his breathing was shallow. Hopefully this was a good sign, more importantly the blood had ceased to bubble through his lips.

Ness asked the question, "What are his chances Chris?" "Slim, very slim indeed." "If the wounds stay clean, if he heals inside, who knows" The Doc replied, "Crane really is in the hands of God now." "How do you know that antiseptic stuff works? Asked Ness. Doc replied, It's made from herbs and leaves an old Indian medicine man showed me how to make and use, after he had taken a bullet out of my leg. "It was amazing, you have seen the wound, he used it when it looked like I would almost certainly lose the leg" "I didn't lose the leg so I that's how know it works." The Doc went on to say "You are a good nurse Ness if Crane survives it will be due in no small way to you. "While I'm saying this, let me add that you are a good woman, you really do make my life complete." "It is times like this, that make me think how lucky I am.

It was dark outside so Ness lit the lamp saying, "You are tired Chris, you must go and rest while I will sit with Crane. "You know that I will call you, if there is any change. The Doc thanked her and then he left the room. When he had gone Ness busied herself with cleaning and tidying up. Having done that she got Chris's instruments and put them in a pan of water leaving them to boil, so that they would be completely clean. Then she picked her sewing, something to keep her occupied while she sat and watched over Crane from her seat in the chair beside the bed. Ness sat, sewed and waited for and waited for morning, sometime during the night she fell asleep.

Ness came awake with a start, she opened her eyes and saw the Doc sitting in another chair smiling at her. When he saw that she was awake he said, "I don't sleep very well you are not beside me, so I came to sit with you." Ness smiled at him, then she looked at Crane. "Hows he doing?" She asked. The Doc replied "there is no real change, except that his breathing seems better, but he is still deeply unconscious." "It's incredible that he kept going when that bullet hit him in the head because most men would have gone down. But somehow Crane kept going. Then he should have definitely been finished when the bullet hit him in the chest but he still kept fighting. Somehow he pulled the strength from somewhere deep inside of him, he just wouldn't quit. It is like Josey Wales said The kid eats the pain and draws strength from it. If he can find that strength inside him again, he might pull through but I wouldn't bet on it. As a doctor I find I can only pray for it." Ness nodded sadly, "I'll make you some breakfast." She paused, then she said "Hey Chris, where's Utah?" The Doc shrugged his shoulders before replying, "I don't know, I haven't seen him since we were out in the street."I don't think he got shot." So he must be around somewhere." Ness went out of the room and into the kitchen to rattle some skillets and fry bacon and eggs.

CHAPTER 11

While this was happening Utah picked himself up from the hay at the back of the empty stall that he had slept in. He had been unable climb up in to the loft with a broken leg, so Larry had let him bed down in the stall. Utah was feeling a bit groggy when he woke up so he got on his crutches and hobbled out to the water trough. When he got there he lent his crutches on the trough so taking his weight one leg and with his arms on the edge of the trough, he lowered his head into the trough. It was a shock to his system because the water was very cold and it caused him to rise up and shake his head vigorously.

Utah heard Larry coming up behind him saying, "Mornin' Utah, this is not a good day." "No, you are right it isn't, is there any word on Crane? Asked Utah. "Nothing, I thought I'd mosey on up to the Doc's in a while, I just don't want to hear that he's gone. Replied Larry "I know what you mean." replied Utah, "Because you only have to know Crane a short time and you like him.""He makes you feel better about yourself, even if you don't deserve to." I know" said Larry, "The way Crane rode to help Big John and the others was a rare thing, as he was riding he must have known the likely outcome was that he would get shot down but he never hesitated, that is the mark of the man"

The two men stood in silence staring in the corral, lost in thoughts of Crane. Then Larry said, I had better get on because I need to put salve on Dancer's wounds," There was no doubt that the name suited the black stallion, since his brave deeds had become known, Devil Dancer was the only name that suited him, especially after his efforts had been seen the day before. They both looked at him, seeing that there were cuts and abrasions on his legs and he had been creased by bullets that had grazed his neck and flanks. "This horse will have scars" Said Utah. "But I think they will suit him." replied Utah, "You are right because he is like Crane, a true warrior." Replied Larry. "But that said, how am I going to get near him to put some salve on the wounds?" Utah replied I'll go in to the corral with him, but first bring the other stallion out to him, Dancer may respond to the familiar."

Larry went into the stable and came back leading the other stallion, when he took him up to the rails of the corral, the two stallions whickered and walked towards each other and nuzzled each others necks. Utah opened the gate and hobbled into the corral, he approached Dancer and reached up and patted his neck. The stallion trembled but did not turn on Utah. So Utah spoke,softly "Easy boy, we ain't lookin' to hurt you none." The horse seemed to be quiet and more interested in his sire than he was in Utah. Larry stepped into the corral with a tub of grease and proceeded to apply some to Dancer's flanks. The stallion trembled again and stamped his feet, but he let the salve be put on. As the two men left the corral and closed the gate Larry said "I don't know what good the salve does except it stops the flies getting on the open wound." Having said that he led the other stallion back into the stable.

Then Larry and Utah went back to Larry's place for coffee and some breakfast. Although it has to be said that neither man had any appetite for food. As they drank their coffee their conversation was sporadic, because each man was lost in his own thoughts. Then Larry said, I'll hitch a team to the buggy and we will go up to the Doc's together and check on Crane. Utah nodded and they went back to the stable. Utah stood watching while Larry put the harness onto a horse and hitched it up to the buggy. Then he led the horse and buggy out on to the street and then he helped Utah up onto the seat. Having done that he climbed up himself, he then picked up the reins shook them and the two horses set off up the street at the walk.

They arrived and pulled up outside the Doc's office. Larry jumped down leaving the horses standing while he went round to help Utah down from the buggy and back onto his crutches. Then he helped him up onto the side walk and they went into the Doc's office together. They saw the Doc in the treatment room and then they saw Crane lying there on the bed. He was looking pale and drawn and there was no sign of movement. "How is he "asked Utah, the words were catching in his throat. "To tell the truth I just don't know" The Doc replied. Larry and Utah looked down on their fallen friend and each said a silent prayer. There had to be some hope while a spark of life was still burning.

Larry spoke, "I don't know who said it but there a quote that pretty much sums up fate, it goes something like this," "A man crazy to live takes a chance and dies." "A man who doesn't really care much, whether he lives or dies takes the same chance and lives." "The problem is, I just don't know which category applies to Crane." The other two just nodded sadly and silently there was nothing else to say. Utah and Larry left the Doc's office feeling pretty low.

As the two men came out onto the side walk they met Big John McCane on his way in, "How's Crane" Asked Big John. Utah shook his head, "I don't know." "Even the Doc doesn't know the answer to that question" he replied. "It's looking bad because he still hasn't come round and the Doc doesn't know if or when he will. Big John shook his head. Then he said "After that great fight Crane put up the bank didn't get robbed, there was no one from town who got killed or hurt but the towns people have turned against him." "What!" replied Larry. "Why?" "It's because they are frightened, the fact that he definitely saved Neil's, John's and mine and Dave's lives, when we were pinned behind the water trough and none of us could get a shot off means nothing. We would have been shot full of lead in the next five minutes. Even when the Missouri raiders were at their peak we never saw anything like what Crane did that day."

Larry said, "I won't stay in this town if people can't see that Crane did his best for people here." "He could have ignored the call to arms but he didn't hesitate, he rode to help people he hardly knew, because by the code he lives by it was the right thing to do." "I know" said Big John, "This town will be needing a new sheriff whether Crane lives or dies." Utah said, "It's not my town and now it never will be, I'll be movin' on when my leg heals." "There is nothing for me here."

Big John said, "I'm going to see the Mayor and give him my badge' he is one of the men who has a down on Crane, so I can't work for him." "Right" said Larry. "While you are doing that, we will go and see John Eckert, he will have an opinion this." As the three men arrived at the barbers shop they met John and his wife Doreen coming out of the door of the shop in the company of the store keeper Neil Crossland his wife Maureen and Dave Selley. Larry said, "This is good, we want to talk to you all about Crane." "Yeah replied, John, that's what we here are about, how is he doing?" "Not good" said Larry, "The Doc doesn't know if he will come round." "But whether he does come round or not me, Big John, his wife Susan and the boys will be movin' on, "Utah ain't staying either." "Same goes for us" said Neil's wife Maureen, "Doreen and me would be widows now if not for Crane yet to hear our customers at the store talk, Crane is the Devil himself." As they walked down the street they met up with the Doc. He greeted them saying, "No need to ask were you are going, I had to leave Ness to watch over Crane, she really wants to be in on this, but Crane can't be left on his own." Doc looked at Utah, who was struggling along sweating on his crutches, he asked, "Are you doing OK?" "You are on your feet sooner than I expected." Utah replied "Pretty fair, you did a good job setting the leg, thanks for that," "You are welcome, Doc replied. "I just wish I could hear the sound of Crane's voice, thanking me." The all walked on,towards the Town Hall, each one lost in their own thoughts.

They arrived in the Town Hall just in time to see an enraged Big John McCane throw his sheriffs badge in Tom Brady's face in front of a large noisy crowd of towns people. Tom who was sitting behind his big desk banged his gavel and shouted at Big John. "Why do you care about a no account drifter, like Crane?" "How dare you raise your voice to me, I'll see you in jail, for disrespecting me" !Big John looked down at him saying, "You will play hell trying to get that job done." He turned on his heel and walked the back of the room. A voice from the floor said "We don't want killers like Crane in our town." Big John turned and spoke again, "Well that's OK I'm taking my family and moving on." "Good riddance" replied Tom Brady. "Yeah well, Maureen and I will be going to" said Neil "Me too" said Dave Sully, "You can find yourself a new barber as well, because me and my family will be moving on." Added John Eckert.

Tom Brady banged his gavel on the table, "This meeting is out of control come to order and speak through the chair" Doc Black responded, "If we did that we would all be speaking out of our backsides ." Then he said "Through the chair, tell your no account citizens that the doctor and his wife are movin' on to." Before Tom could reply Larry Richards spoke, "You will be needing someone to run the livery stable, because I'll be blowing this town off as soon as I can." There was complete uproar in the room now. Tom was banging his gavel in a frenzy, he was shouting, trying desperately to gain control of the room. Eventually as the noise from crowd subsided, he was able to speak and be heard. He said "You losers and misfits can go, this town doesn't need you!" "Just tell me one thing why do you care about a no account drifter?" "That no account drifter stood up for this town when no one else would, none of you good citizens came to help us stop the bank being robbed." "You can be damned sure if anyone else tries to rob the bank again, we won't be putting our lives on the line to stop them. Said Big John.

Tom blustered, "I think it's highly unlikely that anyone would try that again, when word gets out of the wholesale slaughter that took place on the street here." Big John and the others looked at Tom with complete contempt and walked out of the room, out of the Town Hall and out on to the street. Neil said, "I think we should all go up to the bank and draw our money out, because I'm not as sure as Tom is that someone won't try and rob the bank again."

The others agreed with him and they all set off together to close their accounts.

CHAPTER 12

As they all huddled round a camp fire the group of men that had survived the attempt to rob the bank a few days earlier sat in sullen silence as they listened to Mexican Joe. He was grumbling and cursing about everything. He had always been a bitter and angry man but know since his thumb had been shot off and the wound had become infected causing him to lose his hand above the wrist, he was worse than he had ever been. He blamed Crane and he blamed Utah. Utah had betrayed him, for which he declared that he would kill him very slowly and very painfully. The other men sighed and groaned, they had heard this diatribe over and over again but they were afraid to complain case Mexican Joe turned on them. It wouldn't be the first time, he had turned on them. One of their number had complained that he was sick of listening two days ago and he had died shot, before he could finish speaking. Mexican Joe had shot him without warning, as he put it, "As an example to the rest of them."

Mexican Joe was sure that Crane was dead by now, he knew that he had shot him in the head and some else had shot in him in the chest. Crane had been seen lying in the street under another dead man. Word from town was that Crane had lain unconscious for the last week, there seemed to be no way he would come round. The other good news was that there was no sheriff, the one the town had on the day of the robbery had resigned and the mayor was doing the job himself. Mexican Joe said to his men, "We are going back to rob that bank, the sheriff they had is gone, Crane is dead or dying, they won't expect us and the towns people won't stand against us."

The remaining men agreed, they were glad to be doing something, they were sick of the sound of Mexican Joe's voice. "He spoke once more, "Saddle up and we ride." They did just that mounted their horses and rode in silence until they reached the edge of town." Nameless faceless men who leave nothing to mark their lives passing, but misery and despair wherever they go for as long as they lived. One spoke, "OK Joe what's the plan?" "It's simple" replied Joe, "We ride in pull up outside the bank Len can hold the horses, we go in take the money and kill anyone who speaks, what could be more simple?" "Let's do it," replied the men in unison.

So Mexican Joe and his men rode in town, stopped in front of bank, dismounted and stepped up on to the side walk. They all drew their pistols and entered the bank, the cashier blanched when he saw them walking in and back pedalled away from his grill. The outlaws went round the counter leaving two of their number facing the door, Without hesitation Mexican Joe pistol whipped the cashier, who fell to ground unconscious. While he was doing that one of his men rifled through the drawer under the counter taking the cash that was in there. Joe burst through office door the manger stood up then sat down again. "Open the safe" Mexican Joe snarled. The manager staggered to his feet walked across the room, then he knelt one knee and opened the safe. As he did so he looked up full of apprehension, Joe just clubbed him to the floor with the butt of his pistol. The robbers had brought a couple of burlap sacks in to the bank with them so they quickly emptied the contents of the safe into the sacks. "Lets go" said Joe. They strode out of the office, the robbers were smiling, "There are less of us, since the first time so we all get bigger shares, this is good news all round." Mexican Joe behind was behind the excited man, so he levelled his pistol and shot him in the back saying, "Even bigger shares now, because no one likes a smart ass." As the robbers stepped out on the street, Tom Brady bumped in to the first one, he spoke, "What's all the commotion?" One of the robbers clubbed him to the ground, then kicked him in the face. The rest of the outlaws stepped over him and mounted their horses then they rode out of town.

The town was quiet, if the people had heard the single shot fired by Mexican Joe, they ignored it.. People who might have come running like John Eckert, Neil Crossland, Dave Selley and Big John McCane were down at Larry Richards livery stable, planning where they would all move to. They heard the sound of the shot, but thought it may have come from the saloon and thought nothing of it.. As Big John said, "If someone is shooting the place up it's not my problem any more"

Talking among themselves the men with plans but nowhere to go all thought they might move down, to New Mexico. Utah said he knew of a valley there that would support three or four big farms and then some. He said that he had registered his ownership of the valley with the land registry, when he had drifted that way a few years back. At that time he was wondering if he would ever settle to a normal life again. Utah spoke to the others, "I feel that Crane has given me a second chance on life, I owe it to him to try and make good." "If helping you guys find a place to live can help me to do that then I will be happy." The others listen in silence. That kid, Crane had sure had got under their skin, they were all very worried about him.

They all moseyed back on up through town, as they got close to Doc's office they saw three men being helped to the Doc's place. They crossed the street and a very bloody and groggy, Tom Brady spoke to them saying, "Big John you need to get a posse together the bank has been robbed." Big John replied, "You are wearing the badge Tom, it's your job now, not mine." "But the town is in real trouble, the money is all gone." Tom said, "Like you told us Dallas does not need our kind" said Neil. They all walked on, leaving Doc to patch up the wounded.

Doc Black looked at three wounded men, "I told you all that you needed to find a new doctor in this town." "Then you told me that it was good riddance, that you didn't need me, so what are you doing in my office." "But I'm bleeding!" Moaned Tom Brady. "Yes," replied, The Doc, "Strange isn't it Crane bled for this town and you didn't want me to treat him." "So I'm telling you now, get out find a vet, I sure as hell don't treat vermin." The manager of the bank and his cashier started to follow Jim out the door. The Doc put his hand up and stopped them saying, "I will treat you two, you didn't bad mouth me." The Doc sat them both down and Ness came in with clean water and towels and put them down on the table. Then Doc and

Ness set about cleaning the two men's head wounds, after which Doc stitched them up.

"We will have to give some thought as to where we are going to go and live, when we leave here" Said the Doc to Ness when they had treated the two men and let them leave. He continued, "We can't go until Crane comes round but we need to be ready when he does." They both fell silent, hardly daring to think of the alternative, even though the Doc was starting to think that with each passing day it was more likely that Crane would not recover. He said to Ness, "You go down to Larry's stable and see what is happening with those other guys, Big John, Neil and the others, maybe we can tag along with them when they leave Dallas." "I need to stay with Crane in case there is any change in his condition." So Ness put on her bonnet, kissed him on the cheek then she picked up her purse and set off to walk to the other end of town.

When Ness arrived at the livery stable she was a little flustered because many of the ladies in town had ignored her greetings as she passed them. Some of them going so far as to actually turn their backs on her. Larry and Utah saw her and moved forward to welcome her. "Larry spoke, "Hey Ness good it is to see you" He and Utah smiled at her, "How is the Doc?" "Chris is fine." she said, then in answer to their unspoken question she said, "there is no change." Then she asked, "Did you heard about the bank being robbed?" Yes they replied, "John Eckert sent his son, Joey down to tell us," "We were all mighty glad that we had drawn our money out" "Added Larry," "Chris and I were relieved that we did that as well," Responded Ness.

"So""Asked Larry, "What can we do for you?" "The

Doc, that is Chris and I wondered if there would be any point in us riding along with the rest of you when we leave town?" Larry replied, "Well we would sure like to have you with us." "Utah said, "We are all going to settle in a valley that I have registered in my name on the other side of the Sacramento Mountains down in New Mexico, it is in between the Pecos River and the Rio Grand, near the town of Las Cruces, "There is another town there Alamogordo." "Some of us are going to farm the land maybe run a few cattle, we will catch and break a few horses." "But from your point of view I am sure that one of the towns will need Chris to be their doctor." "Neil has already said that he might open up a store in one of those towns, because that is the work that he knows best,""Yes I think we would like that" Said Ness.

"We are all hoping that Crane might ride down there with us when he feeling better." "Yes," Replied Ness, "Please God" Adding "I will tell Chris, I am sure he will want us to come with you'." As she walked away Tom Brady pulled up in his Buggy, his face battered and bruised, "You people need to come to a meeting at the Town Hall now" he shouted. Ness stopped and looked at him. Larry also looked at him and replied, "I don't think so, you have already told us we are not wanted in Dallas, so we are only waiting for Crane and we will be moving on."

"God damn you all" replied Tom, "This town is in trouble and you owe it something" Utah let his right hand crutch fall to the ground and his hand hovered near the but of his pistol. He spoke to Ness, "I would really like it if you walked round behind me" Then as she moved Utah spoke tom saying, "I'll ask you only once to moderate your language in front of a lady, otherwise you had better pull that pistol I see under your arm and we will have at it. Otherwise you can apologise for your disrespect and drive away. Tom blustered "Well I, Of course I didn't, what I am trying to say is I meant no harm," Then he turned his horse and buggy around and drove away'. Larry spoke to Utah, "I never liked that man or the way he treats women I'm glad you told him." Ness smiled at Utah and she thanked him, then she set off home

CHAPTER 13

Ness arrived home to find the Doc sitting in what had become his usual place beside Crane's bed. She walked in and started to tell him about New Mexico. Suddenly Crane sat upright, he flailed with his arms, his eyes were blazing, he was still fighting he was still out in the street. Doc Black had to use all of his own great strength to try to hold him down. "It's OK he said it is over, you won Crane, you won." Crane focused on him and relaxed back on to the pillow. "There are a few people who will be mighty glad to hear that you have come round." The Doc said. "So did they succeed in robbing the bank today?" asked Crane. "Yes they did" replied Doc Black, but you are no part of that, your today was two weeks ago and you stopped them two weeks ago." "I don't understand what you are sayin" said Crane "The last thing I remember is a big guy falling on me in the street, surely that can't have been two weeks ago." "It sure was replied the Doc. "You were hurt real bad, so badly I had started to think you wouldn't make it."

Crane considered this information in silence for a few moments, Then he asked, "What about Big John and the others?" "All fine" replied Doc Black "Thanks to you. You decimated the robbers before you went down." "Crane said "My throat is dry and sore, could I have some water?"

"Sure" replied the Doc and Ness will let you try some of her tasty soup. Ness went out coming back with a cup of cool water Crane took it and drank gratefully. Thank you he said, I feel very weak though," "You will start to feel better after you have had some soup" replied Ness.

Crane's mind was starting to clear, "My horse he said, did I go down alone or did he go down with me?" "Dancer is fine." Replied Doc Black, "In fact he carried on fighting after you passed out, there is no need to worry about him he is back in the corral at Larry's. "That is good news, and Utah? Asked Crane. "He is good" replied the Doc. "He played his part that day in helping to route those robbers. I'm mighty glad to hear that, Utah is a better man than he knows" said Crane.

Ness came back in with the soup, it was Beef broth actually, "Try and eat some of this before you talk any more, because you have a lot to catch up with." "There have been a lot of changes in Dallas since you got shot." Ness put the tray down on Crane's lap, he picked the spoon and dipped in the broth, then put it in his mouth. It tasted amazing, he hadn't tasted any food like that in a long time.

At the same time that Crane was coming round Utah was explaining to Larry how he came to find the valley in New Mexico. "It all started when things went sour for me in back in Utah, I had nothing, my deputy sheriff's job was gone and I just kinda drifted east. I went into Colorado then I headed south down into New Mexico. The first place I came on was Gallup, then I drifted back up in a north easterly direction to Los Alamos I crossed the Rio Grande and found myself in Santa Fe. I stayed there for a week or so drinking and carousing in the saloons, until the sheriff said it would be better for my health if I moved on. So I rode down through Albuquerque, sleeping on the trail, until I got to Alamogordo. After I left there I came on this lovely valley I noticed there were some caves and caverns part of the Sacramento mountains I think. If I had just kept going I would have been in Texas but then I thought I might go back up and see more of Colorado."

"As I rode back to Santa Fe the valley kind of played on my mind with it's streams and wooded areas and good grass. The location seemed kinda out of place in New Mexico so by the time I reached Santa Fe I decided I would see if the land was free to settle on at the land office, it was. In order to lay claim to the land I needed to establish boundaries. With that in mind I used the Sacramento Mountains on the East side and the Rio Grande at Las Cruces on the West as my markers.

To make sure I could choose who my neighbours were, I also ran the southern boundary across from Las Cruces to the Caves in The Sacramento mountains. Northern boundary just below Alamogora."

"My plans all changed when I killed a fella in a pistol fight and I had to light out of town. At that time it was in my mind to head for Mexico before the law caught up with me. It was a fair fight but the guy I shot was the was the town mayors son." When I got down near the border I met up with Mexican Joe and his gang, sadly I chose to ride with them Then as a gang we rode down into Texas and killed Crane's family.

Larry had listened in silence during Utah's explanation, So when he had finished speaking, Utah looked at Larry and said, "Does that change things between us?" "No" replied Larry, "Crane brought you into town and said that you are his friend" "So if he says that, you are a friend to all of us." Larry went on to say, "We all have a past, things have happened that we wish hadn't happened, but it's how we live our lives now that counts.

CHAPTER 14

Crane was feeling pretty chipper, he said to Chris the Doc, I think I should be getting up I haven't laid in a bed for as long as this since my Ma held me in her arms. "OK" replied Chris "But you need to move real slow." Crane swung his feet onto the floor and stood up. Feeling dizzy his legs buckled and he fell back onto the bed. Chris grabbed him saying "Whoa fella let's try that again, this time slowly." With Chris's support Crane got on to his feet again. This time he was able to remain standing. He took a few tentative steps forward he began to feel better. "Thanks Doc" he said, "I owe you, I'd better get my shirt on." "Best you call me Chris we are friends now and glad to be so. It is no good looking for your shirt because it has been thrown away, but, Neil has left you another, he says there is no charge." Doc took the shirt, dark blue in colour down off the shelf behind him. "We did wonder if you'd ever wear it." Crane took the shirt, unfastened the buttons and put it on, he winced as he put his arm in the right sleeve. The Doc seeing this said, "Take it easy Crane, you are have healed very well but you haven't moved for several days and you will be stiff.."

Crane got his boots on with some pain and difficulty then stamped his feet to make them fit right. "You might want to look in a mirror before you go out" said Chris, there's one on the wall over there." Crane walked across the room, taking a step back when he saw his reflection. "Well" He said with a smile, "First decent hair cut I had in my life" He smiled again, looking at the scar where the bullet had gouged it's way under the skin. "That's a mighty good looking scar, it is good thing that my hair will grow back over it." "That's the thing, it may not, some times it doesn't. Replied Chris. "But if you grow the hair around it long it won't show."

"Yeah well, I'm not what you could call good looking so one more scar won't make much difference." Crane decided it was time he went down to the livery stable and checked on his horses. He buckled on his guns, put on his jacket, noticed his Bowie knife on the shelf, sat down and put it in his boot. He left his throwing knife in a pocket of his jacket, he was starting to feel weary. He couldn't be bothered to fasten it to his arm. "See you soon Chris, and thanks again, you and Ness have done me proud" Crane said. And then he walked through out of the building out on the side walk. He moved slowly and steadily down the street, stopping occasionally to rest against the wall or a post. He was feeling quite weak but he needed to get moving.

Crane noticed that people were not smiling or saying hello as he passed by. In fact some people actually crossed the street to avoid him. He wondered if it was his appearance that was putting them off.

It took him a while to get to the stable because he felt quite weak and lacking in energy, but finally he arrived at the corral outside the livery stable. Both Stallions were in the corral. Dancer saw him and cantered across from the far side of the corral, he was showing his pleasure at Crane's presence. The other stallion just ambled across.. Dancer pushed his head over the top rail nuzzling his head against Crane's face, Crane patted his neck saying, "Easy boy you will have me over, I'm feeling quite weak just now. He felt the ridges on the horse's neck were the cuts were starting heal over, Crane ran his hand along the side of the horse's body and down his flanks. "We are a pretty pair aren't we?" Crane said. Dancer nodded his head and the muscles trembled in his legs.

Crane heard Utah's voice behind him. "Damn it Crane, it's good to see you. We have all been mighty worried about you." "I would have been worried about myself if I had known what was going on." Crane replied. "Dancer is looking good, his cuts healed well once Larry greased the" said Utah "You all call him Dancer now do you?" asked Crane," I'm mighty grateful to you both for taking care of him, I never really named things but I can see why people call him Dancer." "Well" said Utah, "As you know it's Devil Dancer really after his battle the other day. Did you know he seemed to fight even harder after you went down?" "No" replied Crane, "But I'm not surprised everything and everybody seem to do better without me around."

"So how is your horse doing Utah?" Crane asked changing the subject. Utah looked at him a worried look on his face, "Did you forget, we left my horse lying dead on the trail? You pulled him off my leg. I'm not talking about your old horse, I'm talking about your new horse." Crane replied, pointing at his other stallion. "But he is yours" Replied Utah. "No he isn't replied Crane, "He has been yours since

I put your saddle on him and attached the litter to the stirrups to bring you in town." Utah looked at him and swallowed, filled with emotion. "Thank you" he said with a gruff edge to his voice, "But why?" You are my friend, I can't ride two horses and the other thing is I wouldn't be here without you." Because Mexican Joe would have left us both dead on the trail if you hadn't shot his thumb off. Replied Crane. ""It was a lucky shot" replied Utah. "Needed making" said Crane. Larry came up behind them saying, "I think I should break this up before you two guys start hugging each other." Utah and Crane smiled ruefully, Crane spoke, "Thanks for taking care of Dancer and Utah's horse for me you've done a fine job." I'll straighten up the money with you soon."

"Like hell you will" replied Larry, "I don't charge friends and you have proved to be a true friend to this town and the people in it." "Even if they don't appreciate it" Crane looked at him with a quizzical expression his face, "What's all that about?" "Although I did notice a few people crossed the street to get away from me. Larry said "Come back to my shack with me we will eat, drink some coffee and we will get you caught up on what's been happening during the last couple of weeks."

The three men walked through the stable and out the back heading for Larry's shack. They ate in silence for a while then Crane pushed his bowl away from him, he picked up his mug took a swallow of coffee. Then he pushed back his chair and spoke, "This pot luck stew of yours is real good, I really enjoy it" You wouldn't say that if you had eaten it every day for years like I have." Replied Larry, Then he added, "Best if we bring you up to date, we are all going to New Mexico, there's a valley down there that Utah has the rights to. We are all going to live there." "Just who the heck is all?" Asked Crane. "Well"replied Larry, "There's me and Utah, Big John and his family, Neil and Maureen, Dave Selley, John Eckert and his family, Doc and Ness, he paused looking straight into Crane's eyes, "And you if you want to." Crane looked back at him, then asked, "Why would anyone want me to go with them?"

Utah looked at him, then he spoke, "Crane friendship is a two way street, you raced to help us when the raiders hit town, so you must have been concerned for us as friends, we want you in our company, we want you with us.. "Well I don't understand" replied Crane, "What happened to make you all want to leave town?" Larry explained about the towns people being frightened of Crane. Going on to tell him about the mayor turning against Big John and the rest of them and then the Raiders coming back and robbing the bank. That didn't happen until after our group had all withdrawn their money. "Some People" Said Crane, "You can't ever figure them out, the more you do for them" He stopped short, "Why are they afraid of me?" "I only shot the robbers." Utah said, "They had never seen anything like you, your face was a mask of blood, you and Dancer laying waste to all around you, they were quite simply terrified." "You are the man they need when there is a war, but when they want things peaceful and civilised, you just don't belong in their town."

Crane thought about this, "I just wanted to help people who had been good to me" He said. Then he went on to say "I would be mighty proud to travel with you all, I don't know if I will settle with you in the valley though," "Why not?" asked Utah. "Because I think the folks in this town are probably right, I am not fit to be part of a civilised community." "The three men sat in silence. There was no way to tell Crane he was wrong, they would just have to prove it to him.

CHAPTER 15

Another week passed and during that time, wagons were bought, made and repaired. Draft horses were bought and bargained for. Belongings were loaded into the wagons and stores of food were packed for the trip. These covered wagons would be the means of carrying everything the outcasts from Dallas possessed to their new home. There were all the hopes and dreams for the future in these wagons, the lives of each person were changing, they believed good times were ahead. There was an undercurrent of excitement and apprehension bubbling in the hearts and minds of each of the seekers of this better life.

Crane and Big John McCane were talking outside Neil Crossland's store, Neil had called them in to let them know he had manage to sell the business lock stock and barrel as the saying goes, John Eckert had been renting the barbers shop so no problem there, he could move as he pleased. Doc Black had taken his shingle down he and Ness were ready to go. John McCane said, We are all real pleased that you are going to be riding with us Crane, we are mighty glad you came town.

Crane nodded and moved of down the street back to wards the Livery stable Big John went back in the store. Two men stood out in the street, "Hey Crane" One of them called. Crane turned towards them and stepped down off the side walk into the street. "Cat got your tongue?" Another one shouted. Crane looked at them as they moved sideways trying to outflank him and put the sun in his eyes. Crane pulled the brim of his hat forward and studied the two men, the one who was just to his left would draw first, he knew that because the guy was nervy and doing the talking, there was no doubt he would draw first, but his nerves would make his first shot miss. The guy on the right was quiet and steady he might be slower on the draw but he would shoot straight. Crane adjusted his position, he needed to be ready. The one on the left, spoke again, "Joe, Mexican Joe that is said to say hello if we saw you "he laughed nervously, "He said to say that will also be Adiós." His right hand flashed down to his pistol grabbing and pulling it clear of his holster. Crane saw this on the periphery of his vision, his own pistol leapt in to his left hand he fired just as the man to his right cleared leather. The bullet struck just below the breastbone tearing the life from the man, he was dead as he hit the ground. Crane was turning and diving left. Firing all in the same movement. The guy on the left died in the dusty street as his own bullet hit the hitching rail behind where. Crane had been standing.

Crane stood up and went to each man in turn emptying their pockets of cash and taking their weapons. A crowd was gathering and someone spoke, "Dear God he is the Devil, look he even robs the dead" Crane threw 10 dollars on one of the bodies, "That will pay for their funerals" He said. Tom Brady arrived huffing and puffing his pistol in his hand, "I'll have to take your pistol Crane, I am taking you to jail, "Good luck with that" said Crane. Then he turned and walked away." Brady's finger tightened on the trigger as he moved to shoot Crane in the back. He would have done but for the barrel of Big John McCane's pistol pressing against his temple. "You yellow scum" Big John grated, "You call Crane uncivilised yet what you planned was cold blooded murder, if there is a devil in this town it is you, you evil swine." "I'm the sheriff" wailed Tom Brady, "Yea" said Big John "Well as Crane said, good luck with that."

Big John looked at the two bodies, You have posters on these two in the office $500 apiece if I am not mistaken, dead or alive. I will come back to the office with you and you can give me Crane's bounty money. They walked back to the sheriff's office and went inside. Big John went round the desk and opened the drawer in the middle. Tom Brady said, "You carry on as though you own the place." Big John ignored him, rifling through the posters. He stopped putting two out on the desk top, told you he said Sneaky Bill Hawes and his partner Steady Stevens, as I said $500 a piece." I'll make out a chit, Crane will have to take it to the bank"Tom said "Wait a minute" said Big John, "I meant to sort this out for Crane, I don't know about the others in the gang that killed his parents but this Lattigo was another $250." "How do I know Crane killed him?" asked Jim." "You don't but I know he is dead because Utah told me" said Big John. "We had to send for and have money brought in by Wells Fargo for the bank after the robbery and now you and Crane are robbing it again" Tom grumbled. He signed the chit for $1,250 and handed it to Big John, "Here take it and you and your friends get out of town" "We will be gone tomorrow, you can be sure of that." Replied Big John. He took the chit and walked out of the office, and headed down to see Crane at the livery stable.

When he got there Larry, Utah and Crane were leaning on the corral poles, Crane had told them about the two pistol fighters who had come looking for him. Big John said, "How come you shot Steady Stevens first?" "I would have shot the fast man, Sneaky Bill Hawes first." "It was something Josey said to me during our time together, it came back to me in the street the twitchy ones will be fast they won't shoot straight, The quiet thoughtful ones usually do,." "I didn't know who they were but it seemed like a chance, so I took it" replied Crane.

Big John nodded thoughtfully, "Anyway this is your money," He handed over the chit to Crane explaining how the money was due to him. "But I didn't kill Lattigo, Dancer did" Replied Crane. "Same difference" said Big John, "If you don't take the bounty, Tom Brady will." "Okay" said Crane, I will give a $1,000 to you Utah call it relocation money you can share it out any way you think fit." He smiled saying, "I will saddle Dancer and ride up to the bank, you never know when the banks going to be robbed in this town." While he was talking Crane unfastened his shirt cuff and strapped his throwing knife in place.

When Dancer was saddled up and Crane had ridden away, Utah said, "That man is an enigma, he has a code of honour like no one that I have met before." The other three nodded. Thinking to themselves, I wouldn't like him to be against me. As if he could read the others thoughts Utah added, "I ran from him for more than four years and then instead of killing me as he had every right to do, he saved my life then he made me his friend. Go Figure."

Crane reached the bank in double quick time, he hadn't ridden Dancer for a while and the stallion was raring to go. As he rode Crane spoke to the horse, "I think I will take you out of town when I get the money and let you run." Crane dismounted, stepped up on to the side walk and walked into the bank, he stepped up to the counter and gave the clerk the chit, saying the words, "Would you cash this please." The clerk said "Yes sir Mr Crane" then he went back into the managers office. The manager looked up, the clerk handed him the chit. He read it got up and went to the safe opened it and took out a pile of notes they were in bundles of $500, he took three, split one and counted out $250, he relocked the safe and went out front saying, "Mr Crane this is a lot of money, would you like to open an account?" "No" replied Crane, "I have no confidence in this bank, it is always being robbed, I'll just take the money. Crane reached out his hand took the money; unbuttoned his shirt and put the two $500 bundles inside, then he re buttoned the shirt, then he divided the $250 between his pockets.

Then Crane turned and walked back out of the bank, got his canteen off his saddle, he worked the pump at the horse trough in the street, then when the water was running he removed the cork and filled his canteen. Crane hung the canteen back on the saddle horn, then mounted Dancer turned the horse and rode back the stable. When he got there the three men were waiting for him, he opened his shirt and threw the two $500 bundles down to Utah saying, "I'm going to give Dancer a run." Then Crane gave the horse his head and he galloped out of town. The hot wind burned his cheeks Crane felt good to be moving again, Dancer was fairly flowing over the ground, his powerful strides fairly eating up the miles, he was just born to run and he was making the most of the chance.

After a while Crane slowed him down to a walk and let him blow, then he stopped him and dismounted. He took the canteen from the saddle horn took off his hat pulled the cork and poured water from the canteen into his hat and held it under Dancers nose the horse drank steadily and gratefully. "That's enough boy "said Crane, "I wouldn't want you to founder, by drinking to quick." Crane looked ruefully at his hat, "First new hat I ever had" he said as he looked at the bullet hole in the brim. Then Crane put the hat back on his head, took a swig of the brackish water himself and hung the canteen back on the saddle. Then he unfasten the girth straps and took the saddle off and rubbed the horse down with the saddle blanket. When that was done Crane refolded the blanket put it back on the horse and then he replaced the saddle. He mounted up they were ready to return to town.

As Crane turned Dancer, back towards town he smelt smoke on the wind, so he changed his mind and turned the horse and rode in the direction the smell was coming from. He hadn't ridden far when he saw what he took to be a sod busters cabin on fire. Crane put Dancer to the run, as he entered the yard he saw an elderly couple tied to the corral rails. There was young woman about five feet tall she looked to be between 25 and thirty years old to Crane, she was wrestling with a tall man easily six feet six with a scar on his cheek. The man was holding a knife in his hand, determined to cut the girl. It wasn't his day because he died with a curse on his lips as Crane shot him in the throat. The man took the woman to the ground with him as he fell.

Two men came out of the barn behind Crane as he leapt from the saddle, "Just let that pistol drop, feller," one of them said. Crane let the pistol fall from his hand, but as he turned towards them his right hand was already on the butt of the pistol under his left arm, Crane faked a stumble and as he fell to his knees he drew and fired. His first bullet hit one of the men between the eyes, Crane's forward movement took him to the right and his next bullet took the other man just above the belt buckle. The man's own bullet grazed Crane's shoulder, the shock causing him to drop his pistol.

Crane was one knee his throwing knife in his right hand when he saw his Nemesis, Mexican Joe come from behind the barn door leading a horse, reins in a hand that was missing a thumb in fact his whole hand was gone,the reins were actually tied to his wrist. He was holding a pistol in his other hand. "Now I will kill you" Snarled Joe. As the throwing knife left Crane's hand, he shouted at Mexican Joe, "You talk to much." Mexican Joe fired and missed as Crane fell forward from his knee. The knife nestled in Joe's left bicep, he screamed in pain and rage as his pistol fell from his hand. He used the stump of his missing hand to knock the knife out of his arm, after what seemed an age it fell to the floor, then Mexican Joe leapt into the saddle, his horse moved off at the run heading straight for the young women who was struggling out from under the tall dead man. His intent was clear he was going ride her down.

Crane was feeling week and groggy, he clearly was not fully recovered from his previous wounds, there was blood was flowing down his arm as he fumbled for the Bowie knife in his boot, but it was plain he would not make it in time to save the girl. Suddenly a scream of rage rent the air, Mexican Joe looked and saw Dancer hurtling towards him ears laid back, teeth bared. In panic and desperation Joe's horse reared and nearly fell back, Dancer flew past, as Mexican Joe fought for control, somehow he stayed in the saddle and fled the yard his horse flat out on the run.

Dancer spun back looking for a battle but he couldn't find one. Crane stood swaying slightly as the young woman walked towards him. Crane turned and walked towards the corral, his Bowie knife in hand. He cut the older lady free and her daughter as that is who the young women was, just managed to catch her mother before she fell, with her knees buckling. Crane heard her say the words, "It's OK Ma" from behind him as he freed the man, whose face was bloody from a scalp wound. "Mighty glad you came along young feller" the old man said. "I was plumb out of ideas, myself." The older man's eyes sparkled as he spoke, with a smile playing on his lips."Yeah, you seem like a tough old boy" Crane replied. "I didn't get it right this time though, I've fought Indians and bad men times gone by but this time they took me by surprise." Said the Old man. "It happens" said Crane, "That Mexican Joe, killed my Ma and Pa, he just keeps doing these things, I've been on his trail about four years now but I can't finish him. "Sorry to hear that" the man paused and said, "By the way my names Fred Hall" he turned, saying "This my wife Flo and our daughter Maggie, we are beholden to you stranger."

Crane replied, "No problem, I'm just glad I came along when I did, people call me Crane." Flo said, "Let me see that arm of yours" Crane turned to her and she took hold of his arm unfastened the sleeve on his shirt, took his Bowie knife and cut the sleeve up and round, "I will have to use this for a bandage" said Flo. She then tore the shirt further exposing Crane's chest and shoulder. Crane smiled, "That's another new shirt gone" he said. Flo was all business now said, "Maggie get me a pail of water" and tear some strips off your petticoat. Maggie silently obliged turning away from Crane as she tore the strips from her petticoat.

Flo worked quickly and efficiently cleaning the wound and making a pad from the remaining strips of petticoat. When this was done she then bound the pad on with the shirt sleeve. "Thank you mam" said Crane. "You were lucky young man the bullet gouged you but didn't go in."

"Well" said Fred "It's over, the house and all our belongings are gone, we might as well head for town."

There were two horses in the corral and Crane could see a wagon over by the barn. He said"I'll help you hitch up your team." Then he and Fred set about that job. Although Crane's arm was starting to stiffen up so he wasn't as efficient as usual. After she had washed the blood from her husbands face Flo and her daughter Maggie had set about loading useful items, tools and the like on to the wagon. Crane got the harness from the barn as he went in through the doors he saw the carnage left there, Every animal had been slaughtered, mindless killing,pigs, milk cow, calf, chickens all killed by Mexican Joe and his gang, for no other reason except that they could. Crane left the barn with the harness, he felt sick to his stomach. When the horses were hitched to the wagon, Crane helped Maggie and Flo finish load the wagon. Then he saw Fred set fire the barn. "Fred saw Crane looking at him, "Nothing else to do" he said hopelessly." Crane nodded silently and turned away.

"Maggie spoke to Crane for the first time, "I'm glad you came when you did, I thought we were done for." Crane gave her one of his rare smiles. "You were giving that tall feller a rough time, I think you might have done for him if he had kept on." "Maggie smiled in return saying, "I was trying to get hold of his pistol, if I could I would have shot him." "You were doing right, when things are looking black and you think your life is over, mentally or physically, you have to fight with all your strength and with anything you can find. You did that and I am mighty proud to know you and your family, each one of you has spirit and grit.." Replied Crane.

Fred spoke, "You were saying that half breed feller and you have history?" "Yeah as I said Mexican Joe he killed my Ma and Pa at our farm a few years back. I've been on his trail for all that time the men who helped him have all died along the way. Said Crane. Fred looked at him saying, "Yeah I can see how they the might." The family got on their wagon, then Crane mounted his horse and they left the farm behind.

CHAPTER 16

As the Hall family approached the outskirts of town Crane brought his horse alongside the wagon and spoke to the family, "I'm taking you to meet my friends, we are all intending to head to New Mexico. We want to start a new life so, if you are serious about leaving your farm for good you can come with us. The family didn't reply, lost in there own thoughts about this strange warrior who had come to their rescue in more ways than one. They thought of Crane in this way because that is how they saw him riding high on his war horse, he and his horse were warriors. There was no other description that would fit this pair.

When the group arrived at Larry's Livery Stable, and Utah and Larry were there to meet them. Crane stepped down from Dancer and explained the situation to them both. "Then he said, "I've told these good people that they can come with us if they want to. I have decided that I will help them set up a new home if they decide to come with us." "What happened to them?" Asked Utah. Mexican Joe had Ma and Pa Hall tied to the corral and a scar faced rider was attacking Maggie when I rode in" said Crane. It was a really bad situation, Mexican Joe had slaughtered all their livestock in the barn and their house was on fire," "Things were going to get much worse, I was only just in time." Then he added bitterly, Mexican Joe got away again!" "Because of my weakness from my old wounds, Maggie nearly lost her life, luckily Dancer took the fight to Mexican Joe, without him doing that there would have been a very different outcome. Flo spoke, "Never mind your old wound, you need to see a doctor with that new wound because it was only a temporary dressing I put on it." "Thanks Flo," Replied Crane, "I will go see Doc Black because I need to tell the others about the additions to our travelling party." With out another word he remounted Dancer and rode off up the street.

"What kind of a young man is this Crane?" asked Fred. "He fought and killed with an intensity that I've never seen before, but then he has been gentle and kind with us and continues to try to help." Utah replied, "He is what life has made him, the only way I can describe him is to say he is an enigma. I was part of the gang who killed his folks, yet he saves my life and makes me his friend." I don't understand him but I would ride in to hell to save him if he needed me. I can only tell you that he has given me back my self respect and I have gone from wishing I was dead, to having a reason to live."

"Anyway," said Larry "Let's get you folks settled in the barn, we will water the horses for you and get you all some food." "I have to say that since Crane came town this place is turning in to a hotel" Then, he added with a smile, "I have stopped being lonely." Then he unhitched the team from the wagon and turned them into the corral. Then the group of five wearily trudged back to Larry's cabin, to eat some of Larry's now famous pot luck stew. The family were weary as a reaction to their ordeal. Larry said, "Right Flo you and Maggie can sleep in here Flo, us guy's will sleep in the barn." Thanks were murmured by the group, as they tiredly got on with eating their food.

Crane called at the store when he got into town, he brushed aside Maureen's concerns for his clearly visible wounds and then brought Neil Crossland Dave Selley up to date,. When he heard that the Hall family had lost everything Neil he said, "I will send take some clothes down to Larry's, some for the two ladies and some for an elderly man, "Please charge the clothes to me." Said Crane." Crane also asked them to let Big John and John Eckert know what was happening. Then he went to see Doc and Ness. When he got there the Doc looked at him saying, "Look at the state of you, you will be needing my services full time if you keep on like this." He called out, "Ness, get some water please and we will clean Crane's wound and put a proper dressing on it." "Thank you" said Crane. "I just wanted to let you know that we need to have a meeting down at Larry's, there is another family going with us to New Mexico and they will need our help." Then he told them both about his run in with Mexican Joe and his gang earlier that day. "How that man keeps surviving his run ins with you I don't know," Replied the Doc. "Yeah" said, Crane "One day one of us won't walk away, it remains to be seen which one."

As Crane was leaving Doc's place Maureen Neil's wife came in with two shirt's. She smiled at Crane, "Neil said to bring you these shirts, we have never known a man go through shirts the way you do." Doc laughed and said, "You might be worried about his shirts, but my concern is his skin, he's only got the one and he keeps getting holes in that." Ness, Maureen and Doc were laughing uproariously, their laughter was releasing some of the tension that had been building up over the last few weeks. Then Crane took off his ruined shirt and put one of the new ones on, he smiled ruefully, then he said, "I'll let you dispose of the old shirt Ness if you don't mind and I'll leave you good folks to your fun and go back and give Dancer a rub down." Crane went out on to the side walk and put his other new shirt in to his saddlebag, then unhitched Dancer, mounted up and rode back down to Larry's stable.

When Crane arrived back at Larry's he set about unsaddling and rubbing Dancer down. Afterwards he let him drink from the trough and then walked into the corral with him. The Hall's team of draught horses were in the corral so he thought that he would see how Dancer settled with them. Crane closed the gate and then he climbed up and sat on the top rail. He watched as Dancer wandered up and down, paying no attention to the bay geldings. It was mighty quiet and Crane was feeling tired so he pulled his hat forward over his eyes and he dozed, leaning his back against the high post that hinged the gate.

Crane didn't know how long he had been asleep when he heard, Maggie Hall's voice saying, "Hello Crane" he opened his eyes turned his body and saw Maggie standing there, looking very pretty, she was wearing a blue gingham dress. Maggie spoke again, "I just wanted to thank you for the new clothes the three of us are all beholden to you, Pa says he will pay you back, but he doesn't know how or when." "No problem" replied Crane. "None of you owe me anything, friends help each other where and when they can, I know you all helped me and you and your Ma cleaned and dressed my wound."

"Right the reason I came out was to give you a message" said Maggie "Larry said to tell you there is some stew on the stove if you are hungry." "Yeah" replied Crane "I would enjoy that because I am feeling very hungry. Do you know that pot has never been empty since I arrived here, I don't know what he puts in it but what comes out always tastes mighty good." "Yes it does" said Maggie, "I think it must be a man thing, women usually cook a meal from the start every meal time, I suppose it is because he works all day and just wants to eat when he is ready and not have start preparing a meal."

As they walked through the barn Crane and Maggie met the guys coming back the other way. "You are looking better Crane" said Big John, the others nodded. Crane smiled, a more frequent habit for him recently and said "yes it's surprising what a new shirt will do." Larry spoke, "We will be pulling out at dawn tomorrow, if you are happy with that." I don't know about happy" Replied Crane, "I just seem to have upset every bodies lives since a came here."

Doc Black's voice came from behind him, "No such thing, you have behaved as a good citizen and friend should, it as not your fault that this town has scum like Brady in positions of authority. "Here Here" said the others in unison. "Thank you" replied Crane feeling quite emotional, "I'll go and get something to eat, if none of you mind." Crane walked on towards Larry's cabin. Maggie was the only one who followed. "Utah smiled knowingly at the others and said, I think that Maggie is rather taken with our young friend." Maggie's father Fred said, "Well in my opinion she couldn't do any better for herself, Crane is a fine young man and from what I've seen and he has a good sense of right and wrong, his Ma and Pa clearly taught him well. They all nodded and John Eckert said, "I wouldn't argue with that assessment."

Crane and Maggie arrived at Larry's cabin just in time to see Maggie's Ma coming out, "Oh Crane" she said, thank you so much for the clothes, she held her skirt and turned around, this is the nicest dress I've had in years. My pleasure ma'am Crane replied. "It suits you, you look mighty pretty." Flo smiled and blushed bobbing her head, "You go in and serve Crane Maggie, I'm going to see what your Pa is doing, he has to go see the bank because we owe the $100 that they lent us against the farm and we can't go with you unless the bank take the farm." Crane said "Just hold on a minute" he went in his pocket and took out two $50 bills. "Now you take these notes to Fred and tell him to pay the bank and then he must ask them to buy the land, you are not going to leave here empty handed." Flo looked at him the money in her hand, she was going to speak, but Crane put his finger to his lips saying, "Shush, there is no need, just go to Fred." Flo hurried away and Crane followed Maggie into the cabin.

Crane sat down at the table and Maggie put a steaming bowl of stew and a hunk of bread in front of him, she also handed him a spoon, to eat with. Crane started to eat then he looked up at Maggie standing by him and said, "Maggie will you please sit down I would like to tell you something.." Maggie sat down beside him, "Crane was blushing as he spoke, "You are a very lovely woman, in fact you are the most beautiful woman I have ever seen." I know that we only met today but I would like to get to know you better, because I think you are very special." It was Maggie's turn to blush and she said, "I know how you feel because I think you are special to, but you do realise that I am twenty seven years old and no man has wanted to marry me yet, nor have I wanted to marry." Then she said, I know you are only about twenty one because I heard the others talking and you may like me now but how will you feel when I am older?"No one knows what the future may hold" replied Crane, "But I know you are special so, if you will, let's just take one day at a time, for what it is worth I think we will grow old and happy together." Crane went back to eating his stew, they had an understanding and they both felt happy about that.

When Crane had finished eating Maggie took the bowl, and with cloth wiped the table clean of crumbs. Then she went outside to wash the bowl and spoon. Crane got up and followed her outside, "I'm going to see where the others have got to." He said, Maggie nodded and Crane walked towards the back of the barn. He hadn't walked far when he met Flo and Fred coming back from their trip to the bank. Fred spoke, "Crane thank you for the money you sent with Flo, I paid the debt and the bank bought the land for $1,125 I came out a little ahead." He held out $100, Crane took the money, because he knew it would hurt the man's pride if he refused. Crane didn't count the money, he just put it in his pocket, saying "Thank you" as he did so. *These are very good people* he thought.

"We must go and tell Maggie the good news." Said Flo, "Please wait for a moment" said Crane, "I want to talk to you both if I may." "Sure," replied Fred. "If anyone deserves our time it is you." "The thing is" said Crane, "I would like you permission to court Maggie." Fred looked at him before replying, "The thing is we like you fine son, it's just that a couple of things worry me, one is you only met today and the other is you are a mite younger than she is" At this point Maggie had joined them, "She spoke saying, "We have covered this ground Pa, and we know that we all only met today, for that reason we would like to take things slow, one day at a time." "I agree with you." Replied Crane. Fred held out his hand saying, "Then we will shake on it son, because I can't refuse Maggie anything." Flo hugged them all and then they went to tell Maggie the news about the bank and how they all had something to move forward with.

"Strange how things can change" said Fred, "First thing this morning our home was burning and it looked as if our lives were over, then you rode in Crane and suddenly we have a future." Crane smiled and replied, "I haven't had a future for more than three years and then I meet a few good folks, starting with Utah and life is full of hope again." Going on to say "Well I guess we all need to hit the hay, literally for us men, because we are sleeping in the barn, we have to be early so that we can get on the trail before dawn.

CHAPTER 17

The next morning it was still dark when they all got together and set about preparing to get on their way. Maureen, Neil and Dave arrived in separate wagons, carrying the things they would need to start a new life. As Dave got down from the wagon he saw Crane and said, "I wonder if you would be kind enough to accept a present for you and Dancer, I hope that you won't be offended by it." Crane was intrigued and followed Dave round to the back of his wagon. Dave lifted the most beautifully worked saddle out of the wagon and held it out to Crane. He took the saddle, Crane was struck dumb, struggling to find the words to speak in the face of such generosity. He looked at the hand tooled black leather admiring the workmanship, the soft lining that was on the inside, the stirrups straps were slightly longer than normal, but adjustable. The saddle had breast and girth straps, and the breast strap had dark metal heart shapes worked into the leather the biggest one of these was in the centre. The saddle horn had the same dark metal on the side. Saddle bags, rifle boot and bridle were included. It was an amazing piece of workmanship.

Finally Crane was able to speak, "I can't accept this, it is clearly worth a fortune, it is magnificent." Dave smiled and said, "I made it for myself, but I never had the horse who could wear it, Dancer must have it and I would be proud to see it on him." "I based it on the silver mounted saddles that I have seen some of the Mexican riders use, but I always thought them to flashy so I decided on the dark metal." Crane said, "you are right, also the sun flashing off the silver could get you killed." "Good point" said Dave. Crane thought to himself, this guy really wants to give this to me, I can't refuse it and still remain his friend. "! So he said "Thank you, I will never be able to repay you, but you can call on me any time and I will be there." "Crane hefted the saddle as he walked towards the corral, "It's a lot lighter than my other one Dave, Dancer will appreciate that."

All the wagons were harnessed and goods had been previously loaded so dawn was just breaking as the small wagon train pulled out of town. Each on of them felt that they were carrying enough but not to much to start their new life. They had all heard tales about overloaded wagons and broken axles leaving settlers stranded in the middle of nowhere, where they often died, so they had not overloaded their wagons. There was a small herd of horses which Crane, Utah and John Eckert's son Joey would ride with, Big John McCane was up front on his horse riding beside his wagon, his wife Susan was driving it, he was leading the train because he had a map that Utah had drawn for him to show the way. The plan was that Utah would ride ahead for a couple hours to check for problems on the trail, so that he could sort out any problems, or plan a diversion if it was necessary.

The travellers encountered no problems in the first couple of weeks of their journey and it was a very relaxed group who sat eating round the camp fire one supper time.

Utah said, "This is a fairly easy trail to follow, their are no real obstacles. I have heard of wagon trains having to lower their wagons and horses over cliffs were the trails have run out in earlier times, but not on this trail. This was I think an old buffalo trail in years gone by they would travel north and south on it depending on the time of year. In those days Buffalo meat was a real staple diet for the Indians. Those Buffalo seem to have cleared the trail very well for us. Crane nodded saying, "You amaze me, I have drifted around this territory with no thought of a destination, or who or what had been here before. On the other hand you seem to have picked up the lay of the land information about it everywhere that you have ridden."

"Well you had other things on your mind at the time that you were riding these trails, I think you will find it different now." Replied Utah. "You may be right about that" said Crane. He got up and took his plate and cup over to the back of the chuck wagon. Where he found Maggie washing the dishes. "You are looking real good" he said. Maggie smiled, "You would say that when all you look at all day is the back of those horses."

"You know that I think you are the best of the best Maggie don't you?"said Crane. "You are biased, but I think about same of you" replied Maggie. Crane kissed her on the cheek and then he walked away.

Utah and Big John smiled at each other, Utah said, I think there will be a wedding there pretty soon." Big John nodded, "Those two were born to be together" he said. Fred came up behind them, "I'd have to agree" he said, "There was a spell there when I wondered but the more we see the easy way they are with each other, the happier

Flo and I are. Maggie never took to any of the other young men she met, but with Crane she just seemed to know that he is the one." "It seems to be the same with Crane," said Utah, I just know that this relationship is good for him. If things go well he may just stay off the vengeance trail, I think he will just settle down now and let Mexican Joe find his own end. He has been talking about building a home for the two of them." Fred said, "I think that you are right he needs to settle down, because he can't go on living the way he has been."

The following morning Utah rode on ahead as usual, he really did relish these morning rides on his own. This stallion, that was a gift from Crane was the finest horse he had ever owned or ridden. The big long striding horse just ate up the ground and as it did the miles just seemed to fly by. Utah liked having the time to think and reflect on how good his life had been since he had taken the decision to turn against Mexican Joe. Even the occasional painful twinge from his recently healed broken leg failed to take the edge off his enjoyment of life. On this day his morning reverie was disturbed when he came to a fallen tree that was lying across the trail. His first thought was, this could be a set up for an ambush so his eyes scanned the surrounding terrain for signs of trouble. Utah saw nothing, there were no flashes off the sun which could have been catching belt buckles or bridles, there was no sign of anything that might suggest someone was watching the trail. After looking around carefully for several minutes Utah saw nothing that gave him any reason to feel nervous.

It was quite clear that a lone rider would be able ride round the fallen tree, but Utah knew that the wagons could not pass this way with the tree lying across the trail. So Utah dismounted, leaving the reins trailing, he knew his horse well enough now to know that he wouldn't stray. Utah looked at the tree roots, it was plain that the tree had fallen some considerable time ago. The reason for this assumption was that there were small plants growing in the ground between the old roots. Looking at it Utah could see that this tree was going to take some moving, so he went back to his horse and unhooked the lariat from the saddle, he walked back to the tree and put the rope around it. Having done that he then turned and mounted his horse, he wrapped the end of the rope round the saddle horn then he backed the horse up. The stallion took the strain and the rope went tight but the tree didn't move. The horse was a powerful animal but no matter how he strained his muscles and sinews nothing happened, the fallen tree did not move. Then the rope snapped and the horse who was taken by surprise when the strain came off, reared staggering backwards twisting his body so that he didn't fall. In that moment Utah was thrown from the saddle, he hit the ground hard and as his head struck a rock the world went black. Utah lay motionless in the hot sun with blood trickling from the deep wound in his scalp. The stallion puzzled by this turn of events bent his head and nuzzled Utah's face The man didn't stir. Not knowing what he should do next the horse stamped his feet and then stood still in the heat of the day. The afternoon passed and the evening dusk came then it was dark and still Utah lay unmoving on the ground.

CHAPTER 18

The wagon train had stopped it was time for the noon break, a time to rest and to water the horses. Crane dismounted and walked over to Doc and Ness saying, "I'm starting to worry about Utah, he has usually turned back and joined us by now." Doc said "We will have a cup of coffee and then if he's not back I will ride out ahead with you to see were he has got to" Crane nodded and then took Dancer to get a drink of water. There was still no sign of Utah half an hour later so Doc saddled up his horse, a big white gelding. Crane spoke to Joey, "You'll be OK with the horses I know, so I'm going to ride out with the Doc and look for Utah." Joey who was growing in stature and maturity with each passing day said, "Sure that's no problem." The Doc and Crane told the others where they were going and then rode on ahead. Big John took the decision that they would remain at the noon camp until The Doc and Crane returned, or until the following morning which ever occurred first.

As Crane and the doc set out on their way to see if they could find Utah someone else, a miner, by the name of Alan Crowe had found Utah. Alan Crowe roamed the territory always looking for the gold strike that he had never made and probably never would. He had just been drifting along in his normal way. Alan was approaching the fallen tree coming down the trail from another direction. As always Alan was travelling aimlessly he had no real place to go and no known place to be. These things were as usual and he was thinking about where he might camp that evening when he came up on the fallen tree. "Whoa mule, Alan said, It seems that we have an obstruction, really we should have stopped sooner because it is getting dark.." Alan talked to his mule all the time, they had been constant companions for may years. Alan mumbled on, "This fallen tree is no problem to us so we will carry on regardless." As Alan and the mule came round the tree, the rough ground off to the side was no problem to the sure footed animal as he picked his way steadily past the obstruction. As they got to the other side Alan saw the horse standing still in the growing dusk and then he saw the man lying on the ground. Alan dismounted from the mule and he went to the fallen man's side, dropping to one knee and as he reached him, he was looking for injuries and making sure that the man was still breathing. When he found a pulse Alan went back to his Mule and got his canteen, as he did this the horse stamped and fidgeted.

Alan was pouring some water on to a rag so that he could wash the blood from the man's face. When Alan passed the horse it smelt the water and snorted, stamped his feet and pushed against him. Alan spoke to him, "You want a drink boy, have you been here a long time?" The horse nodded his head more in anticipation than reply. Alan took off his hat and poured water into it, the horse drank gratefully and drained the water from the hat. "You sure were dry fella, you must have been standing in the sun all day. The horse just nodded his head up and down, as if in reply.

When the horse had finished drinking, Alan went back to the man on the ground, when he got to him he knelt down and started to clean the man's head wound, the man stirred and moaned but did not come round. Then Alan took off his own jacket and folded it into a pillow and put it under the man's head, when he had done that he got up and went back to his Mule. Alan got a blanket from his pack turned round and went to cover the man. As he bent down to cover him suddenly the darkness was filled with sound. Alan looked up an gasped in horror, there was a huge black stallion rearing up over him. The stallion was so black that Alan could barely see him in the dark.

As the stallion was brought under control Alan saw the rider jump down from the saddle all in the same movement. He realised with horror that he couldn't see the riders eyes. "Oh sweet Jesus" he said, "The devil himself rode in" The devil spoke, "You don't have to worry I can see you are helping my friend Utah, I'm sorry I startled you but the Doc an I just didn't see you in the dark."

While this was going on Doc Black had dismounted and was tending to Utah, "Light a fire" he barked, "I need to see what I'm doing." Crane worked quickly gathering brushwood, then he flicked a Lucifer with his thumbnail and set light to the wood he had piled up. The flames quickly lit up the area and for the first time Alan saw that the devil had eyes. He spoke, "I thought you had no eyes, I thought you were the devil." "You are not the first one to think that, Replied Crane. "The name is Crane, That's Utah on the ground and Doc Black is tending him." "Right" replied Alan, "Alan Crowe" is what they call me and there is only me and my mule."

Utah stirred, "My dammed head" he moaned, Doc Black replied, "It is certainly thick enough." "There it is again," Said Crane, "Doc Black's famous bedside manner." Doc Black snorted, saying" I am a very good sawbones for a man who is by nature, a pistol fighter." Crane shook his head saying, "You are a whole lot better doctor than that, the fact that I'm alive and here is testimony to that." Then Alan said, "I will get some more wood or the fire is going to go out," When he came back Alan built up the fire and Crane got the makings for the coffee and the coffee pot out of his saddlebag, poured water from his canteen into the pot with the coffee and set it on a rock at the fire, moving the fire around it so it could boil then, Crane unsaddled Dancer, and Utah gave them all a drink of water from his hat. He rubbed them down, and unsaddled them, as they would all clearly need to camp here tonight.

Alan asked, "Are you guys hungry?" "I've got beans and some jerky, to share" The three men agreed they were hungry and they thanked Alan. So Alan set about heating the beans in a smoke blackened pot. The men were soon sitting by the fire eating and then the Doc asked Utah, "What in the hell were you trying to do when you fell off your horse?" Utah replied, "I tried to move the tree that you can see there so that I could unblock the trail for the wagons to get through, the trouble was the tree didn't move and the rope snapped." "I don't remember anything after that." "You are lucky you landed on your head, if you had landed on your leg it might have broken again," Replied the Doc. "There it is again" said Crane, "The famous bedside manner" the Doc laughed, "I only meant to say he shouldn't have tried to move it alone."

"The wagons will have stopped by now, they will be camped up for the night" said Crane, "One of us can ride back in the morning and let the others know." "Three of us should be able to move the tree at first light, I say three, that's if you will help us Alan" ? Crane left the question hanging in the air." Alan replied, "I'm the man who is going nowhere and everywhere, it doesn't matter when I get there, So I will help you in the morning." They tidied the camp and settled down for the night/ Utah, tried to go to sleep, hoping that he would wake without the banging headache that he had been suffering since he recovered consciousness.

All was quiet around them and they had all drifted off to sleep very quickly, so it was almost a surprise when dawn broke. Crane was up first and he set about watering the stock. Then he stirred the fire and set the coffee to boil. By this time the others were stirring and they all looked forward to drinking coffee, the smell of it was pervading the air. Utah, spoke, "I think I should help you to move to the fallen tree." Doc Black replied, "If you could think we wouldn't be in this mess, so leave the thinking to us, more especially to me" then he added, "I am saying this because you may become light headed if you exert yourself after the bang you took that knocked you out." "So please just do as we said last night and ride slowly back to the others." Utah stood up quickly and felt dizzy, almost falling, Crane at his side supported him, saying, "Sit down, I will saddle your horse." Utah nodded, Then he sat down saying, "You are right Doc." Doc Black just nodded.

Crane saddled Utah's horse and led him forward, Utah

rose up on to his feet, slowly this time and Crane boosted him up in to the saddle, Utah picked up the reins and touched the brim of his hat, turned his horse and left the camp at a steady walk. As he left Crane set about saddling Dancer and the Doc's horse, ready to attempt moving the fallen tree. Alan got his mule ready and in position, while they were doing this the Doc put out the fire. They decided all three ropes would be best looped round the top end of the tree away from the root. So the three men tied their the ropes round the tree, mindful of what happened to Utah, they looped the ropes round their saddle horns. When they had done that they pushed their horses and the mule backwards till they took the strain. They had put the mule between the Doc's horse and Dancer, the Doc and Crane decided they would get round on the other side of the log and add their weight, by pushing. Crane said to Alan, "Don't get near Dancer but keep the three animals moving back."

The tree groaned as it resisted the pull of the horses, whose muscles bunched and rippled, and the added push of the men. The tree started to move and suddenly the attached roots which were still in the ground came apart and snapped with a loud crack. The horses shied a bit but the mule remained steady and probably averted a disaster as the tree started to turn and swing. Crane and the Doc leaned their weight on the tree and steadied it. The tree swung round to the left and the horses and the mule dragged it to the left side of the trail. The three men removed the ropes and took the horses and the mule, to the other side of the trail, all of them, men, horses and the mule were sweating heavily so Crane swiftly unsaddled and rubbed the animals down. Then he lead them round in a circle to let them cool down, after they cooled down he gave them all water to drink from his hat.

The Doc said, "It is no wonder that Utah's rope snapped, one man with one horse would never have moved that tree, if they had week to do it." "You're right" agreed Crane and Alan. "I would just like to say" said Alan, "You're good with the horses Crane, you really care for them and you took care of my mule as well." "My Pa taught me to always put all the stock first" replied Crane. "I don't know anything about you" said Alan, "But I judge a man by how he treats his horse and by those standards you are clearly a good man." Crane smiled and said, "I don't think there many would agree with you." Doc spoke for the first time, "There are more who agree than you think Crane, in my eyes there are none better than you. You are a kind, loyal, thoughtful and considerate man and you would never let your friends down. Putting it simply you are a good man to ride the river with." Crane couldn't speak in response to such praise, he walked away to give Dancer a rub down, because he was unable to believe he was so well thought of. The Doc broke the silence saying, "I reckon Utah will have reached the wagon train by now so it won't be long until they get here."

CHAPTER 19

Utah reached the wagon train, it was called to a halt when the people saw him and they as watched Utah approach they were pleased to see him. Larry said, "Well, you are looking a bit battered and bruised, did you meet trouble? "Only of my own making" Utah replied ruefully as he dismounted. Joey, stepped forward and took the reins, saying "I'll unsaddle him rub him down and give him water." Utah nodded his thanks. He stepped away from the horse and someone passed him a tin cup of water. Big John's wife Sue said "I think we should noon here" and the others agreed.

The people busied themselves, watering and caring for the horses. The ladies made sure that cold cuts of meat were plated up with hunks of bread, they would not be taking time to light fires, so the food would have be washed down with water.

Big John asked Utah about Crane and Doc Black, "How come they haven't returned with you" he spoke between mouthfuls of food. Utah replied, They are moving a fallen tree, it blocked the trail, I tried to move it alone and knocked myself out." That is how they found me." Big John nodded, "By the looks of your face, you were lucky that is all that happened to you."

They ate in silence for a while and then made ready to move on. Then Utah, told them about the guy who had come along and helped them, "Alan Crowe is his name. A miner who has been roaming the territory for a long time and had found me unconscious. He tended me, but I didn't come round. Alan is a good man and he has stayed to help the Doc and Crane move that fallen tree." By now the wagon train was ready to roll again so those who were riding horseback, saddled up then mounted their horses and they all set out towards Crane and the Doc.

They hadn't been on the move for more than fifteen or twenty minutes when there was the sound of galloping hooves followed by a volley of gunfire. The lead horse on John Eckert's wagon went down, this caused the wagon to be dragged around and it nearly tipped over. At the same time Neil took a bullet in his shoulder falling back in to his wagon, the team bolted and there was pandemonium. Maureen, Neil's wife seized the reins and pulled back hard on them, but her efforts were to no avail because the horses had their bits between their teeth and because of all the noise from the gunfire and men shouting, they were scared and ready run so they did.

Utah and Big John wheeled their horses and came running back towards Neil's wagon as it careered towards them. Each man caught the bridle of the lead horse on their side of the wagon and their weight and the weight of their horses going in the opposite direction managed to stop the runaway. With their pistols then in hand Utah and Big John joined in returning the return fire with other travellers who were unleashing gunshot on the raiders. A couple of those raiders went down shot and because of that there was plenty of cursing from the remainder. The travellers were fighting back hard now and with the raiders element of surprise gone, the travellers were holding their own. Then the balance swung in their favour, Joey had stampeded the remunda and the loose horses swept among the raiders and the wagons. Several of the raiders were unseated and found themselves being trampled under foot. In the end it was a complete route, the raiders that remained in their saddles made their escape.

Utah and Big John helped Joey to round up the horses, they did this while the ladies tended to Neil and dressed his wound. Larry got busy and cut the fallen horse out of Big John's team and then he moved the wagon with three horses back from the dead animal. Big John said, "You did well Joey, how did you think to stampede the horses?" "Well," Joey replied "It was partly luck, the raiders sent two riders to take care of me, but they mistimed things, I heard the shots from the attack on you before the two got to me, so I had my rifle out and I shot both them out of the saddle before they knew what had happened." "The horses panicked and ran like the wind, the rest you know." "Good job" replied Utah and Big John, "You have surely grown up since we started out on this journey." "Thank You," Replied Joey.

Doc Black, Alan Crowe and Crane came up on them at the gallop saying, "We heard gunfire" said the Doc, we thought we had better get to you. ." "No problem" said Utah. "These raiders hit us but Joey got rid of them." Crane smiled saying, "We will look forward to hearing about that."

Enough time had been lost from the day's travel so Joey

and Crane quickly harnessed a horse from the remunda and buckled him into Neil's team. When that was done with Maureen driving they got Neil,s wagon back in line, this meant that once again the wagon train moving was forward, they kept the horses plodding on steadily at the walk. The Doc treated Neil's shoulder wound on the move, in the back of a wagon. The bullet had passed straight through his shoulder, luckily missing bone, so Doc was able to clean the wound and dress it, putting the arm in a sling. He said, "Right Neil just rest it you will find that your shoulder will heal with time." Neil replied, "I don't know how Crane stands up when he gets shot, I went down hard and stayed down." "We may never know the reasons why" said Doc. "Crane must have been born that way, he keeps going when most of the rest of us stop, but even he has a limit." Neil nodded and the Doc dropped down out of the moving wagon. Alan now that he was back on his mule spoke, "I think I would like to ride along with you Utah, wherever that takes me if it's OK." "I have got no problem that" replied Utah, "We will be glad to have you along."

Big John and Crane rode together at the head of the wagon train as they rode they spoke of the events that had happened earlier in the day. Big John said, "I think they were Mexican Joe's riders that attacked us." He carried on speaking, saying "I have to say that man is like a bad penny he just keeps turning up." "Tell me about it" said Crane, "I have been on that man's trail for years now and somehow he always rides clear when the going gets tough, I am starting to feel that he is my nemesis." Crane continued. "I don't know how I can settle down and have a family and a home life, as I would really like to do now, with Mexican

Joe always out there somewhere behind me. "Yeah" Replied Big John, "I know about the history between you and Mexican Joe, Crane and I don't think he will ever let you go. In his eyes you have caused him trouble, he thinks he should have killed you at the start. Even if you stop trailing him now, he will still come looking for you." "That may be his mistake" replied Crane. "As long as I am on my metal I may be able to bring feud this to an end." There was nothing else to be said on the subject so Big John and Crane rode on in silence.

Florrie and Fred Hall were talking with their daughter Maggie as they rode their wagon. "So Maggie are you and Crane set to marry?" asked Fred. "You could do worse." Said her Ma before Maggie could answer. "I will marry him, if he asks me." Replied Maggie. Going on to say "Things just feel right when we are together." "Well you make sure he knows it, men are mighty slow when it comes to romance." Replied her mother. Maggie just smiled and then became lost in her own thoughts.

CHAPTER 20

The travellers made good time over the next few days and with no further problems they found themselves on the edge of the valley that was their destination. Fred Hall sighed as he looked down on it, "It sure looks like Gods own country" he said. Utah smiled as he pulled his horse up alongside their wagon, "That's just how I felt the first time I saw it" he said. "I think we should head into Alomogora, first, we will be able to get some equipment such as log splitting tools so we that can start building straight away." John Eckert and Neil said, "We need to look at setting up our businesses in town. So we think we will part company temporarily when we get there."

Crane who had turned back from his position at the front of the wagon train rode up to the Hall's wagon and dismounted. He spoke to Maggie, "I think we should see if the have a preacher in town" he said. Maggie blushed and asked, "Why?" Her Ma and Pa smiled. Crane said, "I have a mind to marry you if you'll have me?" Maggie went a deeper shade of pink, "If that's your way of asking me, the answer is yes." "Well that's a relief" said Crane, "asking you that was the scariest thing that I have ever done in my life." "While my courage is still strong, I have another question, "Utah, will you be my best man?"

"I'd be proud to" replied Utah.

They all headed into town it was about noon when the arrived, so they hoped that places would be open. As they were coming through the outskirts of the town they came on a sawmill. The wagons and riders stopped and the men climbed down, from their wagons or their horses and went to speak to the two men they saw working at the sawmill. Big John spoke, "Howdy fellers, my names John McCane, we looking for log splitting equipment to hire, we've got some building to do." "We are the Thomas brothers, it's on the sign," one of them said, pointing behind him up at the board above the entrance. Going on to say, "I'm Jubal this is my brother George, we have the tools and we will work with you, we will give you a price when we know the work needed." No further talk was necessary, so handshakes were shared all round and the travellers moved on into town.

The first thing that caught Neil's eye on the town's street was an empty store building so he, Maureen and Dave pulled up got down from their wagons and went to look at the paper note that was pinned to the door. The note said, ' 'I've gone East, just can't make it pay, good luck if you try'. The keys were in the lock so the three of them went inside the store and looked around. They walked through to the back, where they found the living quarters, After looking around the place Maureen said to Neil, "This can be our new home."

Dave went out back, when he got there he found a lean to. "I can live in here and it will big enough for a workshop as well, it just needs some work to get it set it up."

The Hall family, Crane and Utah headed on into town until they saw a small chapel with a cross over the door. When they got to the chapel the Hall family got down from the wagon and Crane and Utah dismounted from their horses. They all walked inside, as they did the men removed their hats. At first sight the chapel appeared empty, just as they were about to turn and leave a stocky dark haired man came through a door at the back. As he approached them it was clear that all though he wasn't tall he was a very powerfully built man indeed who very deceptively for a man of his build, was very quick in his movements. The man came towards them with short quick steps, he moved like a coiled spring, seemingly ready to leap into action. With his quick and powerful movements he seemed an unlikely clergyman.

When he spoke, it was in well modulated tones, "The Reverend Peter Leonard at, your service, how can I help?" Crane and Maggie stepped forward, Maggie being an independent woman spoke first, "We want to get married." Crane nodded in agreement. The Reverend said, "Do you intend to attend this church?" "Might be difficult in the beginning" replied Crane, because we have homes to build before the winter, so time is of the essence." "In that case," said the Minister, "I will come and perform services at your home site. In fact I will come out and help you with building the property, I'm quite handy with a hammer and nails."

"Well that is very kind of you," Said Crane, "But our question to you was, Will you marry us?" "When do you want to be married" Asked the minister, "Now" replied Crane. "What's the rush" asked the minister. Crane's patience was being stretched very thin. "You ask a lot of questions without answering one" He replied. "Yes or no will you marry us, I won't ask you again?!" "It is not the way of the Lord to rush at things." Said the minister." Crane half turned away, his patience exhausted, but Maggie gripped his arm and he stopped. Utah spoke for the first time, "Look Reverend, these people have been through hell to reach this point in their lives, so can't you just do the job?" "I feel I have a duty to ensure that they understand the seriousness and sanctity of marriage" replied the minister.

Crane looked as if he would explode, Utah knowing the signs shrank back, but the minister stood his ground. Crane spoke "I've just about had all I can take of you!" He said "Don't raise your voice in the house of The Lord" replied the minister. "Look" said Crane, "We will be living together as of tonight and I want her to have the respect of being a married woman before that happens." "Fine" replied the minister, "Yes in that case, I will marry you now."

As they all moved into moved into place in front of the alter, the minister asked the question, "Who gives this woman?" Fred Hall stepped forward "I do" He said. The minister went through all the questions "Do you take this woman?" and the *take care of her in sickness and in health*, parts, then he said, "Who has the ring?" Crane and Utah looked at each other, they were helpless and speechless, they simply hadn't thought of a ring. Maggie's mother Flo stepped forward taking a ring off a finger on her right hand, she handed it to Utah saying "This was my mothers." Utah took the ring and passed it to Crane, the minister then took it and placed it on the bible he was holding. He said a few words then held the ring out on the bible to Crane who took it and slipped it on to Maggie's wedding finger, it was a perfect fit.

The minister said "You may now kiss the bride." Crane kissed Maggie gently and lovingly. Then he pulled a five dollar gold piece from his pocket saying to the minister, "Thank you, Reverend." "I would have preferred to call the bans and followed the correct procedure," replied the minister. Crane's eyes flashed and he said, "Just shut up for God's sake, I explained why we wanted to do this now." "Do not take the Lords name in vain" The minister, replied. Crane shook his head and said to Utah, "You never get the last word with this man." As they turned to walk out Utah replied. "That's because this man has God on his side.

Maggie and her parents walked out ahead of Crane and Utah, they were smiling and chatting happily. As Utah and Crane reached the door the minister who was following them out said, "I'll be in touch, I am sure the brothers at the sawmill will be able to tell me where you are building. I will ride out and help you to build your homes and of course preach a sermon." Crane who was unnerved by, and unsure, of this man replied "You don't need to trouble yourself Reverend." The Reverend replied, "It will be no trouble at all and you can call me Peter, my wife Lynda and I will see you in a day or two."

As the five of them proceeded away from the chapel Crane and the others met Big John and his wife Susan with their boys, they took one look at the Hall's smiling faces and said, "Well it looks as though congratulations are in order, Mr and Mrs Crane." Maggie blushed and nodded as Susan hugged and kissed her. Big John shook Crane's hand vigorously "Well done" he said, "I know that you are both going to very happy." "Steady with that handshake," Said Crane, "You don't know your own strength my teeth are starting to fall out" they all laughed and continued on their way.

They all met up back at the sawmill, Neil and Dave needed work done at the store, Neil would require alterations made to the store, he wanted new shelving and counter space and improvements in display areas. Dave would require a living area to be created where he could sleep cook and relax. Then he would need work benches and storage space for, equipment and materials. The talk between the friends turned to the valley and building homes there, the consensus was that the Hall's and Crane's places would be built first. Crane said, "What we need is one place with two cabins, Ma and Pa Hall should have their own place and me and Maggie would like to start out our lives under our own roof." "OK" said Utah "But you will still have two sections." "In fact you and I own the whole valley between us, there is no argument about that." "We will only allow our friends to build places on the land." "When he saw that Utah would brook no argument Crane agreed to what was being said."

Everyone agreed that they would rest up for the night and then ride out and choose places to build their homesteads in the morning. For the first time Maggie left her parents wagon and slept with Crane on his bed roll. They slept contentedly through the night in each others arms. Dawn came and they were all soon the road, the future looked bright for everyone. When the travellers reached the valley, it looked peaceful, it was a really green an pleasant land. Crane and Maggie Florrie and Fred picked out a lovely spot with cabins to be built with in walking distance of each other,. The cabins would be built on a raised slope which had a stream running down from a wooded ridge which would be above and behind the cabins when they were built. The farm had so much land that it could easily be considered a ranch. But unlike cattlemen who ranch, Crane and Fred intended to raise crops as well as horses and cattle. They set about marking out the areas that they required for the cabins and barns.

CHAPTER 21

The following morning work began on in earnest on the Crane homestead and barns, there would be two corrals and mother and daughter Flo and Maggie would have a garden for flowers outside their respective cabins. Both Cabins would have root cellars with a trap door over the steps that would lead down in to the cool area to keep things fresh. There would be tunnels leading from both of them, they would lead to the barn, as Crane said, You never know. True to his word the Reverend Peter Leonard arrived with his tools and bible in hand after giving what was to become a daily thanks giving service he displayed his remarkable carpentry skills. As the time went on Crane got over his initial annoyance with the man and they became the best of friends. The carpentry work that Peter, as he came to be known rather than Reverend, was of a very high standard. So when the exterior of the cabins was complete, Peter set about making functional and attractive furniture. This pleased Crane because all though he himself was, as mentioned before, a pretty fair carpenter thanks to his Pa, his own work was functional and robust. Quite simply it was clear that Peters work had a refinement that Crane's didn't. When the structures of the cabins and barns were up It was left to Peter, Fred and Joey to apply the finishing touches, while the rest of them moved on to Big John McCain's place to build his Cabin and Barn.

They had been working for twelve months and they all, including Utah and Alan had a home. In town the alterations had been made at Neil's store, business was steady and his friend Dave had his living accommodation sorted and his workshop up and running. Alan Crowe had decided to stay and work with Utah. It was no surprise Larry had built with everyone's help a fine livery stable that was already doing steady business. Life was good and Crane was not restless because he was happy with his wife and the family. Things got even better when Maggie told him she was expecting a child, Crane felt that his world was complete. On the stock side Crane, Fred and Joey were breeding horses, and with Dancer as their sire they were fine ones. Land had been ploughed and the first crops had been sown. Unbelievably Crane hadn't buckled on his pistols for months and Maggie smiled one day when she saw him wrap them in rags and put them under the floorboards, only his rifle was kept out for occasional hunting trips. Crane had put the vengeance trail behind him.

One bright morning with the air crisp and as winter approached Utah rode in dismounted and came into the Crane's cabin. As they sat drinking coffee while eating a piece of Maggie's apple cobbler Utah said, "I need to ride up to Santa Fe and register all the deeds for the different sections in the relevant peoples names at the Land Office." "If something happened to me there could be trouble and I have seen folks lose their homes before." Crane nodded, "I agree with you, but you are not going alone I will ride with you, apart from anything else Dancer needs the exercise." Maggie agreed with him saying, "You should go with Utah, your son and I will be waiting when you get back." "Son" said Crane, "How do you know it's a boy?" "I just have a feeling that it will be" replied Maggie.

"Right then we will go next week" said Utah, "Alan will look after my place." "Yeah," replied Crane, "Fred and Joey can handle things here." "OK we will meet in town in the morning, pick up the Larry's paper work, I've got Big John's you've got yours so we can get on the road."

When they met next morning Dancer was full of vim and vigour ready to run. If Utah noticed the absence of Crane's pistols he didn't mention them. They rode side by side, they were friends with a future and they were happy in that knowledge. The trip took them a steady week and all went well in Santa Fe and every body's homes were registered. The whole valley was re-registered in both their names. The two men felt secure, now that this was done and this was a new feeling for both of them.

As Crane and Utah were riding home they came on a rancher who was herding cows and calves. Utah and Crane looked at each other, here they knew was an opportunity. So they stopped, "Howdy boys" The rancher said. "Howdy," Crane, replied. Will you sell us any calves?" "I sure will I have to many this year, I won't have the grass for them." Said the rancher, "Come back to the ranch with me we will talk a deal." Three more riders approached, the rancher said to them, "Keep rounding the cattle up boys and then drive them back to the ranch,".

The rancher, Utah and Crane got to the ranch and dismounted and watered the horses. The rancher introduced himself and his wife who came out to join them, "My names Mick Andrews and this is my wife Jill." It was almost noon, Jill served them coffee and bread and cheese. Mick said, I can let you have a hundred head of these calves for two dollars a head, I haven't the grass or water to sustain so many this year." Crane replied, "I'll take them for a dollar fifty a head, cash money." "You know they will die on the hoof, if you don't sell to me." "This way you will have money in hand." The rancher shook hands on the deal and Crane gave Mick three fifty dollar gold pieces, from the money he always carried, Mick gave him a bill of sale.. They agreed that the calves would be picked up in a month when they were strong enough to travel. When the deal was done Crane and Utah rode away.

Utah and Crane made camp that first night out on the trail home and they talked about how life had changed. Neither of them had ever thought that a normal life was going to be possible. In fact Crane had thought he would ride the vengeance trail till he was killed or he had killed every last one of the men in Mexican Joe's gang. Crane said, "Utah you do know don't you that it was Josey Wales and you that started me down the right road again?" "Well" said Utah, "I understand Josey's input but I don't get mine." Crane replied "Well you showed me a lot when you warned me about the ambush that Mexican Joe had set up. That let me know that Josey had been right about many things. For instance I blamed myself for Ma and Pa being killed, but as Josey said it was fated to happen and I couldn't change it." "You showed that given the chance you would always do the right thing." Those things sent me down the road that led to me marrying Maggie" Utah shook his head and said, "So that is why you are not carrying a pistol." Crane nodded, "I hope I never need one again, now go to sleep" he said "We have talked enough."

When the morning came and Crane and Utah broke camp then saddled up and headed home. They had just stopped for a noon break so that they could water the horses when they heard the sound of hooves, the looked and saw Joey galloping up to them His horse was lathered in sweat so was he. When Joey dropped down from the saddle he was pale face and the first thing they noticed that his arm in a sling. Joey nearly passed out when he dismounted, Crane caught him as he swayed and began to fall.

Crane lowered Joey gently to the ground and Utah offered him some water from the canteen. Joey drank gratefully and sat up, "Crane I'm sorry" the boy said. "They have taken Maggie and the baby." "Crane's mind whirled he couldn't comprehend what was being so he said, "Please Joey, start again at the beginning ." The boy took a breath, and started talking, "It was two days ago, a gang of outlaws hit your place. Maggie had not long given birth to your daughter and Doc Black and Ness were with her." "Eight riders rode in and asked if they could water their horses, Fred said they could." "Then he noticed that the Mexican looking feller was missing a hand, at that point he said, I know you, you are Mexican Joe, you attacked my farm." Crane's heart sank, as he listened quietly. Joey continued, "The guy just turned and clubbed Fred down." "Then he pulled a pistol and went to shoot Fred while he was on the ground." I saw what was happening so pulled my pistol and fired." "I missed the Mexican and hit the guy next to him, he fell dead but the Mexican shot me, the force of the bullet took me off my feet, I fired again on the way down and hit another guy in the thigh." "I found out afterwards that the guy I shot had bled to death, I hit my head on a corral pole on the way down and passed out." "When I came to Flo was tending to me." "The Doc was lying on the porch, Ness, Maggie and the baby were gone." "I could see that there were three more outlaws down, all dead. The Doc must have got them before someone shot him."

"OK" said Utah, "But what about Doc and Fred? Fred's alright, his head was split open but he came round. The Doc was shot through the right side of the chest, the bullet went straight through with touching anything major we think. He was not frothing blood when he was breathing anyway. He is laid up but both Fred and Flo think he will live."

While they were talking. Utah had readied the horses, Crane helped Joey back in the saddle then he mounted Dancer, the great horse sprang forward at the run. "Bring Joey home" Crane shouted to Utah. Dancer it seemed was sensing trouble and flew, running flat out, Crane thought that wildfire had never travelled so fast across the prairie. So Crane rode on through the rest of the day and night he arrived home and dismounted in front of his cabin at about eleven the next morning.

Fred ran to him saying, "I'll take care of Dancer" he said, leading the horse into the corral. Crane went up the steps into the cabin. He saw Flo caring for Doc, "Crane" she said stepping forward, "They were alive when they were taken" she said. "I think they would have killed us all if Maggie hadn't said she was your wife and the baby your daughter. "That is when that Mexican Joe said it would hurt you more to know they were alive with him than if he killed them." Crane looked over to the bed where Doc Black, lay, Doc spoke in a low weak voice, "I'm sorry Crane, I let you down, Joey did real good but he is only a kid." Crane looked at him, "You did fine no one could have done more, Joey told me how you fought. I will bring Ness back to you if I can. I'm riding out in the morning because Dancer needs to rest and I think I'm gonna need him this trip, no other horse will do." Doc smiled weakly, "By the way you have a lovely daughter" he said, "Maggie named her Mae Florence for both your Ma's." Crane smiled in spite of himself, Maggie had been so sure it would be a boy.

Crane went to the floorboards by the fire place bent down lifted the boards and took out his pistols, then he checked and loaded them. After he had done that he gathered all things he would need for the trip and packed his saddlebags, this could be a long trail. Fred came to eat the cold meal of bread and cheese that Ma had made them. Fred told Crane that it looked like the remaining outlaws had headed for Texas. Crane nodded Saying "You know I'll do all I can to bring the girls home safe.

The following morning just as Crane was ready to leave Utah and Joey rode up, As they dismounted they both said. "We will ride with you." "No" said Crane, "I'm going alone the only one who has a right to go with me is the Doc and he can't make it." "I don't want to be looking behind me when I make my play, I don't want to be worrying about other people." Joey said "But." Utah shook his head "There are no buts Joey, I've seen this look on his face before and I hoped I never see it again, Crane rides alone." Crane mounted Dancer he looked down, "If anyone asks for me just say I've gone to Texas."

Crane rode away from the farm, with Flo shouting after

him until he was out of sight, but he never looked back. Flo held on to Fred, "I just wanted to tell him that he should come home to us whatever happens, because he has become more than just Maggie's husband, he is a son to us." Fred replied, "He knows Flo he knows." But he thought himself Crane won't come back alone, of that I am sure. Utah called after him "Don't worry I'll go for the calves, they will be here when you bring the ladies home."

Big John, Neil, Dave, John Eckert, Larry, and Alan Crowe all rode up "Where's Crane?" Asked Big John. "He said to tell you that he had gone to Texas" replied Joey, "He also told us that he don't want anybody going with him." "This is very very bad" said Larry, "because of what Mexican Joe has done, a lot of people are set to die." "Yes that's right" said Big John "Worse still because he will feel that he has to finish this for good, one of them could be Crane."

"Let's try to be positive" said Larry, "The best we can do for Crane and the girls is to keep things going here and make sure they have good things to come home to."

Peter and his wife Lynda came to visit and they prayed for the Crane family The Doc and Ness. Everybody there took part in the service. When he heard that Crane had ridden after the gang alone, Peter thought about it and then he said, "Vengeance is mine sayeth the Lord, but in these times and this place maybe Crane is the one chosen to carry out the will of God."Then he went on to say, "Crane has been in my experience, a good man who has a clear understanding of right and wrong." "I'm sure he will follow the right path and that path will bring him home." Not sure if they completely understood what Peter was saying, the others remained lost in their own thoughts.

Doc Black was in a frustrated mood, "I need to be up and on my horse riding after Crane, because he will be taking risks on my behalf." Utah and Big John shook their heads, Utah saying, "You as a doctor know that in your state, you would die before you got a mile down the road." "You also know that we all wanted to ride with him but you know what he's like he would ride over everyone of us to get to Mexican Joe." "Right now he is blaming himself for not staying on Mexican Joe's trail until the end, he is just not in the mood to take advice or help." Doc Black nodded, "I know do that but I am still frustrated because I want Ness home. "Big John spoke, "If anyone can make that possible it is Crane."

CHAPTER 22

Crane was riding steadily, because speed was not the plan, he knew that as much as he wanted to race to Maggie's aid. He knew that he had to slow and steady because that was the only way that he could catch Mexican Joe. Gradually Crane made his way back to his parents home place. He stopped and looked down on it before he rode in. As he sat there in the saddle his eyes took in all the changes. Crane was surprised to see that there was a new cabin, it was not built on the site of the old one but over to right of were the Crane's cabin had been. As he looked around he could see that the site of the old cabin was taken up by a garden of cactus and desert flowers. There was a white picket fence, with a latched gate around it. Crane could see that a new barn had been built on the site of the old one. It was clear that the whole place looked well worked and cared for. Crane moved on and rode into the yard, he stepped down out of the saddle and stood beside the well. A stocky powerful looking man came towards Crane saying, "Howdy stranger how can I help you." Crane replied, "I'd like to water my horse," the man stepped forward and lowered the bucket into the well, then pulled it back up and put the full bucket on the ground, Dancer dipped his head down to it and drank gratefully.

Crane nodded his thanks and then said, "Is this your own place?" The man looked at him and answered, "Very Nearly," "I am putting money in the bank in Jacksboro for the owner." "I have a few hundred dollars put by." Crane asked, "Who is the owner?" "The place belongs to a kid called Tony Crane. "We heard that his parents had died in terrible circumstances. Things got worse because the kid was treated badly by a crooked sheriff and the kid killed the sheriff." "Before he left the kid put his parents and his dog in the cabin, then he burnt the place down like a funeral pyre." "When he had done he saddled up and he rode out, to try and find the killers." "The sheriff we have now, name of Don Liston told us the story."

"We do get news of the kid from time to time, although haven't heard anything for a while." "The last thing we heard came from a feller called Edge who was passing through." He said that this kid who is just calling himself Crane now had fought a pistol fight from the back of his magnificent Black Stallion against a band of outlaws." The man paused looking at Dancer, then he continued, "It seems that Crane was heavily outnumbered but he made that gang of outlaws run." "Edge didn't know if the kid had died that day but he had seen him go down badly wounded." "The other thing Edge said was,that he thought if anyone could live after receiving those wounds Crane would, because he had a real fire in him, that fire drives him on, when other men stop."

Crane looked at him, "That is a fine looking garden." They moved towards it, "Yes the man said it's a memorial garden for the Crane kid's family there's a cross in it, do you see it?" Crane nodded. "I can see it, it says *In loving memory of Len and Mae Crane.*"

Crane was silent. The man said "My wife Amy insisted we did this." Crane asked, "What's your name?" Mike, Mike Preston, me, Amy and our two boys Jim and Joe, live here now," He paused and then said, "Funny thing, that Edge feller said that the Crane boy rode a huge black stallion, who was a fighter like him" He looked at Dancer, then back at Crane. Crane spoke, "I can see that you have guessed, I'm Crane and you don't owe me anything for this farm, you paid for it with this garden." "I'll go and bring Amy" said Mike, "She will want to meet you." As he walked away Crane sank one knee, leaning on the picket fence, "Well Ma and Pa" he whispered, "These good folks have done better for you than I did. I think you would agree, they should have the farm" There were tears in his eyes.

Crane stood and gathered up Dancer reins, the horse had followed him across to the picket fence. He was just about mount up when Mike and Amy, reached him. Amy spoke, "Won't you stay and eat with us?" Crane shook his head, "No thank you Mam, I have to ride on, but I am mighty pleased that I met you folks." "God bless you and your family, be happy and be lucky." He swung up in the saddle touched brim of his hat and rode out at the walk, "God Bless you" He heard Amy and Mike say. *Not much chance of that* Crane thought, *God blessing the devil, that won't happen.*

Crane rode into Jacksboro, and dismounted outside the sheriffs office, he looped Dancer's reins on the hitching rail, stepped up on the side walk and walked through open door and went inside. He spoke, "Howdy Do" he said to the man sitting behind the desk. The man looked and said

"My God Tony, I almost didn't recognise you." He got up came out from behind the desk, grabbing Crane in a bear hug. Crane spoke, "It's not Tony, he died that day back at the farm, it's just Crane now." "OK" replied Don, "I guess you'd like to know why I'm not attempting to arrest you for killing Ben Shaw?" Crane looked at him with eyes that chilled Don to the bone, then he said in cold flat tones, "With what I have got to do you would play hell trying to do that job. But you can tell me if you like"

Don swallowed, "It's right what they say about you, you must be the Devil in human form." "Anyway it goes like this Ben Shaw was blackmailing a few of our good citizens and half the town was living in fear, because he was a bully and a bad man. So I told them what had happened and how Ben had provoked you by bad mouthing your Ma and Pa who were lying dead on the ground." "When they heard about that they decided that you had done the town a favour by killing so you are facing no charges. The townsfolk made me Town Sheriff and things have been fairly good around here until now. By the way the people on your farm are good people. They have put money in the bank so that they can buy the farm from you."

Crane said, "There is no need to say any more I know about them, I met them on the way into town. I've given them the farm and I don't want their money." "You have grown into a strange man" Said Don. "One minute I think you are going to kill me, the next you are giving your farm away." "What has happened to you to make you like this?" Crane told him quite a lot of the story about life on the trail. The friends he now had and about the fact that he was married, ending on the point where Mexican Joe had taken his wife and as yet unseen daughter." "I can see how that would make a man mean" Replied Don. "Have you got any news about Mexican Joe?" Asked Crane. "We hear he has men at a ranch, The Triple X on the north side of town, he comes and goes here as he pleases." "You don't stop him?" Asked Crane. "I'm the Town Sheriff my authority ends at the edge of town, there is a ten thousand dollar bounty on his head but no one is keen to collect it." Replied Don. "Why can't you arrest him for what he did to my parents?" "Well I can't prove he did it, so there is no point in arresting him, no judge will let me hold him."

"Then it looks as though I will have do something myself." Said Crane. Suddenly Crane changed the subject asking, is old Amos still running the livery stable?." "He sure is replied Don, "He is a fixture in this town." "Why do you ask? "I still owe him a dollar." Said Crane. "I am going to see Amos now, I might see you on the way back" he added. Don nodded and Crane left the office mounted Dancer and rode down the street to the livery stable. He dismounted leaving Dancers reins trailing as he stepped forward to see if he could find Old Amos. As Crane approached the man himself came out of the barn, "What can I do for you stranger?"Amos asked. "I'm no stranger Amos, I owe you a dollar" replied Crane. Old Amos peered at him through rheumy eyes, "As I live and breathe it's the Crane's boy" he said.

Crane handed him a dollar, following it with four more, "call that interest" he said. "Also I would like to put my horse up and sleep in the barn tonight, if that's OK with you? Old Amos replied, "Sure you can, but I'll need $1.50 cents in advance." Crane smiled and paid him the money.

Then he led Dancer in to the barn, took him to a stall, unsaddled him and rubbed him down. Then he gave him water and a feed of oats. That will be another fifty cents for the oats, said Amos. Crane paid him and then went and found a few bales of hay so that he could make his bed and lie down. He was tired after his long ride and he soon fell asleep.

When morning came, Amos came to Crane with a cup of coffee, Crane thanked him for it and drank it. Then he took his canteen and walked to the water trough and stuck his head under the water. After a moment Crane came up out of the water and ran his fingers through his hair. He got his canteen and filled it then he closed the cap. When these things were done Crane went back into the stable and saddled Dancer hung the canteen on his saddle. Putting Dancers bridle on Crane led him out of the barn, mounted his horse, nodded to Amos and rode away.

As Crane rode along the street, he noticed Don Liston stepping down off the side walk into the street. Once in the street Don continued walk towards him. "Crane" he said, Crane stopped Dancer beside Don, Asking, "What can I do for you?" "I just want to warn you, there might be up to twenty riders out there at The Triple X and there's only one of you." Don replied. Crane looked down at him, "I will try to give them an even break, but they must not come between me and my wife." Don shook his head in disbelief, maybe just maybe he thought, the rumours about Crane that came from drifters who passed through the town were true. Don touched the brim of his hat and stepped to one side, "Good luck" he said. Crane nodded and rode out of town.

As Crane rode he looked around him, seeing that the terrain was made for an ambush he decided to be more cautious. Crane felt that Mexican Joe had to know he was coming looked around again and he could see a dust cloud approaching from the north. Rather than be on the move Crane sat slouched in the saddle and waited. He had his arms folded with one hand on the but of the pistol in his shoulder holster. Crane could see that there were seven riders approaching him, as Crane watched them one rider moved slightly in front of his fellows. Then the seven stopped in front of Crane. One of them said, "We all ride for The Triple X, his horse shuffled sideways, perhaps he was being made nervous by the close proximity of Dancer. As he moved Crane saw the brand on his on his horses flank, XXX, "So I can see drawled" Crane. Then he said, "Have you got a name?" "The rider looked flustered, "Why?" He asked. "Because I may need to have it put on a tombstone," replied Crane.

The rider blustered, "There is no need to take that tone, stranger, we don't mean you any harm, it is just that we have orders to stop a feller called Crane." Crane looked at the rider with his eyes flat and hard, "Well then you have a problem because I am Crane," he replied. When he realised what Crane had said, shock registered on the riders face, there was delay and then he reached for his pistol, Time seemed to have stopped and the air was still, when Crane drew his pistol and shot the rider between the eyes., The other riders scattered, trying control their horses and draw their pistols at the same time.

By now Crane was moving, fast, he had his reins in his teeth and without hesitation he rode Dancer straight into the panicked group of horses and their riders. Now he had a pistol in both hands and he fired right and left, two riders fell from their saddles dead before they hit they ground. One of the horses stumbled and went down as Dancer collided with it, it's right front leg snapped it's rider was trapped under it, the riders head bounced of the ground he took no further part in the fight, Crane shot the fallen horse so that it would not suffer. Dancer reared and spun on his hind legs and then hurtled back towards the remaining three riders. They fought for control of their own mounts,who had been terrified by the screams of the fallen horse, incredibly no one but Crane had got a shot off yet.

One of them never would because a bullet from Crane's right hand pistol took him through the chest and he fell backwards from the saddle, his left foot caught in the stirrup and as his horse ran it dragged his bouncing body behind him. Dancer spun again and the rider on Crane's left got a shot off, it took Crane's hat sending it spinning through the air, Crane fired right and left and the remaining two riders fell from the saddle. Crane halted Dancer and shot another broken legged screaming horse between the eyes. Crane took the reins from his teeth and stepped down from the saddle and walked to rider trapped under the now dead horse. Clearly he was still breathing, but unconscious. Crane cursed, "Damn it, now I will have to move the horse off him. He turned back to Dancer and took his lariat from the saddle horn, he put the loop over the horn and walked back to the dead horse, he tied the other end of the rope to the saddle on that horse, then he gripped the shoulders of the fallen rider "Back up Dancer" Said Crane. Dancer backed up and Crane pulled the rider clear. He laid him down, walked and untied his rope then gathered in up and put it back on his saddle.

Crane got his canteen an splashed water on the unconscious riders face, the man stirred and opened his eyes. He lay there quietly for a moment, getting his bearings, then he said, "I think my ankle is broken." He sat up and looked around him, he saw his dead horse and is fallen comrades, "Dear God" he said to Crane "What are you?" "I've been called many things including the devil in human form, but right now I'm just a man who wants his wife and child back," Crane replied. The man said. "She told us that you would come riding in like the angel of death and kill us all, we thought that she was exaggerating but..." he paused as he looked around at the destruction Crane had created. "...Now I see that she wasn't." Then he said, "I have to tell you that Mexican Joe gets real angry when he hears your name, I wondered about that, but now I know why."

Crane asked "Are Maggie and my daughter OK?" "Yes they are as far as I know" The man replied. "What about Ness?" "Well that is different, she is taking it really hard because Joe killed her man." Replied the rider. "Well he is wrong about that, Doc Black lived, there no surprise there, Mexican Joe never could carry a killing plan through, he's been trying to kill me for years." "Having seen you in action I'm not surprised." Replied the man. They were silent, Then the man spoke again, "I suppose you will kill me now?" "Not unless you make me" said Crane.

"Then Crane noticed that one of the loose horses had drifted back, so he went and caught it. He picked his up his hat on the way. Crane led the horse back, when he got back to the man, he showed him his hat, "I get through a lot of these" He said ruefully." "Do you think that you can ride?" "I can if I can get up on the horse," The man replied. "Don't worry I will help you" said Crane. With that h e put his arm under the man's armpit and pulled him to his feet. Then he helped him to the horse. When they got there the man reached up and wrapped his hands round the saddle horn, and Crane hoisted him into the saddle by his good leg. "Thanks Crane," the man said looking down on him, "I surely thought you'd kill me, I'll tell them how it was when I get town." He went on to say, "My name is Jim Cassidy and I owe you." "Oh and I should tell you that there are still at least four riders at the ranch, five with Joe, not that he does anything except drink all day.."

As Crane watched Jim Cassidy ride away then he started to check the fallen men for useful kit. He collected about two hundred dollars from their pockets. Cartridges and holstered pistols he put in his saddle bags along with a couple of knives.. He found a hat that fitted without a hole in it, then reloaded his pistols. When he was ready he remounted Dancer and rode on. There were buzzards circling high in the sky. They have to eat, same as us he thought as he moved away. Before long Crane came in sight of the ranch, he paused and checked the loads in his pistols then he rode into the yard as he did he put the reins in his mouth and drew his pistols, Dancer just stood there like a statue, as Crane's eyes swept the scene.

A man came out the barn his rifle at the ready, he sighted on Crane and went to pull the trigger. He was to late, Crane shot him with a bullet from his right hand pistol. At the sound of the shot two men burst out of the house firing their pistols, bullets tugged at Crane's sleeves and he dropped his right hand pistol as one of the bullets burned his arm. He fired twice with his left hand pistol, instinct taking over as the two men collapsed and fell from the veranda. During this time Dancer never moved. Crane dismounted and bent to pick up his pistol as he did a rifle shot sailed over his head. Crane tumbled forward and rolled, coming up one knee still with his pistol in his left hand bullets peppered the ground around him Crane fired just once and the rifleman fell from the loft, crashing to the ground.

Picking up his dropped pistol he put it back it's holster and replacing the other, he looked at the blood on his arm and thought how careless he had been. It was clear that if he hadn't bent to pick up the pistol that first shot from the loft, would have cut him in half. He would need to take more care if he wanted to see Maggie again. While he was thinking he reloaded both pistols, there was only one shot gone from the right hand pistol but that one shot might save his life. Where was Mexican Joe? This was a question he could not answer, if he were still here he surely would have taken his chance at Crane by now. Crane mounted the veranda steps and entered the ranch house his eyes adjusting to the change in light. As his vision adjusted to the gloom he saw a human shape on the floor in the far corner. Crane crossed the floor and there bound and gagged he saw Ness. He pulled his knife from his boot and cut her free, then he took off the gag, picked her up and carried her outside.

Crane sat Ness on the steps and Dancer walked towards him, and stood next to him. Crane took his canteen down from the saddle and as he turned he took the of the cap and then while holding Ness's head he poured the brackish liquid it contained into Ness's mouth. She, swallowed and reached for more. Crane held it away, "Easy" he said "Just a little at a time." Ness nodded, "Maggie knew you would come" she said, "I believed her but for myself I didn't care" "Now that Doc is gone, there is no point in me going on." "Doc isn't dead," Crane replied. Ness jerked forward, "I saw him go down hit in the chest." She said. "That is true, he was hit hard but he is recovering" Answered Crane, then he said "You need to get home to him." Ness nodded an took another swig of water.

"Where are Maggie and the baby?" Asked Crane. "Mexican Joe took her and the baby to Larado last night, he wasn't sure his men would be able stop you, if you came." Crane started walking to the barn saying, "I'll saddle you a horse, we need to get you to Jacksboro. And then I will follow Mexican Joe." Crane went into the barn and saddled a strong looking bay mare. As he was leading the mare out, he heard Dancer squeal with rage and a shot was fired, he ran pistol in hand in time to see Dancer reared up towering over a horse and rider as he came down and his hooves drove horse and rider to the ground Then he reared again, smashing down with his hooves and both horse and rider lay still. Crane ran to Ness, "I'm all right "She said. It's one of Joe's men, he must have sent him back for me, he was all right till Dancer saw him pull his gun, then the world went dark as Dancer went to war."

Crane went back the barn and brought out the mare, then he helped Ness to get mounted. After that Crane picked up his canteen and mounted Dancer and as the dusk gathered and turned to darkness they rode to town. They arrived to find fire baskets burning to light the streets, they both dismounted outside the sheriff's office there was a water trough and Crane let the two horses drink. Then he and Ness went into the office. Don Liston was sitting in his chair he jumped up as they entered, "Crane good to see you." He said, That Cassidy feller told me what happened out on the prairie, Then he asked, "Who is this?" "This is my friend Doc Black's wife Ness, she was taken when they took my wife." Replied Crane. "I would like you to put her in the hotel till morning." "Can I just get our doctor to look at you both? Asked Don. Crane looked at Ness as if seeing her for the first time, her face was pale and bruised her hair dishevelled, and her shoulders were slumped, she was clearly exhausted. Then he looked at his right arm, the shirt sleeve red with blood. "Crane shook his head, "Yes he can see Ness, first, because this was my own fault, he said, "I was careless." Don pulled chairs out for both of them, and they sat down. Then Don brought coffee for them both from the stove saying. "You just sit there and I'll bring Doc Evans." With that Don left the office.

The warmth in the room made Crane and Ness sleepy, and they dozed on their chairs. Because of this they were both surprised when Don spoke them, "This is Doc Evans." Crane stirred and looked at the two men saying, "Howdy doc, you need to take care of the lady" The doctor replied, No unlike yours the ladies injuries appear to be superficial, so I have arranged a bath and a room for her at the hotel, I will examine her after she has had a chance to freshen up. "You on the other hand clearly have a gunshot wound, I need to treat that." "Well," replied Crane, it is just a bullet burn, I never even noticed that it was bleeding." Don took Ness away to go to the hotel as they left, Crane stopped Don and gave him ten dollars, "Please take this to pay for the hotel and bar" he said. Don nodded. "Here's another five dollars, if you could ask some to take the horses down to Amos at the livery and pay him. Please tell whoever takes the horses to keep in front of Dancer at all times where he can see them and they mustn't make sudden movements. Amos will be able to unsaddle him because he has watched me do it."

After Don and Ness had gone Doc Evans said can you take that shirt off, or do I tear the sleeve?" Crane replied "Tear it Doc it full of holes anyway" Doc Evans took his scalpel from the bag and tore the sleeve. He had a bowl of water beside him that had been brought in from the trough and put on the stove while Crane and Ness were dozing. The water was tepid, warm enough to wash away the congealed blood, Doc Evans did this with a clean cloth took from his bag. As the congealed blood washed away it became clear that Crane's wound was a gash, the bullet had torn his right bicep, The Doc quickly and efficiently worked cleaning the wound, Crane jumped when he poured some spirit on it, then the doctor bound the wound.

The doctor spoke as he worked, "You don't remember me do you?" Crane looked at him and started to say, "No " then he checked himself and said, "I remember you took care of me after that fight years ago." "Yes" said Doc Evans "I thought you wouldn't come round after that. Sometimes working with medicine can be a puzzling thing." "I've been unconscious for longer than that, after I got shot one time" said Crane, "My friend Doc Black thought I wouldn't come round then" "But you did, you are strong on the outside but something inside you is stronger." "Maybe in the years ahead these things will be understood but right now I don't know, I just a country sawbones." "Anyway just be careful because this arm will be stiff for a few days, but if you keep it clean and it will heal fine.

Don came back in with a clean shirt, "I took the liberty of getting this from your saddlebags, Crane gave Doc Evans five dollars, "Thank you" he said. Doc Evans looked at the money, a dollar is enough," "No it isn't because I owe you for your looking after me last time" replied Crane. "Plus you need to make sure Ness is OK.""I'm on my way to see her now" said Doc Evans and he left the office. Crane unbuckled his shoulder holster, and leaving holster and pistol on the desk he followed the doctor out through the door. Crane went to the water trough outside and having removed his torn shirt with difficulty he washed his body, while he did this he trying to keep the bandage on his arm dry. Then he rubbed the shirt over his body to dry himself. Then he went back in, when Crane got back inside the office he opened the stove door and threw the ruined shirt in. Then he picked up his clean shirt from the desk were Don had left it and put it on. Crane buttoned it with difficulty, his arm was already stiffening up. The last thing he did was put his shoulder holster and pistol back on.

"Right Don" Crane said, "I'm going to sleep in the barn tonight" Then he said "Before I go, here is a hundred dollars if the undertaker will go out and bury those fellers who welcomed me to The Triple X land, he can have this." Don replied, "After what Cassidy told me, you really must be a pistolero. "Well if I am I hope I'm the last of the breed" said Crane. He went on to say"We need a world where the law takes down the Mexican Joe's and all the scum that destroy peoples lives.." After that Crane left the office and he wearily walked to the livery stable. He was ready for his bed, he called at Dancer's stall just to check that his horse was settled for the night. Crane found him with an uneaten pail of oats, so he picked up the pail and held it under Dancers nose, the horse ate hungrily. "You wanted to wait till you knew I was OK did you boy?" Crane put the pail down and took another to the water trough and brought water for his horse, rubbed his nose and left him for the night. Then he checked on the bay mare, saw she was settled so Crane then settled himself in the hay for the night. He was bone weary and he soon fell asleep.

Suddenly Crane was awake there was a the smell of smoke in his nostrils, he was alert and on his feet in an instant. As he got up he could see a smouldering glow near the double doors at the entrance the stable. Dancer was stamping his feet and charging the door to his stall. There were doors at the back of the stable so Crane ran and opened them At a rough count Crane thought there where about twenty horse in the stable and they were all starting to become agitated. There was no time to lose Crane ran down the line of stalls letting the horses out and driving them through the back door.

Suddenly there was a crash and the crack of splintering wood Dancer had broken out of his stall, he came to Crane and stood beside him. Crane threw his saddle on, but did not fasten the chest straps, the fire was catching hold and the front doors were burning, clearly the fire had been started against the outside of the doors. Crane knew that the water trough on the other side of those doors was the only chance of putting fire out. Crane was pretty sure that the door would be barred from the out side. Thanking the lord he had slept with his boots and pistols on, Crane leapt into the saddle and bending low he sent Dancer out through the back doors.

As he rode through the doors Crane heard a rifle crash, once twice, lying low along Dancers neck he drew and fired the pistol from his shoulder holster, he fired aiming at where the rifle flash had come from, he got lucky because he heard a cry as his bullet stuck flesh. Crane was out of the barn and into the corral, with the other horses milling round and he spun Dancer and the horse leapt the corral fence he went round the side of the building to the front entrance. Dancer's saddle was starting to slip as Crane leapt down beside the water trough, leaving the reins trailing. Crane was right, there was hay piled up the door and it was barred and burning. Moving very quickly Crane filled a bucket from beside the water trough and he starting throwing water up the door. More people arrived with buckets and set up a chain, one guy worked the water pump keeping water in the trough. Some how they managed put out the fire without the whole barn burning down.

As dawn was breaking Crane and Don who had been among those fighting the fire, went round to the back of the barn, Dancer walked behind them. The first thing they saw was Amos slumped against the corral, they checked him over because he was groggy and bleeding from a cut on his temple. A couple of the townspeople had followed them round and they took care of Amos. Don and Crane moved in the direction that Crane had seen the rifle shots come from, they saw figure, lying face down on the ground with a rifle beside him. Crane turned him over the blood on the front of his shirt showed he was gut shot, he was barely alive.

Don brought water and he gave the man a sip, drinking water is not good for stomach wounds but the guy was dying anyway. He was a Mexican, he wanted to talk, Mexican Joe had left him in town a few days before to wait for Crane, but he had been drunk in the saloon, when Crane had come and gone. He had seen Crane's return as a chance to put things right for Mexican Joe. He coughed blood as he tried to laugh. As he said it had been a good plan, no one could get out of the fire and not get shot, then he looked at Crane saying one word "Devil." He died with the word on his lips.

Don looked at Crane saying, "The devil would have left the horses in the barn to die and saved himself.""Amos wouldn't have a barn if it wasn't for you, I think you are a strange man but, a good one." Crane turned and went to Dancer and took his saddle off and put it on the top rail of the corral there was no answer he could give. Don said "What hell you were doing saddling up with the fire coming I don't know." Crane replied, "That saddle was a present from a very special man and a good friend, Dave Selley. I would never leave it behind if I could help it." "I have to say that one of the best saddles I've ever seen," replied Don.

They walked back round the building to find Doc Evens just finishing dressing Old Amos's head wound. Amos spoke saying, "Hey Crane, I owe you, you saved my horses and my barn." "I'm sorry to say it's my fault the fire happened, if I wasn't here your building would not have been set on fire." "I'll pay for a new door" replied Crane. "You don't have to do that." Said Amos. "No but I will, no argument" said Crane. "You heard the man" said Don. Amos nodded thank you.

Doc Evan's smiled and said, "Ness and Cassidy are waiting for you at the hotel Crane," "I'd better get over there if she is fit, I need to get Ness on her way home." Crane shouldered his saddlebags, he had things he wanted to sell and supplies he needed to buy "Don said, I will come with you."

The two men walked down the street together and went to the hotel. They found Ness and Cassidy in the lounge area and went over to them. "Howdy Crane" said Cassidy, Howdy Jim, Crane replied. "Ness are you ready to go home?" "I sure am, I need to get back to Chris." "Well that's the thing," said Crane, "As you know I have to go and get Maggie and my daughter Mae, I can't take you home." He turned to Jim Cassidy saying, "Jim, I know it's a big ask but would you ride along with Ness and see her home?" "If it wasn't for the person you are Crane, I would be dead out on the prairie, of course I will take her, I owe you." Cassidy replied.

"Right then" said Crane, "Here is the deal, I will write a note for my father-in-law Fred and tell him that he can pay you fifty dollars, or if you prefer to stay and want a job you can have one, you can sleep in the barn. There is just one thing, Joey the kid who is there is my top hand, in the note I will tell Fred is to give him a raise and build him a cabin. If you don't think you can work for kid, no problem, you can just take the $50 and just drift, no hard feelings." Jim replied, "I can't believe you would give me such a chance, I'll take the job," "Good" replied Crane, "Also I want Fred to mail some money to Don for Amos's door." "I will outfit you for the trip back to my home, then I've just got to go."

Crane borrowed a pencil and paper from the hotel desk and wrote the promised note and gave it to Jim Cassidy. After Don had gone back to his office, Crane Jim and Ness went back up to the livery stable, calling at the general store on the way, to buy food and equipment for their respective trips. While Crane stocked up on cartridges, the store keeper looked at and bought the pistols and holsters that Crane had taken from the men who had attacked him on the prairie. When he had everything that would be needed Crane packed beans, jerky and coffee in his saddle bag, the rest of the purchases, he put in two burlap sacks, for Jim and Ness. Jim was limping on what had turned out to be a badly sprained ankle and knee but he was doing OK. Crane looked at him with a wry smile saying, "Maybe we should start calling you Hopalong," Then the three of them started walking back to the livery stable. Crane had his saddlebags over his shoulder and in spite of his arm being stiff he carried a burlap sack in each hand. Ness and Jim followed him.

When they all got back to the livery stable, "Crane said, "There is no reason why you both shouldn't use the horses you rode in town on" he added, I don't think Mexican Joe is going to be charging you with stealing horses." Then Crane caught up Dancer and saddled him after that he filled his canteen and a new one that he had bought at the store, hanging them both on his saddle. Crane got his bedroll jacket and hat from the stable. He found that they smelt of smoke but a few days on the trail in the fresh air would fix that.

When he was prepared, he jammed his hat on his head and turned to Ness and Jim saying, ride safe and sleep warm. Ness ran over to Crane and hugged him, she said, "I'll never be able to thank you, if you hadn't come I would have given up because I believed that my Chris, the Doc was dead and I couldn't go back to being without him." Crane, replied, "No problem, the Doc would have done the same for me, just make sure that get home safe to him." "Bring your wife and daughter home" Ness said. Crane nodded, unable to speak and rode away without a backward glance.

Jim and Ness watched him go, Jim said, "He is a strange man, but I like him." "I've been on my own for twelve years, since I was ten years old and nobody ever treated me right before. Ness said "Crane is a good man, but bad things happen to him, he has a default mechanism for trouble and that mechanism kicks in when he or those he cares for are threatened." "When that happens he goes on the attack and he doesn't stop till it's over." "Or he didn't until he stopped trailing Mexican Joe to marry Maggie and have a life like the rest of us." "He blames himself for what has happened, now he will never stop till it's really over, one them Mexican Joe or Crane is going to die." Then deciding that there had been enough talk, Ness said "Let's ride, I'm going home, I need to be with Chris.

CHAPTER 23

Jim Cassidy and Ness, rode long hours keeping their noon and night breaks to a minimum and they were tired and weary when they rode into the yard of Crane's farm. Joey saw them and shouted to the Doc "Ness is home." Doc appeared on the porch and Ness urged her horse over to him, she jumped down from the saddle and ran into his arms. "I thought you were dead you weren't moving when they dragged me away, I'd given up all hope when Crane found me," Said Ness, "I would have come if I could" relied the Doc, "I'm only just up and walking around now." Then he said "I love you and I've missed you. I'm glad you didn't come for me, I know you are an old time pistol fighter," said Ness, "But I don't think anyone but Crane could have done the job alone." "Including those out on the prairie, and four at the ranch, he fought and with Dancers help killed ten men, he let Jim Cassidy there live." Ness pointed over were Jim was talking to Fred and Joey. Doc leaned on Ness and they walked slowly to the three men, Joey said, "There's a note from Crane, he says I'm his top hand, I going get a raise and I am going have my own cabin. Jim gets my room in the barn." "Don't worry, you don't have to sleep in the hay Jim, you get a room at the back of the barn, it has a bed and everything. "Tell me Jim, why do you get a job here after you rode against Crane?" Asked the Doc.

Ness answered for Jim, "Because he brought me home, if you need to understand any more of the reason think of Crane's best friend Utah." The Doc nodded, saying, "Crane has his own ways."

Jim said, "Let me tell you Crane was hell on wheels, not one of us got a shot off, out there on the prairie. That horse of his frightened our horses and paralysed us with fear" "I have never seen the like of it and I was riding with some bad men. Men who had fought and killed people before. After we tried to fight him, Crane must have seen something in me I think. All I can say is Crane has given me a chance, I won't let him down." Ness said, "Crane was wounded when he rescued me and he didn't even notice that he had been shot until he got me back to Jacksboro. Putting it simply we have all seen that Crane is a fighting machine." "At this point everyone nodded, they had all seen Crane in action. Fred said, "Anyway he has sent this note so we will just get on with things. So we will build another bed for you Jim,instead of a mattress for the time being we can make a straw palliasse for you to lie on." "You are going to stay with us are you?" asked Fred. "Oh yes I'm staying, no one ever gave me a chance or a home before." Jim replied. Jim looked pale and drawn, he was clearly in pain from his leg and tired from the rapid journey he and Ness had just made. Then Joey said, "Come on Jim let's get you, settled in, you can sleep on my bed tonight, we can sort another bed tomorrow." "You look played out after all you have been through.." Jim thanked him, asking, "Where will you sleep tonight?" "No problem there, I will just bed down in the hay"There was nothing more to say, so they both headed for the barn.

After Jim and Joey had walked away Fred said, "Well we are all glad to see you got home Ness, we all hoped and prayed for that, now all or prayers will be for my daughter and grand daughter come home soon." Fred looked very sad, Because I know that Crane will never come home if he doesn't get them both ." Ness put her arm round him, saying, "Don't worry Fred, "You know that Crane will never give up on his girls." He is on his way to Larado now, Mexican Joe will know he is coming, he won't harm Maggie or Mae while Crane lives, because he knows they are his bargaining chip." "Mexican Joe isn't smart but he is a cunning man." "Believe me he will every ounce of that cunning to live through what Crane is bringing to him." Ness continued speaking, saying, "I had to live with Mexican Joe and I can tell you, he is terrified of Crane, no one has ever lived to cause him trouble before." "But he thinks Crane is a ghost, because every time Joe is sure he has found a way to kill him, Crane still keeps coming."

Mexican Joe drinks all the time and when he drinks, he shouts and screams and threatens, the threats he makes are all against Crane." While they were talking they heard Flo call out, "There is food on the table, come and get it while it is hot!" Adding, it is Larry's pot luck stew, he has given me the recipe.." They all headed for the cabin, even Jim came with Joey, saying, "I will eat first and sleep later, because I haven't had a home cooked meal in years." They all went in to the cabin and sat down at the table. Flo served the stew and she had left hunks of fresh bread by every plate. "They all sat and ate in silence, each one lost in their own thoughts. Although they were all thinking of the same people and wondering, if they would ever see any of them again.

They all turned in for the night, Joey had made a bed from the straw in the barn. Doc and Ness were sleeping in Crane and Maggie's bed, they had fallen asleep in each others arms. Flo and Fred always content in each others company, went back to their own cabin, although content they were both weighed down with worry for their family. Fred said to Flo, I can't believe we are faced with these problems and I'm to old to be any use in solving them." "Now Fred you know that ain't true, "Florrie replied, "You will keep this place running and Crane knows that, because of you, Crane, Maggie and the baby will have a place to come home to." "You are a hard worker, Joey understands the horses and Crane has sent Jim to help with everything else." "Crane is relying on you, he is trusting you with all the money that he has for all our futures." So let's have no more about you being useless." Flo hugged him fiercely and they went into their cabin, tomorrow would another day, the beginning of better times for them all, because they believed in Crane."

The morning came and Fred started work early, but as he walked through the yard he saw that Joey and Jim had started work before him. Fred spoke to them saying, "I will have to go town this morning to sort the money that Crane wants sending to the sheriff in Jacksboro. "Don't forget that Utah and Alan Crowe will be bringing in those calves that Crane bought on his way back from Santa Fe." Please put them in that south pasture section we fenced off, until we think that they are ready to roam." Joey said "Don't worry, we can handle that." I never doubt you, neither does Crane," Replied Fred." Then he hitched up the wagon and readied himself to go town. He called Joey back over, "I'll call at the saw mill and arrange for the work to be started on your cabin." "You had better pick a place you want it to be built." "Oh Mr Hall, I know were I would like it to be." "I would like it to be built in my favourite place on the whole farm." "Well then tell me where that is boy, another thing how many times must I tell you to call me Fred?" Replied Fred. "Well" Said Joey, "About half a mile north of here there's a rise and at the foot of the ridge there's a stand of trees, there is a stream running by the trees. I always ride out there when my work is done and I want to think and be quiet. "OK, then that is were we will build it, I know Crane will be happy with your choice." Said Fred "I must go," So he climbed on to the wagon and drove out of the yard.

As Fred left the yard Joey turned to Jim saying, "These are good people, I can tell you that you will never regret coming here, you haven't met my folks yet, they will like that you came here." They head Flo call out to them, "It's time you boys ate, I have eggs ready for you." Joey and Jim followed her back into the cabin, to eat breakfast with Ness and Doc. As soon as they had finished their meal they heard the sound of cattle moving in the distance, so everyone went outside. They saw a dust cloud coming towards them, it could only be their calves. Then through the dust they saw Utah, Alan and Dave Selley riding into the yard. Is there news about Crane?" Asked Utah. Then he saw Ness, he dismounted and went to her saying, "It is great to see you, is everyone home" ? "No" Said Ness, "Just me Crane has ridden after Maggie and his daughter Mae, he has gone to Larado, because Mexican Joe is there."

"OK" Said Utah "Please tell me tell me about the thing's that have happened." "Also what about the new guy over there?" "That's Jim" Said Ness, "After he met him out on the prairie, Crane tasked him with bringing me home, in return he has given him a job and a place to stay."

Utah turned to Jim, "So Jim how did you meet Crane?" Jim replied I was riding with the men that Mexican Joe sent to kill Crane." "I went down under Dancer's charge on the prairie outside Jacksboro not just me, my horse as well." "My horse had a broken leg and even in the heat of battle Crane heard it screaming and shot it even though he could still have been gunned down himself." "When the fight was over there was only me and Crane still left alive, the six I was riding with were all dead." "I don't think any one of us managed to get a shot off."

"I was sure Crane would kill me but he pulled the dead horse off me caught up another one put me on it." "I have never seen anything like it." Then he said, "Do you what was the strangest thing?" Utah shook his head, "It was what he said to our leader, Waco, who was fastest gun I had ever seen, until I saw Crane. "Crane asked his name" Then Waco said, "Why?" Crane replied to him saying "I may want to put it on a tombstone." "I thought to myself this guy is mad, and then all hell broke loose." Utah nodded, "I have seen him in similar situations, he saved my life in a similar way." "He is my best friend now, yet I rode against him like you." "I promise you that you will do well if you stay here."

Utah saw the Doc and said, "You are looking better than the last time I saw you Chris, but it is clear that you are not ready to ride yet." "I have to go and help Crane so I am going in the morning, I have to I'm Crane's best friend he may have face an army even Crane can't do that alone." "Alan I know I can rely on you to take care of our place?" "Our place? Asked Alan, "What do you mean our place?" "What I mean is that we have been partners, since you took care of me when I was unconscious on the trail. So I registered you as a joint owner of our farm when I was in Santa Fe."

Alan was speechless, Utah added "The point is that if you hadn't come along that day on the trail I might not made it, then nobody would have had anything. We are friends Alan and friends share. All Alan could say was "Thank you." At this point Dave entered the conversation, saying, "I will be riding out with you in the morning." "I don't think so" replied Utah. "I do," said Dave "Because Crane is my friend to and I will be going, even if I am riding behind you. Utah nodded, then he said, OK we will leave at dawn.

CHAPTER 24

It was almost dawn when Crane was woken from his sleep by an incessant howling, the sound of an animal in agony. Crane got up and walked through undergrowth towards the sound, with a pistol in his hand. As Crane got deeper in to the thicket the dawn light was breaking through the trees above him. Because it was becoming lighter, he could see ahead of him in a small clearing, a dog or possibly a wolf caught in a steel trap It was clear that it's front leg was trapped and bleeding. The dog was already starting to gnaw at the leg, Crane knew from past experience that a wild animal would bite it's leg off in it's panic to be free. Crane put his pistol back in his holster then took his bandanna from round his neck. Crane could tell that the animal was tiring, but being tired would not stop it from biting him if it could. Approaching the dog from behind, speaking in a soothing voice, Crane put his bandanna over the dogs eyes, then he knelt down and laid his hand on the dog's back. This was done while he was talking softly to the animal. As Crane spoke the dog began to breathe easier, it sagged and lay quietly.

Crane scanned the ground around him, there was nothing strong enough to help him open the jaws of the trap. He would have to rely on his own strength, although all the while knowing that the dog could try to bite him as Crane released the trap. Crane moved towards the dog's trapped leg slowly on his knees. When he was in position Crane gripped the jaws of the trap in his strong hands. Crane moved his powerful arm and shoulder muscles and pulled hard, the dog's leg fell free from the trap but the dog still lay with his head under Crane's bandanna. Crane stroked the dog again, it lifted it's head, the bandanna slipped off and the dog looked straight into Crane's eyes. It was clearly the old story, one wild thing knows another and the dog recognised one of his own kind looking back at him.

As Crane looked at the dog, he could clearly see that it wasn't was much more than a pup, probably between eight or ten months old. But this dog was huge, he was long and lean with a massive chest, and he had paws the size of a big man's fists. The only way Crane could tell that it wasn't a wolf was its colouring, it was Sable and Black. But as he was looking at the animals gaping jaws, Crane was sure there was wolf in him.

Crane stroked the dog, now the sun had come up and he could see that there were scars on the dogs head and across his shoulders, scars that could only have been made by a quirt. Rage burned inside Crane, if there was one thing he couldn't stand it was cruelty to animals. Only a coward who was afraid of the dog would have beaten him like that. Crane continued to stroke the dog saying, "Never mind boy I'll look after you, staring with that leg." Then Crane said, "Lets see if you can get up," Crane stood back and said, "Come on boy up you get" the dog manage to get up and stand on three legs. Crane knew the dog would walk and follow him, so he set off back to his camp.

As he walked along Crane turned and saw that the dog was following him, so Crane continued on his way back to his camp. When he got there Dancer looked warily at the dog, he hadn't been this close to one since the time he was living at the Crane's farm and that dog had been shot. Crane got his canteen, and some cloth from his saddle bag, it was part of yet another shirt that he had ruined. As an after thought Crane also brought some jerked beef out of the saddle bag. He put a piece in his own mouth and then gave the rest of it to the dog. The dog ate hungrily, but Crane noticed something strange, unlike many dogs this one chewed each mouthful, instead of just swallowing it down. After that Crane poured water into his hat and held it for the dog, the dog lapped at the water gratefully. When the dog was finished Crane poured more water in his hat for Dancer, who drank from the hat and then stepped off to one side.

Seeing that the dog was licking his wound, Crane said, "Right we had better take a look at that leg." The dog eyed Crane warily as he was tearing the old shirt into strips. When he had done that Crane poured water from the canteen on to one of the strips of cloth and bunched it up. Crane approached the dog, it was watching him very carefully, Crane knelt down beside it leaning his body into the dog, the dog turned it's head and they went nose to nose. Then as Crane gently washed the wound, the dog growled low in it's throat, but it made no attempt to attack him.

When the wound was clean Crane made a pad put it on the dogs leg and tied two strips of cloth round it. He spoke to the dog, "If you want to travel with Dancer and I you can just follow on, or if you want to go your own way that's OK." Crane turned and saddled Dancer then he packed up his camp, when he was ready he mounted his horse and rode out. When he looked back and the dog was limping along behind them.

They had not been going long when Crane saw that three men were standing on the trail, blocking his way. They were holding rifles across their chests, trying to look as it they meant business. The men were about to speak as Dancer stopped and the dog came up beside him on his left side, there was a low evil, growl in his throat. "The man in the middle spoke, "You opened my trap and stole my dog." Crane looked down at him, "I didn't steal him, I asked the dog and he said he wanted to come with me."

The three men looked at each other, Then one spoke, "This feller has a smart mouth, we should close it for him." Crane replied, "You need to be very careful what you do next, wrong move could be fatal" The men laughed and one the one in the middle stepped forward reaching for Dancers bridle, for a second the world seemed to stand still, then Dancer reared up to his great height, when he came down his right hoof, crashed through the man's head and the man died before he fell. The other two men readied their rifles, but they were to late Crane' pistol was in his hand the right hand man took a bullet in the face. On the his left side on the periphery of his vision, Crane saw the dog flying through the air, all four legs off the ground the left hand man screamed as the dog hit him driving him backwards, it was the last sound he would ever make, as the dogs powerful jaws tore his throat out. The dog let go and sat down with blood dripping on his jowls, he just looked up at Crane.

As Crane dismounted he reached his hand out and he rubbed the dogs forehead, then he reloaded his pistol. Then Crane went through the men's pockets, they all had few dollars, but they had nothing else of value. Their weapons were poor and not cared for, these rifles couldn't be relied on in a fight. So Crane remounted Dancer and rode away, leaving the men for the buzzards. He looked down at the dog, "You fight like a grizzly, I think I will call you Bruno Bear or just plain Bruno." For the first time since Crane had known him the dog wagged his tail.

Crane was riding along pondering on life and the delays it always seemed to put in his way. It was impossible for him to describe how desperate he was to get to Maggie and their daughter, but he knew that he had to be patient. Past experience had taught him that things had a habit of going wrong when he rushed at them. When he reached a fast flowing stream with a still pool of water beside it he decided to stop and take a short noon break. So Crane wearily, although it has to said reluctantly stepped down out of the saddle, as he did Dancer lowered his head into the stream and drank gratefully. Crane took the saddle off the horses back, he looked at it and not for the first time he admired Dave Selley's workmanship. Dave had proved himself to be loyal and true friend he though, someone that I hope to see again. Crane rubbed the sweat off Dancers back and then he laid the blanket on a rock so that it could dry in the blisteringly hot sun. Then Crane took off his hat, he bent forward and filled the hat with water from the stream. Having filled it he poured the cool water over Dancer's back, the horse shivered with appreciation as the water it ran down his back and over his wither's, Crane did this twice more, while Dancer snickered in his delight after a hard mornings ride.

Crane looked for the dog, he saw that Bruno was standing in the fast flowing stream, letting the water clean his leg wound. Somewhere at sometime during the morning journey he had lost the makeshift bandage that Crane had put on. Crane spoke to the dog, "It looks as though you are a better doctor than me, Bruno." He said as he bent and drank from the stream. The dog looked at him and Crane would have sworn he was smiling, he turned away from the stream and went and picked up his two canteens he loosed the caps and emptied the brackish water that remained in them. He filled them from the fast running water, then replaced the caps and put them under the shade of the saddle to keep the water in them cool and out of the sun. Then Crane called Bruno to him, when the dog came he gave him some beef jerky from his saddlebags. The dog sat looking at him while Crane chewed some of the meat himself.

Crane slowly reached out his hand stroked the dog between the ears, he knew that sudden movements would startle the dog, making him think he would be hit. Bruno looked at him seeming unable to believe these acts of kindness. "No one will hurt you again, if I can help it Bruno." Crane said.

Then Crane looked across the stream where he saw an Indian couple watering their horses. They had a nice little calico pony and a very fine Appaloosa Stallion. They had made camp off to the right of Crane's position, but on the far side of the stream. It was likely that they would be

Comanche, Crane thought. The Plains Indians had become isolated now with the spread of white settlers coming to take the lands that the tribes had historically roamed. Crane could see that the Indians wife, for so he termed her, he would not call her a squaw, was heavy with child. They two of them watched him very carefully. Crane lifted his hand waved, then he lay back on his saddle and pulled his hat over his eyes. By doing this he was showing that he had no intention across the stream, or of riding through the heat of the day. Crane knew that he could settle comfortably, because there was no chance that anyone could approach without either Dancer or Bruno warning him. The dog lay down at Crane's feet and they both dozed.

Then suddenly shouting disturbed Crane' siesta, He pushed his hat back on his head and stood up, He looked across the stream in the direction of the voices. He could see that there were four men arguing with the Comanche brave. The braves wife was lying on the ground, it was clear that she had gone into labour. Crane called Dancer to him, when the horse came he gathered up the reins, as he did so Dancer dropped a knee and Crane vaulted up on to his back. They went across the stream at the gallop and angled towards the disturbance, with Bruno in hot pursuit.

As he got to the scene Crane could see two of the men were holding the Comanche while one of the other men approached with a knife. "Hold it." Said Crane he asked. "What is all this about?" "Nothing that needs to concern you," Replied the man with the knife,. But we can't allow this son of Satan to drink our water." Crane stared down at him, "I've been drinking, your water." He replied. "I think this man and his wife deserve a share." "They get nothing"

Snarled the man with the knife.

Suddenly a shot rang out Crane went backwards off Dancer a bullet in the fleshy part of his left shoulder, the fourth man who had fired his pistol shouted as he pulled the trigger "It's the Devil, It's Crane!" At that moment all hell broke loose, Dancer screamed with rage, as he reared and sprang forward trampling the man with the knife under his hooves. Bruno leapt forward seizing the pistol shooter's gun hand, the weight of the dog drove the man off his feet, fell backwards going to ground, he was screaming but the dog would not let go.

Crane was down one knee as the two men threw the Comanche Brave to the ground. They grabbed for their pistols but Crane's pistol was already in his hand. He fired twice hitting one of the men in the chest and then he hit the other in the throat they both went down and they stayed down. The Comanche brave went to his wife, she was as Crane had surmised in labour the screams of the man being mauled by Bruno were growing faint as he weakened from loss of blood. Crane spoke saying, "Leave!" Bruno let go and sat down his eyes on the man.

The man's arm was torn to shreds the hand hanging by a piece of skin from the wrist. There was nothing that could be done to save him he was bleeding out fast. Crane looked down at him saying, "Do you know me?" "I sure do." The man replied, "I rode on a bank raid with Mexican Joe, and you and that damned horse killed nearly all of us." "I left Joe after that, but-------, the man's eyes glazed over as he breathed his last breathe.

Crane turned when he heard the baby cry, as he did he stumbled, blood was dripping was dripping down his left arm it dripped from his fingers it was dribbling to the ground. He ignored his pain and spoke to the Comanche Brave. "Are you and your wife OK" he asked, The brave nodded, his face was battered and bruised but otherwise he was fine, he was holding the child in his arms. He passed the child down to his wife then pointed at Crane, "You though are not, that bullet must come out." Crane nodded, "I would be grateful if you could take it out for me ." The Brave nodded saying, "I will build a fire, while you sit, he looked at Dancer and said, I will go I'll go and bring your saddle across the stream. Crane nodded as he sank to the ground. "You need to approach Dancer real slow if you need go near him." Then he took his Bowie knife from his boot because the brave would need that. Crane knew that it was extra sharp.

The brave came back from the other side of the river with Crane' saddle and his other possessions he put them down and then he started a fire. He brought the saddle to Crane and let him lie back on it. Then he took the Bowie knife from Crane and heated it in the flames. "I have seen white doctors do this" He said. Crane nodded. The brave gave Crane a piece of wood, "you must bite on this" he said "There will be much pain." "Just a moment" Said Crane, then he spoke to Bruno, saying "Bruno stay!" Adding, "Dancer Stand." "I worry if they think you are hurting me they will attack. Then he bit down the wood and the brave took the knife out of the fire and replaced it with his own.

The brave tore Crane's shirt and probed for the bullet, Crane bit down hard on the wood, the pain was extreme but suddenly it was over as the bullet popped out. The Brave put down Crane's knife and took his own knife out of the fire, "You must bite down again" he said. Crane did, this time as the pain hit him hard as the wound was cauterised. The pain was so great that Crane bit right through the wood. He sank back against the saddle feeling weak, gradually his breathing returned to normal. He spoke, "I think that I should know the name of the man who took the bullet out of me."

"They call me Rides the Wind" Replied the brave he continued, "This is my wife White Dove and our son, who will be called Standing Crane after the man who saved all of us." You stood and fought when all other men would have ridden away, you are my friend and you will always be able to call on me." Crane said "Well there is one thing" "Anything" replied Rides the Wind. In my saddlebags there is coffee, beans and jerky I think we should all eat, I can't go any further tonight" Both men both smiled and Rides the Wind nodded.

Then he said "First I am going to move the camp down wind of the dead. "While you are at it said Crane, "Go and pick up that good Henry Rifle and any shells there are for it." "You may need it." As he pointed, Crane saw that the men's horses had wandered back. "Hobble those horses he said, "They are yours now." Rides the Wind did as Crane said. While he was doing it he was thinking, this is truly a great warrior because, he gives the things he wins in battle to his friends.

Rides the Wind moved quickly and efficiently and soon had the new camp set up, He had unsaddled the horses and turned one of the saddles over so that his wife could sit comfortably and rest her back in it. Food was prepared and they ate together enjoying the food. Crane spoke,

"I hope you don't mind but I am just going to call you Rider, I thought about Windy but decided against it." The Comanche smiled saying, "One word name like yours, I like it." Then he said, "Why are you a friend to the Comanche?"

Crane said, "For two reasons, one is, I like people for who they are, not for their race, I saw how you cared for your wife when you arrived at the stream, you were gentle and considerate, I like that in a man." "Two, I am a quarter Comanche on my Grandmothers side, My Pa was half, so I figure if the tribe was good enough family for my Grandpa, then they are good enough to be friends of mine." Rider answered him, "You are not just our friend you are part of the tribe, you are my brother."

Crane nodded saying, "I agree with you." Then because he was feeling tired he closed his eyes and went to sleep. Bruno lay at his feet and Dancer was close by. Rider made his wife comfortable and settled down beside her and his child. He thanked the Great Spirit that Crane had travelled to meet them on his journey. Rider had not wanted his son borne on the reservation so he and his wife had left so that the boy could be born free like his ancestors.

That decision would have seen the three of them killed if Crane had not come by. He would always help his brother Crane. Rider closed his eyes slept, he was a happy man, roaming free he had a wife a fine rifle and three new horses, he wasn't that awful term, a blanket Indian, he had his pride again, he was what he always should have been, a warrior. He could roam and hunt, provide for his family. He fell asleep, he was content for first time for a long time.

They all awoke early, Crane's wound looked good, if a

little inflamed, Rider said I will go and find plants along the bank of the stream to make a poultice, it will help your wound heal. His wife, White Dove had her baby in a wrap which was over her shoulder and round her neck. She had got the fire going and had coffee boiling on it. The smell was good and Crane was looking forward to a cup. He was surprised to see a jack rabbit at his feet Bruno sitting by it looking at him. He said to him, "Good boy, I haven't enjoyed fresh meat for a while." Bruno wagged his tale and stepped into the river again he enjoyed the cool water on his bad leg.

Crane said to White Dove, "I would be grateful if you would cook this for us all." White Dove nodded smiling saying, "You are very kind to share with us ." Crane replied, "Whatever there is will be ours while we are together." A few beans and some rabbit went down very well and they washed the meal down with coffee.

Afterwards Bruno enjoyed stripping the bones of any remaining meat. Rider had come back with some leaves which he chopped up in boiling water on the fire he stirred it up and let it cool then he drained the water and made a paste which he allowed to cool. Then when it was cool he applied it to the wound on Crane's shoulder saying "This doesn't smell to good but it will heal the wound." He looked at Bruno, "You can put some on his leg, I would do it for him but I would like to keep my hand." Crane did, he gently felt the leg while applying the paste, "It is as I thought" he said, "The leg wasn't broken, there was just some ligament damage, as well as severe bruising and the skin was broken, which caused the blood to flow." Then he said,"All being well the leg should be as good as new in a few days."

Crane looked ruefully at his torn shirt, "Typical," he said this is my last shirt." Then he said, "Rider can I go through the dead men's saddlebags?" "We will share everything" said Rider. Crane went through the belongings in the bags, one of the men was pretty much his size, actually he had carried more weight, but that was no problem. There was two shirts in the saddlebag so Crane claimed them, taking his torn shirt off and putting the clean, if wrinkled, one on.

He made two piles of any useful stuff that he found, Beans, coffee, piggin string, a couple of knives and some cartridges. He went over to the bodies, He found twenty dollars and forty cents and divided it equally between them. He brought the pistols back and said to Rider, saying "Pick the best of them, you never know when one might come in handy."

He gave the bedrolls to Rider saying, "The blankets are quite clean and they will help to keep Dove and the baby warm and dry at night." Then Crane said, "Look I have to keep going and get to my wife and daughter, they need me," he explained about Mexican Joe and how he had to keep riding to get to his wife and daughter so that he could take them home. Rider said, "I should go with my brother Crane," but he waved his hand towards Dove and the baby.

"No problem," Replied Crane "Where will you go Rider?" He asked, "I don't know, we will not go back to the reservation." Crane said "don't worry I will write a note, I have a pencil and paper in my saddle bag, My father in law Fred will let you stay on our land." Crane wrote quickly explaining to Fred about Dove and Rider and their baby. He also told Fred that he was still riding to find Maggie and Mae. Then Crane saddled Dancer and gathered his belongings, he put his Bowie Knife back in his boot. Then having checked the loads in his pistols and rode out. Before he left Crane looked down from the saddle at Rider and said, "Do one thing for me let that fine stallion of yours run with my mare's, we will share the money when we sell the colts."

Rider and Dove watched as he rode away, Then Rider said, "Crane is a great warrior, he is our friend we will see him again." They set about breaking camp and headed out to find Crane's farm. It seemed that anyone could go to Crane's home with the exception of Crane himself.

CHAPTER 25

Rider and Dove, rode for many days finally arriving, at Crane's farm. Joey saw them a way off and he shouted "Fred, Jim, Indians!!" They came running with pistol's in their hands. Fred said, "It's just a man and a girl with a baby." They rode into the yard, the Indian brave jumped down from his horse, as he did so he struck his chest saying, "I am Rides the Wind and my brother Crane, says that we should come here to live, he sends a paper" Then he held out the note that Crane had given him.

Fred took it and he read it, then he spoke, "Crane says we are to let Rider," he looked at Rides the Wind who nodded, "Live on our land forever. Crane still trailing this man Mexican Joe." Rider said, He continued, "This is my wife White Dove and my son Standing Crane, so called for the way my brother Crane stood with us." "Crane says my Appaloosa should run with his mares, So I will let him free." "If you do that, you can have your pick of the horses in the corral as a riding horse" replied Fred.

Flo had come over, "You will eat with us, she said, in Crane's house" Everyone followed her back to the cabin, They were glad that Peter Leonard had made the long table, and more chairs, because he had realised that friends would often meet round this table. They all ate and talked at the same time, because they wanted news of Crane. Fred asked, "How did you meet Crane?" Rider, told them how Crane had ridden to their rescue, how Crane his horse and his dog had fought bravely, how Crane had been wounded.

Joey, eagerly asked the questions that were on everyone's lips, "How is Crane?" "Is he still fit for the task ahead." Rider, nodded "He is a great warrior you know this, he will ride his trail while his heart beats." Then he said "I have never seen a warrior horse like Crane's he fights with and for him."

"When Crane was shot he went down, Dancer still attacked and won his battle. "Crane's dog, Bruno is a new friend but he to would lay down his life for Crane" "I felt the fear in the air when the three of them attacked, the men who were trying to hurt us. I never known this before and I have fought in many battles."

Joey said, "We have all seen that from Crane and Dancer but this dog Bruno is something new." Mexican Joe is in more trouble than he knows, one of the three if not all of them will definitely get him." "Yes" said Fred, "And hopefully Utah and Dave will get to Crane in time to help." Then Rider asked a question, "Why do you all accept Comanche when so many of your people are against us?" "We accept you because you and White Dove are good people, and that is all we care about." You will roam this valley put up your wicki-up anywhere you wish," Said Fred.

"This is so typical of Crane" Said Flo, "He shares the good things in his life with all of us." "I pray to God that he finds our Maggie and Mae and is able to bring them home so that he can share in what he has done for us all." "We all agree with that said Jim, you know I think that Crane is the best of men." "While we are talking Rider," Said Flo. "I think that you and White Dove should stay around the homestead with little Standing Crane, until he is older." Rider nodded, "We would like that, being alone did not work for us at this time, if it had not been for Crane we would not have survived."

Riders horses were turned into Crane's Corral were they mingled with the other horses. Then Rider and Dove pitched their camp in sight of both cabins. Rider said, "It is true Crane said we are a people who are one tribe, there is no Indian and strangers from another land" When Crane and his wife and daughter come home we will all make one big happy family."

At his point Peter Leonard arrived with Big John, John Eckert, Larry and Neil. They were eager to get the work on Joey's cabin finished. When Peter heard the news about Crane and met The Comanche family he held a thanksgiving service for such good news. He also offered to baptise Standing Crane. Although Rider and White Dove did not understand the religion, they did recognised that baptism would be a good thing so they all went down to the stream, Ness and Doc stood as Standing Crane's Godparents. The Doc was getting stronger every day but he realised he was best staying at Crane's farm, as much as he wished to ride to join, Utah and Dave, in helping Crane.

All the men rode out to work on Joey's Cabin, It was taking shape and Peter was making his usual functional but attractive furniture. Joey said, "You know Peter, I can't help but think that you are a man of God, now Jesus's father Joseph was like you a carpenter, it makes me wonder, having a good man like you here with us, what is Gods plan?" Peter smiled, "God has a plan for us all, I sometimes think he guided me to carpentry in order to teach me patience, I was sometimes angry but now I work with my hands, I am at peace with everything ." "Then again I think he has guided Crane and all of us to be together, so you are right to wonder, because we are enjoying a special life."

Neil spoke, "I sure hope that Crane can get Maggie and the baby home soon, they don't deserve what's happened, I know that life doesn't have be fair but they have been given more than fair share of bad luck." John Eckert said, "I agree, I never saw so bad many things happen to a man as have happen to Crane." Peter Leonard said, "It's all in the plan, God never gives any of us more than we can bear." Also let us not forget Crane that has had many good things in his life

They were all working hard now, because it was time to get the roof on Joey's cabin and they were sweating and straining getting the timbers in place. Jubal and George Thomas from the sawmill had arrived in their wagon, they had hauled fence posts and poles to build a corral. They pulled up and got down and began to unload the wagon. The others stopped working and came to speak to the brothers.

Joey said, "You fellers, have done me proud, everybody is making me a great place to live. Fred said, Flo has sent cold food for us, we will eat before we do any more. They all sat together enjoying their food the way only those have worked for their appetite can. After their lunch. They all worked until dusk and then packed up their tools, and made ready to head to their respective homes.

They were ready to head their different ways when Joey's dad John Eckert stumbled off the porch and fell heavily he put out his arm to break his fall, he hit he ground with the heel of his hand it jarred his arm all the way up to his shoulder. It cracked and he twisted over with a cry of pain escaping from his lips. Joey ran forward, "Dad" he cried. He helped his dad to his feet, John's right shoulder seemed to have dropped and he was clearly in great pain. Joey unfastened the front of his dad's shirt, then he gently bent the arm at the elbow and put his dad's hand wrist inside the open shirt. This eased John's pain a little, because it took the dragging weight off his shoulder. Peter said, "Help him onto my buggy, he can't possibly ride his horse like that. It was a painful experience for John, but they got him up on to the buggy. When they had him up there John sat back and closed his eyes.

Joey tied his dad's horse behind the buggy, saying to Peter, "We had best get him back to Doc at the farm," Peter nodded, I will drive as slow as I can because the vibration over the ground is going to be painful for him. At least it is not to far to get back to the Doc at Crane's farm. Joey said, then he added, "Jim, Fred, Larry and I will ride ahead and let the Doc know that you are coming." The others all wished John well and headed for town. After a short but painful trip Peter and John arrived back at the farm, Doc, Joey, and Jim helped John out of the buggy and took him into Crane's cabin.

Doc made his examination, "Well John" he said "It could be worse, it is not broken but you have dislocated your shoulder, I will have to put it back in place, it will be painful." Doc then said to Ness, "Get him something to bite down on." Ness did and then she distracted John by standing off to his other side and speaking to him. The Doc quickly and efficiently, put John shoulder back in place. The colour drained from John's face but gradually he relaxed, he was in far less pain. Doc fashioned a sling from a cloth that Flo had brought him and put it on. Then he said to John, "I would rest up here to night if I were you will feel better tomorrow. Joey said, "I will ride into town and tell Mom that you are OK" "Thank you Son" replied John.

Then he said, "This is not a good look for a barber is it Doc?" The people in the room all smiled and laughed. There had been a lot of tension in the cabin and that one joking remark lifted the mood. Joey left for town and every one else prepared to turn in for the night.

CHAPTER 26

Mexican Joe was drunk, mean drunk, mad drunk in this condition he was losing all reason. All his madness, meanness and rage were aimed towards Crane. He was shouting, "How is this possible, how is this worthless piece of scum still alive, Crane is not human, he is the devils spawn, but I will stop him!" Mexican Joe threw an empty tequila bottle against the wall, then grabbed another, he pulled the cork with his teeth and spat it out on the floor. He took a long pull of the fiery liquid, Then turned his attention to Maggie who was sitting on a bed in the corner of the room, with one ankle chained to the floor. "Mexican Joe shouted, "Fear me!" "I am the most dangerous man in Texas, I hold your life in my hands."

Maggie held Mae close to her as Mexican Joe ranted and raved about her husband. On and on he went shouting almost crying with rage and frustration that the men he had left to kill Crane were dead themselves. After all this, Maggie said, "You are not a man,you are a fool and a coward, you have come up against Crane before and you know can't win, yet you take his wife and daughter. Knowing that he will come and now he will never stop until he has killed you."

Mexican Joe, cursed Maggie and said, "I will kill him,

I will have many, many men waiting, he will die." "If you kill him, you know that his horse will kill you," Said Maggie, "You know that you can't win, you are not the most dangerous man in Texas, You are nothing but a joke." "I am not a joke, I can kill you," Said Mexican Joe, "If you do that you will still die" Said Maggie, "If you hurt us at all Crane will find you and kill you, in fact he is going to do that anyway, you sealed your fate when you came to our farm and took us prisoner." "The stupid thing is, from your point of view, Crane had put his pistols away, because he wasn't going to ride after you any more."

Mexican Joe, stormed out into the street, he walked down the street, then turned and went through the swing doors into a crowded Saloon. As Joe went through the doors someone bumped into him on their way out, This caused Mexican Joe to drop and break his bottle of tequila, Joe drew his pistol and with no hesitation shot him, the whole room was stunned to silence. Mexican Joe spoke, "A man comes riding a big black horse, I will pay $1,000 to the man who kills him, $2,000 if you kill the horse as well. "How will we know this man?" a voice asked from somewhere in the room. "You will have never seen a horse like his," said Mexican Joe, "This man is called Crane, he is the devil." There were some bad men in the room, many of them had ridden with Mexican Joe in the past, they were the type who would do anything for money." "How do we know that you can pay?" Someone asked. Mexican Joe, put his good hand inside his shirt coming out with a thick bundle of $20 bills. "I have plenty more" he said, then he strode to the bar, "drinks for everyone" he said throwing two of the $20 bills on to the bar. The men in the room were all clamouring to get to the bar.

Stuffing the money back in his shirt and taking a bottle from the bar for himself, Mexican Joe left the saloon an went down to the livery stable. When he got there, he said to the ostler, "Saddle my horse, I'm going to Mexico." Then he said, "There is a woman and a baby in my hacienda, you will feed them and see that no harm comes to her or the baby until I come back. Here's $20, You know I will kill you if she is harmed," the ostler nodded. "Now fill my canteen," the man did, and Mexican Joe put the bottle of tequila in his saddlebag, mounted his horse and rode out.

Mexican Joe was sure that when he returned Crane would be dead, no one could be lucky for ever. He smiled grimly and thought and then I will kill the fool who killed Crane, as if I would actually pay the money. Mexican Joe was unaware how lucky he was on this day, because he hadn't been gone five minutes when three men and a dog came into town.

Utah and Dave Selley had finally caught up with Crane as he made camp for the night about thirty miles away from Larado. To say Crane was shocked was an understatement. He said, "I am mighty glad to see you two, how are things back home?" Utah said "Things won't be right until you Maggie and the baby are back where you belong." Dave said, "everybody wanted to come but in the end you got me." "You are just man we need" Said Crane, "I couldn't ask for a more loyal and reliable friend, I know you've got my back." Utah said "We recognised Dancer not you, because your hair is halfway down your back and you have a beard like a mountain man." "Crane smiled, "I just keep going and I don't look at myself." He replied.

They were all tired, Crane was still little weak from

his shoulder wound so they bedded down saying they would talk in the morning. When dawn came while they got themselves together Crane explained why he wasn't rushing, he needed to try and recover his strength after the wound, after all he did not know what he would face, when he got to Laredo. They continued to talk as they rode, "How was Ness, when she got back?" Asked Crane. "The Doc and her were so pleased to see each other, I don't think they wanted to let each other go." "You know that the Doc wanted to ride with us, but he is just not fully recovered. Replied Utah. "I know," Crane said. "People have to be allowed to live their lives, this really is my mess, but I am glad you two are here."

Utah looked down at Bruno, "What is the story with the dog?" Crane told him about the trip and the two bits of trouble the dog had helped him with. Dave said, "You seem to have made a real friend of him." "Yes" replied Crane. "I am very lucky in all the people who choose to be my friend, Bruno is one of those friends." "I wouldn't be alive this time round if Dancer and Bruno hadn't fought beside me." The he told them about Rides the Wind, White Dove and their baby.

Utah said, "I have to say that the Cassidy kid seems to be the real deal, all he needed was the chance you gave him." "Yeah" Replied Crane. "I also think Rider is going to be a good man to have around as well. "Yeah I agree," said Utah, We are really making a family in that Valley." "You bring good people with you Crane, I'm glad we got together." What they did not know was that big John McCane was riding three horse into the ground to catch them.

Big John had said to his wife Susan, "I'm sorry I have

to go, Crane is our friend and seeing John Eckert have his accident has reminded me that we are all only human, even Crane." He had selected three horses for their speed and stamina, because as he said, "I am a big man and one horse can not carry me as far and as fast as I need to go." He took limited supplies to keep the weight down for the horses, he was carrying more water than anything else. He set off at the gallop. Big John was covering a lot of ground leading two horses and riding one. He cursed the time it took him unsaddle one horse and saddle another, but he knew he was making good time, he rode at a steady loping gait rather than a flat out gallop. He knew he would kill the horses if he went to fast and that would get him nowhere,. He managed to swap horses at two ranches that he came on along the way.

After his tremendous ride Big John arrived in Larado about two hours after Utah, Dave and Crane, although he did not know this because he was exhausted. Big John had been riding for three days and nights and he had not slept, although he had dozed in the saddle. So he was glad when he stopped at a water trough on the street and his horses were able to drink gratefully. When then they had finished drinking, Big John plunged his head and shoulders into the water. Slightly refreshed he set about finding out if his friends were in town. His first port of call was the saloon, his entry was treated with suspicion. He walked the bar, "Whiskey" he said to the bartender, Big John drank it in one swallow. He tapped the glass for a refill, when he got it he turned and looked round the room, all eyes were on him.

A couple of guys sidled over to him, "You got a name

stranger?" They asked. "Yeah," Replied Big John, "Well" asked one of the men, "Very," answered John, He towered over the men who were asking questions, but one of them became belligerent, and went for his pistol, he never cleared leather, because Big John's fist crashed into his face and the world went dark for him. In the blink of an eye Big John's pistol was in his hand, "We don't want to be silly now do we?" He asked the others in the saloon, "No" came the reply, "It is just that we are on the lookout for guy named Crane, "So am I" replied Big John. One of the men said, "So you heard about the $1,000 Mexican Joe put on his head, with another $1000 for the his horse. "I have now" Said Big John.

Unlike Big John, Crane, Utah and Dave had not chosen the saloon as their first port of call, for them it was the livery stable. They dismounted and asked the Ostler if they could turn the horses into the corral. He nodded and they unsaddled and turned the horses loose in the corral. Crane said "I'm looking for Mexican Joe, do you know where he is,?" "He just left town" replied the Ostler. Crane's heart sank, He asked, "Do you know where he's headed?" "Mexico" came the reply. The three men looked at each other. "Was he with anyone," asked Crane. The Ostler shook his head. "Well he was travelling with my wife and daughter" said Crane. "Do you know where they are?" "I do" said the Ostler, "But Joe would kill me if I told you." Crane's pistol leapt into his hand, "I will kill you now if you don't and then I will tear this town apart looking for them." The hostler told them and directed them to Mexican Joe's house.

Crane, Dave and Utah ran through the streets with

Bruno loping behind them, till they came to the single story house, Crane burst through the door and he saw Maggie on the bed in the corner, holding the baby, She looked up at the sound of the door bursting open, Crane she cried, "I knew you would come for us ." Crane fell to his knees and swept her and the baby gently into his arms. "I'm sorry, I was so long getting to you, there have been a few hold ups along the way." "I never doubted you, replied Maggie, Then, she said, "Mae say hello to your Daddy," the baby looked up, and something broke inside Crane, the love he felt for these two was like nothing he had ever known. Dave and Utah came in and said, "We are mighty glad to see you ma'am."

Crane looked at the chain and said, to Maggie,"We need to get that chain off your ankle. "That's easy" said Maggie. "Joe was always drunk so he kept the key to the padlock on the window ledge so that he could find it when it was needed." Crane crossed the room got the key and set Maggie free. Then Crane took Mae in his arms for the first time, he was sure that she was smiling at him. He said to Dave and Utah, "I need you to support Maggie when she first gets up, I don't know if she will be dizzy." They did as they were asked, but it soon become clear that Maggie was made of strong stuff and she was fine.

While all this was going on, Big John was making his way from the saloon to the livery stable with his three horses. He got there and immediately recognised Dancer and Utah's stallion. "The men who ride those horses, where are they?" He asked the Ostler. "They and the feller that rode in with them have gone to Mexican Joe's house" "Where is that?" asked Big John. The Ostler pointed out the way saying, "Second turn along it's down at the bottom end, scruffy looking building." Big John ran, shouting back over his shoulder, "Put my horses in your corral and I will pay you later." The Ostler grumbled, "Nothing happens for days and then all this." He set about unsaddling Big John's horse and turned all three of the horses into the corral.

Big John arrived at the door, he stood one side, he wasn't fool enough to burst through the door of a strange house, he knew his friends if they were in there would all open fire if he burst in. He heard a dog bark inside, it was loud and sounded like rolling thunder. From inside the house Big John heard Crane's voice say "Down Bruno!." He called, "It is OK Crane it's John McCane" The door opened and a huge dog blocked his path, growling low in it's throat,

"You've got a new member of the team have you?" Asked Big John. Crane replied "Yes, that's Bruno." "Bruno this is Big John, he is our friend." Crane stepped forward and shook Big John's hand, when the dog saw this Bruno went to the other side of the room and lay down at Maggie's feet. "We have a lot of things to tell you" said Utah as he and Dave shook hands with Big John. "It will have to wait" Said Big John. "Because there are twenty or thirty people down at the saloon, the number could grow, all wanting to kill you and Dancer, because Mexican Joe has put a $1,000 on each of your heads." "We had better move." Said Crane. They headed out the door, back to the livery stable.

Down at the livery stable all hell had broken loose, half a dozen of the men from the saloon had followed Big John to the livery stable and heard what the Ostler had told him. They had a plan, they would kill Dancer and then get Crane at Mexican Joe's house. The first mistake the drunken clowns made was when one of them fired into the corral hitting the wrong horse. The next mistake they made was not deciding to run.

Because as soon as he heard the first shot, Dancer took off and he leapt the top rail of the corral then he charged the men and their pistols. As the next shot was fired the man who fired it was under Dancer's hooves, he would never use a pistol again. Knocking another man down as he ran through, Dancer seized the shoulder of yet another man he lifted him in the air, the great stallion's teeth biting deep into the flesh. Dancer was shaking the man like a rag doll, the man's screams were terrifying. The other horses were milling round and neighing. Crane and the others were coming as fast as they could. Crane said to Dave Selley, "Stay with Maggie, I know you will make good use of Henry Rifle you carry, if anyone threatens her or the baby" Dave nodded, "You know it" He said.

Bruno raced ahead in the direction of the noise, as he came round the corner to the Livery stable he came up on a man with his pistol levelled at Dancer, Bruno leapt through the air and took the man down. Then he ripped his throat out, he went for another of the men and this one panicked and tried to run, but it was to no avail, he died with a scream on his lips. Dancer was kicking biting and lashing out wildly with his hooves. All the men who had made the plan to kill him, died.

Crane and the others arrived and looked at the scene of devastation. Big John said, "Bruno, is the same as you and Dancer" He said, he fights for survival and takes no prisoners" Crane said "Right let's get saddled up, the men in the saloon will want to know what has happened, I want to get Maggie and Mae out of town." The Ostler came out of the barn, shocked and silent. "Crane said, "Sell me a saddle." The Ostler went back in the barn, "I will need a horse for Maggie." Big John said, "She can ride one of mine I have three." "That explains how you got here so quick." Said Utah.

They all worked quickly and efficiently and they were soon saddled, canteens were filled and then they were ready to ride. Dave and Maggie arrived with the baby they looked without surprise. Big John spoke to the Ostler, You get the horse I am leaving in exchange for the saddle, and whatever else we owe you, OK." The Ostler nodded, he was still in shock.

Back in the saloon there was uproar, something is badly wrong they were saying, listen to all that noise it can't be right. None of them could decide what to do. Eventually they started to come out of the saloon to the street some of them had already drawn their pistols. They had decided that they would all head down to the livery stable.

Crane marshalled his men. "Right Dave, he said, you will take Maggie and the baby out of town we will meet you where we camped last night." "He looked at Dave saying, "I am trusting you above all men with the safety of my wife and child, I know you would want to stay here and fight, but I need you to do this." Dave was choked with emotion, all he could do was nod. Crane turned to Maggie hugged her and the baby and lifted them into the saddle. There were no words they both knew how the other felt.

Dave and Maggie rode out of town away from the saloon they would circle back around the town and get to last nights camp. Crane, Utah and Big John mounted their horse's just in time, a crowd of men were approaching. Some of the men were excited and started firing their pistols even though they were out of range. Any bystanders rushed inside to safety. Crane, Utah and Big John, all put their reins in their teeth drew their pistols, one in each hand and charged, Bruno was with them doing his expected damage.

The sound of gunfire and the smell of cordite filled the air. Crane an his men were driving forward and men were falling before their attack it was impossible to say who was shot by the terrible three and who had been ridden down. The three riders burst through the line and then spun their horses and rode back at their assailants. The brave men from the saloon, gave up when they saw that half their number were down dead or wounded. Those who remained standing dropped their pistols and held up their arms in surrender. Crane dropped the reins from his mouth, "Get back in the saloon." He said. The men walked away chastened by the ferocity of the three riders attack. Still mounted all three, Utah, Big John and Crane reloaded their pistols.

As they did this a man with a sheriffs star, stepped off the side walk into the street. He looked up at Crane. "I take it you're the man who Mexican Joe will pay $1,000 to have dead." Crane looked down at him his eyes flat and cold, "Are you looking to collect?" He asked. "No" replied the sheriff, "I hope to live a while longer and having seen you in action, I wouldn't rate my chances very high if I stand against you." "I just want you to leave town."

Crane nodded, "We will just get supplies from the store and be gone." "I will be back though, when I bring Mexican Joe in for the bounty." He turned Dancer and rode up the street followed by Big John and Utah. They all stopped at the general store dismounted and went inside for their supplies.

"The three friends rode out of town with their supplies which included things for the baby, towelling nappies, clothes, even a doll. They also bought clothes for Maggie including a dress and trousers the trousers were for comfort when riding, Crane had a good idea of the size Maggie would need they also bought a hairbrush, soap and a couple of towels. Their other purchases included beans, two sacks of coffee and a couple of boxes of shells. When their shopping was done, they headed for their rendezvous with Dave, Maggie and the baby. Dave had set up camp when they got there. He was on guard with his rifle in hand, when they rode up to the camp. Crane said, "Thanks Dave you are a good friend."

Then he said, "We have food and things for Maggie and the baby. Maggie was delighted with the clothes soap hairbrush and towels. "She said Mae and I will go down to the stream and clean up." Maggie took Mae and set off, Crane went with her to carry the clothes, soap and towels for her. While she washed the baby and herself, Crane washed and shaved off his beard with his straight razor. He kept an eye out in case there were any intruders on their privacy.

"Well" he said when he saw Maggie in her new blue dress, she was brushing her hair, "You look beautiful." Crane said. "You are biased," Maggie replied, "But I am clean for the first time since Mexican Joe took us." Crane nodded, "He is going to feel pain for that, I intend to kill him, but not until he regrets what he has done to you and Mae. Men who hurt or abuse women and children should be castrated before they die." "I can do that for him." "Maggie said. "I warned him over and over that he would regret what he had done, that you would follow him into hell if you have to."

"Well never mind Mexican Joe" said Crane, "He is for another day. I have to say that you and Mae sure look good to me." He carried on speaking, "Mae sure is a good baby, I haven't heard her cry yet." They gathered up their things and went back to camp. Dave had cooked bacon and beans, there was a coffee pot on the fire boiling. He looked up and said you are just in time this food is ready to eat. Utah, said, "I knew I brought you with me for a reason."They all laughed and helped themselves to the food.

Big John said, "Well Crane, now you have shaved you look almost human" Crane smiled and said, "Funny thing shaving has been the last thing on my mind for a while." After a while Maggie had gone out of sight for a few minutes while she fed Mae. When she came back they gave Maggie and Crane news from home and they all chatted about good things and the future. Then when they were talked out, and well fed, they turned in for the night, Dave took first watch followed by Utah and then Big John, he took the last watch because after his titanic ride he needed some sleep. They would leave Crane and Maggie to sleep the night, in peace, together again at last.

So as they settled down together with Mae beside them, Maggie said "It has been way to long. I have really missed you." "I have missed you too" said Crane. They fell into a contented sleep with Bruno at their feet. It was a quiet night and morning came without incident. Dave had the coffee on and they all enjoyed breakfast, Maggie fed Mae, they all knew what was coming. "Crane said, "This is where we have to go our separate ways" "You know I have to end this, I'm going to Mexico, to find Mexican Joe, I didn't follow him last time and look what happened."

Utah said, "I can't let you go without me." "I know" said Crane "But you Dave are taking Maggie and Mae home for me and I'd be obliged if you went with them Big John, because you need to get home to Susan and the boys." "Also there is no way of knowing what Dave will meet on the way back. He may need your guns." "I want you all to get home alive." Big John and Dave agreed, because they knew that Crane was talking sense. So they divided the supplies and saddled up, Maggie and Crane hugged and he kissed his daughter Mae. As they rode their different ways Maggie said to Utah, "Bring him home safe to me." "You got it" replied Utah."

CHAPTER 27

Dave and Big John rode with Maggie and the baby just behind them. They were talking about Crane and how loyal people and animals were to him. Dave said, "That dog, Bruno is hell on wheels, he clearly thinks his reason for living is to protect Crane. Between him and Dancer they have a formidable attack and defence force for Crane." "True" said Big John, "It's as if they have all been together in another life, the three of them act on instinct, they move individually and they act together." I certainly wouldn't want to be Mexican Joe, when Crane gets to him and this time he will get to him. "You are right, no one would ever give up on getting scum like Joe who abuse and use woman and children, only a slow painful death will suffice in his case" Said Dave. "Utah will be in at the kill as well, I sure wish we could be there" said Big John.

They were making good time when they made camp that night and even though she had the baby to attend to Maggie insisted on cooking supper, "I'm not helpless" she said. Both men knew better than to argue.

The next day or so passed without incident and the two men were hopeful of having a trouble free trip. As they rode Dave said to Big John, "You know I can't believe Crane picked me to protect Maggie and Mae back in town." Anything could have happened, we didn't know if Mexican Joe would come back." "He chose you because you are a good and loyal friend, he knows that you would lose your life before you would let harm come to his family, in fact he all of us regard you as family." Replied Big John. The emotion welled up in Dave, he found himself unable to speak, so he didn't try. They rode on in silence

They stopped for their noon break and decide to have a fire and make coffee. Suddenly there were five men riding into their camp, "Howdy boy" said the first rider., "Sure would be obliged for some of that coffee." Big John and Dave were not pleased that the riders had come in unexpectedly. They nodded as the riders stepped down.

Then one of them saw Maggie, holding Mae, "Well now boys, we have a mighty pretty little lady here." "I think we should show her how much we appreciate her." He moved forward and put his arm round Maggie, trying to kiss her. "Now don't be greedy Jedadiah, we are family and we all share everything." For Dave it seemed that time was standing still. He was in no man's land between the fire and where his Henry rifle was leaning against a rock. One of the men said, "Watch the big man, his eyes look as dangerous as a rattler that is about to strike." Three of the men moved towards Big John, one of them said. "Don't make any sudden moves, big man, if you do those moves are likely to be your last."

At that moment Maggie raked the nails on the fingers of her free hand in the eye of the man mauling her, He screamed and cursed, "God damn," He never finished, the men had made the mistake of ignoring Dave, He dived for his Henry, rolling and levering a shell in one movement, his first bullet took Maggie's attacker in his throat, His second hit the next man in the left arm, just as he fired his pistol, his bullet hit Dave in the leg above the knee, passing right through his leg just as he was getting up into a crouch he fell back, Maggie had turned away with Mae getting out of the line of fire.

Big John didn't need a second invitation, he drew and fired twice in quick succession, two of their assailants who had turned toward Dave with pistols in hand went down. The third man spun back his pistol levelled ready to shoot, Big John, "The back of his head exploded as Dave fighting for consciousness, fired for the last time. Big John was moving and he shot the man that Dave had wounded in the arm, through the chest. Maggie ran to Dave putting Mae on the ground beside him. She patted his face he stirred and looked at her, pale faced "Did we see them off," He asked. "Yes you did, Dave," Maggie replied, "Now you know why Crane trusted you to take me home."

Big John looked around making sure the strangers were all dead, they were. He came over, "Are you and the baby OK Maggie," He asked, "Yes, thank you John." She replied. Mae was wailing loudly and she picked her up saying,"Mae doesn't often cry, but when she does they can probably her in New Mexico." Then she said "We need to dress Dave's wound because he is losing a lot of blood."

Big John set about boiling water, he checked Dave's wound and was glad to see it wasn't near an artery. He drew his knife and tore Dave's pants on both sides. Dave looked at the knife apprehensively, seeing this Big John smiled and said, "Don't worry Dave, the bullet went right through your leg, I just need to heat this and seal the two holes.

"I'm just as worried about that" replied Dave.. Maggie said, "I will have to tear my new petticoat for bandages." She turned away and set about it.

Big John put his knife in the flames and began to bathe wounds. Then he picked up a stick, he handed it to Dave saying, "Bite down on that." Dave put in between his teeth and closing his eyes bit down hard. His flesh sizzled and beads of sweat sprang out on his forehead, Then Big John said, "We are done." Dave relaxed and let the wood fall from his mouth. Maggie worked quickly and efficiently putting a pad on each side of the wound and bound the leg with strips of her petticoat.

We will have to move away from these bodies and remake our camp, Said Big John, "We will be here for the rest of the day and over night, while Dave rests up" he and Maggie moved things away then Big John helped Dave to move. Maggie cooked some food and boiled up the coffee. They all ate, Dave said I'm feeling better all ready, then they settled down for the night. All except Big John, he let the others sleep but he remained on watch while the others slept. One mistake the only one they had made, which they had been lucky to survive, was one mistake to many.

Morning came and Dave awoke to the smell of bacon and coffee Maggie had breakfast ready. Big John asked, "How do you feel about riding today Dave?" "You may have to help me up into the saddle but, once I'm up there I'll hang on." They ate their breakfast and drank coffee.

Afterwards Big John said, We are lucky to have you with us Dave, if you hadn't reacted the way you did, I think we would all be dead now." "No" replied Dave "We all did it together." "Not so" Said Big John, "They caught me cold, your actions gave us an edge, very important." "You definitely saved my life when you shot my third man." "Well, said Dave "You saved mine." "Crane knew what he was doing when he told me that you would look after Mae and Maggie, I will never forget what you and John have done for me" said Maggie "I'm on my guard now" said Big John, "I've spent too long living in town and on the farm, I would never have let anyone ride into my camp unexpectedly, in the days when I lived on the trail." They packed up the camp, Big John, linked the horses that their five assailants had ridden in on, then tied the lead rope to his saddle horn. He helped Dave in to the saddle and they headed out for home. As they did Big John said, "There is no point in leaving these horses behind."

Progress was slower than on previous days, because Dave was in a lot of pain, but gradually his leg improved and they were finally in sight of Crane's ranch. Fred saw them coming and he called Flo, "Our girls are home Flo!" He shouted. Flo came running, and Maggie handed Mae down to her. Then Maggie dismounted and it was hugs and kisses all round.

Dave dismounted with difficulty, and there handshakes and thanks for himself and Big John. They watered their horses, and John turned the riderless horses into the corral. As always Flo was the good hostess providing coffee and cold cuts. Maggie was delighted to be back in her own home, she wandered round picking things up, then putting them down and touching the furniture. She was happy to see Mae in her own cot, the months away had been really hard. All she needed now was her husband home, but she knew that could be a while.

Joey was quick to tell her about his cabin and he introduced her to Jim Cassidy. Big John and Dave were pleased to hear that Doc Black and Ness were back home in town, with Doc finally fully recovered. Dave said, "I think I will be calling on him to get this leg checked." Big John said "I really need to get home to Susan and the boys." They all moved outside, Dave and Big John mounted their horses and headed out together for their respective homes.

Maggie said to her Ma and Pa, "I knew big John was a fighting man, but Dave really surprised me, I knew he wouldn't let us down, that he would stand fight. But you should have seen the way he took the fight to the five guys who used to have the horses that are now in the corral. Quite simply we would not have made it home without him." "We want to hear all the news," said Flo. "How is Crane?" "Well he has had another wound, so that means yet another scar. Having said that he is over the moon with his daughter, I am so pleased that they have met each other. Then there is this huge dog, Bruno he has attached himself to Crane and like Dancer he fights with and for him. If it's possible, I feel more confident of Crane coming home safe to me now Bruno is with him."

Fred said, "I wish he could have come home with you, but I understand that he has to end this thing with Mexican Joe. Otherwise none of us will be able to sleep easy in our beds." The three family members, four with Mae, went back to the cabin and Joey and Jim got on with their work.

Rider, Dove and the baby, Standing Crane entered the farm yard, saying, "Dave and Big John told us you were home, we are happy to meet you." "Me to,Crane spoke well of you" said Maggie hugging White Dove and the baby, "Come into the house and meet Mae, we have a lot to talk about." The cot was big enough for two and they sat Standing Crane at one end and Mae at the other, the two children were smiling at each other. Maggie said, "I think these two are going to be great friends." Maggie and White Dove were soon engrossed in conversation, Rider just sat drinking coffee. Maggie, said, "I am so glad we can speak the same language." White Dove said, "Living on the reservation we needed to be able to communicate with the agent. We resented it at first but since we met Crane, we have been glad." "We are a family now" said Maggie, "That is what Crane told us, he and I are brothers." Replied Rider.

"Is the reservation going to be a problem?" asked Maggie. "Well" said Rider "If they find us we can be taken back, maybe thrown in prison or even shot." "I don't know if they would follow us here or if anyone would recognise us." "None of us especially Crane would allow that." Said Maggie. "He told me that he is a quarter Comanche, if anyone asks we will say you are his true brother and that you have a stake in this land." "Crane is right" said Rider, "We are one people. We will be your true family, our thanks to the Great Spirit."

After they had been riding for about 15 minutes Big John, said to Dave, "I'm heading home, so I will leave you to head on into town, let the folks know the news and I will see you soon." They went their separate ways and Dave soon saw the town coming into sight. He waved to the Thomas brothers, as he passed their Sawmill. Dave stopped at the livery stable and brought Larry up date with the news, glossing over his part in saving Maggie and Mae.

Then as he passed the church, Peter Leonard came out and called to him. Dave turned his horse towards him and stopped. He told him that Maggie and the baby were home, and that so far he, Big John, Utah and Crane were safe. I will perform a thanksgiving service at Crane's farm on Sunday. "I'm going to see Doc Black now, but I will attend the service." Dave touch the brim of his hat and rode on.

He made his way up the street until he reached Doc and Ness's place. He dismounted and limped in. "He saw the Doc and Ness and said, "Just to tell you both, Maggie and the baby are home." "Thank God" they both replied. "You are wounded," said Doc, "Let me look at that leg." Dave hobbled into the medical room and Doc helped him on to the bed.

"Is Crane back?" Doc asked as he cut off the makeshift bandage. "Sadly no," replied Dave, going on to explain about Crane' continuing search for Mexican Joe. He explained that Utah had continued on with Crane, while he and Big John had brought Maggie and Mae home. He told them how he had been wounded but he underplayed his own role in the incident.

Then he told them about Peter Leonard's, thanksgiving service out at Crane's farm on the coming Sunday. Doc and Ness said they would be there. The Doc redressed the wound on Dave's leg, saying, "Big John did a fair job of patching you up, the leg should heal well, although you will have to ugly scars. Dave thanked him and nodded.

At that moment Neil and Maureen, came through the door,. Neil said "I'm mighty glad to see you in one piece old friend." "Peter came by and told us you were back."

He held up a pair of pants, "Peter said you looked like you would need these." "Thanks" said Dave he got down from the bed, "I think I will need help getting my boots off, my leg is a little stiff." He sat down in a chair and Neil pulled off his boots, then Dave went behind the screen and put on the new pants. With some difficulty he stamped his way into his boots. He came out from behind the screen, "These are a good fit, Neil," he said, "Thank you.

Maureen spoke, "Peter told us about the service, we will be there, we all have a lot to be thankful for." "We will go and see John and Doreen Eckert and tell them the news, they will want to come to the service as well."

Big John was home, Susan and the boys were relieved to see him return. "I was worried I wouldn't see you again" Said Susan. Big John held her in his arms, "If it had not been for Dave Selley, I would not have made it home this time." He told her about the attack that the five riders had made on Maggie and how Dave's actions had saved them all." "I have will give him my thanks when I see him." Replied Susan. "Tomorrow I must ride over to Utah's farm and let Alan Crowe know what's happened and where Utah is now" said Big John. "But now all I want to do is go to sleep in my own bed."

CHAPTER 28

Crane and Utah, rode on in silence, the miles passed steadily. Then Utah spoke, "I know you want to go home and be with Maggie and Mae." "That being the case I want to you know that I would go on after Mexican Joe alone for you." "Crane replied, "I know you would, but friends like you are hard to come by, I wouldn't sleep nights, knowing that you are on this trail alone." He continued. "You wouldn't let me do it alone and I won't let you." Then he said "I think we are about twenty miles over the border into Mexico now." "So we need to be on our guard."

As they were riding along they could see a shack smouldering, in the distance. When they got closer they could see lying on the ground, the bodies of a cow, a donkey and two of human form. They rode up to what remained of the corral and dismounted. Bruno sniffed at the fallen bodies, then he moved to another body that he saw on the corner of the shack, he barked and pushed at the body with his nose. Crane and Utah went over to him, then Bruno stepped back and sat down. "It's a young woman," said Crane. "She is breathing, bring me your canteen quickly."

Utah ran back to his horse grabbed his canteen and came back. He pulled the cap and splashed water on the young woman's face, she stirred and moaned, "Try her with a drink" said Crane. Crane was holding her up in a sitting position. Utah open her mouth and slowly dribbled water from the canteen into her mouth. The woman coughed and spluttered and then she opened her eyes, there was fear and panic in them. "It's all right," said Utah, "Crane and I are here to help." "My mother and father are they all right?" She asked. Utah shook his head, "I am sorry" he said. There was blood running down the young lady's face from a wound on her head. Crane looked at it and could see crease along her skull that had been caused by a bullet. "Is it just your head that is hurt? He asked. The young lady nodded, "Yes, I have a really bad headache." "You are lucky that is all you are suffering" said Crane. "If that bullet had been any lower, you wouldn't be talking me now."

Utah said "I am Utah, what is your name?" "Maria Gonzales," the young woman replied. "Do you know who did this?" asked Crane. Maria shook her head, "Not really I heard shots and ran from our shack, my parents were already on the ground." "The man who shot me was missing his right hand." Crane looked at Utah. "Mexican Joe" he said "That man has got to be put down." Utah gritted his teeth, "He will be soon," he said.

Crane and Utah spent the rest of the day burying Maria's parents. They fashioned two crosses for markers from the broken corral poles, they tied them together with piggin string from Crane's saddle bag. The two men removed their hats and stood in silence while Maria said some prayers over the graves. As they moved away Bruno was following them. Crane and Utah, got their horses, and the three of them walked away from the shack."We will make camp and have supper." Said Crane. "I think we will have to take you with us Maria, because we certainly can't leave you here said Utah. Maria nodded, "I haven't any choice but to leave, there is nothing left here for me."

When they were rested the three set out on the next stage of their journey, Maria was riding double with Utah. Maria had told them that there was a small shanty town a couple of miles south so that was where they were headed. As Crane said, "If Maria is going to travel with us we will need to get her a horse." Utah agreed although, he said that unfortunately he had left in haste and was not carrying much cash, certainly not enough for a horse. Crane told him not worry, he had the funds to cover their costs.

As they rode into the shanty town it was dusk as they went through the narrow streets looking for the livery stable they found it at the far end of town. The three dismounted and Bruno sat beside Dancer. A small slightly stooped elderly man came out of the stable, He spoke, "Ho-la, Señor's, Señorita, I am Juan Montoya at your service, I am the proprietor of the livery stable and the undertaker for the town."

Crane spoke, "Howdy my name is Crane, we are looking to buy a horse and saddle" "You are in luck Señor I have a fine Palomino mare, the owner unfortunately fell under someone's gun, he did not get up after I had buried him, I took his horse to pay for the funeral." He went back into the stable when he re-emerged, he was leading a very fine mare.

"I like the mare very much" said Crane, "How much is a funeral?" "$5 señor. "I see" replied Crane, "I will give you $25 for the horse and the saddle and bridle, which I am sure came with it." Oh but Señor" said Juan, This horse is worth maybe $60 or $70 in Laredo." "I'm sure it is," said Crane, "But we are not in Laredo are we?" "If we take the horse, we will stable our horses here and sleep in the stable ourselves and give you another $5." "The two men shook hands. Utah and Crane led their horses into the stable, unsaddled them and put them in stalls. Crane paid Juan his $30 then he asked, "Is there anywhere to eat in this town?" "Si señor" Crane replied to Juan. "There is a Cantina back up the street there, he pointed, then he said, "Very good beans and sometimes beef ". "Thank you ," Replied Crane.

As they walked to the Cantina, Utah, Crane and Maria talked about what lay ahead. "It could be dangerous for you to ride with us Maria, perhaps you would prefer to stay here." "I have no one here or anywhere else, if you don't mind I would prefer to ride with you and Utah." "OK then ." Replied Crane. They had arrived at the door of the Cantina, "he said, "Let's go in and eat." They went in it was dark and dingy inside, the only light coming from, a couple of oil lamps on each side of the room.

Nobody was paying much attention to them as they found a table where Crane could keep his back to the wall and then they sat down. Crane spoke, "I don't normally come in these places, but I've heard tell of a pistol fighter called Hickock, a good man by all accounts, went into a saloon to play a game of cards, he sat down with his back to the door." "Some feller came in and shot him in the back" "Utah nodded saying, "I think I heard about that."

Then Utah said, "I almost laughed out loud Crane, when you asked Juan how much a funeral cost, you left him no where to go on the price of the horse." Crane smiled, then replied, "Well I knew he would want to negotiate the price up, but at the same time I wanted to give him a fair profit, I hope I succeeded." "I'd say so," said Utah, "Juan would have been lucky to get $10 for that horse in this town, that is if somebody hadn't just come taken the horse away from him."

A man came to the table and asked, "Do you want food?" "Yes please" replied Crane, "Four plates of whatever you have that is good to eat and a pot of coffee, with three mugs." The man looked at Bruno lying at Crane's feet, "The dog can't stay in here, you will have to leave him outside" Bruno stood up snarling, Crane said "Be my guest, feel free to take the dog outside." The man shook his head and walked away, Bruno lay back down and closed his eyes. Even Maria smiled at the dog. The pot of coffee arrived first and Utah poured three cups, "I was ready for that said Crane as he sipped the scalding hot brew."

They sat and waited for their food each one lost in their own thoughts. When the steaming plates full of beans and some sort of beef stew arrived with, spoons to eat with, Crane, said, "The dog don't need a spoon." The man just walked away leaving the extra spoon on the table. Crane looked down at Bruno saying, "You will have to wait for this until it cools." Bruno looked at him balefully then lowered his head between his front paws, "That's the sign of a good dog" Said Utah. The three companions began to eat, "This stew is surprisingly good," Said Crane. When the food had cooled sufficiently Crane put Bruno's plate down for him. Maria said, "Your dog is surprisingly gentle when he eats." Crane nodded in agreement.

Crane called the man who had served them over to the

table, "How much for the food" he asked, "$3 dollars" The man replied. Crane paid him, saying "Bring a bowl of cold water for the dog please." The man nodded and went away returning in a moment with water. He nervously put it on the table, Crane thanked him and put the bowl down for Bruno who drank from the bowl gratefully.

"I think we will mosey on back to the livery stable and get some shut eye now" said Crane. He added, "In the morning we will find a store to buy some trousers for you to wear when you are riding, and anything else you need, Maria." "Thank you she said, I am so lucky you rode by our hut." "I have no idea what would have become of me otherwise." They went into the stable and made beds on the straw, Utah gave Maria a blanket from his bedroll, they all had a saddle now, so these were used as pillows. Bruno as had become his habit, slept at Crane's feet.

They slept for a while and then Utah woke to the sound of Maria, weeping softly. She was sitting up and he went over and comforted her, he put his back against the wall of a stall and put his arm round her. Maria laid her head on his chest, and gradually she dozed off. When Crane woke up in the morning he saw them there. He smiled to himself and went out when he got outside plunged his head in the water trough, the shock of the cold water that certainly freshened him up for the day.

Utah woke up at almost the second as Maria as they looked in to each others eyes they both felt a spark ignite in their hearts. Without either of them saying a word they both got up and went outside where they saw Crane. "Good Morning" Said Crane,. Utah nodded, Maria, more vocal replied with her own, "Good Morning." Like Crane before him Utah plunged his head in the water trough. Marie being a lady was more decorous about her ablutions, she just washed her hands and face. When their morning ablutions were completed, they decided that the three of them would head for the Cantina.

They sat at the same table they had occupied the night before, feeling very hungry. Crane ordered four plates of ham and eggs, the man who took the order, looked at but did not mention the dog. Crane also ordered a pot of coffee, which as it had the night before arrived first. At the same time Crane also ordered a bowl of water for Bruno. The three of them sat quietly and drank their first mug of coffee.

When their food arrived and Crane shared the eggs from Bruno's plate between the three of them, then he put the plate containing just the ham down on the floor for him. Bruno ate surprisingly slowly and methodically chewed each mouthful. Crane watched him, saying, "You don't often see that in a dog, in my experience they usually swallow each mouthful whole." The other two nodded their agreement. Then they all concentrated on enjoying their breakfast. When they had all finished eating, Crane asked Maria, "Do you know were the store is in this town?" Maria nodded saying, "I will show you, Crane paid for the food and they left the Cantina.

When they all got to the store, Bruno lay down on the side walk they went inside and once they were inside they left Maria to get the things she needed, while the two men replenished their own stores. Crane said, "I think I will get another couple of boxes of shells, you never know when they might be needed." Utah agreed with him because he knew that there was still the job of bringing down Mexican Joe.

As they went to leave the store, there were three men blocking the way out through the door, One of them said, "Mexican Joe said that you would drop by, so he left you a message." Crane let the bag he was carrying fall to the floor, Utah pushed Maria behind him, then Crane spoke, "What is the message?" The man on the right said, "He said to tell you goodbye as you were dying." The man's hand flashed down for his pistol, he never made it to the pistol grip because Bruno was flying through air, the dog hit him and knocked him off his feet. As the man fell he caused his companions to stumble, just as they reached for their own pistols. Crane leapt through the door a pistol in each hand, the two men had their pistols out by now, one of them pulled the trigger but because he was in panic that shot missed Crane. Crane didn't miss, he was firing both his pistols at the same time, the two men fell into the street, they were both dead before they hit the ground.

Behind him Crane could hear Bruno growling and the first man screaming, he spun and saw that Bruno had the man by the arm and he was shaking the man like a rag doll. Crane spoke saying, "Bruno leave!" Bruno let go and sat beside Crane, who marvelled how the dog responded to him after knowing him for such a short time. Then Crane looked down at the man saying, "You need to tell me where Mexican Joe is"

"Your dog has nearly ripped my arm off." The man replied. "You have been lucky on this occasion" replied Crane, "Bruno seems to be off target, he always goes for the throat." Then Crane continued "I asked you a question, please don't make me ask you again, I wouldn't like Bruno to get a grip of you again, he might not let you go next time." ""I can't tell you," the man replied, "Mexican Joe will kill me if I tell you." Crane looked at him then he said, "Bruno." The dog got up and came and stood over the fallen man, he was growling low in his throat, as he stared down balefully at the man. "Get the dog away from me" came the cry from the fallen man. "Only when you tell me where to find, Mexican Joe" Replied Crane. Bruno's jaws opened and the saliva from his mouth dripped down on to the man's face. "OK, OK, I will tell you, there is a ranch 10 miles south of here, it belongs to Manuel Cardosa, you will find Mexican Joe there."

"OK Bruno, leave him ." Said Crane, Bruno turned away and then went and sat behind Crane. After the dog had moved Crane pulled the man to his feet,, he was a lucky man, Bruno had been holding the man by his shoulder, so although he had been mauled, his injuries were not life threatening. Crane asked the question, "Did Mexican Joe pay you to kill me ?" "Yes he did, he paid us a thousand dollars apiece" the man replied. "Well I'll be taking that" Said Crane,. "I don't think-----" The man started to say, "No" replied Crane, "You don't think, otherwise you wouldn't have taken this job." "Utah, help the man out he has only got the use of one arm and hand."

Utah came forward and rifled through man' s pockets and pulled out all the money he found. He made a quick count and said, $1,067 and a few cents that he counted out," he said. "Put the $67 and the few cents back in the guys pocket" Replied Crane saying, "A man has got to live, although if he wants to keep doing that, he really needs to find another job." Utah nodded and put the money back in the man's pocket. Crane picked up the man's pistol and emptied the shells from it then he dropped the pistol into the man's holster. Having done that he pushed the shells into the man's pocket, Then he said, "If I were you I'd go and find a doctor so that you can get that shoulder fixed up." The man walked away, he must have known how lucky he was.

Utah offered Crane the $1000, Crane declined it saying, "You had better hold on to that" Then Crane bent and took the money from the pockets of the two the fallen men. He counted out enough money for two funerals, and put it back in the men's pockets, saying, Juan will get the horses and the effects so he will be happy." He counted out $500 and handed it to Utah, then he put the remaining money in his own pocket. Utah said, "I don't know if----"

Crane interrupted him, "Mexican Joe paid them with this money to kill me. I can tell you that he is going to get my company at least, so the money is mine. Because you are my friend I can share my money with you. Utah nodded his thanks, realising that Crane would brook no argument so he just put the money in to his pocket. After they had finished speaking Crane reloaded his pistol, he was well and truly in survival mode, Utah noted silently. As expected Juan arrived to claim the bodies, Crane told him that he did not want the horses or anything else. Juan was pleased he said, "It is very good for me, with you in town." Then he asked Crane hopefully, "Will you be staying in town?" Crane shook his head, "Not a chance." He said.

Utah, Crane and Maria made their way back to the livery stable and prepared for the journey ahead, they the saddled their horses. The saddle for the Palomino was hanging on the side of the stall the mare had been stabled in so they had no trouble finding it. Maria went behind the wall and put the new trousers on under her dress.

While she was gone Crane divided the supplies, he spoke to Utah, "We have part company here my friend." Utah responded "No you know that I will ride with you until the end." "I know you would like to be with me ." Said Crane, "But Maria being here changes everything, I can tell you are very taken with each other, we can't risk harm coming to her, so you should take her home and marry her." Utah couldn't argue with Crane's logic, so the two friends shook hands and they hugged each other. Maria came back looking puzzled, so Utah explained what was happening to her, saying, "I would like to marry you and take you home to my farm." Maria smiled it was her turn to hug both men. Then Crane said, "We had better find the Chapel and the priest, otherwise Peter Leonard will give you a really hard time when you get home." Utah laughed and they all agreed. A quick trip to the store again made sure that Utah would not have the same problem as Crane, they bought a ring.

Of course the first and perhaps the only problem came when the priest asked for the names of the couple who wished to be married. Maria had no problem, Maria Gonzales she said, Utah looked helplessly at Crane, "I can't help you with that." Said Crane. "Well it's the first time in about ten years that I have said or heard this name, Fred Liston." Utah blurted out Utah finally admitted. "Well I know a Don Liston," Said Crane. "Never heard of him," replied Utah

When the ceremony was over, Crane had a quiet word with Maria and shook hands with Utah, then Crane mounted Dancer and made ready to ride away. Utah stopped him and tried to give him the $1,500 back. Crane shook his head, "You can call that a wedding present he said, and rode off. Utah and Maria mounted their own horses and rode in the opposite direction leaving the town behind them.. Utah was feeling happy and sad in equal measure. As they rode along Utah said to Maria, "I feel glad, indeed happy to be with you, but I feel I that am letting Crane down." Maria said, "You must not worry, Crane told me that you would feel like this and he said to tell you that he started this alone, that you have helped a lot along the way but it is his destiny to finish this alone." He has to for the memory of his Ma and Pa." "Well I can't argue with that," replied Utah.

CHAPTER 29

Maria and Utah, made their first night camp seven hours later, Maria said, "Now I will cook for you, This will be my first time doing it as your wife. While I am doing that will you unsaddle the hoses." "I like the sound of that" said Utah. After they had eaten their meal the couple sat contentedly drinking coffee. Maria looked at the palomino and said, "Do you know that this is the first horse I have ever had, she is beautiful." Utah replied, "Yes I feel the same about my stallion, once again a he was gift from Crane." "In fact he was Crane's fathers horse, and on top of that he sired Crane's horse Dancer. "Please tell me how you and Crane met," said Maria. "Well" replied Utah "It is not a meeting that I am proud of."

Utah went on to tell her the whole story. He started by telling her about is having been part of Mexican Joe's gang when they attacked Crane in the street when he was a boy in Jacksboro, Utah went past that through the gangs murder of Crane's parents. Then Utah told her how Crane had pursued the gang to try and gain some justice for his parents death, he took the story right to the point where Crane had saved his life. He made little of his own contribution to event by warning Crane of the ambush and the fact that was Utah himself who had shot Mexican

Joe's thumb off.

Maria was amazed, "But Crane really admires you now." She said, "No one would know that you had ever been on the other side from him." "He must have seen the good in you that I see now." Utah put his arm round her and they settled down for the night. Dawn broke and Utah woke up to the smell of coffee and bacon cooking. "He looked across at Maria and smiled, "I think I'm going to enjoy being married to you." Maria smiled back and replied, "I am sure that we both feel the same."

Utah hugged her and kissed her forehead saying, "We will have great times, you are going to have your own brand new cabin, the one we built for Alan and I, is just a basic shelter for two men more like a bunkhouse than a home. "You can choose everything you want to have in it because our friend Peter Leonard, you know the man that Crane and I mentioned, made some fantastic furniture for Crane and Maggie, I am sure he will do the same for us.

Utah and Maria rode side by side chatting about their future, Maria said "It won't upset Alan, you and I being together will it?" "No replied Utah, Alan Crowe is my friend, he will be happy for us." "Plus the fact he gets the cabin we have sharing, to himself." The days went by quickly and without problems and they arrived at Utah' farm one afternoon just before dusk, Utah called out, "Hey Alan, I'm back and I have got a surprise for you,"

Alan came out of the barn, Saying, "Utah if you ain't a sight for sore eyes." He stopped as they rode up to him, He smiled, "That is a mighty pretty Palomino pony the lady is riding, do you want to tell me about it?" Maria and Utah dismounted, Utah said, "Alan, this Maria, she is my wife."

"Well, I am mighty pleased to meet you Maria" replied Alan,. he stepped forward and hugged her, then he stepped back and said to Utah, "You are full of surprises, you left to find Crane and came back with a wife." "I rather think that you have a lot to tell me." "I sure do," replied Utah, "Let's unsaddle we will put the horses in the corral then we will get some food and then I'll bring you right up to date. "The main thing I have to tell you is that Crane is still alive, and is still hounding Mexican Joe.

While Utah and Alan attended to the horses Maria got supper on the go. Later on as the three of them sat round the table, Utah told Alan about al the events that had taken place, since he had headed out after Crane. Utah went on to explain how Maria had come into his life and how her coming into his life had meant Crane and Utah had to ride different trails, "You see Crane just wouldn't risk Maria's life by letting her ride with him after Mexican Joe."

Alan said, "The thing is Crane lives by a set of rules that mean women and children must always be protected and treated with respect." "It doesn't matter if that belief puts his own life at risk he will live and die by that code. Alan said, "We would all do well to follow him in that belief." Utah nodded his agreement, "It was a good day for all of us when Crane came into our lives." "Right" said Alan, "I am moving myself in the barn." "That's good of you" said Utah, "I will be staring to build a new cabin for Maria and I tomorrow, on the rise behind the trees at the back of this cabin. "This is your home not ours, you have spent more time in it than me, so it is yours by right. "Well that is mighty generous of you," Replied Alan, "I would have been happy to sleep in the barn."

In the morning after the had all enjoyed a good breakfast Utah said to Alan, "I'm leaving you with all the work again, because I'm going into town with Maria. She really needs to buy some clothes at Neil and Maureen's Store. Then I will need to stop at the sawmill, I will need Jubal and George Thomas to help on the building of the new cabin. Also I need to see Maggie, I have to explain to her that I couldn't keep my promise to bring Crane home safe to her. I'm sure she will understand" replied Alan, "She will know that Crane is his own man and that he will always doe things his own way."

When Utah's stallion and Maria's mare were saddled, the two of them mounted up and rode out. As they were riding Utah said to Maria, "We need to go to Crane's farm first, I have to see Maggie and tell her about Crane." "OK" replied Maria, "I want to meet all your friends." "They are going to be your friends as well, in fact we are all more than friends, we are family. As they rode Utah showed Maria various landmarks. Maria was blown away by the lush pasture, the groves of trees and abundant water supply, "Wow" She said, "This is beautiful land that you have, not like the dirt farm my parents scratched a living on, I have never seen anything like it." "My share of this land is your share as well ," Replied Utah, "You are my wife the farm is ours." Maria smiled happily. Before long they were in sight of Crane's place, Utah was worried that Maggie would feel that he had let Crane down, by coming home with Maria. So it as with some apprehension that he rode into the yard with Maria at his side, When they had both dismounted. Maggie came out of the cabin, with a smile on her face. "Utah" she said, "does this mean that Crane has come home? Crane is fine, but he just couldn't come home yet, he wouldn't let me stay because of Maria." "This is Maria she is my wife now, I need to tell you all about it." By this time Flo and Fred had come across from their cabin, Utah introduced them to Maria and they all went into the cabin and sat down. Then they all congratulated Maria and Utah.

Utah told them about Maria's parents, then he told them about how Maria and he came to be married. He also told them about the three men that Mexican Joe had paid to kill Crane, Utah continued to explain that he had still wanted to ride with Crane, but that Crane had been adamant that Maria would not be safe if they went on together. Then Utah said, "I know I promised to bring Crane home safe and I know that I have let you down."

Maggie, smiled and said, Utah, you are a good friend and we all know that Crane knows his own mind, you have nothing to apologise for" Then she said "We are very pleased to meet you Maria, we are all family in this valley, so welcome to the family." Maggie said, "I must tell you about Dave Selley, "What a man he is, If it hadn't been for him Big John and I wouldn't have got home." She told them the whole story, about how the robbers had got the drop on them and how even after he had taken a bullet himself, Dave had saved Big Johns life.

While they were talking Joey and Jim Cassidy came in and they were delighted to meet Maria and more than pleased to hear that she had married Utah. Utah said "I am mighty glad you have taken things that way, now Maria and I need to get into town and start the arrangements for building the new cabin."As they rode away Maria and

Utah, were feeling much happier, it was good to know that there was no ill feeling about Utah coming home without Crane. They stopped at the sawmill and brought the Thomas brothers up to date and told them both what they needed. Jubal said it was a good day for us when you and your friends came the valley, we ain't never had so much work.

Then Utah said "We must go and see Peter Leonard and his wife Lynda, we will need their help with the fancy work and the furniture"

As they rode up to the church, they saw that Peter was outside on a ladder putting the finishing touches to a cross over the door. He looked down at them, "Good to see you Utah, I see you have brought a new member of the congregation for me." Utah, smiled, "This is my wife, Marie" he said. "We would like you to make some of that fine furniture, like you made for Crane for our new cabin." Peter sprang athletically down from the ladder, "I would be happy to, he said, "But first come into the Church and we will pray together for God to bless your union." Utah thought of, saying no because he had many things to do in town but he knew that resistance was futile so they both dismounted and followed Peter into the church.

Peter and his wife Lynda, who cleaning the church were effusive in the welcome they gave Maria and then they prayed together and Peter, gave them a lecture on the sanctity of marriage, assuring them that a road travelled together would be more rewarding than one travelled alone. Then Peter said prayers for Maria's parents, he told her that they were already happy in the house of the Lord and that they would all meet again on that glorious day.

Then they all prayed for Crane's safe return. After that Utah and Maria thanked him and Lynda and then took their leave.

As they rode further into town Maria said to Utah, "I can't believe how welcome your friends have been making me." "I never doubted them," Replied Utah. "We have all been through a lot together, we are like family and you are part of the family." "They pulled up outside Neil and Maureen's store and dismounted, stepped up on to the side walk and went in, Maureen saw them first, she was talking with and serving Doreen Eckert. "She and Doreen came over to Utah and Maria, "Utah you're home safe," she looked at Maria, saying, "That is good to see, and who is this fine lady that you've brought with you?" "This is my wife Maria," Utah replied proudly." "I would like it if you would outfit her with all the fripperies and everything that she will need." "Come along with me said Maureen, I will help you choose, so will I said Doreen, the three ladies went to the feminine apparel section of the store, chatting to each other as they went.

Neil came through from the back in the company of Dave Selley who was walking with the aid of a stick, thanks to his leg wound, "Howdy Utah, what is the news on Crane?" They asked. "He is good" Replied Utah, "But he sent me home when Maria," he gestured towards where the three ladies were standing, "And I got married," Dave and Neil shook hands vigorously with Utah, "Congratulation" the y called to Maria, "We ain't even met you yet, but we know how good you are going to be for this old cuss." Utah said, "I want to shake your hand again Dave, Maggie told me what a warrior you are, I just want to say that I always knew that you were and so did Crane that is why he wanted you and John to take Maggie home." "My mistake was thinking you wouldn't have the stamina to make the ride with me to join Crane, I'm sorry for that because I was wrong." "You don't have to apologise, I wasn't sure I could do it myself, but I knew I had to." "As usual he made light of the part that he had played in protecting Maggie. So Utah said, "We will have a new cabin Maria and I, Crane won't be here to see it built because he is still trailing after Mexican Joe." Dave replied, "If it wasn't for this damned leg I would go after Crane again, but this time I really wouldn't make it." "No" said Utah but I would and I have been thinking about going back down to Mexico." "Funny you should say that because the Comanche brave Rides the Wind has been saying the same." "Mind you" said Dave "I don't think your lovely new wife will be pleased about you going back down there.." "No I suppose you are right" replied Utah. "What is this Rides the Wind's reason for going to help Crane?" "Well he says that it is a matter of honour, because Crane saved his wife, child and him and for that reason he is determined to go." "Right Neil," said Utah, outfit me for a trip to Mexico, enough for two men." "Now why am I not surprised to hear that" ? Asked Dave. Maria and Utah picked up their packages, some of Maria's clothes would be delivered when Neil Maureen and Dave came out to help with the cabin. As they rode back through town, Utah said to Maria, "I'm sorry but I have to go back and help Crane." "I know" Maria replied, "Maureen, Doreen and I were talking about it." "I would rather you didn't go but I know you will never be happy if you stay." "Amazing,"Replied Utah, "You already know me so well."

They stopped outside John Eckert's Barber shop, he came out, "Utah" he said, "You are back," "Yes but I am going again, I just wanted you to meet my wife Maria, before I went." "Good to meet you" said John, "I just met your wife in the store," replied Maria, "she was very kind to me." Larry came out of the shop, he had been in for a haircut, "I think it is my turn to take a trip to Mexico" he said, "I will ask Joey to look after the livery stable for me." "OK" said Utah I think we will ride out from Crane's farm in the morning, three horses apiece so that we make good time." Then he said "I will have to find Rides the Wind on our way back now." When Utah and Maria reached Crane's farm Rides the Wind was there, he was catching up his Appaloosa ready to make his journey, Joey saw Utah and came over to the corral "Utah" He said this is "Rider, Rider, meet Utah." "Howdy" said Utah. "It is mighty good to meet the brother of my brother Crane" Replied Rider. "If you don't mind we will go to Mexico together Rider," Said Utah, "Larry is going to ride with us." "This is good" replied Rider, "Crane is on his own, he is a great warrior but he is still on his own, I know he would come for us if we needed him, so you are right, we must go to him." "We will do what Big John did, take three horses apiece and ride night and day." One thing we won't wear the horses out, like Big John did, because he weighs a much as the three of us put together." They all laughed a lot at that remark.

Rider said, "This is a problem for me," I only have one horse." Fred had come over to see what was happening, He spoke, "That just ain't so Rider, when Crane sent you us you became part of the family, everything that is ours, also belongs to you." "So every horse on this farm belongs to you and me and everyone." "So you pick two of the best horses that you can find." Anyway have you forgotten you were leading three horse when you arrived here, so that would be four horses anyway. Joey said I just brought two fine strong bays in off the range, they are there in the corral you must take those ." Rider, said, "You have my thanks" said Rider, "and I must also say that you are a good judge of horseflesh, Joey."

"Right now that is sorted out I'm going home" said Utah, "I will be back in the morning, if you don't mind I will leave the supplies for our trip here in the barn tonight." "We have will have to ride home now Maria and explain to Alan that all the work round our place is on him again." Maria waved to Flo and Maggie and then she and Utah rode out of the yard. They made good time and when they got back to their farm they found Alan waiting for them with supper on the stove.

Utah said, "I have something to tell you Alan." "I know" said Alan, "Don't tell me, You are going out after Crane to help him again." "How did you know that?" Asked Utah, "You are loyal and a good friend, you would do the same for me, the best thing I can do is look after things here, otherwise I would ride with you." Replied Alan "Thank you" said Utah. "I wouldn't leave Maria here if you weren't here to take care of her." Enough said" replied Alan. They ate their supper and discussed the new cabin. "You must have everything the way you want it, Maria, just tell the guys how you want the cabin built and what furniture you would like" said Utah. "I know you are going to make us a lovely home." Maria just smiled and nodded. The following morning Utah saddled his stallion and led his other two horses out of the corral. Maria and Alan had their horses saddled and they all rode out to Crane;s ranch together. Alan said, "I thought it best to come and bring Maria home rather than let her ride back alone" "Good man" said Utah. They arrived at Crane's farm and Larry and Rider were ready to go. The supplies had been split into three gunny sacks, one had been fastened to Rider's saddle and one to Larry's so they fastened on the other one on to Utah's saddle. Maggie said, "You make sure you give Crane my love, and all of you come home safe." The three men nodded, then they said their goodbyes and rode out.

CHAPTER 30

Crane was frustrated because he still hadn't found Mexican Joe. He had got to Manuel Cardoza's ranch and found that house and barns had been burned down. Manuel Cardoza had his arm in a sling. When Crane asked him about Mexican Joe he was told, "That man is crazy, he shot me and burned my home, then he rode out with more than half my Vaquero's." When he heard Cardoza's tale of woe Crane decided that his best choice would be to ride back to Laredo and find out what he could about Mexican Joe's current whereabouts.

When Crane got back to Laredo he called in on the town sheriff, he left Bruno outside with the untethered Dancer. Crane walked across the side walk he opened the door and went into the office. Crane's eyes swept round the room when he entered the office, The sheriff spoke, saying, "You are a man I never wanted to see again." Crane just nodded. There were two deputies in the office they stood up and moved either side of Crane. The sheriff spoke again, "I think you should turn in your pistols while you are in my town." Crane looked at him, "Does this rule apply to everyone who comes town?" Asked Crane. "No I have made this rule just for you." The sheriff replied "So what you are asking me to do is commit suicide?" Crane responded. "Well I must say that I wouldn't be sorry if you died" Said the sheriff." "So I suggest that you hand those pistols to my deputies, we have you out manned and out gunned." Crane looked at him, "So how much did Mexican Joe pay you for setting me up like this" ? "More than enough!" The sheriff sneered. Crane stepped back across the floor and closed the door. Then he locked it, by fastening the bolt across it. The sheriff and his two deputies looked at each other in disbelief.

There was a moments delay and then two deputies went for their pistols, but they were a day late and a dollar short, Crane's pistol's leapt into his hands as if by magic. Remarkably Crane shot the deputies pistols from their hands, one guy lost a thumb the other lost his trigger finger. Crane looked over at the sheriff who was still sitting in his chair. "Please get up" Said Crane as he re holstered his pistols, "Because I always believe in giving a sucker an even break." The sheriff stood up very slowly, "You can't make me draw on you Crane" He said. "I wouldn't dream of it" Replied Crane.

"Look I will give you the money Mexican Joe gave me" said the sheriff and he reached in his pocket. As his hand came out of his pocket it was clear there was a weapon in his hand he levelled that weapon at Crane. But once again he was too slow because a bullet from Crane's right hand pistol went into his shoulder. The derringer he had reached in to his pocket for fell from his fingers as he fell back over his chair. Crane came round the desk and opened the drawers, in the top right hand drawer he saw a wad of money without hesitation he took the money out and put it in his pocket. Always alert Crane reloaded his right hand pistol and then his left, returning them both to their holsters. "Then Crane looked down at the sheriffs derringer and picked it up, I seen better men than you use one of these," He said. Without saying another word Crane went to the door unlocked it slid the bolt back then he opened the door and he walked out of the office without a backward glance.

As he walked down the street, with Dancer plodding beside him on one side and Bruno on the other Crane felt the eyes of the townsfolk on him. All the people stepped aside as he went past them. When Crane got to the saloon he went inside walking through the bat winged doors. Crane stopped as he viewed the room and people in it, seemingly satisfied with what he saw carried on walking over to the end of the bar, when he got there he stood with his back to the bar so that he faced the room. The bartender asked him "What will it be?" "Nothing I just want to know if anyone has seen Mexican Joe" Crane said "Can any of you tell me if he has been back in town lately?" "I wouldn't tell you if he had" The bartender replied.

Crane raised his voice, "$50 for the man who points me towards Mexican Joe." No one took him up on his offer, so he thought to himself, my next port of call is Mexican Joe's house. Before Crane had moved away from the bar a tall lean man came into the saloon, he walked over to Crane then he spoke, "I take it that you are Crane?" "That's right." Crane replied. "Well I'm Johnny Boone." As he spoke the man pulled his jacket to one side, to show a badge, I'm a captain the Texas Rangers,I have sent here to investigate allegations of corruption in the sheriff's office. "Why should that interest me?." Asked Crane. "Well it's lucky for you I have already proved that corruption, so I won't be taking you in for shooting the sheriff and his deputies. I left the three of them in the cells receiving medical attention." "Lucky for me, is it?" said Crane, "That remains to be seen."

Crane looked at him, "The question I am asking is what do you want with me?" "Let's take a seat and I will buy you a drink." The ranger replied. Crane shook his head saying, "I don't drink." They found a seat anyway one where Crane could keep his back to the wall, "Well talk to me?" Crane said. Captain Boone replied, "I want to induct you into the Texas Rangers, I have heard about you over the years and you fit the bill." "We want you as a ranger because we want Mexican Joe as well. The man has been on the loose for to long, to make matters worse he has killed the last five Texas Rangers that we sent out after him ." Crane looked thoughtful, then he spoke, "I don't think I am the man for you. "I just want to kill the son of Satan and go home."

"I can live with that" Said Captain Johnny Boone, "The plus points for you are that there is no chance of you getting stopped by the law, because you will be the law and you get wages, 50 cents a day, when you get the chance to collect it ." Crane laughed saying, "I could get more than that punching cows." "Then again I was going to pick up the reward money when I get Mexican Joe." "Well you can't do that as a Texas Ranger," replied Captain Boone. "I guess we will have to cross that bridge when we get to it." Said Crane. Going on to say, "I want it in writing that I ride home after I get Mexican Joe, you don't try to hold me in the Texas Rangers." Captain Boone agreed. Saying "If you can do this job you will deserve to go home."

Captain Boone took a rangers badge out of his pocket

then he pinned it on Crane's shirt and swore him in. Crane took the badge off his shirt and put it in his pocket, "I don't like targets Captain, they can get you killed," he said. The Captain nodded, "I don't like titles, so you can call me Johnny." The two men got up and walked out of the saloon, mounted their horses and rode down the street. Together. They were heading for Mexican Joe's house, when they got to the house they made a cautious entry through the front door, Bruno went in first The place was empty,there was nothing there that offered any clues as to Mexican Joe's present whereabouts. Crane said, "I think we will go up to the livery stable and see Juan." "We may get some information there." They went out remounted their horses and rode up to the livery stable. They got lucky when they got there because three men were beating on Juan and another twenty men led by Mexican Joe were still mounted, watching the three men hand out the beating.

Crane shot the two men who were holding Juan up, before Mexican Joe even cleared leather. When he finally did get his pistol out he shot the guy doing the beating, "Another failure" Joe screamed. The other riders drew their pistols, but Dancer was in full flight by this time and he was heading straight for them, everything happened very fast because as Crane knew, if you stand still in a pistol fight you die. His quick movements saved the Ranger Captain's life because the nearest rider was sighted on him, but just as he was pulling trigger Dancer collided with him and his horse, this caused his bullet to fly wide and in that instant, the rider died under Dancer's hooves.

As usual Mexican Joe whirled his horse and ran fleeing through the crowd of panicked horses and riders. Crane was firing both his pistols right and left, Dancer was plunging and rearing and horses and riders were falling underneath him. The Ranger Captain was picking off the fallen riders who were able to continue the fight. Bruno was wreaking havoc among the fallen always going for the pistol hand The mounted riders fled the scene, because Crane and his Devil horse ably abetted by his dog were striking fear and panic into them all.

Crane jumped down from Dancer and began reloading. Johnny said, "My God I can hardly believe my eyes, I heard stories about on the trail and in some of the towns but I only half believed those stories, but you the dog and that horse are terrifying. I can tell you I fought at Bull Run and I never took a backward step, but if you charged me on that horse, I'm sure that I would turn and run." Crane just shook his head and went to look after the badly beaten Juan.

Dancer and Bruno followed him and Crane took the canteen from his saddle and after removing the cap he splashed water on Juan's face. Juan groaned and sat up,. "Why did Mexican Joe have his men do that to you" Crane asked. "This was the first time he came back since you took your wife from his house and when he found that she was gone he blamed me." Juan replied. Crane helped him to his feet saying, "Well you are still alive so it seems to have worked out well for you. There will be six funerals and there are four horses that haven't run and you get their saddles" I'm making you rich man." Then he went to each fallen rider and checked their pockets, $973 and few cents he took $500 of it, and gave rest to Juan. He looked at the Ranger Captain, "I have to make my expenses somehow."

He said. Captain Johnny Boone looked at him, "I wouldn't argue with you about money or anything else." He said.

Crane looked at the weaponry dropped by the fallen men none of it impressed him until he saw a short rifle with a revolving chamber below the barrel, he picked it up hefted it, reload it with .44 shells. Then he saw the scabbard for it hanging from one of the saddles on the standing horses so he unbuckled it and took it over to Dancer and fastened it to his saddle. He put the short rifle in the scabbard. "So then," Said Johnny as he watched Crane he was thinking about the future, "What do we do next?" Crane said, the first thing I'm going to do is leave Dancer here for the night." "I'll be sleeping here myself, Juan I don't expect you will be charging us."

Crane led Dancer to the water trough and let him drink his fill and then he took him to a stall and unsaddled him and rubbed him down. He saw Johnny doing the same thing with his horse. He called Juan over saying, "Please give both horses a feed of oats he said, no charge for the Captain here either." When he got close to him Crane noticed that one of Dancer's shoes had come loose, so he said, "Is there a Blacksmith in town?" "Yes, Seth, he works out at the back"

Crane took Dancer through the stable and out to the back of the stable. When he got to the forge, he saw a huge black man working there, his arms were as big as a normal sized man's leg's and he must have weighed 300lbs and was Crane guessed, about six feet nine inches. Crane spoke to him, "Seth, my name is Crane" he said, "Would you shoe my horse for me please ?" Seth looked at Dancer then he stepped forward and gently rubbed Dancer's forehead, speaking quietly to him, Dancer lowered his head and nuzzled Seth's chest. Crane was amazed to see this, no one but Crane himself had ever been able to get so close to Dancer. Then quickly and efficiently Seth set about changing the shoe, then he checked the other shoes and trimmed Dancer's hooves for him. Crane offered to pay for the work, but Seth refused saying, "No thank you, for two reasons, one you said please, people never say please to me." "Two, It is a privilege to work with a horse like yours who is full of spirit and allowed a mind of his own. Crane said, "Well please Seth come and eat with us." Seth nodded and said, "I would be pleased to eat with you." The two men shook hands then Crane went back in to the stable.

Crane brought Dancer back to his stall, then he asked "Juan, do you have paper and pencil around here "? Juan nodded then he went away and came back with the items. Crane said right Captain, write up the duration of my time in the Rangers, and sign it. "Make sure it's right because I can read." "I wouldn't try and cheat you Crane." Replied the Captain. Crane said, "This way there is no room for manoeuvre and I like it that way." Seth walked up to him while he was talking Crane added, "By the way Johnny this is Seth, he will be eating with us." Then Johnny and Seth shook hands and then Johnny wrote down the words that Crane had asked him to.

Seth the Captain and Crane headed for the Cantina. When they got there they all went in and sat down, Crane as always sitting with his back to the wall he spoke saying, "The food, here is not bad at all" said Crane. Just as they were about to order the door opened and three men who Crane was mighty pleased to see. Utah, Rider and Larry came up to the table and sat down with smiles on their faces. "We knew you were here" said Utah, "Juan at the livery stable told us when we were stabling the horses." Right said Crane, This is Seth, and Captain Johnny Boone, Texas Rangers, please meet Utah, Larry and my brother Rider." There were handshakes all round as the waiter approached the table."

Crane said "We will all have steaks, including the water for the dog, no trimmings with his steak and a pot of coffee. Crane paused, looking at the waiters face, "You know that you serve my dog, don't you?" "The dog is not the problem." Replied the waiter, "We don't serve Negro's or Indians in here," he looked at Rider, and Seth, then he said "Get out!." Crane stood up, then he stepped out from behind the table "You serve me he said, I am Crane, I am a Comanche and Rides the Wind is my brother as is Seth, he is Seth Crane." The waiter stepped back, "I will bring the food, I didn't know." Crane said, "But first I am sure you wish to apologise to my brothers" The waiter nodded, then he looked at Seth and Rider, "I am sorry" he said and rushed back to the kitchen.

All the men ate their food and talked about what had happened to them and in the case of Rider, Utah and Larry gave Crane news of home. Crane was pleased to have Maggie's message of love and really appreciated Utah leaving his new wife and setting out once more to help him. He also thanked Rider for leaving his wife and new baby. Crane was most surprised and pleased that Larry had come. From the day I came to your livery stable, you have been a good friend then when I brought Utah in with his broken leg you proved that you could be relied on but I never expected you to come to Texas and help me.." Larry said, "you know that the feeling is mutual." They all decided to sleep at the stables. With the exception of the Captain who said, "I have to sleep at the jail until the federal marshal arrives to take over the running of the town."

In the morning, when the horses were saddled and canteens were filled, Crane said, "Larry you and Utah should go the store for supplies, Here is the money he handed Larry $25. Then he said "The rest of us will go to the sheriff's office and talk to Johnny." As they were talking Seth came through the barn leading a huge plough horse, It was saddled and bridled, clearly it was the only horse that could possibly carry Seth. Crane spoke to him, "Where are you going Seth?" He asked. "With you, Crane." "Why" Asked Crane. "You stood for me as you would for any other man, I will be there for you always as the brother you claimed to be. "I won't disrespect you by saying that it would be dangerous" Replied Crane, "What I will say is that I would be proud to have you ride with me." "You got it," Said Seth. They all mounted up, then Juan spoke, "I hope you come back soon Crane, if you do I will get rich very quick." "Sorry Juan," Replied Crane, "I really hope that I never have to ride to Laredo again."

The Crane Gang because that is what they had become rode to the sheriff's office, Utah and Larry turned left and went to the store for supplies. Crane stopped, "Do you have a firearm Seth? He asked. "No Seth replied, I have never needed one." "You will if you ride with me" said Crane. Reaching down his horse Dancer, Crane unfastened the short rifle he had recently acquired and handed it to Seth. "Seth took it, took the rifle out of it's scabbard and examined put it back, saying "Thank you." Then he fastened the short rifle to his belt." On him the rifle hardly looked bigger than a pistol. Crane dismounted and took a length of piggin string from his saddle bag he went over to Seth, as he went over he drew his throwing knife he reached up to the end of the scabbard and holding it with one hand pierced the leather he threaded the piggin string thou the hole. He put the knife away and said, "Tie it round your thigh when you dismount then the rifle won't flap around when you are walking." Seth thanked him, stepped down and tied it off, then they both remounted.

As they both remounted they heard gunfire up the street, so all of them, Rider Crane and Seth took off at the gallop with Bruno at a full run. As they neared the sheriff's office they saw that it was under siege. Rider and Crane got there first. There nine men were firing on the jail, clearly only one was returning fire from inside the office, but he had shot one of his attackers down. Bruno shot forward he seized a man by the throat, he savaged him let go and caught another by the shoulder. Crane's pistols were in his hands, he fired and two men fell. Riders Henry rifle took another one down, then they were on top of them. As Crane leapt from the saddle Dancer trampled someone under foot as Crane shouted "I'm coming in Johnny" hitting the door on the run, Crane burst through the door falling flat, he rolled to the side hearing Riders rifle boom twice behind him. Then he heard the rapid fire that had to be coming from Seth's short rifle. Crane came to his feet to see the fight was over. Johnny was down bleeding from a leg and a shoulder wound. Crane sent Seth for the doctor because he knows his way round the town and Rider doesn't. "What happened here, Johnny?" Crane asked the wounded Captain. "Turns out the sheriff and his deputies are all Mexican Joe's men, so he sent these guy's to get them out, they would have got the job done if you three hadn't turned up." Johnny replied.

Utah and Larry had arrived and were helping Rider herd the wounded men back into the cells. When the doctor arrived he tended to Johnny's wounds first, telling him, "You are going to be laid up for a while. "Well Crane" said Johnny, "I'm sorry but as your Captain I have to ask you to stay here and guard the prisoners until the US Marshall arrives." Utah said "Captain, what the hell is going on here." "Crane is a Texas Ranger until we catch Mexican Joe, so I need him for this duty." Replied Johnny. "Unbelievable I go home for a few days and everything changes" "I know that Crane is the ultimate lone wolf and now I find that he is part of the most important group of law enforcement agencies in the Texas. "I look forward to hearing how this came about" said Utah. Johnny smiled ruefully saying, "Well, Utah,there is no real explanation, I just got lucky." Crane took up the conversation saying, "I did not expect this turn of events but, I gave Johnny my word and I took the fifty cents a day. So that means I will have to stay here for as long as I am needed. I would suggest Utah that you, Rider and Larry ride out and see if you can pick up any news of Mexican Joe's whereabouts." "If you find anything out, please bring the information back to me, that information may save us a good deal of time later." "Do not for any reason at all try to take Mexican Joe on without me." "You've got it." Said Utah. The he laughed saying, "Fifty cents a day? I have heard it all now you can't get a cup of coffee for that, what a good deal,"

Some time later it was decided that Larry and Utah would be the ones that would ride out and look for Mexican Joe, Seth and Rider would stay in town with Crane. "But remember you two must not take Mexican Joe and his gang on, under any circumstances." Said Crane. "Agreed" his two friends replied. "Right" said Crane "So all being well we will see you in about a week." "I think that we had better leave will leave our spare horses here" said Utah, "We will also leave half the supplies with you." With these verbal arrangements in place Larry an Utah mounted their horses and left town. Rider said "I will take the spare horses back to the corral at the livery stable." "Good idea," replied Crane.

Juan arrived, very excited because more work for his undertaking business, "I told you, you are going to make me a rich man Señor Crane." "In return for this I promise you will get a fine free funeral if I bury you." Crane smiled, "Well thank you Juan, that is an offer I've never had before." Seth said "I will go and get some of Juan's timber I with that can make some bunk beds for the three of us to sleep on, because there is there is no room for us in the cells so we can bed down in the office." "There will only be a small charge for the wood" said Juan. Seth stepped forward and picked Juan up by the back of his jacket, he was dangling him in the air, with his feet well clear of the floor "Of course, of course, there will be no charge for the wood" Juan stuttered. Seth nodded and put Juan down and then he set about helping him by putting the bodies of the fallen on to the cart that Juan had arrived on.

By nightfall Seth had built the bunks and made mattresses

from sacks filled with straw. Johnny was propped up one of the bunks, the doctor had removed the bullets from his wounds. The wounds had been dressed and although Johnny was feeling weak he was feeling much better. The Cantina had sent a boy over with food for Crane, Seth, Rider, Johnny and the prisoners. This apparently was an ongoing arrangement that had set up by previous sheriffs. The amount of food provided dependant on the number of people at the jail Breakfast and evening meal would be brought in. The payment came out the stipend paid to the sheriff by the townsfolk. As the resident law man Captain Johnny Boone was temporarily in receipt of the stipend. As he was still there in spite of his wounds, there was no need to change the arrangement. After they had all eaten their food Crane spoke, "I should have known better than to sign with you Johnny, based on past experience it could take five years to catch Mexican Joe at this rate." "I want to get home and be with my wife and daughter." "As it is I could waste time, for no other reason than the fact that I signed up to be a Ranger and I could be with you for months" "But I am telling you now I won't be spending years as a Ranger and I assure you, that I will fight the Rangers as hard as you've seen me fight anyone if the Texas Rangers make the mistake of coming after me.

Johnny said, "Please Crane, don't let us get ahead of ourselves, I won't let this situation come to that." "You are a good man and the Texas Rangers have enough outlaws to go chasing after, without us turning you into one." "I think Mexican Joe could even come back to Laredo if he thinks you have left town. "I won't hold my breath waiting for that to happen." Replied Crane. Then Rider spoke saying,

"We will just have to wait for Larry and Utah to get in touch, I am sure they will find news of Mexican Joe."

As they days went by Crane, Seth and Rider and Johnny got to know each other very well. Seth told his new friends that he had been born into slavery before the war between the North and South of the country. He went on to say his life had been miserable because, apart from being treated to harsh punishment, he had been sold away from his parents at the age of eight, he never saw or heard of them again. He had never been able to find a trace of their whereabouts, although he had tried to look for them after the war. Seth said "I had a brother and sister but again I had no idea if they are dead or alive." When he was set free after the war, he just had just drifted finding nothing hearing from nobody, so he had finally settled in Laredo because as he said himself, "It was as good as place as anywhere else." He told them that his name was not really Seth saying, "I made the choice because from the beginning of my life to being sold away from my parents I remembered that the name I had been called was Otis. Then he said, "My new owners had called me Seth and I found that I preferred Seth." Going on he said "I am immensely proud to be your brother Crane." "I will be Seth Crane for the rest of my life."

Crane replied, "let me assure you that I am just as proud to be a brother to you and Rider." Then he asked Seth, "Where do you intend to go when we have finished the mission to get Mexican Joe, Seth?" Seth shrugged his massive shoulders then he said, "Who knows? somewhere, anywhere it does not matter." Crane shook his head saying, "That won't do, We, Rider, Utah Larry and all the others you haven't met yet, would like it if you came with us and settled on our place in our valley." Rider nodded, "Yes we would like that, it is a good place to live." He said. Seth replied, as he hugged both men in turn, "I would not want to live in any other place."

The three men agreed that Seth coming to the valley was a great idea then after a few moments the conversation turned to Rider's life before he had been as he put it, "Herded on to the Reservation." His life had been wonderful he said. "He said that his life was good because his tribe had Summer and Winter homes they were a happy people. The reason for that happiness was that the land gave them all they needed and living as they did was a good learning ground for a young lad who was eager to be a warrior." He described himself saying, It seems that I was born to be fast in everything that I did." So father called me Rides the Wind. "It soon became clear that I could run faster than the other young lads." "For some reason every horse I ever got on ran faster with me on their backs. There was something else that actually puzzled him he said, "I had a speed of thought that led me to a good decision making when hunting, or in later years in battle." "So" he said "that explains why he was called *Rides the Wind*," but now he said he was glad, indeed proud to able to add the name Crane to his own. Johnny said, "This is turning out to be a real love-in, I can't wait to hear your story Crane."

So Crane told them about his own childhood and in telling them that he told them how he had been blessed with the most wonderful parents. He went on to tell them, how every day was hard work but it was worth all the hard work because there was always something to show for it. He told them of his quick and unreasonable temper, of his father and mothers' love and patience in teaching him to read and write and most all teaching him the important values in life, such as being honest, having integrity and being loyal to friends and family. "That is the way I continue to try and live my life." Said Crane. "The operative word" he said, "being try." Crane then went on explain about his first meeting with Mexican Joe and how his parents had been murdered. Then he told of his reaction to what had happened, how he had shot the Jacksboro sheriff and then burning own his home and riding on the vengeance trail. He could have said more but he left it at that. There was nothing more for any of them to say they sat in silence, This had been the very first time Crane had really spoken on the subject. He paused deep in thought and then after a few moments, he said, "If I don't make it back alive, you two must still live in the valley, make the valley your home." Rider said, "You must make it back Crane, Maggie and Mae need you." The subject was then just left alone, because they all knew that living his life the way he did, Crane was always just one bullet away from the end of it. In one respect things changed very quickly after about ten days, the first thing that happened was that a tall determined man with quick movements and fast hands rode into town on a stocky strong bay mare. You could just tell from the horses stride that it would travel far and eat up the miles every day. This man as wearing two pistols in the cross draw style and he had a badge on his chest. He came into the sheriffs office, saying, "I'm looking for a Captain John Boone, of the Texas Rangers, is he here "? Johnny back on his feet at last hobbled forward, "That would be me." "He said" "Good," the man replied, I am Marshal Chris Evans, "I've come to take over the office here until the town elects a new sheriff" He looked at the crowed cell area, "Another thing," he said, "The circuit judge will be here next week to try the former sheriff and his deputies."

He looked a Crane who had risen to his feet, "Well now who might you be" he asked," "Crane" was the reply. "Really, I've heard tell of you, a stone cold killer by all accounts, I expect I will have to take you down before I leave here." Seth spoke, "You would play hell trying to do that." Bruno who had been lying quietly at Crane's feet growled his hackles rising. "Down Bruno" said Crane, the big dog complied lying down by the side of Crane, he still continued growling. "Marshall Evans said, I will silence that dog, the surly mutt. Evan's right hand flew in a blur and drew his left hand pistol, his right hand came across he was intending to fan the hammer. It never got near to the pistol because Evans was howling with pain as his pistol flew out his hand. There three shots in quick succession the second and third shots sent his pistol spinning through the air. The pistol finally came to rest on the side walk outside the office door. Evans looked in disbelief into Crane's face, He spoke saying, "You broke my God damned trigger finger." Ryder spoke, "You are lucky that is all he did, Crane didn't start to draw until you pistol was halfway clear of leather, he fired both his pistols just as your pistol came clear, he hit your pistol with all three shots." "If he was the stone cold killer you said he was you would be dead now." Evans blustered, "I could arrest you,and anyway you blind sided me, no one can outdraw me." Crane who was reloading his pistols said, "Please try, you have another pistol." He put both of his pistols away and stood looking at Evans. Johnny spoke saying, "Marshal Evans," Crane is a Texas Ranger, and you do not have jurisdiction over a Texas Ranger who is in pursuit of his duty, I won't be responsible for what happens to you if you draw on Crane again."

Crane spoke again, "I've seen show boats like you before, you strut round proud as a peacock carrying two guns, but you can only use them one at a time." "Let me tell you this, if you want to stay alive you need to work on getting the proper use of one sorted out." He continued, There are many men who can draw and fire a pistol faster than me, there are even more who are faster than you. "There will be another time, I will take you down" said Evans, "Not if you are facing me" replied Crane, then he said "Oh you should know that if you do succeed in back shooting me, my dog or my horse will kill you." "If they don't," said Ryder, standing there with a look as cold as ice, "There are a few of us who will line up to do the job." "You are a fool Evans" said Johnny, "I don't know how long you have been a Marshall but unless you change your attitude quickly you won't last long."

Seth picked up the Marshall's pistol, "This is scrap metal now" he said. Then he directed the Marshall to the doctors office to get his finger set. After Evans left the office Crane spoke saying, "It beats me the differences that there are in the people who wear a badge. Most of them in my experience are brave and honest men, who do the job with pride and dignity." "Many, indeed most of them are not good with a pistol but they are trustworthy and reliable." "Then it seems that you get the crooked few like that guy in there he pointed at the Larado sheriff, and the clowns like this Marshall." "When the history of the west is written, I would like to think it will be the good guys who are remembered."

The second thing that happened was that later that day was that Larry and Utah arrived back in Larado with news of Mexican Joe. Utah said, "Mexican Joe and his gang have robbed the bank in Jacksboro they killed the teller and two passers by. He also shot and wounded your friend the sheriff, Don Liston, now I know where you know the name from, he added. Larry took up the story saying, "After he robbed the bank it seems that Mexican Joe headed for his ranch The Triple X to lie up for a while. "Right" said Crane, "It is time for us to hit the trail." The five friends, Seth, Larry, Rider, Utah and Crane gathered their supplies, and made ready to leave."

Johnny spoke saying, It was good to meet you guys, By the way Crane, don't forget if you do take Mexican Joe, as a Texas Ranger you can't claim the reward." "I know I can't," said Crane, but Utah can and he will." Johnny smiled and nodded, "I knew that you would find a way round it." Crane touched the brim of his hat and the five riders headed out on what they hoped would be the final leg of their journey, to take Mexican Joe down Bruno trotting behind them.

CHAPTER 31

They made good time and when they made camp on the second night, Crane said, "I know that we will make the Triple X Ranch tomorrow, having been there before I think we should come in from four sides and take them by surprise, because they might be expecting me but not you three." They agreed that it was a good idea and bedded down for the night, each man was lost in his own thoughts. In the morning they all saddled up and rode out. When they were about half a mile from the ranch, Utah spoke, "We will hobble the spare horses and leave them here." "We can come back for them later after we take Mexican Joe." Crane replied I will come in from the North, Utah from the South, Larry from the East and Seth from the West, we ride in slow and steady, I think you should let me go in first, it might lull them in to a false sense of security." Crane rode up to the house, He came in slow and quiet, with Bruno on his heels. The cowboys who were working around the corral ignored him at first. A guy came out of the house and stood on the top step, "What can I do for you?" He asked. "I'm looking for Mexican Joe" Replied Crane. "He ain't here" The man replied, "So who might you be." Crane just gave a one word reply, "Crane." He said. The man went for his gun and Crane shot him were he stood, Another man came out of the house with a rifle in his hands but he never got to use it because, Bruno hit him at full speed his jaws fastened round his throat, the man died quickly. At the same moment Crane spun Dancer towards the corral and return the fire to the cowboys who had joined the fight, Utah, Larry, Rider, and Seth sent fire in from each direction and several cowboys fell, the rest dropped their pistols and surrendered. The four friends dismounted while they kept their pistols trained on the cowboys.

Crane asked the men who had surrendered a question, "Where is Mexican Joe and the rest of the crew?" One of the cowboys replied "He went down to Larado to rob the bank there, he said the town treated him very badly." Then he said that he was going to your farm to finish off what he started. How many men are riding with him?" Asked Crane. "Twenty maybe twenty five, he usually manages to pick up more men after a successful raid." Came the reply "I don't know why because he doesn't give shares from the raid money, only wages." "He isn't very regular with the wages either." One of the other cowboys said.

"Right said Crane, "I am a Texas Ranger," he showed them his badge, "I should arrest you but I don't have time. So get your gear all of you and ride, I don't want to see you again." He noted that were there were three or four bodies in the yard, including the two on the step. Then he added, "So bury your friends, tend to your wounded, and get on your way." Crane went into the house followed by Utah, the searched the house and found a safe with a large padlock, Crane had already reloaded, he drew his pistol and shot the padlock off the safe door. He reloaded again then replaced his pistol in it's holster. He opened the safe door, the safe was stuffed with bags of coin and bundles of bills of various denominations. Crane Said, "It looks like the proceeds of the robbery in Jacksboro, see if you can find a couple of gunny sacks, we take it in town on our way home." Utah asked, "You are not going to Laredo?" "No" replied Crane, "We will likely miss Mexican Joe there, it is better if we try and get home before him and give him a surprise.

They loaded the money from the safe in to the gunny sacks that Utah found and went outside. When they got outside Crane said to Larry, "While the rest of us head for Jacksboro, it would help if you go back and collect the spare horses, then meet us in town." "You got it" Replied Larry leaping into his saddle without hesitation gathered his reins and rode off.

"No" said Crane re-thinking, "Seth and I need spare horses, Dancer would run his heart out for me, but that wouldn't help if he foundered." They went to the corral. Once there they picked three of the biggest strongest looking horses in there, "I can ride any of them but neither of the others will carry Seth far, but we will have to make the best of it." Saying that they all mounted and rode out leading the spare horses, as they left the noticed that six graves had been dug, clearly two of the wounded had died before the cowboys had finished digging.

Crane and his band of brothers, headed out along the trail to Jacksboro, when they rode into town they went straight to the sheriff's office. When they entered the office Crane was pleased to find Don Liston sitting behind the desk. Don's right arm was in a sling, but otherwise he looked well. The bags of money were dropped on the floor,

Don looked up questioningly at Crane, who said, "That is the money Mexican Joe stole from the bank, so we thought we would return it." Don said to his deputy, "Go and get the banker and bring him back here. While Don's deputy went for the Banker, Crane showed Don his Rangers badge and brought him up to date with all the events since they last met. Don was pleased to know that Maggie and Mae were home safe and he was fascinated by the relationship between Crane and Bruno. He was just giving Crane his own information when the Banker arrived, he looked at the bags on the floor and got the teller he had brought with him to look inside the bags The teller said, "There is nearly $100,00 dollars in notes here not counting the bags of change, that is much more than was stolen." "There must be proceeds from other robberies here." "We will pay ten percent recovery as a reward, call it $10,000. Said the banker, Crane replied saying, "As a Texas Ranger I cannot take a reward but Utah, Seth, Larry and Rider can, so I want you to divide the money by four then give the share that would come to me, to the families of the three men killed in the robbery." The others said,"Please give a $1000 of each of our shares to the same people." "The banker nodded, Saying, "That's very good of you, it will be done." Then Utah said I want you to pay the rest of the money into our bank in Alamogora. "We can do that." Said the banker.

Then Crane said to Don, "We have to go, I've got to get home before Mexican Joe gets there" Don agreed that they should ride on immediately. As Crane and his companions were leaving the office Captain John Boone arrived in town as he rode up to them. Crane said, "Johnny, what brings you here?" "I'm taking leave to ride with you into New Mexico" Johnny replied. He was leading a spare horse. "Well that is great news," said Crane "Lets ride." As they were riding Johnny told Crane and the others, that Mexican Joe and his gang had robbed the bank in Laredo and while Marshall Evans was trying to deal with that, a group of Mexican Joe's riders broke everybody out of the jail. "So it looks as though it's down to us to take Mexican Joe down." Johnny concluded.

Crane said, I think we should call at my Ma and Pa's place, the new owners are good people and I want them to be sure that I will never want their money for the place." As they followed the road to the farm, Crane couldn't help but let his mind run on the last time he made this journey and what he found at the end of that journey. His reverie was disturbed by the sound of gunfire. They all put there horses to the run, Crane thinking, dear God don't let what happened to my family happen to the Preston family, he really feared for Mike, Amy, Jim and Joe, please God let us get there in time he silently prayed. As they galloped into the yard, Crane weighed up the situation he could hear and see, three rifles being fired from the windows of the cabin, across the yard a lone rifle was being fired from the barn. That was clearly the defence, around the corral and behind the water trough there were twelve men who were unleashing repeated volleys of fire on the cabin and the barn. Crane and Utah who knew the border riders style of attack thundered in reins in their teeth, firing their pistols right and left, Dancer was knocking men of their feet and trampling them under foot, one reckless attacker stood his ground and found Dancers teeth sunk to his shoulder as he was dragged along.

Johnny and Larry had dismounted and were laying down fire with their pistols, While Rider was showing remarkable dexterity by lying along the side of his horse, firing his rifle one handed under the horses neck. Seth was just walking towards the men around the corral firing his short rifle, when he had emptied his rifle he grabbed two of the men by the neck and cracked their heads together then he dropped them. Bruno of course was just tearing anyone who was holding a pistol pointed at him, to pieces. The men who were attacking the Preston's farm soon gave up, those who could still move threw their pistols on the ground. Mike Preston came out of the barn, he walked over to Crane, "I am mighty glad to see you again, Crane, I thought our number was up, then you came charging in and the whole situation changed in our favour." Amy, Jim and Joe came out of the cabin and the family hugged, the relief that they were all alive, was clear and the relief that Crane felt not to have found this family the way he had found his parents, was indescribable.

Utah and the others had herded the men together, Crane walked over and asked the nearest man, "Why did you attack this farm?" "Well," The man replied, "When Mexican Joe got back to the Triple X and found the safe had emptied he went berserk, He couldn't ride on himself because he was wounded during the bank raid in Laredo, so he decided to that he would send us here to were he said it all started, he said it would hurt you Crane, if people died here again." "He is not wrong there," said Crane, "I want this family l to live here as happily as my family did, but hopefully for much longer." "Anyway you seemed to be holding your own when we got here Mike." Crane added.

"Yes but I don't know how long we would have lasted If you hadn't turned up." Replied Mike. They noticed that, Jim was bleeding profusely from a head wound that his mother Amy was using a cloth to staunch. "Are you hit?" asked Mike, this was a seemingly stupid but concerned question. "No" replied, Jim, "I got clipped by a wood splinter that flew from the window frame." "I will be just fine when it stops bleeding." This was the only wound suffered by the family in the defence of their home. The question was what to do with the captured raiders. This problem was solved by the arrival of a cavalry patrol who were out looking for Comanche's who had fled the reservation, but their arrival would lead to another problem.

The Lieutenant who was in command agreed to take the raiders into Jacksboro. He refused to dismount so he was talking down to Crane. Crane took exception to this state of affairs and so he called Dancer to him. When he came Crane leapt up into the saddle, now he looked down on the Lieutenant and they continued their conversation. Then the Lieutenant saw Rider, "Sergeant" ! he said, "Take that Comanche in charge." The sergeant moved forward. Crane blocked his path, "Stay where you are!" He snarled "You don't touch that man" ! His left hand pistol leapt into his hand, in his right hand he held his Texas Rangers badge out so that the Lieutenant could see it. "I am Crane, I am a Comanche, this man Rider is my brother, if you try to take him you have to take me" Then Crane looked at the patrol saying, "Most of you will die trying." As if to emphasise his words, Dancer reared up causing the soldiers to back their horses away nervously. Bruno positioned himself beside Dancer, snarling and barking.

"The Lieutenant spoke, "Look it is my job to put you and your brother back on the reservation." Crane put his badge back in his pocket and as Rider rode up beside him, Crane said, "This is a good day to die," Then he drew his right hand pistol and put his reins in his teeth the great stallion Dancer just stood as did Rider and his horse. The confusion showed on the Lieutenant's face, nothing in his military career had prepared him for this eventuality. Suddenly another horse stepped between, Crane, Rider and the soldiers. A voice rang out, "The name is Captain John Boone, Texas Rangers I am the state authority here and you will not take my men into custody."

The Lieutenant, spoke, "Comanche's from the reservation must be returned to the reservation, I will not tolerate any argument" Mike Preston spoke saying, "This is Crane's Farm, he and his family grew up here, he kindly lets my family live here." "You have been given a chance to live you need to take it," said Captain Boone, "This is Crane, he is one of the deadliest guerilla fighters the west has ever seen and I can assure you that you and your men will all die if you persist in your attitude." "Can anyone else verify that Crane grew up here?" Asked the Lieutenant. Surprisingly, one it was one of the prisoners who replied, "It's true," he said Mexican Joe killed Crane's parents here and Crane has been on his trail ever since." The Lieutenant decided that he would conceded the point, so he gathered the prisoners and got them mounted, and rode away with out a backward glance.

Rider and Crane dismounted and Rider embraced Crane saying, "When you say we are brothers you mean it, I could hardly believe when you told the Lieutenant that it was a good day to die." "People say that I am strange man, that I live by my own rules, and I do" replied Crane. "I will never let friends or family down while I can breathe." "You frightened me to death" said Johnny, "I knew you would kill all those soldiers if they fought you and that meant you would have had to run until the day they hung you." "Crane said, "That Lieutenant would always follow the last order that he received and once we were on the reservation we might never have got free again" "That is why I can't be a real part of any organisation, I always try to apply common sense and I will not follow anyone blindly" "I admire anyone who can follow orders but I am not wired to do so." My loyalty is to individuals and definitely not to any of the organisations." It doesn't mean that I am right in my beliefs, I am just different."

"Just one thing Mike," said Crane, "Make no mistake this is your farm and I have left paper at the bank saying that I have ceded my rights on the farm, to you." "We surely do thank you" said Mike, "We are very happy here, and we are glad to know that you are the kind of man who puts people before everything else." "You and your family live right" said Crane. "You deserve only good things in your life." "Anyway we had better ride on, because we don't know when Mexican Joe will be heading for our valley and we want to be there to welcome him." There were handshakes all round and Crane and his friends rode away from the farm he had grown up on for what, he thought would be the last time. But he knew from past experience that his life's journey life could take him in strange directions.

CHAPTER 32

The journey was completed in double quick time and after an uneventful few days and nights, early one morning after parting company with Utah who rode on to his own farm, Crane found himself home. As he rode into the yard at the head of his band of brothers, he saw Maggie with Mae in her arms, run out from the cabin. He moved Dancer in that direction and was out of the saddle in time for Maggie to hug him excitedly with one arm, while holding Mae in the other. "At last" she said, "You are home safe, thank God." Crane nodded saying, "yes, I am where I want to be." Flo and Fred came and added their hugs and handshakes of welcome to Maggie's enthusiasm. Rider's, family Dove and Standing Crane had moved their Teepee close to Crane's cabin, so they were enjoying being back in each others company. There was much to talk about so when Joey and Jim had arrived, they took the returning travellers horses. The horses were unsaddled and then turned them into the corral. Maggie and Flo made breakfast and there was much to be discussed.

Crane was amazed when he saw two riders in particular walking towards him, one he recognised instantly, a quick wiry man with a scarred face, "Josey Wales" he said, "what brings you to our home?" "Well" replied Josey I'm down in

Texas now, me and a guy called Forest Carter are running a ranch together, "Like you I have a wife now, so also like you I am trying to live a quiet life." "Then we kept getting word about some mad rider with an even madder horse who has been tearing up Texas and leaving bodies in his wake." "When I heard that I knew it had to be you Crane, so I thought I would come and see if I could help." "On the way here I met Edge who was riding to find you with the same idea."

Crane looked at Edge, "Why would you do this" He asked, "I don't know you." "No" replied Edge but I know you. Because I was in Big John McCane's town when you took on those bank robbers, I thought then that you deserved an edge, so I thought I would travel up and try to give you one." Big John spoke, "He gave you an edge on that occasion in town as well, he brought his pistol to the game when you need it most." Crane looked at the tall, taciturn nan whose clothes had once been black but, because they had been washed so often they were a shade of grey. "I guess I'm already beholden to yo" he said, He held out his hand they shook hands, "I'm mighty glad you are here" said Crane. "Well he said, I have a friend, a real gentleman by the name of George G Gilman and he said he thought this was something I should do, so here I am."

While they were having their breakfast, Crane told everyone about Seth and how he was going to be staying with them. Everyone was pleased to meet Seth and they arranged his accommodation. "There is plenty of room for two in the barn, we will share everything," said Jim Cassidy, "Please come with me Seth and we will get you settled in. While the two of them went to sort out Seth's sleeping arrangements Larry said, I will go back into town and make the others aware of Mexican Joe's plans to attack your farm and ask them to come out here, they will want to come and help. Flo took Mae over to her cabin so that Crane and Maggie could spend some time together. That was something they hadn't been able to do since Mexican Joe took Maggie and Mae away with him to Texas. They spent a very pleasant afternoon together discussing their hopes and dreams for the future. It was early evening when all the guys rode in to the yard, every one was eager to see Crane and here how he planned to defeat Mexican Joe. When they saw the people arriving Crane and Maggie came out on to the veranda of there cabin and welcomed their friends. To Maggie and Crane's surprise Flo and Fred together with Joey, Jim, Rider and Seth's help they had put trestle tables and benches out. The tables were laden with good food, Dove and Maria, Utah's wife who had returned with Utah and Alan earlier, had helped Flo prepare the food. Everyone was pleased to see Crane, they were all eager to shake his hand welcome him home. Crane greeted each of them in turn, he was especially pleased when Dave Selley came forward, He hugged Dave saying, "Thank you so much, Dave," "Utah told me how Big John and Maggie would not have made it home if you hadn't stepped up to the mark and put your life on the line." Dave was embarrassed, as he replied "I could do no less, you put your faith in me, I couldn't let you down even if I died in my attempt to do what you expected." "How could I have come to you and said that I had failed?" Crane looked at him and said, "You went above and beyond the anything that friendship could have expected, I knew you had that in you when I asked you to take Maggie home."

They all gathered round the tables then sat down and started to eat. Crane said, "My plan for the battle is that we ride out from the farm, say about a quarter of a mile so that we can stop Mexican Joe before he gets near the houses or the barn." Crane looked around him and then spoke saying, "I didn't expect the ladies to be here but I'm very glad to see you all." Susan McCane spoke, "We have all been in this together ever since we met you Crane, If you hadn't made that unbelievable charge when Big John was the sheriff,some of us would have been without husbands when Mexican Joe staged that bank robbery" Doreen Eckert, Ness Black and Maureen Crossland agreed with her, we are all part of a team, indeed as we have said before we are a family. After that they all said, "Quite simply we have to be here." "That brings me to the second part of my plan" said Crane, "In case they break through our attack, we are going to need a rear guard, "So Dave. I am asking if you will organise that, you will have the ladies, Fred, Joey, Seth, Larry and Neil, they will be with you to form that rearguard." Dave just nodded, he was proud to choked to speak." Peter Leonard who had arrived with a pistol strapped on each hip, spoke,saying, "I will ride with you Crane, I have been into battle before, during the war between the states."Crane looked at him, then he said "I will be glad to have you there beside me." He replied.

Crane gathered his friends together, by the corral. He spoke to them saying, "I didn't want the ladies to hear this but we are going to be heavily outnumbered, Mexican Joe is likely to have as many as forty men with him we will have to attack him like border raiders The plan is to try to break them up and then hopefully we will kill him and try and scatter the rest of them. "Well" said Johnny, "You Big John, Josey, Utah and Edge should have no trouble with that but the rest of us have only seen it done, by you." "Are we up to it, "You will be fine." Replied Crane, "We will just attack them from different directions, don't forget that the noise is our friend, with all the gunfire, men shouting with all the horses milling round, unnerving those being attacked and this time we will be attacking."

"Right then we had better get saddled up" said Utah, Crane said I will go and organise some iron rations for us, Mexican Joe could be arriving here in an hour or a day, we just don't know." He walked across the yard to speak to Maggie and Flo. As he came back it was starting to rain. "Utah said, Crane, I might have forgotten, to mention the rain." "What do you mean?" Asked Crane. "Well you know it is unusually green, with all the good grass around here, that is because it can rain for a week at a time" Replied Utah.

"Well that might just work in our favour" Replied Crane. They all put on their long slicker coats and pulled their hats low over their eyes. Neil called Crane over saying, "I have something here for you Crane, a guy traded them with me for a rifle in the store the other day." Crane came over and looked at what Neil was holding out to him, two huge revolving pistols in saddle holsters. Crane took one of the pistol's out of it's holster, he found that it was well oiled and looked cared for, he tested the heft and balance, the pistol was heavy but the balance was good. Neil spoke again, "The guy who traded them with me said that he had them specially made during the war by a gunsmith in Santa

Fe. The problem that he had with them was the recoil. He was saying that the one time he tried to fire them the recoil was so strong it blew him backwards, right out of the saddle" Crane said, "I will buy them from you Neil, thank you for bringing them." "The only person I have seen with anything like them is Josey." "You can't buy them from me Crane, because they are a gift," Replied Neil.

He continued, "Anything that helps you to take down Mexican Joe is good for all of us. The other thing is that you need to make your own loads. There are 150 rounds that I have made up and I have bought the equipment to make more. You get it all"

Crane, put the spare rounds in the pockets of his slicker then took the pistols over to Dancer and fastened the holsters on to his saddle, on either side of the saddle horn. "I will have to try them out, I can't ride into battle without knowing how they work." Josey stepped forward, "I don't need to tell you but if I were you, I would fire them alternately not together." Crane nodded, then he mounted Dancer and galloped out of the yard through the pouring rain. As he rode he put his reins in his teeth and drew the pistols. He fired at a tree to his left and one on his right, the pistols roared and both trees were split down the middle, even Dancer who was always cool under fire shuddered.

Back in the corral horses were rearing and bucking because the two loud reports had frightened them and five miles away Mexican Joe, who was already cursing the rain, heard the sound and said, "Now it thunders as well, this weather is foul I will make Crane and the others pay for causing me to ride in this weather" At the same moment that Mexican Joe was speaking, Crane rode back into the farm yard and dismounted, he reloading the pistols, "These pistols are lethal, I have never seen such devastation, I imagine the cannons they used in the war would have a similar effect." He said. Utah smiled and said, "We will all need to make sure we are well behind you when you fire them." The cabin and the barn had been well fortified and the rearguard took up their places. This was no time for goodbyes so the advance party rode out in search of Mexican Joe. Bruno took up his place at the rear of the troop.

Josey rode ahead of the others, alone. He would use his experience to find Mexican Joe in the driving rain, so that Crane and the others could mount a surprise attack. Any misery that Crane and the others were feeling due to the weather was nothing to the distress that Mexican Joe's men were feeling. Mexican Joe's sorry crew were not riding in defence of a home and family, they were just riding in search of plunder so that they could continue their perceived easy lives. It was not long before Josey saw through the pouring rain the spray that could only indicate a crowd of men travelling. Obligingly the lightning flashed and lit up the group of thirty or forty men. There was no doubt in Josey's mind that this was Mexican Joe's gang, so he turned his horse and rode back to find Crane.

When Josey came on Crane and the rest he said, "Just turn to the east and we should come on them in about ten minutes, to quarter of an hour. The band of friends headed east and stopped after a while Crane said, "I am going to ride fast in straight down the middle, you guys come in slower on both sides, the raiders will turn your way when Dancer, Bruno and I drive a wedge down the centre of the group." They all nodded. Crane unfastened his slicker coat to give him free access to his pistols. The lightning flashed and the thunder roared and suddenly through the driving rain they saw Mexican Joe's band in front of them. Mexican Joe saw them in the same lightning flash, "Charge!" He roared, "Kill them all!" As usual he turned his own horse and raced away to the rear of the column.

Crane jammed his reins in his teeth and then he drew his two horse pistols from their holsters on the front of the saddle. Dancer reared he was screaming his rage at the fusillade of fire that came from Mexican Joe's raiders. Then with the wind and rain lashing at them Dancer leapt forward, with Bruno at his heels, the huge pistols in Crane's hands roared as he hurtled forward into the fray. The lighting was flashing and it's light showed him with his slicker coat flying out, behind and around him, his teeth bared and his lips drawn back in a snarl, the boom of his horse pistols, seeming to sound louder than the thunder.

"Grown men were crying out in fear they were saying, "Sweet mother of God it's the angel of death flying out of the gates of Hell." Nothing in their cheating, killing, robbing lives had prepared them for this. Their horses were twisting and turning, trying to get away from Dancer's flying hooves and snapping teeth. One man was more in control than the rest and he would have succeeded in killing Crane had it not been for Bruno's powerful leap up at him, resulting in the dogs great jaws tearing his hand off, while was still gripped his pistol. "Jesus save us" ! Someone shouted "The Devil himself is here and he has brought all his hounds of hell!"

Men and horses were turning right and left as they did

they rode straight into the pistols of Chris Black, Utah, Rider, Captain Boone, Big John McCane, Edge, Peter Leonard, John Eckert, Josey Wales, Jim Cassidy and Alan Crowe. Crane's horse pistols were empty so he re-holstered them and drew his usual pistols as he did so. There was lead flying all around him and a few of the bullets had grazed him and Dancer so they were both bleeding but the rain was washing away the blood. Crane saw one rider try to shoot Bruno as the dog knocked another out of his saddle, he shot him in the throat, the dog was on the ground now tearing into fallen riders, who were just trying to get away. A bullet sliced through Dancers ear and the horse went crazy, he reared up and smashed his hooves into the face of the rider who had fired on him, the man fell from the saddle he was dead before he hit the ground. Crane's pistols were empty again so he re-holstered them, his jaws were aching from biting down on the reins so Crane took the reins in his hands and rode out of the thinning crowd of raiders.

Crane's comrades were still firing at the raiders as he let the reins go and started to reload his side arms. As soon as he got that job done he started on his horse pistols and reloaded first one and then the other. Then he replaced them in their holsters. As he did so two raiders realising he had no pistol in his hands charged at him firing wildly. Bruno took the lead raider out of the saddle with a flying leap. The pistol from under Crane's arm leapt into his hand he fired twice in quick succession, causing the following raider to go down dragging his horse with him. The horse got up out of the mud and stood there chest heaving, his rider stayed down.

The fight had gone out of the remaining raiders and those still able to hold their pistols dropped them and put their hands in the air. Crane and the others looked around for Mexican Joe but,there was no sign of him among the wounded or the dead. Crane asked some of the raiders, if they had seen Mexican Joe, most said no that they had been to busy trying to stay alive, then one of them said that Mexican Joe and maybe ten others had peeled away from the back of the line and looped around the side. Utah said, "They must have headed for your farm Crane, we've got to ride and ride hard to get back there." "No," Crane replied. "We have to rely on Dave, Neil, Larry, Fred and the others to do their job, we just can't get there in time."

Crane walked around his friends in the rain checking that they were all OK, Rider was bleeding profusely from an arm wound, Crane checked it and found that the bullet had gone straight through his left bicep, luckily it had missed the bone, he asked Utah to bind it up. As he continue his rounds of the wounded Crane found Doc Black lying unconscious on the ground, he knelt beside him. After a cursory check he found that his friend was breathing, Crane let out a sigh of relief then he called out to Big John and asked if he were hurt,. It was another source of relief when he heard Big John reply. "No I am fine." Big John went over to Crane's side and the two of them checked Doc Black for wounds, the found that he had none, except for a lump and a dark bruise on his forehead. Big John, with seemingly no effort at all picked the Doc up in his arms and carried him out of the mud, when he got to a slightly drier area he put him down and sat him up against a rock. Crane kept looking around his friends,

Jim Cassidy's horse had been shot out from under him and he had twisted his previously damaged ankle, otherwise he said he was just fine.

Johnny Boone had opened a previous wound, but he said, "I'm OK it only leaking blood, not flowing the way it did before." Peter had taken a bullet in the right leg, unfortunately the bullet was still it was still in the wound. He was propped up against three of the fallen raiders, one of whom had shot him, before he got them. Peter being Peter was reciting the twenty third psalm, he was murmuring, "Yea though I walk through the shadow of valley of death,"Crane interrupted him saying, "How are you feeling?" Peter replied "Blessed," because as he always is, the Lord was with me today." Crane nodded saying "He was with all of us today." Crane was bleeding but in the rain he couldn't tell from where. He thought to himself *no bad wound's bad anyway*. Just like Crane, Bruno had blood all over him, but he was still walking and in the rain it was difficult to tell if the blood was his or someone else's.

Crane spoke to the remaining raiders telling them, to catch up their horses and get themselves and their wounded out of New Mexico. Jim Cassidy caught up everyone of his friends horses and got one of the fallen raiders horses for himself. "He said to Crane, this the second time I have gained a horse in this way." Crane just nodded and walked over to Doc Black. The Doc stirred and started to come round, Crane was worried spoke to Doc, calling him by name, "Chris, my friend how are you feeling?" "Like someone has been dancing on my head, replied the Doc. "What happened" ? Asked Crane. "I made a big mistake I got to close to you and Dancer and you knocked me off my horse when you came charging through." Utah who was listening spoke saying "I warned you all you should never ever get anywhere near Crane in battle, he sees nothing and hears even less." They all laughed relieving the tension they were all feeling.

Doc Black got to his feet, "Are any of us wounded?" He asked, Crane replied to him, Johnny, Rider and maybe me and Bruno, Jim has a twisted ankle. "The question is can we all ride?" Asked the Doc "Because I can't do much in this rain to help any of you." They all agreed that they could ride, with the exception of Peter, who when asked said with "God's help I shall try, if someone can get me up into the saddle." Utah and Big John lifted him up on to his horse when he was in the saddle it was clear that he was in great pain, just one foot in the stirrups because his right leg wouldn't bend. The others mounted and then they all rode back to Crane's farm together, leaving the survivors from the raiders gang to sort themselves out.

CHAPTER 33

Back at the farm the people there had been unable to distinguish the thunder from what may have been gunfire. But they were ready, they wouldn't have to fight in the rain. Behind the barricades that they had built, one in front of the veranda outside the cabin another in front of the barn with Neil and Fred up in the loft able to sweep the yard with their eyes, they would see their expected attackers first.

There was shelter from the weather and the expected raiders bullets. Fred gave the signal to the others by firing a shot in the air, that was the warning that the attackers were on the edge of the yard. When Mexican Joe and his raiders heard the shot it actually stopped them in their tracks, foolishly they started to return fire even though they were out of effective range. The defenders of the farm did not fire any shots after hearing Fred's warning shot. They just waited, Mexican Joe and his raiders came on in to the yard at the walk, it was drizzling, just fine rain now but, it made it difficult to see very far, the flash from Fred's rifle, told Mexican Joe that the defence was coming from the barn. How a man so stupid had survived so long was a mystery. He knew the layout of the yard from his previous visit so that being the case, he said, in fact he shouted to his men, "Charge!" We will make a head on attack on the barn, there won't be many in there,to defend the place, all the men are clearly out on the prairie."

The raiders poured fire on the barn, only to be surprised when they found that they being were fired on not just from the barn but from the cabin as well. They were being cut to ribbons, Mexican Joe cursed and shouted, "Fall back." He just could not believe how well he had been out thought by his enemies. If Mexican Joe thought that he would have time to think about this turn of events, he was wrong because three shots rang out from the ridge behind the house and three of Mexican Joe's men fell from the saddle. This was to much for the bandit, he resorted to his usual tactic, in the face of what he saw as insurmountable odds he turned and fled. As as he put his horse to the run he Mexican Joe shouted to his men, "Go North! Go North!! We can turn South later, we can't go South first in case we run into Crane and his men coming back to the farm"

As they went a lone rider rode down off the ridge into the yard, he held his arms over his head showing that he was no threat to the people on the farm. Dave Selley came out from the barricade in front of the cabin, he spoke saying, "Howdy stranger, that was mighty fine shooting in weather like this" The man looked down from the saddle and shrugged his shoulders saying, "It is a good thing I was using a rifle, I couldn't hit a barn door from ten paces with a pistol." The rider stepped down from his horse, he was not a tall man but he was wiry, clearly strong and his movements were very quick, his eyes were dark and he had a hard look to him, he wore a well trimmed beard. He was the kind of man who you wouldn't want to cross. That said he was smiling when he held out his hand saying, "The name is Barclay, Tony Barclay and I'm looking to find a relative of mine who goes by the name of Crane."

Dave took Tony's hand replied, saying, "I am Dave Selley please Come up to the house there are people who will want to meet you." People were coming out from the barn and the cabin to the rain, all wanting to congratulate the stranger on his remarkably accurate shooting. Dave said, "We can do individual introductions in a while, in the meantime everybody this is Tony Barclay." As he was speaking Dave took an appraising look at Tony's horse, It was a chestnut mare, very powerful in the back end, he knew that it was what is known as a quarter horse, very fast and able to turn on a sixpence. When you looked at the man and horse together you just knew that they were meant to be a partnership. Dave spoke to Tony saying, "Joey will put your fine horse in to the barn, he will rub her down and make sure that she is dry and warm.

Joey took Tony's horse into the barn and took care of her while the others moved on to the cabin. Dave saw, Maggie and said to her, "Maggie, this is Tony Barclay who is it seems, a relative of Cranes, Tony this is Maggie, she is Crane's wife," they shook hands and Tony said "I am pleased to meet you ma'am." Maggie replied, "Call me Maggie please, we will have a lot to talk about." As they went in to the cabin Tony was amazed at the size of the rooms, particularly the one they all went into. The first thing he saw was a long a long trestle table surround by chairs, more than were needed at the moment. Fred noted his surprise saying, "Crane is a well loved man around here, we have all been blessed with his friendship and because of that there are always plenty of visitors."

Food and coffee were being served by the wives of the men who had been defending the farm. Tony looked at Dove saying, "Who is that lady?" That is Dove replied Fred, she is Ride the Wind's wife, We call him Rider, he and Dove are part of our family." They are Comanche, Incidentally, Crane is a quarter Comanche." "Yes, so am I" Replied Tony, "That is our connection, my grandmother was Crane's grandmothers sister. So that makes us some kind of a cousin I think." "The thing is my Ma died recently, now over the years she had told she told me all about her aunt's family and then we heard about them being killed. Then stories about Crane came to us from strangers passing through the place were we lived and I thought I have nowhere else that I want or need to be, so I will try and find Crane and see if I can help him." "Well" Fred replied, "You certainly helped today. That was Mexican Joe, he is a most evil man and you scared him off with that fine shooting of yours. I can say that I have never seen anyone better than you with a rifle, and I have seen a few." There was one feller, Jimmy Stewart was his name, he came from Laramie, and he could shoot the eye out of a needle. Then there was a guy called Adam Steele, he rode with a feller called Gilman, a real straight shooter, he was another who could make a rifle talk but neither of these men could shoot better than you." "Well I guess I was just lucky," said Tony. "Yeah" replied Fred, "I would say that you were very lucky, three times." Everyone laughed at Fred's dry sense of humour

Crane and his friends rode into the yard, they were surprised to be greeted by the sound of laughter. They all dismounted as Joey came towards them. "Things seem to have gone well here then." Said Crane as he surveyed the scene, taking in the bodies on the ground. "They sure have been going well." Replied Joey. Going to say, "A guy called Tony Barclay picked of three of Mexican Joe's riders from the ridge over there, in the pouring rain, unbelievable shooting, three shots, and three raiders went down." "Mexican Joe and his guys high tailed it out of here like the devil himself was on their trail.." "I am!" Said Crane, then he went on to say, "That sounds like very impressive shooting, I would like to meet this guy." "Oh you will," said Joey, "He is in the cabin now."

Joey, Utah and the others took the horse to the barn while Crane went over to the cabin, he noted all the slicker coats hanging on the veranda as he passed them, he left his own with them as he entered through the door. Maggie saw him coming in and stepped forward and hugged him. "Welcome home husband." She said. Crane hugged her back then Maggie said, "Crane I want you to meet Tony Barclay, it seems that he is some kind of cousin of yours." "Really, I didn't know I had any relatives" replied Crane as he shook hands with Tony. Tony explained, "My grandmother was your grandmothers sister, she married a French trapper, called Gaston Leroux, I was told that he lived with the Comanches for a few years. "The tribes chief had two daughters and my father married one of them, so here I am." Crane said, "Well you are welcome here and it sounds like you arrived just in time. At that point Utah came in received a greeting from his wife Maria. Utah I'm so glad that you are back safe" "I am glad to be with you again." He hugged her, then he said, "The Doc is in the barn, he is taking a bullet out of Peter Leonard's leg, he said to ask if you could you go over there and help him Ness?" Of course I can, replied Ness. With that Ness went out to the barn taking Lynda, Peters wife with her. "Are there any serious wounds?" Asked Maggie, "No I don't believe so" replied Crane "Although having said that Rider lost some blood to an arm wound, but he is fine, Crane smiled at Dove, "He really is OK, he is in the barn he is just having a fresh dressing applied to the wound." Dove, nodded followed the other two women out to the barn.

As the other men came across from the barn more food and coffee was brought to the table. As the food was consumed the talk came round to Mexican Joe and what needed to be done about him. Crane said, "I have to get the job done this time, he will go to Texas and then maybe down to Mexico, so I will be behind him." Maggie said, "That may be so, but you won't be going anywhere till tomorrow, I'm sure Mexican Joe is holed up somewhere out of the rain and you will be sleeping here tonight." Crane agreed saying, "Yes we all need rest. I need to clean Bruno up he seems OK but I don't know if any of that blood is his or if it belongs to the people he fought with." Flo replied, "Well there is nothing wrong with his appetite, see how he is polishing off a plate of my stew." They all looked and smiled as they saw Bruno eating his plate of stew.

When they had both finished eating Crane took Bruno outside, he was pleased to see that it had stopped raining. Walking over to the trough he picked up a cloth and a bucket which he filled at the pump. When he had enough water he gently washed the blood of his magnificent dogs body, Neil who was coming out of the barn said, "Would you look at that is Crane, one of the greatest warriors that you will ever see but he is as gentle as a lamb when he isn't fighting." Everyone agreed saying, "You are right our friend Crane is a man of many parts. As he washed the blood away from Bruno's fur Crane was pleased to see that there were no wounds on the dog at all. When he was finished Utah came over and said, "You need to sort yourself out, because I know that some of the blood on you is your own.

Crane nodded and he took off his jacket and shirt, he had deep gouge just above his hip bone and another one more like a weal across his right forearm, he also had a graze along the side of his head,although he couldn't see it himself. Crane emptied the bucket out and then he filled it again, then he tipped it over his head, flinching as the cold water cascaded over him, he repeated the exercise couple more times and then as he turned towards the cabin he found that Maggie was standing beside him with a towel. He took the towel and as he dried himself, he noticed that Maggie had already dried Bruno off. Crane went back inside and walked through to the bedroom were he took his pants, skivvies, boots and socks off, he looked up to see that Maggie had followed him in with a bowl of warm water, she smiled at him and then she bathed his wounds. When she was satisfied that they were clean she put some salve on the wounds then, she dressed them. When she was finished Crane put clean clothes on and went back into the main room.

Peter had limped in to the cabin supported by Jim Cassidy, once again Peter being Peter decided to say prayers, he wanted to thank God for every ones safe return. When prayers were over, Crane said, "You may think that

I am a none believer, but I know that if ever God is not riding with me, I won't be coming back." He continued, "I never doubt his presence even when bad things happen." Peter replied saying, "Your faith is strong and you always try to do the right thing, that is why you are always in my prayers." "It may surprise you to know that you are always in mine."

Neil, Dave Larry, John Eckert and the rest of the people from town had decided to ride home. Crane thanked them for their help saying, "No man ever had better friends." Larry said I have put salve on Dancers wounds, there is nothing serious, but he will always have a torn ear. "Thank you" said Crane. The townsfolk all filed out and made their preparations to head home. "Tony Barclay will bed down in the barn, with Josey, Seth, Johnny, Edge and Jim" said Crane. "Alan and Utah will be going home with Maria." "Big John and Susan will go home, so will Joey which reminds me, I hope to get a look at his cabin soon, adding Rider and Dove are going to stay with Flo and Fred." "So we should all get a good nights sleep." Utah, said, "I will be back in the morning, Alan will sit this one out, otherwise we won't have a farm, plus his own cabin still need to finished. Alan, nodded saying, "I will come if I am needed." Big John said, The same from me with the exception that I will be here in the morning"Having said that he made his preparations to take Susan home. Crane said, "If there is one thing I am sure of, it is that the words 'let down' are not in Big John McCane's vocabulary, I couldn't ask for a better friend.

Crane, walked to the stable end of the barn to check on Dancer, the horse was pleased to see him and was seemingly none the worse for his superficial wounds. The horse nuzzled Crane's chest, Crane smiled and said, "We mustn't let people see this, they will think you have gone soft" he looked at the horse ear and said "I don't think you would let us stitch this wound, so we will just have to make sure we keep it clean for you." As he walked away Crane thought how grateful he was to have such a horse, there as no doubt that Dancer had kept him alive on more than one occasion. As he left the barn Crane looked down at Bruno who walking beside him and said, "I'm mighty glad that you chose to come along with me boy." He patted the big dogs head then they walked back into the cabin together. Crane sat down at the table, for the first time in a long time he felt ready to eat, really eat and enjoy the food.

CHAPTER 34

While Crane and his friends and family, were dry and warm, Mexican Joe and his gang of cronies were sodden an soaked through. They were miserable, even when the rain stopped they couldn't get dry, there was nothing they could light a fire with, the grass foliage and trees were running with water. There was a chill breeze that was so cold that it even knifed through their wet slicker coats. They were cursing and blaming Crane for everything, Mexican Joe was the worst, he was moaning and whining, threatening Crane with the most terrible death Like all the rest of his kind Mexican Joe took no responsibility for anything in his life, it was always the other guy's fault. Mexican Joe was silently plotting his next move, he spoke to his men. "We are going to head back to the Crane's old farm, we are going to take the family that lives there now alive, Crane will come thinking that he can save them. Some of you will make sure he fails, I am telling you wait for Crane out there and then kill him." "I am going to ride to into Jacksboro with the rest of you and wait there, if he gets by you miserable excuses for men, I will end it for him in the town where it all started."

The following morning Mexican Joe and his sorry bunch of renegades were riding down the trail that would lead them back to Texas. They were still wet and they were still cold. After they had been riding for a while they came on some more of Mexican Joe's men who were also making their way back to Texas, after their encounter with Crane and his friends. They rode up beside Joe and the others, making fourteen renegades in total. Mexican Joe spoke to them all as they rode along saying, "This works out very well because seven of you can carry out the raid on the farm, the other six can go with me into town. Seven is a good number because we beat, that kid Crane senseless way back then with seven of us and I only had the likes of Lattigo, Fat Colin, Kirby, Shelby, Ralston and that bum Utah to support me then. You are better men, so we will have no trouble with him this time." They all rode on in silence.

After enjoying a very pleasant evening and night with his family, Crane was up early the next morning. He went out to is tool shed to make some new shells for his horse pistols. The reason for this was that he was worried that the loads he had would be damp and so they might misfire. Crane had been working for about an hour and was ready to pack up when Maggie came out get, Josey, Edge, Johnny, Tony, Jim, Seth and himself for breakfast. Fred, Flo Rider, Dove and their baby were already on their way to the cabin and while they were walking back, Joey rode in as always the young man was ready to eat. The food was tasty and very welcome and they washed it down with copious amounts of hot coffee. Edge said, "I don't know how you ever manage to ride out of here, you have things really good. The others nodded their agreement. "Crane replied "I am hopeful that this will be the last time I have to leave, I just can't sit and wait for Mexican Joe, you all know what happen last time." They all agreed, and slowly left the table, going outside to make their preparations to leave. Joey packed provisions for each man, including spare ammunition. As they all went outside Utah rode in. He dismounted, saying, "Alan and Maria are going to look after things at home for me so I am good to go."

Josey and Edge had saddled up before dawn, the were going their separate ways, "It's been good to see you again Crane, I think you will end it this time" said Josey "So do I" said Edge, "You have backed Mexican Joe into a corner, he can't get out, because you have stopped him at every turn." "It has been good riding with you both" said Crane. "You know that I would do the same for both of you, just call if you need me and I will come." Both men nodded and mounted their horses, they rode out, "Adiós and be lucky" both men said. Via Con Dios Mi Amigos," said Crane.

Once again Crane was ready to ride out from his home as he was saying his farewells to Maggie and Mae, Tony Barclay stepped forward saying, I would really like to ride with you Crane I came try and help and I would be pleased if you would let me. Crane looked at him, "If you ride with me you may not get to ride back but if you understand that and still want to come, I would be happy to have you with us." "I will ride with you what ever happens." Replied Tony. At that moment Big John rode in. "That's it we are all her" said Crane "let's ride." Crane, Utah, Big John, Rider, Seth, Johnny and Tony rode out of the yard, each one saying a silent prayer, "Please God let this be an end to the misery caused by Mexican Joe."

What Crane and his friends did not know was that when

they stopped and made camp that night they were only about three miles behind Mexican Joe. It was the same for Mexican Joe, he and his renegades had no idea just how close Crane and his band of brothers were behind them. If they had been they would have ridden through the night. As it was both parties spent a relatively comfortable night, although it was a cold camp for Mexican Joe's men because they had lost most of their supplies to the weather. Where as each man in Crane's party had set out from the farm, well supplied for the journey ahead.

The other thing that Crane wasn't aware of was that someone was on his trail. A young Mexican boy whose name was Danny Pedrosa arrived at Crane's farm just after Crane and his friends had ridden out after Mexican Joe. The exhausted boy, rode into the farm yard on an emaciated donkey, as the boy tried to step down from the animal his strength and balance deserted him and he tumbled to the ground landing on his ancient musket. Joey who was working by the corral saw him fall and ran to the boy's side. He spoke to the boy saying, "It is OK, son, you are safe here," then Joey picked him up and carried him to Crane's cabin, shouting, "Maggie, come quickly I need your help." Maggie came out of the cabin, when she saw what was happening, She said, "Bring him in here." Joey carried him in and put the boy down in an armchair, Maggie checked the boy over for signs of injury. When she didn't find any injuries she realised that the boy was just not hungry, he was starving.

While Maggie set to work getting food for the boy, Joey went back outside to care for the donkey. When he got there Fred had already taken the donkey into the barn and put it in the stall. He was giving it water and a small amount of food, he knew if he over fed or watered it the animal might die. Joey had picked up the ancient musket, fired looked at and said, "That gun is older than me, it is rusty and if it was fired the only person likely to get hurt is the person holding it." They came back out of the barn and walked over to the cabin and wet in to see the boy eating a bowl of stew. Maggie said "He picked up after he had a cup of water, so I am letting him have a little food, I don't want him to be sick." Then she said, "His name is Danny Pedrosa, he is a Mexican." It seems he set out to kill Mexican Joe, because he slaughtered Danny's family." While he has been on the trail he heard about Crane so he decided that his best chance was to find Crane and join forces with him and then they can kill Mexican Joe together."

"Well" Fred answered, "We had better outfit him if he intends to catch up with Crane he will need a horse, saddle and a rifle with ammunition and some food supplies. We have a few saddles that belonged to the raiders who got killed." Maggie said "If he insists on travelling on he will need a bath, a change of clothes and most importantly a good night's sleep." Jim Cassidy who had been out on the range came back and while he ate they brought him up to date, with Danny's situation. Danny spoke saying, "I must go no one can stop me." Jim nodded and then he said, "If I can have the time off, I think I should go with him, He is not like Crane, he should not go on alone." Fred said, "I agree with you, there is no one like Crane, Danny has done well to get here, we won't let him push his luck."

Then Joey said, "I have some clothes, that I have grown out of that will go near to fitting Danny," he looked at

Danny's feet they were dirty and sore, he only had a pair of rope sandals on, "I think my old boots will fit him as well." They looked at Danny and saw that he had fallen asleep in the chair. Smiling down at him Fred said, "I know just the horse for him." "Do you remember that tough little line-backed Dun, that Crane pulled out of a mud hole last winter?" "That little horse will run all day and all night and never quit, I think that it will suit Danny very well." The others nodded saying "good choice Fred." "I will bring him in and select a saddle for him. Said Jim. Joey went out saddled his horse and rode home to his cabin to get the clothes. Maggie set about boiling water for Danny's bath. Maggie's mother Flo came over saying, "I will give the lad a haircut, we can't take him into town to John Eckert's shop can we?"

The following morning Danny was well rested, clean and with his hair shorn was dressed in Joey's old clothes and ready to go. He came out of the cabin and looked for his donkey, instead he saw Fred standing beside a saddled and bridled line backed Dun. "Where is my donkey." Asked Danny. Fred replied, "He is in the barn, we will feed and look after him until you get back. "Then he said, "This is your horse Danny, he is not being lent to you he is yours, so are the saddle and bridle." "Thank you" said Danny. Joey handed him a rifle "you can put this in the boot on the saddle." "You have everything you will need for the trip in your saddlebags" said Fred. Then he said "This is Jim Cassidy, he will ride with you to find Crane, he knows the territory down there in Texas." Maggie and her mother came forward and hugged the boy. Maggie said, "Whatever happens, you come back here to us, this is your home now"

Danny hugged her, saying, "thank you I don't know what more to say." Maggie replied, "There is nothing more you need to say, come home soon." Jim and Danny mounted their horses and rode out on Crane's trail. Fred, said "I hope they get there to late to take any part in the shooting." Joey replied, I'm sure that is Jim's intention, he doesn't want that boy anywhere near any pistol fights.

Unaware that they were being trailed, Crane and his friends continued there journey down to Texas. There was little conversation between them because everything had been said before. Each man kept his thoughts to himself. It was hard to believe how much rain had fallen so recently because the heat now was intense, Crane ever mindful of the livestock called the noon break. Tony Barclay spoke saying, "Shouldn't we keep going? Mexican Joe, will be gaining time on us." Crane said, "If there is one thing I have learnt in the years that I have been on Mexican Joe's trail, it is patience. It does no good to catch up with him when you are tired out without purpose because in those circumstances he always gets away, so I always take my time." Tony replied, "I'm sorry I am new at this, I don't have a lot of patience, I guess on this trip I will have to learn some." "Don't worry Tony" Utah said, "You will see plenty of action soon enough."

Danny and Jim were not making good time, in fact they had gone slightly off course. Danny asked Jim, "How long will it be before we catch up with Crane?" "It could be some time because we have to call and see a couple of people first." Replied Jim "Who?" asked Danny. We are going to see two of Crane's friends, Maria who is Utah's wife and Alan Crowe who is Utah's partner and a friend to us all." "Why do we need to see them." Asked Danny. "Well they will want to send Crane and Utah a message, a message that we can take to them. They arrived at Utah and Alan's farm, Alan came over to them as they rode into the yard saying, "Howdy Jim, who is your partner on that fine looking horse." This is Danny he is on the trail to get Mexican Joe for killing his family." "Well now it's good to meet you, Danny, please step down and visit a while." As Danny and Jim dismounted Maria came across and Alan introduced her to Danny, explaining why he was there." "Well I'm pleased to meet you Danny, I know how you feel, because Mexican Joe, killed my family as well." "Please, while Jim and Alan talk come in the cabin and have a piece of apple pie."

While Maria and Danny went inside for apple pie, Jim and Alan talked about this new situation, Jim saying, "There is no way I am riding this kid into a pistol fight, so we will just drift down to Texas and hopefully arrive to late for any action." "That is a good plan" said Alan "there is no way that boy needs to see any more violence than Mexican Joe has already put him through." "When they had wasted as much time as they could Jim and Alan went up to the new cabin and joined Maria and Danny." Danny was enjoying his second piece of pie when Jim spoke saying, "If you want to stay here I can go after Crane on my own." "No" Danny replied, I have to go I want to see Mexican Joe go down." So they went outside mounted their horses and restarted their journey to Texas.

As Jim and Danny were riding away from Utah's farm, Crane and his party were just stopping for their noon break. Crane spoke saying "This is were we part company boys,

The rest of his group looked at him. Then Utah spoke, "What in tarnation is happening now Crane? You agreed that we could be with you." "This how it plays out," said Crane "Mexican Joe will have two things in his mind, one is to kill me. He has an overpowering need to do that, the second thing he wants to do is hurt me before I die. He has failed to hurt Maggie and Mae or burn down my home, so he will want to do the next best thing." Big John McCane said, "And what would that be" "Mexican Joe will raid my old home place and kill the Preston family, preferably in front of me."

So Utah said, "OK we can all understand that, but I still don't understand why you have to leave us." "The thing Mexican Joe will really want to do, in my opinion, is kill me where it all started in Jacksboro." Crane replied. "I think you are right" said Utah. "I have ridden with Mexican Joe and he is totally obsessed with Crane, he blames him for every bad thing that happens in his life." "He has tried to hurt Crane, he has lied about him to steal Crane' reputation, he has tried to hurt Crane's family and most of all he has tried to kill Crane, basically he will stop at nothing to destroy Crane completely. Utah's explanation clarified the situation for the others. Utah added, "Basically meeting Crane when Crane was a boy all those years ago in Jacksboro, tipped Mexican Joe's already unbalanced mind over the edge." "So what's the plan?" asked Johnny. "Well" replied Crane, I cannot afford to get this wrong for Mike Preston's family, whatever happens to me. "Because we have got to protect Mike Preston and his family, you will all go to the farm, I will go to Jacksboro just in case Mexican Joe goes there. "Couldn't one of us go with you?" Asked Rider. "Best if you don't because if there is trouble at the farm you will need every man we have got." Replied Crane

Crane saddled up after the noon break then, made his farewells and road East towards town, while his friends headed straight on North to the farm. They were fairly close to the farm so, by early evening they were looking down on it. They were not happy with what they saw, the Preston family were all tied to the rails of the corral. They were looking very much the worse for wear even from a distance. The friends could also see that there were seven raiders around the place. Utah said "Seven riders, I can't see Mexican Joe so it looks as though Crane is right he has gone into Jacksboro, we need a plan to make sure we get the Preston family out safe."

Tony Barclay replied, "I've got a plan, you will have to trust me but it will work." Utah said "OK tell us what you intend to do." "Right, the plan needs me to ride in alone, the rest of you move out and come in from different sides after I make my move." Johnny asked, "Does it really help you going in alone?" "That is were the trust comes in, I can only tell you that it will work and it will help protect this family." "We will go with your plan Tony just give us time to get in position," Seth will come in from behind you on your left, Big John will come in from your right, I will loop round and come in from the far right and Rider from the far left, just give us a few minutes." Utah and Rider moved out wide to ride round each side of the farm. After they had been gone a little while Tony rode down towards the farm, he started his horse dancing sideways, Tony was talking to the mare as he came in to the farm yard, "Whoa, horse silly horse, why won't you walk in a straight line, we will never get to town if you keep going sideways like this." Two of the raiders came forward as Tony and his horse came level with the corral at the point where the family were tied up,

One of the raiders got hold of the mare's bridle close to the bit, The horse stopped and the raider spoke saying, "It seems to me that this is to much horse for you stranger, I think you should give it to me." In a very affected voice, Tony replied, "Oh I say that's not very kind, I'm sure I will be in control soon." Then Tony said, "And what about these poor people, you've tied them up and look some of them are bleeding, you really are unkind." The mare started to dance again getting between the raiders and the Preston family. The same raider spoke again, "You had better get down of that horse before you fall off it." Things happened very quickly then because suddenly the horse was being fully controlled by Tony, it's back hooves suddenly hit the raider who was standing at the back of the horse, in chest and face with all it's power, the raider died without even knowing what hit him. The raider at the front of the horse went down with one of Tony's bullets between his eyes. Tony leapt from the saddle his horse now standing still. He put his pistol away and drew his knife and began to free the prisoners.

The other five raiders rushed forward eager to shoot down Tony down, only to fall beneath the pistol fire being unleashed by Big John, Utah and Johnny and the rifle fire from Rider and Seth. The raiders tried to return fire but the surprise attack was to sudden. The whole thing was over in minutes none of the raiders survived. Mike Preston spoke to Barclay saying, "I don't know were you came from, but we are mighty glad to see you." Tony replied, "My name is Tony Barclay and Crane sent us." "Yes I recognise Utah, Big John, Rider and that ranger feller now I see them." "We thought it must be some kind of a trap for Crane when they tied us up instead of killing us, but we couldn't seem to work out just what it was all about. Big John came across to them and Mike said "So where is Crane?" "He has gone into town to see if Mexican Joe is there, Crane hopes to put an end to all the fighting and hating back where it all started. Utah said we need to start clearing up the mess, we will throw the raiders over their saddles and take them in town. You don't want them out here on your farm."

All the men including Mike's two sons, Jim and Joe set about saddling the raiders horses and tying the dead raiders over their saddles. Mile's wife Amy went into the cabin and prepared food and coffee for everyone. It was quite amazing just how quickly and how well the rescue had gone. Utah said Tony, "That was quite a trick you did with that horse of yours, the raiders were so busy laughing at you they forgot to be on their guard. "Yes, well it wasn't really explainable before hand but, Lady Jane was a rodeo horse for sometime and she is full of tricks." Replied Tony. "That would explain something else I think" said Big John. "What would that be" Asked Tony with a smile. "I would say you were a sharp shooter given your performance at Crane's home place." "You are right" replied Tony. "To be honest what happened at Crane's farm was the first time I had fired a rifle at a live target. "It is a good thing for us that you are a quick learner" Said Utah.

Amy chose this moment to call out "Come and get it!" The men all wandered up to the cabin, where Amy served bacon and beans and of course hot coffee. Johnny said "I am sure Crane get a laugh out of your stunt with the horse." "I just hope that things have gone as well for him in Jacksboro as it did for us her" said Rider. "Yes" said Utah. "I Think we had better get on into town, I am starting to worry about what Crane would find when he got there." The six friends tied the raiders horses together in a train and mounted up with Seth leading what really was a funeral cortège. They thanked Amy for the food, she and her family thanked them and the procession headed for town. The guys were more worried than they let each other know, the idea that somehow Mexican Joe would be able to out think Crane and worse still defeat him. With Utah in the lead the troupe set a very quick pace, all the time knowing that they would be to late. Whatever Crane had met in town, it would be over by now.

CHAPTER 35

As Crane rode in on the outskirts of town he sensed that all was not well it was to quiet. As his eyes scanned the buildings and the street he saw Amos from the livery stable crouched down at the side of a building. Crane stopped Dancer but did not look right or left he just kept looking a head. Amos spoke saying, "You've been set up Crane, the sheriff and his deputy are in jail, there is a rifleman on the roof the general store and one on the other side of the street, he is on the roof the bank." "There is a raider waiting for you on the side walk outside the general store." "The other four are in the general store one of those in the store is Mexican Joe."

Crane put his horse to the run, Dancer exploded of the mark racing along main street with Bruno in pursuit. With his reins in his teeth Crane drew both of his horse pistols, He saw a hat above the sign saying bank and fired his left hand horse pistol, the effect was devastating, all in a tangle the sign, part of the roof, a rifle and man fell into the street, the man lay still. Turning his body Crane looked back at the roof the general store he saw a man sighting his rifle in Crane's direction, Crane fired and fired again. Part of the roof and the store front came down, the rifleman was hit but he didn't fall in the street, he fell back on to the roof.

As Crane spun the rearing Dancer he replaced the horse pistols in their saddle holsters, not great weapons for the close work that was coming. "Crane had wondered about the raider on the side walk, but he didn't have to worry, because Bruno had taken responsibility for that unfortunate raider. At the same second that the first raider was falling into the street The valiant dog was making his own attack, tearing the at throat of the shocked raider outside the door of the general store, the man's scream quickly changed to an incoherent gurgle. Crane and Dancer were racing back towards the general store. There was panic and rage inside the building, Mexican Joe saying, "Right you two, you are going to return fire from in here. You..." he stabbed a finger at a raider that went by the name of Wally Tune, "...will come with me out of the back of the store, we circle round and take that scum Crane from behind, he will never know what's hit him."

Down in the Jail, Sheriff Don Liston and his deputy heard the roar of repeated shots that came from Crane's horse pistols. "That's it" said Don, "Hell has come town, Crane is fighting for his life out there and for an end to what started when Mexican Joe's gang set about him in the street, all those years ago." The deputy looked at him saying, "We had better pray that Crane wins because you know that if Mexican Joe lives he will carry out his threat to shoot us both down in these cells." Don just looked at him and nodded.

Back out on the street Crane, who had dismounted was returning fire to the raiders who were holed up in the store. Dancer was snorting with rage and when one of the raiders open the door of the store to get a better shot, Dancer just charged the double doors as he hit the doors. They splintered sending both the raiders inside back peddling in to the shopping area. Dancer kept going and picked up one of the raiders in his jaws, he shook the man like a rag doll than threw him down on the floor and trampled him. The other raider got lucky and fired his pistol blindly, his bullet hit Crane in the right leg as he followed Dancer through the door. As Crane was spun sideways by the force of the bullet, knocking him back out through the door two things happened, the first thing was he shot the raider who had got lucky though his left eye. The second thing that happen was that Mexican Joe, Wally Tune opened fire from behind Crane, but because he was falling as they fired, Crane got really lucky because, instead of getting three or four bullets in the back, only one hit him. It grazed the muscle on the top of his right shoulder, the shock of the wound caused his right hand pistol fall from his fingers as he hit the side walk half in and half out of the store. Crane dug deep, he was in the zone now living by the creed he believed in, He was walking the walk, He was so mad there was a rage in him that said, *if it is my time, to die I am going out fighting with every fibre of my body.* Crane twisted so that he could see his attackers and as he lay there facing the street he shot Wally Tune in the chest with his left hand pistol. Mexican Joe was shaking with fury and anticipation of victory, He fired his own pistol at the same moment Crane fired again, Mexican Joe's bullet took the top off Crane's right ear, Crane's bullet smashed Joe's left knee cap, Crane fired again, hitting Joe's right arm, breaking his elbow. Mexican Joe was writhing in agony screaming in the street, he cursed Crane saying, "Now I will kill you slowly with my knife." Crane knew that his pistol was empty and with the way he felt he was losing blood he thought his only chance was his throwing knife but he didn't think he could throw it far so he would have to wait for Joe to come to him.

Mexican Joe was dragging himself towards Crane, he had a knife in his only good hand he was raving, the pain and frustration of the years since he first met Crane had overwhelmed him he wasn't just unbalanced he had completely lost his mind. Crane on the other hand was calm and sure this was it, neither of them could avoid the other it would end here in the street outside the general store were it all started. Crane sat himself up against the door frame, he was weak and he was bleeding, but he was at peace with himself and the world. As Crane sat up against the door frame he called out to Mexican Joe saying, "It is a hell of a good day to die Joe." Mexican Joe was bleeding out himself and he raged and cursed at Crane as he struggled, to get to Crane. As he watched him struggle Crane said, "I told you a long time ago you couldn't win and today you lose it all." Mexican Joe roared "No, no!!" I have you, I kill you." As he struggled forward intent on getting to Crane the unthinkable happened, Bruno flew from were he had been sitting beside Crane, It was over so suddenly that even Crane couldn't believe it, Bruno tore Mexican Joe's face off and then sank his teeth in Joe's throat. Crane was drifting in and out of consciousness, he was relieved that the journey that he had set out on as boy was over.

There was an eerie silence in the town, Bruno was lying at Crane's side and Dancer was standing close by. People were starting to come out on to the street., Looking around at the bodies and at the damage to buildings. Heads were being shaken in disbelief. Someone spoke, "I can't believe it, it looks like Crane got all seven of them before he went down." Then Amos shouted, "Get Doc Evans, Crane is still breathing, he spoke to Bruno who was growling, Come on dog your pal needs help, you've got to let us help him." Crane stirred, saying, "Bruno lie down," the dog moved letting Amos get to Crane. Dancer neighed and stamped his feet, Crane said, "It's OK Dancer you know Amos." Dancer stood quiet. Then Amos led Dancer away to the stable, he called to Bruno but Bruno stayed where he was. Doc Evans arrived saying, "You made it Crane, your long battle for justice for your parents is over" "All you have to do now is help me to make sure you don't bleed to death." Crane nodded and Doc Evans open his bag and got out the things he would need to help Crane. He checked for a head wound because there was so much blood, he was relieved to see that most of the blood was come from Crane's ruined ear. He applied a temporary dressing and then he saw the shoulder wound, Doc Evens was working fast but efficiently, he could see that the bullet had gone straight through. Once again he applied a temporary dressing. Doc Evan's then realised that the leg wound was the problem, his examination showed that the bullet was still in Crane's leg, he could not take the bullet out here. He saw a passer-bye on the street outside so called to him.

Please go to the stable and ask Amos to come with a wagon so that I can move Crane to my place. Someone had been down to the sheriff's office and released Don Liston and his Deputy. As Crane was being helped on to the wagon Don arrived, he stood beside the wagon and spoke to Crane saying "Well, you finally got the job done Crane." Crane smiled, "Bruno had to finish the job for me, it just goes to show that you can look at all sort's of ways to get a job done, but it's always the thing you never thought of that gets that job done in the end." "It seems that even the dog didn't like Mexican Joe." Don shook his head, "You have animals that love you Crane, they always help you because you help them." Doc Evans said, "I have to get Crane back to my place, and get this bullet out of his leg, so you will have to finish this conversation later." As the wagon moved away Bruno jumped up on the wagon beside Crane. Don smiled and said, What did I just say?"

Doc Evans got back to his Office and he and to Amos let's get Crane inside, they managed with Cane hopping one keg while they support him on either side, Bruno seemingly happy with the situation, jumped down off the wagon and followed them in. The doctor got Crane on the bed, saying, "I have to knock you out for this operation Crane because the bullet is close to the femoral artery and if you move while I'm cutting, you could bleed to death." "I have some of this chloroform, when you wake up the job will be done. Crane lay back totally relaxed for the first time in years saying, "Just go to work Doc, I trust you, Then he laughed and said, "I don't know what Bruno will do if I don't wake up." Doc Evans poured the chloroform from the bottle on to a cloth, as he held the cloth over Crane's face he said, "You are not putting me under any serious pressure then." There was no reply, because Crane was asleep.

CHAPTER 36

As Utah and the rest of Crane's friends were riding away from the Preston farm the heard a voice calling out to them. As they turned they saw Jim Cassidy with another, smaller rider at his side approaching them. The group reined in their horses. Jim rode up saying, "We have been looking to find Crane, is he with you?" He looked apprehensively at the bodies face down over their horses." "No" replied Utah, "He has gone ahead into Jacksboro, to try and catch up with Mexican Joe." Then Utah asked, "Who is this riding with you." "This is Danny Pedrosa, he is hunting Mexican Joe for killing his family" replied "We are pleased to meet you Danny," "You may find that Crane has done the job for you, when we get town, God knows that he has spent enough years trying." "As long as Mexican Joe is dead, I don't care who does the job," replied Danny. "I am sure Crane will have done his best to oblige." Said Big John.

Rider said, "If I am not mistaken that fine horse you are riding is one of Crane's."" "Yes" replied Danny, "Fred gave him to me." He looked happily at the strong little line back dun he was riding, "he is the best horse I could ever have. Jim said, "Danny is part of the family now." Utah and Seth said "we are glad to have him." The talking was done so they all rode on towards, Jacksboro. Crane's friends travelled hopefully but they were worried about what they might find at their journeys end. So it was a worried group that went into the outskirts of town.

The sights that greeted their eyes amazed them,the damaged buildings and the bodies being carried away from the street. They kept moving up the street until they reached the sheriffs office, when they got there Utah dismounted, stepped up on to the side walk and went into the office,. As he walked through the door, Don Liston, stood up and walked forward hand out stretched saying, "Well Fred, it's good to see a fellow Liston." Utah grimaced, I will only tell you once Don, It's Utah, use that other name again and I will have to shoot you." Don laughed, holding his hands up, "OK Utah, you win, Can't you allow a man his little joke?" "As long as it's the last time." Replied Utah, "I have no happy memories of that name." "Anyway" continued Utah, "What about Crane?" "Can I assume from your good humour that he is all right?" "Yeah he is fine, he survived the shoot out, but last I heard he was unconscious up at Doc Evans place." "Unconscious!" "You mean he is hurt bad?" Asked Utah. "No, he had a few wounds, but the doctor used this chloroform to put Crane out, while he removed the bullet from his leg. "By the way Mexican Joe is dead." "Good news! It's about time." Replied Utah.

The two men went out into the street and Don Liston, gave a sharp intake of breath when he saw the seven raiders bodies draped over their saddles. "Well" he said, "There will be reward money payable on these fellers, no doubt." Utah said "We all share in that, including the new kid, meet Danny Pedrosa, Danny, meet Don Liston." Danny reached his hand down and shook Don's hand. "Oh by the way kid, you are to late, Mexican Joe, has killed his last man, he's done Crane's dog sent him to his final resting place." "That's OK" Replied Danny, "I wouldn't have known what to do if I had found Mexican Joe, I just had nowhere else to go and I didn't know what else to do after he killed my family." "So I set out after him with no hope of anything but because I did that, I found people who care about me." "Sounds good to me Danny," said Utah. Crane is a lot like you, it just took longer for him to find the people who care about him." "I know that if he can be left to live quietly now he will hang up his guns. Because I never met a man who believes in truth justice and the law more than Crane, he just wanted the law to be the law and dispense justice and fairness to all. He will be a quiet man from now on, he has never started a single argument."

"There is the issue of reward money for all of the raiders, not just Mexican Joe," Said Don. "Well as I said I know that Crane will want all of us to share in that, on top of that Crane will want the town to have 10% of any reward money," said Utah, He looked at the rangers captain, Johnny Boone, then he said, "Crane as a Texas ranger cannot claim any reward, but that doesn't stop the rest of us." Don Liston, nodded saying well, you will have to pick up the money for Mexican Joe because Crane has claimed it in the name of Bruno, as he said the dog took Mexican Joe down, so he is entitled to the reward. Utah smiled, saying "That sounds like Crane." "Anyway" Utah continued, "I need to get up to Doc Evans place and see how Crane is getting on." The group of Crane's friends mounted their horses and rode along the street towards Doc Evans office.

When they arrived they all went in, Utah said, "I want

Crane to meet Danny so if you don,t mind I will take him in to see Crane first." Doc Evans spoke to them all in the entrance room, "No more than three of you in to see him at one time," Big John, Utah and Danny walked into the treatment room, to see that Crane was sitting up in bed, Bruno was lying on the floor beside the bed, Crane Looked up and smiled when he saw them, he spoke saying, "Big John, Utah, you guys are a sight for sore eyes, who is the young man you have brought with you?" Utah reply, this is Danny, Danny meet Crane." Utah continued, "Mexican Joe killed his family so he was trailing him." "Yes" said Danny, "But things are better for me now, "I am riding your line back dun, with one of your saddles, everyone is very kind." "If you are riding the line back dun, then the horse and the saddle must belong to you." "I'm really sorry about your family, but I am sure there is a place for you with my family" Danny smiled, "Fred, Florrie and Maggie said my place is with you all now but, I didn't want to believe it until you told me." "Those people speak for me, Danny so you can take what they say as gospel." "Now Utah" Crane continued, "You, Rider and Big John need to go home to your wives, I am so proud and grateful that you three and the others rode with me and for me, no one who ever lived had better friends. Please take Danny with you, he has a home to go to with people who will care for and about him. There is something else, Jim, Seth and Rider, need cabins because they are staying, try and get the building of the cabins started for them as soon as you get back. Also, perhaps you could ask Seth if he would stay in town and look after Dancer and Bruno until I am fit to ride." Seth was just outside the door and he spoke saying, "I'll be happy to do what you ask." He called Bruno and the loyal dog left Crane's side, "Come on boy let's go and see Dancer" Seth continued. Bruno and Seth left the Doctors place and headed to the stable. "Also ask Peter if he will make me a box with a lock on, my pistols are going in there, then the box is going in the root cellar and I hope they will stay there." Then Crane said to Big John, "The only other thing is, please call on Mike Preston and his family and tell them that I would like to call on them on my way home." "I have a long standing invitation to visit with them and I think this would be a good time."

Big John, and Utah left the room to make ready for the journey home, Rider came in saying, "It is good to see my brother Crane and great to know that you have ridden the trail of so many tears for so many people for the last time. I will be there when you come home to welcome you." Crane replied, "I wouldn't want it any other way" Crane saw Jim saying, "Jim you did a good job with Danny, now I need you home being one of our top hands, looking after our horses." Jim nodded. "Then Crane spoke to Johnny, here is your badge, I expect you will go back to being the Ranger captain that you should be now, you will always be welcome in our home." "I will always think of you as the kind of man who always keep his word, because he believes in the truth." "You would have been great Texas ranger Crane, I will see you round the bend." Johnny replied. "Tony Barclay spoke saying, "If you don't mind Crane I would like to wait and ride back with you, it would be a good chance to get to know you." "I would like that" replied Crane.

Utah went and saw the sheriff, to making arrangements

for the rewards to be paid into the bank, there was a total of $24,000 to be divided after the town had been given their 10%. Don spoke saying, "Well Utah I think you are all going home to stay this time, I hope that all of you and especially Crane find peace." Utah, nodded, "It's been good knowing you Don, I will quietly remember that there is another Liston in the world." The two men shook hands and said their goodbyes. Utah mounted and said to Big John and the others, we will pick up supplies at the store, then see Seth at the livery stable before we head home.

The group of friends rode up to the livery stable and they all dismounted and spoke to Amos and Seth. "Before we ride home Seth" said Big John "We need you to tell us where you want your cabin built." "Seth replied, Close to Crane's so I can see the family who have taken me in," "Otherwise wherever you think is best and thank you." "OK replied Big John." "Well Amos" said Utah, "You have a fine new set of doors."

"True" replied Amos, "Because Crane is a man of his word."

"You are right about that," replied Big John, "Crane is the kind of a man who lives by his belief in truth and justice, even if the truth doesn't help him he will stand or fall by it. Crane would rather lose every thing he owns than lie to keep it. If you are always honest with him he will stand by you no matter what."

The others nodded, then they all said their farewells and rode out of town towards the Preston farm, when they got there the family were pleased to see them and asked for news of Crane. "Big John, replied, he is fine, just recovering from a bullet in his leg." "He said that we should tell you that he would like to take up your invitation to eat with you on his way home, he will have Seth and Tony with him." "That is good news," replied Mike, "We will look forward to that." "There is better news" said Utah, "Mexican Joe did not survive the pistol fight in town." "Crane took out all Mexican Joe's men then he wounded Joe and Bruno Crane's dog finished the job."

At this point Mike's wife Amy came out of the cabin, saying, "Please come in and eat with us, we would be glad to have you." They all went inside and enjoyed their food and conversation. Big John finally said "We must ride on, we are to comfortable here, we need to get home." They all said their thanks to the Preston family and mounted up and started out on their journey home. It had been a long time since they had all felt so relaxed and their only thoughts were on home and family. They encountered no problems on their journey and a couple of days later the group of friends arrived at Crane's farm and rode into the yard. Maggie came out of the cabin and ran towards them with a worried look on her face, saying "Crane, is he?" "There is no problem, He is just fine he just has to get over his leg wound before he can travel, it is all good news, Crane put a couple of bullets in Mexican Joe and Bruno finished him off." "We have cabins to build and Crane wants Peter to make him a box with a padlock and put it in the root cellar, the best news is that Crane will be putting his guns in it, he says he doesn't need them any more." "That is great news" said Maggie, "that means he will come home and stay."

Utah said, "We will be building cabins for Seth, Rider and Jim, the other thing is that Danny is here to stay." Flo and Fred had arrived and Fred said, Danny if you get down off that horse Flo and I would like to ask you to live with us, we have been building an extra room on our cabin and we where hoping that you would move in." Danny, dismounted and went over to them saying, "Home at last." Rider and Dove walked away talking together about living in a cabin for the first time, they thought it would be strange at first to live under a permanent roof. Big John and Utah said their farewells and headed home to their respective wives. Fred spoke saying, "I will travel in town and get things moving for the cabins to be built." He harnessed a team to the wagon and moved out town.

Back in Jacksboro, Crane was getting better by the hour, he had moved from Doc Evans place and he Seth and Tony were sleeping in Amos's barn. His leg was still stiff and painful but he was ready to go home. "Tony and Crane had been chewing the fat about family connections and they had built a good relationship, in fact they had become friends. Seth was ready to go home for the first time in his life, they made the decision they would head for Crane's farm the following morning. Making only one stop on the way, they would spend a little time with the Preston's at their farm. Crane said, I am just going up to see Don in the sheriffs office, I need to tell him thanks for everything before we go home.

Crane walked into The sheriff's office, Don got up from behind his desk saying, "Good to see you Crane." "Those are words I thought I would never hear, in this town" Replied Crane. "Well" said Don, "I was wrong abut you, I thought you were the devil himself when you came back." "I'm hanging up my pistols when I get home, I'm weary of it all, I seem to have spent a lifetime on the vengeance trail." "I just wanted to say goodbye and thank you for helping me with my Ma and Pa that day back on the farm and for telling the townsfolk about Ben Shaw." "If it hadn't been for you I would have had a price on my head all this time." "That is all I want to say" Said Crane. "We are riding out at dawn, so this time it's Adios," I won't be coming back." "The two men shook hands,then as Crane left the office Don said "Vaya Con Dios mi amigo. Go with God my friend."

The following morning Crane Tony and Seth saddled up and said their goodbyes to Amos. They left town with Bruno trotting behind them, heading for the Preston place. Crane had explained to the other two why it was important to him to make one last visit to the old place. When they rode into the yard, Mike and his two son's were coming out of the barn, reminding Crane of the morning chores, that he and his father had done together. Before he could dwell to long on the memory, Mike came over to them saying, "Come into the cabin and welcome, Amy will want to feed you all."They all dismounted and turned their horses into the corral, then walked up to and into the cabin, Amy was delighted to see Crane and soon had coffee bacon and beans on the table. When they had eaten, Amy spoke saying, "You know Crane, that our family will never be able to thank you enough, for this home you have given us." Crane smiled before replying "You earned this place with your hard work, it ceased to be mine the day my Ma and Pa died. I made sure of that when I burned it down, I knew I could never live here again. Also with that garden you have made a memorial to my Ma and Pa, I would never have thought of doing that so thank you. Let's just say that we have done right by each other."

Amy kissed Crane on the cheek, there was nothing more to be said.

After a few moments Crane emptied his coffee cup, then he said, "If none of you mind, I would like to go and spend a few moments with my Ma and Pa at the garden." No one spoke and Crane got up and walked outside. He went across to the garden and looking down at the flowers, spoke to his parents, saying, "Well things are good for me now, all except one of the men who came to the farm that day are dead. The one who is alive is my best friend, his name's Utah, he is a good man, I have learned a lot about the character of people during the last few years. I am married now, Maggie is my wife's name, I have a daughter as well, we named her Mae, after you Ma. I never understood why you hung up your gun Pa, but I do now, I'm hanging mine up when I get home. These are good people who are living here now, they have done you proud. I thank you for the values you taught me they have helped me to reach this day alive. Your granddaughter will know of you and love your memory as do I."

That said Crane moved away over to the corral where he made Dancer ready to travel. The others seeing him came out of the cabin and Seth and Tony got their horses ready. Crane mounted Dancer saying, "Long life and happiness to you folks, thank you for everything." Mike Preston and his wife replied, "We thank you Crane for giving us this place and for saving us twice when we were under attack, you and your friends have done so much for us." "You will always be welcome here." Crane and his two friends touched their hats and rode out. Bruno as always was trotting behind.

The trio were eager to be home and they rode day and night until they came in sight of Crane's farm. They were seen coming and family and friends were waiting in the yard for them. Maggie was there with their daughter Mae in her arms. Crane stepped wearily down out of the saddle and hugged them both saying, "Home at last, I am home to stay" Dancer will run free and Bruno can sleep on the porch. Crane unbuckled his guns and handed them to Peter Leonard saying I think you have a place for these." Peter took them saying "Praise the Lord, thank you God for a traveller safe home." They all said, "Amen to that."

The End (of the vengeance trail but ...)

Crane will ride again 2019

INTERNATIONAL PRAISE FOR THE AUTHORS PREVIOUS BOOKS

Have Gravel Will Travel

Dave Lodge's biography about Tommy Bruce *Have Gravel Will Travel,* is an excellent book. It doesn't just tell the very moving story about the life of sixties recording star Tommy Bruce. It also tells about what happened to some of the other sixties recording stars and where they are now. Artistes like Michael Cox, Lance Fortune and Nelson Keene, are in my minds eye again. I am reading *Have Gravel Will Travel* for the fourth time!!
Svein Sorlie Norway.

I believe Dave Lodge's book *Have Gravel will Travel* is more than just a fine tribute to our old mate Tommy Bruce. I think that in time it will come to be regarded as a reference point for the history of Rock and Roll.
Brian Poole Hit Recording Artiste
& Entertainer England

Dave Lodge with *Have Gravel will Travel* has written the best book about an entertainer Tommy Bruce, that I have ever read. The book made me see Tommy Bruce as a great guy who I would really like to have known. You just can not put this book down, page after page it just got more and more interesting. John Eckert Talent Consultant, California, USA.

Have Gravel Will Travel written by Dave Lodge is a great book. I really enjoyed learning about sixties recording artiste Tommy Bruce. I just couldn't put this book down.
Manfred Kulman Author, Drummer, Rock and Roll Promoter. Beilfield, Scholenesh, Germany

The Long Road

I have really enjoyed reading *The Long Road* the author Dave Lodge is my mate and he really cares for the people he writes about.
Tony Crane, hit recording star "The Merseybeats."

The Long Road in which all of us guys from the sixties get a mention is book that Dave Lodge once again demonstrates, that he writes from the heart and really cares about his friends. Thanks Mate.
Brian Poole lead singer with Brian Poole and the Tremoloes.

The Long Road is another masterful piece of writing by Dave Lodge. In this book he shares his felling for his friends in the world of show business, clearly he really cares about his friends. They reciprocate these feeling and many of them have given an insight into the friendship they share with Dave by writing meaningful forewords for their chapters. This book can be read from cover to cover or, chapters can be read randomly, Great work.
John Eckert Talent Consultant. California USA.

Lucky, a Dog's Tale

A read that will touch your heart, This time Dave Lodge shows the loyalty and friendship he and his dog Lucky shared for sixteen years. It is a clever piece of writing as Dave has written it from Lucky's perspective, as though Lucky had written it himself.
John Eckert. Talent Consultant. California. USA

Tin Pan Aspirations

I always look forward to Dave Lodge's books and I have to say that *Tin Pan Aspirations The Golly Goulding Story* is one of Dave Lodge's best works to date. A very good read.
John Eckert. Talent Consultant, California USA.

Dave Lodge writes the kind of books that I enjoy reading. *The Long Road* and *Tin Pan Aspirations* open up the world of show business and the people in it. These two books flow on well from, *Have Gravel will Travel.* His book *Lucky, a Dog's Tale* is different but still a good read.
Svein Sorlie Norway.

MY REASON FOR WRITING
THIS WESTERN

In 1960 just as I was getting ready to separate myself from the most miserable and unhappy time of my life,my school days I decided that as an avid reader of western novels I would write one myself. I had been reading Louis Lamour's books, including his wonderful "Sackett" series, also Zane Grey with his thrilling tales, such as "Riders of the Purple Sage." This book is, according to Frank Gruber, the American author and screenwriter the best western ever written, I would not argue with that assessment.

All the books written by these great authors told of friendship, honour, courage and decency, they gave a young person a code to live by. So filled with my idea of the west and having purchased a few exercise books, I set to work and after a couple of months I believed that I had written a best seller. Eager for approval I showed my efforts to my father. He read the story and then offered his thoughts, he said, "It shows promise but your style of writing is naive, I can help you, this is something that we can do together." I was growing up as a typically resentful teenager, so we had several conversations during which I dismissed all his suggestions and ideas out of hand. Eventually in a fit of childish frustration, I threw the exercise books in a drawer and uttered the immortal words, "I won't write it then!"

About fifteen years later I found the book and read through it again, My father, long dead by then, had been right it was naive. I played around with it for a day or two didn't achieve much and put it away again.

It was probably another twenty years before I looked at it again and it struck me that I had moved away from my boyhood western writer heroes, and without knowing it I had slipped into a style of writing that to my mind was similar to that of Forest Carter. The strange thing was that at the time I had not read his great novel 'Gone to Texas' or seen the film that was based on his book 'The Outlaw Josey Wales' when I had attempted my rewrite. Still I was busy with life and although I thought about the story now and again and even mentioned it to my wife Margaret I had no real compulsion to finish the book. I still continued to read westerns and in doing so I also enjoyed the writing of, Max Brand, Claire Huffaker, A G Fleischman and Larry McMurty among others of the western genre, so when I finally decided to write this book there clearly several influences for me to draw from.

Only fifteen or sixteen years later having written and had published four other books of a total different genre, I woke up one morning just knowing how I wanted this western story to be written.

The story flowed from me within weeks and, all of life's experiences, joys and disappointments, seemed to help me to tell the story.

My wife Margaret and I had enjoyed a great life to that point and we continue to do so. There had been hard times along the way, caused by people who don't recognise my ideals of belief, truth and justice. However none of the misery these people caused, came near the misery I endured in my school days. So to overcome the desperate times these unimportant people caused, Margaret and I relied on the words believed to have been spoken to the Chiefs of the Plains Indians by the then United States Secretary of the Interior, "Endeavour to Persevere." We did persevere thanks to the many wonderful friends we found that we had. Those friends lived by the same code that I live by, the code learnt as a boy reading westerns by amazing men who knew the value of truth and honour.

Because I felt the characters of the calibre of Josey Wales who was in books like 'Gone to Texas' first published in 1973 under the title "Rebel Outlaw" and "The Vengeance Of Josey Wales" published 1976 by Forest Carter, (Asa Earl Carter who died in 1979, to soon, at the age of Fifty Three.) Josey Wales would have been on the trail around Crane's time, so I decided they should meet in my fictional story.

Also I think George G Gilman's character Captain Josiah Hedges, "Edge" would have crossed Crane's path, I have tipped my hat to the authors where this happened. George Gilman Aka Terry Harknett, eighty one years of age at the time I hope to publish this book, who had another great Western character, Adam Steele. I have to say that George G Gilman really is the best and most prolific of British Western and Mystery writers, I hope to have the benefit of his opinion this book.

I am pleased to say that I am still naïve, even though I have spent more than seventy years on this earth. This naïvety still persists in spite of experiences to the contrary of all my beliefs. These experiences which have shown that for some people, truth and justice have no place in the same sentence, have been unable to sour my life.

I still believe that good always triumphs over evil and that truth is the key to a good life. So in this book I have tried to show that my belief in friendship, truth honour and loyalty will always for me win the day. I may be old but hope springs eternal that I will continue be proved right. I have never doubted my friends ability to make this belief come true.

So here it is more than fifty six years in the writing, with influence from my father, my friends and all the great writers of the western genre, my humble offering, '*Crane, The Left Handed Gun*'. I hope you all enjoy reading it as much as I have enjoyed writing it.

ACKNOWLEDGEMENTS

To those who made a difference to my life but are no longer with us.

Ted Lodge, my father who clearly knew more than me about life and writing.

Big John McCane taken too soon, for his loyalty and friendship, you never let me down, John ever. I try every day to live up to the example you set.

Danny Williams a great singer and a good friend, knowing you Danny, made the world a better place, for Margaret and I.

Tommy Bruce one of the great entertainers and more than that our friend. We were brothers from the day we met Tommy, and I think of you every day.

Mac Poole a fine musician, who was another man who knew the true meaning of friendship and proved it every day.

Kay Garner a true friend and a lovely talented lady.

Graham Bodman who called me BF and taught me so much.

Chris Black a great guitarist and a true friend through thick and thin.

Peter and his wife Effie Smith, my aunt and uncle who showed me, with the help of my grandparents what selfless love really is.

Dick and Zena Smith who knew the meaning of team work and cared for others, two people who espoused the meaning of the words "Don't Quit."

Frances Lodge, my stepmother, who was a wonderful woman with great courage.

Roger Day, my uncle who taught all those who would listen the value of Rudyard Kipling's great poem *If*.

Fred and Florrie Hall, my Father and Mother-in-Law who were the best of people.

THE LONG ROAD — Dave Lodge

Have Gravel, will Travel

The Official Tommy Bruce Biography

The amazing story of how a young cockney lad went from 'barra boy' to a teen singing idol. A unique insight into the 1960's rock 'n' roll scene when Tommy Bruce and contemporaries such as Billy Fury, Johnny Kidd and Joe Brown were doing the rounds together. In this fickle world of show business many friendships don't stand the test of time. Not so that of Tommy Bruce and Dave Lodge, his manager, friend and author of this biography. We see how their partnership has endured since the 1960's unhampered by contracts, surviving on friendship through the highs and lows. The book is a testimony to Tommy's affable style both on and off stage making him a well-loved character in the industry for the past five decades.

Price: £6.99

Paperback: 280 pages / 100 B&W photographs
Publisher: Pixel Tweaks Publications (July 2015)
ISBN-13: 978-0992751487

Lucky, a Dog's Tale

The story of a remarkable dog, whose loyalty and love for those in his life may have been equalled but never surpassed. From the moment he came into our lives, abandoned and dishevelled on the Mancunian Way, he was an amazing and unexpected addition to our family. A Newfoundland, Labrador cross, he grew to be a gentle giant who surprised us every day of his life.

This book will appeal to those who have enjoyed the company of wonderful pets of their own; they will understand how much we loved Lucky. I can't say he was the best dog in the world; I haven't known enough dogs to make that assumption, What I can say, without fear of contradiction is, "I have never known a better dog"!

So I leave it up to you, read and enjoy Lucky's book and see if you can answer his question, "A dog can have a life story, can't he?"

Price: £4.99

Paperback: 72 pages with B&W photographs
ISBN-13: 978-09956190-3-6

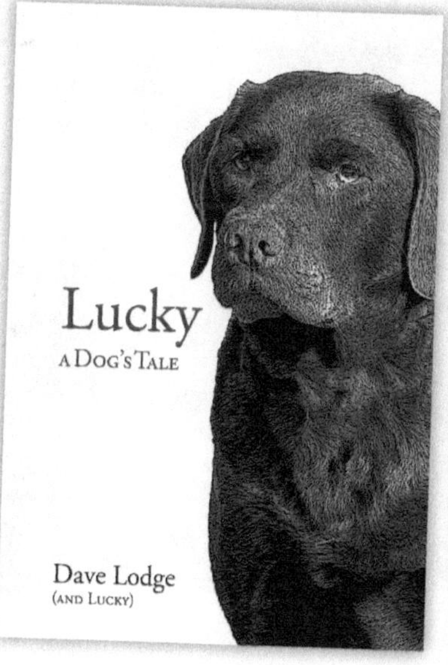

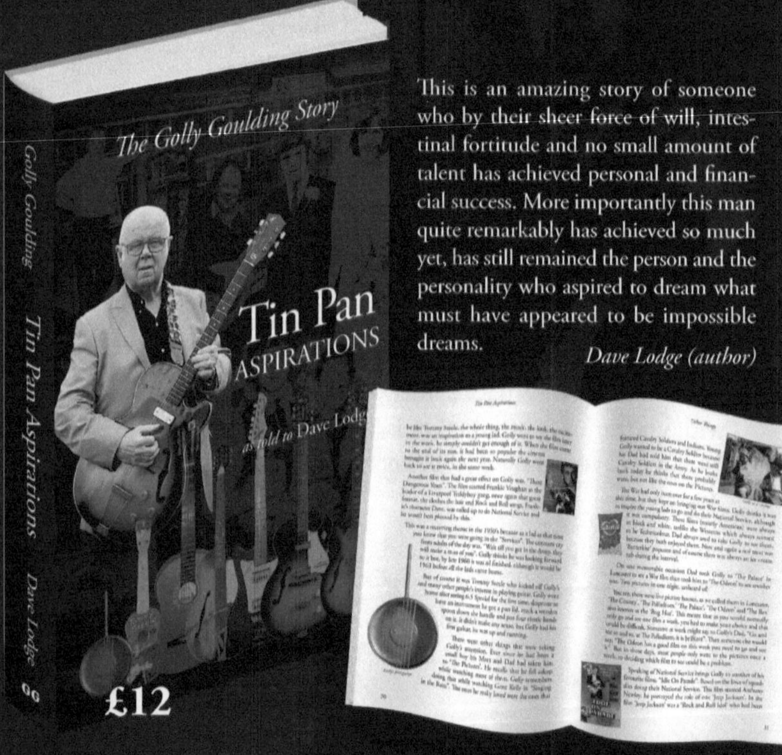

TIN PAN ASPIRATIONS
The Golly Goulding Story

Golly Goulding
Tin Pan Aspirations
Dave Lodge

The Golly Goulding Story
Tin Pan
ASPIRATIONS
as told to Dave Lodge

£12

This is an amazing story of someone who by their sheer force of will, intestinal fortitude and no small amount of talent has achieved personal and financial success. More importantly this man quite remarkably has achieved so much yet, has still remained the person and the personality who aspired to dream what must have appeared to be impossible dreams.

Dave Lodge (author)

All proceeds from the sale of this book will go to New Start Charity
The Wythenshawe Hospital Transplant Fund
www.newstartcharity.org

Paperback: 322 pages
ISBN-13: 978-1-5272-1135-3
Available from local bookshops & Amazon
Tel: 01524 850757 or Email: golly@ggantiques.com